PROPHET'S JOURNEY

PROPHET OF THE BADLANDS BOOK 1

MATTHEW S. COX

DIVISION ZERO PRESS

DIVERGENT FATES
—A— NOVEL—

Cover art: Jackson Tjota • Cover formatting: Alexandria Thompson
Interior art by: Ricky Gunawan

ISBN (ebook): 978-1-950738-00-7

ISBN (paperback): 978-1-950738-01-4

CONTENTS

AUTHOR'S NOTE

Ever since I wrote *Prophet of the Badlands*, readers have often contacted me asking for more of Althea's story. (Usually after they discovered *Archon's Queen* is not a direct continuation from *Prophet*). I've been wanting to write a spinoff with her as the main character for a while, but it would need to be set after the end of that series, so I decided to wait until the final Awakened book came out before writing this.

Prophet's Journey is a continuation of Althea's story, set after the events of the Awakened series. The following contains spoilers for those who have not read it. Please consider at least reading *Prophet of the Badlands* (if not the entire Awakened series) before this book.

The Awakened series

- Prophet of the Badlands
- Archon's Queen
- Grey Ronin
- Daughter of Ash
- Zero Rogue
- Angel Descended

SAND FLOWER

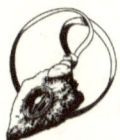

Hope had finally taken root in Althea's mind, though she didn't quite know how to deal with it.

In her old life, staying in one place for more than two months would've been an unusual surprise, either pleasant or awful depending on the surroundings. That she'd been in Querq for about six took her into strange territory, stirring new thoughts and emotions she'd never confronted before, most especially the sense of having a real home, a place that not only offered safety and comfort, but one where she *wanted* to be, not simply appreciated for being a less cruel state of captivity.

It didn't matter that she looked nothing like Karina or Father, pale and blonde to their rich brown skin and black hair—she loved her adoptive family fiercely. So much so that a moment of intense fear had turned her healing power into a weapon.

She still felt guilty about causing Hector pain, even if he had tried to kill Karina.

Lately, her sister had been talking of Althea's birthday. Before arriving in Querq, she'd guessed at being twelve, but she had recently learned that the biological mother she never knew fled a research facility only eleven years ago. No one had a clue as to her exact birth date, so she *might* actually be twelve or still eleven with a few months to go.

Father decided they would officially recognize her birthday as the day he'd found her exhausted and near starved while out hunting.

She smiled at the memory of the emotions he gave off when suggesting that date. Her new life as a person with a family instead of a captive wanted only for her powers *did* begin that day, even if she had some bumpy spots to cope with soon after. This new life did, however, come with one downside: she would remain officially eleven until next year. It made no sense why she disliked being *eleven* and not twelve so much. Perhaps because she had spent so many months thinking of herself that age. She stuck her tongue out. Father had probably done that on purpose so it took even longer for her to become sixteen. He had insisted she not 'do anything' with Den until that age.

Not that she had any interest in being wifed, but she had become somewhat curious at the idea that a woman could possibly *want* to do that. Over her years of being stolen over and over, passed from one raider group to another, she'd seen slaves get wifed and not one of them wanted to. Well, a few truly broken souls aside, none of them did. Den believed that women who weren't even slaves would somehow *want* to be wifed, but she couldn't imagine it. He tried to claim that it happened because people in Querq had babies... and laughed when Althea had asked him what babies had to do with it.

She'd always believed women just sometimes had babies when they wanted one. Den seemed to think that wifeing had something to do with the process. And true, a few slaves she had been around had babies while held captive in the raider camps. Women raiders had some too, but at least they enjoyed being raiders so their desiring a baby didn't seem surprising. At the time, she thought it strange that slaves would want to have a baby in such an awful place, but if Den was right...

Perhaps being alone wasn't good. Her thoughts went places she didn't like. The other children in Querq all attended the school, while the ones too little for that had gone down for their naps. For reasons she couldn't understand, the town elders didn't want her going to school with the others... yet. It had something to do with her barely being able to understand the frozen speech. Father called it 'reading.' Some man the Zero police made her talk to for an 'assessment' said she had the mind of a six-year-old. She'd gasped in horror at that, as she most certainly did not steal any poor little kid's brain. The woman helping him talk to her thought she might have been carrying 'mental trauma,' and didn't believe her when she held her arms out and said she didn't have anything but her dress.

So, for the time being, Althea had to cope with the awful little glowing tablet thing that called her stupid whenever she didn't say the right words. It showed her frozen speech, or sometimes pictures of things, and she had to do the telling of it. Half the time she'd say the right word, but the machine still yelled at her. Like, if it showed a *gato*, she'd say *gato*, but the stupid thing wanted her to say 'cat.'

She didn't so much care if she learned the same things the other kids learned, she just wanted to be with them. Being alone made her sad. She *should* have been home at that moment getting frustrated at the 'learning machine,' but after going to the farm to visit Karina for their lunch break, Althea had taken the scenic route, in no hurry to have a fancy electric tablet from the bad city tease her for being dumb. Yes, finishing the lessons on the device would allow her to maybe go with the other children to school, but she did not like that awful little thing.

It talked to her like she *was* five years old.

"Apple. Ahh-pell. *Good*." She raspberried. "No, it's a *manzana*, not a stupid ahh-pell. Who cares if I know the words?"

Althea meandered down a dusty street at the northwest end of Querq, following the wide stone path marked with the faded remains of yellow stripes. In the Before-Time, cars walked on these strips of rock that the ancients somehow shaped to their whim. People from the bad city had cars, too... some flying into the sky like birds. All the ones the Zero police brought out here flew, so they didn't use the roads. The Watch had two cars they called 'pickups', but only used them for emergencies and never bothered to follow the roads.

She didn't go to this area often, so it still felt new enough to be worth exploring. Being this close to the wall at the edge of a village would once have made her wary of raiders trying to steal her. The Old City that surrounded Querq had lots of bad things like bonedogs and the enormous millipedes. The only safe passage through the ancient ruins went to the main gate, and a small group of raiders trying to steal her would not go right to the front door. But now, she didn't worry about raiders anymore. Even if they did show up, she would protect herself.

Two main reasons allowed her to tolerate captivity for most of her life: one, she had never understood the concept of a true home, so didn't feel a sense of loss when moved from place to place. As long as she could still help people, it didn't matter where she went. Secondly, she had been too afraid to use her powers that way.

Some other Scrags—native denizens of the Badlands—had magic, too. Most of the tribals called those with such abilities 'mystics.' They could know people's thoughts or give them commands that they couldn't resist. Officer David with the Zero police had explained these things she thought of as magic were called psionics, powers that came from the mind. Althea could also *make* people do things. However, Mystics terrified raiders and peaceful villagers alike, and even normally friendly people would often attack them on sight. Worse, common legend said the only way to truly kill a mystic was to burn them alive. If merely shot or stabbed or poisoned, the mystic would come back from the dead and wreak terrible revenge.

Althea didn't want to be burned. And that fear had kept her from using her gifts to protect herself from enslavement—though she feared being wifed even more than being burned. Forcing subtle changes in her captors' emotions often proved enough to convince them not to keep her tied up—her second biggest fear after wifeing—but if anyone looked at her the way they looked at the harem women, she never hesitated to tell them to go away.

Everyone in the Badlands knew her as the Prophet, the great healer, the child with the blue eyes that lit up like stars. Her eyes always glowed, giving away her identity to everyone who saw her, telling them they had found the greatest prize. She didn't know if the Scrags' fear of mystics would overpower their fear of harming the Prophet, but she hadn't wanted to take that chance. She once thought if people learned she could control them with Suggestion, they would kill her.

But, Althea had found confidence and strength. In having a home, in having a family she loved and would do anything to protect, she promised herself she would never hesitate again. If anyone tried to take her away from this place, she would overwhelm them with fear and make them run away, or throw them into such a deep pit of sadness they could only sit there and cry until the Watch arrested them.

She held her arms out to either side for balance while walking heel-to-toe along one of the old painted yellow lines, pretending the paving was a big hole and she had to cross a narrow rope. When the paint ended, she stood normally again, and grinned. It felt good to play. It felt even better not to worry about being taken. Most of all, she adored the people of Querq treating her like any other person—well mostly.

They still respected her as the Prophet, but neither worshiped her nor caged her. Except for that one middle-aged woman who constantly bowed and tried to kiss her feet, but Guadalupe lived in her own little world.

Off to her right, the giant, decaying forms of Before-Time buildings appeared as twisted shadows in a sandy haze. The Old City surrounding Querq often hid beneath a brownish mist, neither fog nor true sandstorm. She knew The Many lurked close, seething in anger at the world that continued in spite of his suffering. Though the entity often appeared as a decrepit old man, he claimed to be made out of the souls of everyone who died in some long-ago great war, the war that separated the now from the Before-Time.

Althea paused at a spot where another road crossed. A box on a pole with three colored lenses by the corner made her think back to being lost in the bad city far to the west. An angry man had jumped out of a little car that almost hit her, screaming and calling her stupid… just like the teaching machine.

I don't want to be a hood ornament.

The three light things here didn't work, all remained dark. Since that angry man had yelled at her not to walk when the red one lit up—and the red one presently remained off—she shrugged and kept going. Of course, none of these road lights in Querq ever lit up. They probably had in the Before-Time, though.

She tried to picture cars on the road here like in the city beyond the wall of fire. That, too, had been a lie—or at least a misunderstanding. No wall of flames stood at the end of the world to keep people away from the place the Ancestors go. She had seen a big metal wall at the edge of the horrible city, though assumed it existed to keep people trapped inside. It didn't seem possible anyone would *want* to be there. However, some of the Zero police who visited Querq did miss it and wanted to go back. Maybe to people who always lived there it wouldn't be bad, but Althea had only scary or sad memories of the place. Her time in the 'modern' city had been an overwhelming flood of negative emotions, so loud she had to concentrate on not letting them consume her.

Picturing working cars in Querq didn't seem right, so she scrunched her nose up and stopped trying to daydream. She didn't really like the fancy city stuff the Zero police brought either, thinking it would turn her home into a small version of the bad city. But, some stuff she had to admit was nice. Like shampoo. But not cars. The bad city had too many cars and too many people.

"Everyone in them was so angry. Cars must make people angry. That's why they have the button so even the cars yell at each other. *Beeeeeeep.*" She made a silly face, then sighed, pitying the poor people stuck inside cars. Honestly, those machines scared her. She didn't understand how they could make a person's emotions go from calm to wanting to murder someone in two seconds.

Officer David with the city police tried to explain to her that not everyone in the big city was always angry or sad, but he hadn't felt what she'd felt. He, too, had the power he called Telempathy, able to read or change other people's emotions, but nowhere near as strong as her. That Awakened word flew around whenever they talked about her. It meant something about her being stronger. Her Telempathy made her far more sensitive than he could understand. In that city, people who didn't even know each other threw off so much anger while sitting in their cars they reminded her of raiders about to kill. She cringed at the truth she'd sensed *less* anger on some raiders when they *did* kill.

She paused to trace lines with her toes in a wash of sand across the paving, smiling as she created the vague suggestion of a flower. Taken by sudden inspiration, she squatted, using her fingers to add leaves and more detail to the petals, then some grass on either side of the stem... and a happy bee about to land on it.

Her little drawing filled her with joy, the perfect complement to a nice sunny day.

A sudden, stiff wind fluttered her long, blonde hair and white dress, eroding her flower and the poor little bee after a moment, scattering it to loose sand that drifted along the pavement in tiny whorls.

Althea frowned. "Why do you have to be so mean? Why do you hate it when people are happy?"

2

STOP

She squinted around at windows and doors, certain the Many had sent that wind to destroy her moment of happiness. He didn't respond, nor did she feel any dark presence nearby. *Sometimes wind is just the wind*, said Father's voice in her mind. The buildings on the right side of the street held little but debris, as they formed part of the village's outer wall. Blue-painted metal ran across at roughly twenty-five feet off the ground, a walkway for the Watch.

To the left, all the buildings held family homes. In the Before-Time, they'd been something called shops. She understood some of the frozen speech still visible here and there in fading paint or broken signs.

Althea approached a window with white letters. "En… tist. Entist? What's that?" She traced her finger around a shape that resembled a tooth, only bigger than a potato. She clamped both hands over her mouth, wide-eyed at what scary magic might be able to make teeth grow to that size. Good thing the Before-Time magic had stopped working. No one here could do that to anyone's mouth.

The building beside it had metal letters on the wall above the window. It looked like other parts had been there before, but broken, leaving only the words 'nkin onut'.

She struggled to say it a few times, but gave up and kept walking down the street.

A man with long black hair, white shirt, and pants made of squealer hide leapt out of a doorway a distance ahead and ran for an alley that led toward the center of the village.

He raised a hand in greeting. "Hi, Althea."

She grinned, knowing she'd seen him before but unable to recall his name, and waved back at him right as he disappeared behind an old store that now served as a home for three families.

"Althea," said the man from the alley. He trotted backward into view, staring at her like he couldn't believe his eyes. "There you are."

"Here I am." She flapped her arms out to the sides and let them fall.

"I was just runnin' to find you." The man jogged up to within a few paces of her. "My little brother Luciano's hurt. His leg."

She nodded. "Okay."

He hurried back down the street to the building he'd emerged from, nearing tearing the door off its hinges on the way inside. She raced in after him, entering what had years ago been a giant open space. Flimsy wooden walls or sheets of thin metal divided it into separate rooms, mostly empty at this hour of the day. Children would be in school, adults at their job things, and the old people mostly all sat around at Tumbleweed's, drinking that pungent orange stuff that made it hard to walk—or even stay standing upright.

The man ducked past an old sheet hung as a door over a hole in a barrier of corrugated metal.

"Nicolás!" yelled an older woman, who proceeded to erupt in rapid-fire Spanish, too fast for Althea to fully understand.

Up to age five, as best Althea could remember, she'd lived at a nice village with people who predominantly spoke Spanish. The Wagon Man had abducted her and dragged her all over the Badlands. He mostly spoke English. Scrags, settlers, and raiders farther north generally favored English, while the more southerly people spoke Spanish. As Father explained, her being dragged 'all the hell over the place' left her with a language part English, part Spanish, and part 'made up.' If people spoke too fast in English *or* Spanish, she'd end up confused... though she'd long ago gotten into the habit of reading their minds without even realizing it to understand their meaning even if she didn't grasp the words.

She pulled the sheet aside and crept into the room, standing demurely at the edge while a sixtyish woman angrily scolded the man. Althea managed to pick up that his grandmother believed he'd ignored her request to go find her because he'd come back so fast.

"Excuse me," said Althea.

The old woman glanced at her and froze statue still, a look of shock on her face.

"Luciano is hurt?" Althea padded into the room. "Where is he?"

"She was right outside. I didn't have to go anywhere to find her." Nicolás gestured at the door, then pointed at a cot at the back corner of the room. "He's there."

Althea ducked around the grandmother, scurrying over to the old olive drab bed covered in a mishmash of blankets made from ancient shirts sewn together. The Zero police had been supplying Querq with some 'modern' things, but the fancy stuff hadn't spread everywhere yet.

A younger man, not quite twenty, lay in the cot, his left leg — or what remained of it — hanging over the side. Someone had improvised a tourniquet below the knee, a few inches above where the limb ended in a tatter of ripped up muscle and splintered bone. An alarmingly big pool of blood covered the floor beside the bed, still dripping from the leg.

He moaned, lost to the delirium of pain.

"Bonedog," whispered Althea before kneeling, sitting back on her heels, and grasping the damaged limb in both hands.

She closed her eyes, concentrating on the sense of his life essence. Amid the void of darkness, a red silhouette faded into view, cut short at the point the leg had been severed. With a brief glance up toward his thought-shape, she commanded it to cease registering pain. In response, the tense muscles in his calf relaxed in her grip, and the whitish forms of his air bags shrank.

His body responded to her power, new muscle growing over new bone. Althea clenched her jaw, pouring her psionic energy into Luciano. Over the course of the next fifteen minutes, the missing half-leg gradually reappeared. She vaguely noticed a distant yell and a heavy *thud* shake the floor under her.

Once his toes finished growing, Althea relaxed her concentration but didn't break the link. The effort to make his leg regrow had winded her like a hard sprint all the way across Querq. She paused for a few seconds to catch her breath, then checked over his life shapes to make sure he had no other hurts. A few shallow cuts marked his arms, which she fixed before coaxing his body to expel several pieces of concrete debris embedded in his other leg. Nothing else appeared wrong, so she started to release the link — but stopped herself.

A bonedog bit him. He's gonna have a sick. They always give people sicks.

In her mind's eye, she floated like a little bug around a giant body, searching over his various life-shapes. Eventually, she noticed a thin yellow thread drifting within the blood-presence.

She commanded his body to purge itself of the sick. The wispy thread of disease migrated around at her urging, gathering in Luciano's bladder. Fortunately, he hadn't been attacked very long ago, and the sick didn't have the time to grow and spread everywhere.

Confident no more hurts or sicks remained, she released her link and opened her eyes. Nicolás crouched beside her, one gentle hand at her back she hadn't noticed before. The twenty-something man wept like a small boy, grinning from ear to ear while staring at his younger brother's intact—and somewhat pink—lower left leg.

"Is someone else hurt?" asked Althea.

"No, child." Nicolás slid his hand to her shoulder and pulled her into a hug. "We will be forever grateful." He radiated so much awe and gratitude it made Althea uncomfortable. It made her feel ashamed of herself when people worshiped her. Though, he didn't take it *that* far.

"Did something heavy fall?" She peered down at her knees, surrounded in blood that had dribbled from the formerly shredded leg.

"Our grandmother fainted when Luciano's leg began to grow." Nicolás wiped at his tears with the back of his arm and chuckled. "She is all right."

Althea nodded, then stood, peering at her legs, smeared in blood from the knees down. It didn't bother her. She'd ended up far dirtier than that many times. Some raider groups that captured her had been so violent, she'd end up covered head to toe in gore by the time she passed out in exhaustion from healing them. Grown men would occasionally throw up from watching her grab life shapes that had fallen out of their friends and stuff the bits back inside with her hands. More than once, after she finished making all the hurts go away following a vicious raid, she'd look like she'd gone for a swim in a bathtub of blood. At least back then she didn't have any clothes to get dirty. Blood didn't like to wash out of clothes. Few tribal Scrags who lived where the weather remained warm all year round bothered to waste energy on making or scavenging things to wear.

Karina might be upset with her for getting some blood on the bottom of her dress, but Althea kept forgetting to be careful whenever someone needed help. Dirty didn't matter—helping people did.

"Gah!" Luciano sat up, grabbing himself between the legs.

She pointed at the door. "You had a sick. You need to let it out."

The younger man groaned, nodded, and dragged himself out the back door. She endured several minutes of exuberant hugging from Nicolás and his grandmother until Luciano returned and joined in the embrace.

"You are truly an angel," said Luciano.

She giggled, thinking about what Aurora told her. "Only like half."

"Aww." Grandmother kissed her atop the head. "You are so precious."

The brothers got into a mild argument over Luciano going into the Old City on his own, even if he had become old enough to go scavenge. Althea stood there, looking up at the men, turning her head back and forth like she watched two boys throwing a ball to follow their debate.

"Just a bonedog," said Luciano. "I would've been okay, but I fell."

Nicolás shook his head. "And what happens next time? The fiends are becoming bolder, angrier, and there are a lot more of them."

"The Watch should go out there and clean it up," muttered Grandmother.

Althea fidgeted. While bonedogs *were* a menace to people, and they likely had more than a little dark energy to them, she still thought of them as animals. The idea of the Watch going out there to kill them off bothered her. Of course, the Old City held worse dangers than simple bonedogs. The Many dwelled in the dark abandoned places of the Badlands, embodying half-living creatures like bonedogs or attracting mutated monsters like the part-living part-machine canids, massive roaches, or other horrors she had only heard of as rumor.

After what happened nine weeks ago, she figured The Many would be angry with her. Though she had chased him off, and had no desire to destroy him, he probably wanted to attack her again. Creatures massing in the Old City sounded like him being angry with her. Instead of the Watch going out there to shoot animals, maybe she could try doing the same thing she'd done when he had last confronted her. If she radiated enough of that white light she could make, perhaps the bonedogs and other monsters would find somewhere else to go, and no one would have to do any shooting.

She sighed silently out her nose. All she'd ever wanted was to help everyone she could. Why did The Many hate her so much?

"Please tell that father of yours that we are concerned about the dogs," said Grandmother.

"I will." Althea smiled up at her. "I should really go do the learning. Father wants me to."

Another round of hugs and head-pats later, she headed out the door, hooked left, and fast-walked to the end of the block. Guilt needled at her heels, urging her home as fast as possible so she could do the learning she'd been avoiding.

At the spot where the narrow 'people road' bent a corner to the left, she encountered a strange object that resembled a creature with a broad octagonal face and no arms, only one stick for a body. She'd seen them here and there before for years, but only now did it occur to her that it had frozen speech on it. Prior to her being forced to suffer with the learning machine, she had no idea the white marks had any meaning.

Curious, she stood on tiptoe and examined the four letters.

"S-t-o-p. Sah-toe-pee?" She scratched her head. "No, that doesn't sound like a real word. "Stoop? Umm. I don't think that's right either. Need two round ones together to make an oo. Stope?" She scrunched her eyebrows in thought. Never in her life had she ever heard anyone say 'stope.' Soap, yes. But not stope. A few seconds of staring later, she grinned. "Stop!"

The sign didn't react.

"Umm. Okay." She looked down at her blood-smeared feet. "I stopped."

Minutes passed. Althea stared at the sign expectantly. It still didn't say anything, so she kept waiting. After a while, she noticed the need to make water—pee as Karina called it—but the sign hadn't done anything... so she held it and kept standing there. Minutes later, she glanced at the lengthening shadow on the road and whined.

"Please? Can I go?" Althea squirmed, biting her lip. "Water wants out."

The sign didn't change.

After another few minutes, she gave serious consideration to simply letting the water out where she stood. Before she could make a decision, the scratch of boots approached from behind. She twisted to look at a man in a flannel shirt and jeans carrying one of the new city rifles the Zero police had brought here to protect the city.

Recognizing him as a member of the Watch, she waved with a big smile. "Hi, Miguel!"

"Hello, Althea." He started to smile, but his expression became one of concern. "You okay? That blood all over your legs?"

"Yes. Luciano was hurt and I sat in blood on the floor while making his hurt go away. I'm going home now."

"All right, sweetie." He started to walk off, but paused, raising an eyebrow at her.

She resumed watching the sign, but glanced over at Miguel when he continued to stare at her.

"Are you going home?" asked Miguel.

"Yes."

He scratched his chin. "Why are you just standing there?"

Althea pointed at the sign. "It told me to stop. And it didn't tell me I can go yet."

Miguel burst into laughter. She tilted her head in confusion. The look she gave him made him laugh harder, tears streaming from his eyes. Since he couldn't talk past his laughter, she peered into his thoughts. He'd never seen anyone actually stop for one of those old signs, and had no idea why the Ancients even made them. They certainly didn't mean for people to just stand there... and he thought of her as beyond adorable.

Althea blushed, feeling a little dumb. "Umm. Oops."

Miguel patted her on the back. "Thanks. I haven't had a laugh like that in years."

She looked down. "I thought it wanted me to stop."

"Aww. It's okay. Go on home."

"I will!" She smiled at him and hurried off down the street, running as fast as her need to make water allowed.

Upon arriving home, she raced to the bathroom and jumped on the strange chair with the water in the bottom. It still felt weird to sit on something while making water, but Karina and Father wanted her to use the thing they called 'toilet,' so she did. After, she wet a cloth at the sink and washed the blood from her legs and feet, then scrambled back downstairs to the couch where the annoying learning machine waited.

She flopped on the cushion, picked the book-sized thin plastic slab up, and swiped her finger at the top. A ghost of a blue cartoon rabbit appeared—a hologram according to the Zero police, who had strange words for everything. It rotated a few times before smiling at her.

"Welcome back, Althea!"

The rabbit changed into a picture of a classroom. Frozen speech on the 'chalkboard' read: 'Reading and Spelling – Grade 2 ages 6 to 8.' Althea frowned, mostly at herself, but a little at the machine for making fun of her again. Much younger children than her did 'grade two,' but she still struggled with it. That made her feel stupid.

She *really* wanted to learn from a person, not a machine. Or at least have some time each day to learn from a person and then deal with this machine afterward.

A crowd of children's voices approached outside, then, rapid thudding of feet on the porch. After three knocks, the door opened and Kim poked her head in, black hair hanging long to one side due to her leaning so far over. The thirteen-year-old had been one of the kids Archon rounded up for his gang. They'd met when she'd been ordered to bring Althea food. Kim didn't dislike the big city in the west like Althea did, but she also had nothing there to go back to. Her father was something called a senator, which meant he hated her for being psionic. The former city girl who'd grown up in the modern world now looked like most other kids in Querq, barefoot in a plain dress.

"Hey, Thea. Wanna play." She held up a dingy white ball.

Althea glanced at the teaching machine. Father would be disappointed in her if she didn't put in her time on it, but she *had* mended Luciano's leg. Even if she'd gone straight home from the farm, she wouldn't have been able to do much learning before Nicolás arrived to ask for help. The stop sign ate an embarrassingly long amount of time… but.

She also wanted a living teacher. And she'd been alone far too long today.

Father would understand… and she could still do her learning time after dinner.

"Yeah!" Althea turned off the electronic pad dropped it on the cushion, then ran off to play with her friends.

3

PICNIC

Althea played soccer with her friends until the daylight began to weaken. One by one, parents or older siblings called children home. Eventually, Karina's voice carried over the buildings, looking for her.

She waved to the other kids and ran off, racing down the road, over a dirt lot, and through a narrow gap between two patchwork houses to the street her house sat on. Karina waited on the porch, hands cupped over her mouth, still shouting her name every ten seconds.

Althea sprinted into a hug.

"Where have you been?" Karina spun her around once and set her down on her feet. "Is that blood on your dress?"

"Yes." Althea gripped the hem and pulled the fabric taut. "Luciano went into the Old City. A bonedog bit him."

Karina shivered. "You didn't go out there?!"

"No." On the way to the kitchen to wash her hands, Althea explained how her day had gone, including confessing to not doing her electronic learning.

Fortunately, the stop sign incident made Karina laugh too much to chide her for avoiding the lesson. Father walked in to find them clinging to the kitchen counter to keep from falling over from a severe case of the giggles. He paused in the doorway, watching with two raised eyebrows for a moment before grinning and crossing the room to hug them.

"It is wonderful to see my daughters so happy." He, too, noticed the blood on the white dress. "Thea? What happened?"

Althea repeated her explanation while helping Karina assemble enchiladas. Father looked down and sighed at her confession about not doing schoolwork, though he did chuckle at the stop sign story.

"I'm going to have the learning after dinner. Why do I have to use it? Can I please have a person teach me?" It would be as simple as making raiders leave her alone to force the Ravens—the town elders in their big black robes—to let her attend the school, but doing that didn't feel right.

"That is the plan, Thea." Father brushed a hand over her head. "But, you need to catch up first. Otherwise, you will not understand what they are teaching you."

"I think I will catch up faster with a person." She clasped her hands in front of herself. "The learning machine sounds happy, but it can't be happy. It makes me feel stupid."

"The machine doesn't mean to call you anything." He swiped at her stomach, tickling her.

She grabbed his finger in both hands, grinning.

As soon as they put the food in the oven, Althea went to the living room to fetch the learning machine, bringing it to the kitchen to work while dinner baked. Frozen speech appeared, and she had to read the word. If she didn't get it right in a few tries, it made a holographic picture of the object and let her try again. Father watched over her shoulder for a little while, saying soothing things whenever the chirpy rabbit voice told her she said the wrong word.

"Hon, do you feel a mind the way you do with people when you look at this thing?" asked Father.

"No." Althea shook her head. "It's not alive."

"You don't feel its emotions?"

She stuck out her tongue. "It's a machine."

"A machine that cannot feel happy because it makes fun of someone, or frustrated at you for not knowing answers."

"Yes." Althea nodded.

"The machine is not making fun of you. I believe you think it is because you want to learn faster and you're becoming frustrated. Stop thinking of yourself as dumb. You are not."

"But the other kids know more than me! Kim can even hear the frozen speech in books that don't have any pictures!" Althea slouched and emitted a defeated whine.

Karina grinned, removing the enchiladas from the oven.

"Perhaps, but does she know which plants she can eat? Or which critters out there are dangerous?"

"No. She's from the big city."

"She doesn't know more. You both know a lot, only different things." He patted her on the head. "Time to eat. That can wait for after."

"Okay." She grinned, shut down the device, and picked up her fork.

That—eating with utensils—at least, she had finally mastered.

ALTHEA SPENT MOST OF THE NEXT MORNING SITTING OUTSIDE ON THE porch with the learning machine.

As much as the thing frustrated her, Father's words rang true. It couldn't make fun of her or call her stupid. She imagined it doing so because *she* called herself stupid. But, those other kids had been going to school their whole lives—or at least from like age six. When they'd been learning how to understand the frozen words, Althea had been locked in a cage, hauled back and forth across the Badlands. The Wagon Man had taught her speaking words, but not frozen words.

Several abductions after she'd been taken from him, she'd spent a while with a nice man named Reed who taught her about plants and fishing and how to hide in the woods at an age when the other kids were learning stuff like farming or numbers. As best she could guess, she'd been eight then.

I do know stuff. Just different stuff. She huffed in determination. Her life had changed from one of feral survival to attempted civilization. That required learning more stuff. And really, what did it matter how much she did or didn't learn? No way could she ever see herself going to the bad city and trying to do bad city stuff with all the modern fancy complicated machines. She'd most likely live in Querq forever, mending the hurts and sicks from anyone who asked. Maybe she'd someday agree to let Den wife her—if the idea ever ceased being icky. The touching lips thing he did still felt weird, and she didn't completely understand why people did that. But it also kinda make her feel squirmy and tingly.

Good squirmy or bad squirmy, she hadn't yet figured out.

But, she had several years before she'd have to worry about

anything like that. Karina sometimes teased her that she might not even still like Den by the time she grew up enough to do more than touch lips with him. She frowned, tapping her feet on the wooden steps while thinking. Drawing flowers in the sand, running around with children her age or younger kicking a ball, or playing hide-and-seek made her happy. Even sitting around with littler girls pretending to drink tea and talk to dolls thrilled her because it made her feel like a normal child and not some possession to be shuttled around. She liked doing stuff some people might call her 'too old' for.

Althea closed her eyes, shivering at the memories of women screaming.

She'd also seen things no child should ever witness. Or most adults for that matter.

Once she realized she could command people when emotional manipulation didn't work, she stopped whatever wifeing she could. Even if some of the raiders suspected she had controlled them, they hadn't gone crazy or tried to burn her. Perhaps they valued having their inner bits put back together more than wifeing. Most of the adults here in Querq and with the Zero police found her non-reaction to gore disturbing. That, she didn't understand. No one got upset at seeing a person covered in grease while armpit deep in a machine to fix it; she thought of people the same way.

Dr. Ruiz in the clinic didn't mind looking inside people either, and no one thought it weird. Perhaps because he wasn't eleven. She'd been literally elbow-deep in bodies for as long as she could remember and associated the sight of horrible wounds with the awesome happiness she experienced after she stopped people from dying.

However, for the time being, she had a different job—she had to learn how to 'child.'

And generally learn.

So, she resigned herself to working with this electronic device. Maybe she should use the city people's word for it, 'datapad,' instead of calling it the learning machine.

Nah. She didn't like anything about the big city.

Not even its words.

LATE THAT AFTERNOON, ALTHEA RECLINED ON THE GROUND A SHORT distance from a fast-flowing stream. Den stretched out beside her, also gazing at the clouds. She leaned against a steep hillside, ankles crossed, smiling up at the clear, cloudless sky.

Whenever she spent time with him, she'd pull the agate arrowhead pendant out from under her dress so he could see she kept it. He had worn it since he'd been old enough to walk, a gift from his father, the chief of his tribe and sign of his claim to the throne. When the raiders had snatched Althea in front of him, he had given it to her. Soon after she had returned home from the bad city after helping stop The Many from killing all those people, Den had told her what the pendant meant. In that moment before the raiders took her away from him, his giving her the agate arrowhead had been his way of saying he chose her over his title, his tribe, even his family.

Althea glanced down at her chest, brushing her thumb over the green stone.

Den laced his fingers behind his head. He'd taken his boots and socks off, though still wore his shirt and jeans. Despite his being a bit on the young side at fourteen, he had joined the Watch. So far, he hadn't had to shoot anyone.

He'd packed a few empanadas for their 'lunch outside,' as well as a jug of water.

Althea had brought up the lip-touching thing soon after they'd finished eating. In an effort to figure out the point of it, she looked into his thoughts right after asking. He didn't entirely understand why people did it either, but had seen many people in his old tribe doing that when they liked each other. Also, Den suspected they did other things, but had no idea exactly what. The boy had never observed raiders wifeing their captives and couldn't understand why the idea of it disgusted Althea so much. It did confuse her that he thought of wifeing as something permanent that happened between two people. That worried her quite a bit since the longest she'd ever seen anyone wifed had been a little over an hour—and the poor woman had been hurt by it.

Permanent didn't even seem possible. Wouldn't that kill them both?

Eyes closed, she stopped trying to understand and simply listened to the rush of the water going by. The stream didn't work for swimming since it only came up to her knees in the deepest spots, had lots of sharp rocks, and a strong current that could knock her over if she didn't make herself stronger. Most people in Querq came out to this spot to wash clothes, but it also offered nice, peaceful scenery for a picnic with a boy she liked.

It didn't even bother her being so far away from town that they'd even gone past the edge of the Old City—now that she wouldn't hesitate to *make* raiders leave her alone, she didn't worry about them showing up to kidnap her. Besides, after six months, any raider group in the area tempted to abduct her from Querq would have tried already. It didn't seem likely that the largely disorganized, impulsive bands of marauding nomads would set off from far away and commit to an attack on such a well-defended place.

"It's so quiet," said Den. "Except the water."

She smiled. "It is loud."

"Do you like it here?"

Althea nodded. "Yeah. A lot."

"It is much different from the village." He sat up and poked at the dirt beside his knee. A waft of sadness emanated from him.

She also sat up, squinting at the sun in her eyes. "You miss your father?"

"He was mean to you."

"Not as mean as Palik." Althea frowned, thinking of the wannabe chamán who at first wanted to kill her, then objected to the tribe allowing her out of the cage.

Den dug a little hole with his finger. "He had the envy of you. Called himself chamán, but couldn't remember what powders to use."

"Yes. Palik thought himself important. He wanted people to have the fear when he looked at them."

He glanced up at her. "You can give people the fear if you want."

"I can." She held her head high. "But it doesn't give me the happy. Being with you does."

A bit of blush darkened his cheeks.

"The tribe didn't like me. Half had the fear, and half had the wanting. They thought having me in the village gave your father power. Only you…" She furrowed her brows trying to think of the right words. "I don't really have the speaking for how I feel. To them, I was a thing to have. But to you, I was me."

Den took a deep breath and sighed it out. "I did not care of anything but to find you. Not the tribe, not becoming the next chief, not being chased by bonedogs or shot by raiders. You speak truth. My father was mean to you. And to me as well."

She brushed a hand at his cheek. "You have the sad."

"As his son, I cannot hate *him*, but I hate what he did."

Anger mixed with his sorrow, but both faded to happiness when he looked over at her. At least until the shame welled up. No matter how many times she tried to tell him that he couldn't possibly have done anything to stop that man with the strange name and sword, he didn't believe her. Den had no way to understand psionics like that. She didn't exactly understand it either, but Officer David said the guy could make himself as strong as a machine. He'd even thrown Shepherd through a cinder block wall.

"I'm happy because you are here with me." She took his hand, her fingers pale against his rich sienna skin. "I know you have the like for me because you walked so far to find me."

Den smiled… perhaps for the first time in months. The sun at his back shadowed his face, but his wide, brown eyes reflected the glow from hers. She reached up to caress his cheek, a gesture she had seen some young women in Querq doing with men. He appeared to expect her to do the lip-touching thing and half-closed his eyes. Althea grinned to herself and started to lean closer, but paused just shy of contact when a strong sense of worry fell on her.

She leaned back with a gasp. Old feral instincts kicked in; she scrambled from sitting to squatting with her hands braced on the ground between her feet, staying low while being ready to dash away. Like a spooked squealer, she twisted side to side, gazing at their surroundings, but nothing in sight appeared to be the cause of the inexplicable dread.

"What's wrong?" Den rested his left hand on the rifle he'd brought with them.

"I have a seeing," whispered Althea. "The clairvoy ants talk to me. Bad is here…"

"Where?" He shifted to one knee and picked up the weapon.

"I don't—" She froze when the odd warning sense evaporated. For no particular reason, she looked straight up. Yet, nothing dangerous appeared to be falling toward them. Somehow, she believed the sky had a connection to the bad feeling, though nothing presently struck her as threatening. *It isn't now, but soon.* "Umm… It's gone."

The sorrow and homesickness that had been clinging to him

disappeared under a wave of protectiveness. He thought she appeared small and frightened, mistaking her wariness for fear. Officer David called those strange feelings clairvoy ants, but she didn't think bugs had anything to do with it. Since that man with the white fire on his arms had nearly killed Den, the boy had been preoccupied with feelings of inadequacy. Pretending to be scared and wanting him to protect her would make him feel better, but it also felt too much like speaking the false.

She wouldn't act scared, but she didn't have to correct his assumption either.

Before either one of them could speak again, the scuff of footsteps approached from the east.

Althea leaned closer to Den and grasped his right arm with both hands. Though she touched him with the intent to give his body a psionic boost if needed, he again mistook her for being scared and gripped his fancy city rifle.

Four men walked into view out from behind the ruins of a Before-Time building some distance away on the opposite side of the creek, the outermost edge of the Old City. All appeared to be adults, neither old nor young. They wore clothing mostly of animal hide, though here and there, a scrap of scavenged pre-war fabric added color. All four were on the darker side of brown with black hair, like many people in Querq. The one leading the group carried a shotgun. The two behind him wielded long scrap metal spears, and the fourth man pulled a large cart made from the back end of what Father called a 'pickup truck.'

"They will not take you," whispered Den.

Althea nodded once. She had no intention of letting anyone take her.

The man with the shotgun spotted them, gesturing in their direction. The two with spears looked, muttered words too faint to hear, and the group veered to their left, walking straight toward them. Squeaks and rattles came from the cart the fourth man pulled.

Since she'd been spotted, Althea rose to her feet, released Den's arm, and stood tall, chin high. He scrambled upright, rifle held sideways in a nonthreatening—but ready—manner. She read the men's emotions: mostly worry from the three in front, and exhaustion from the man pulling the cart, tinged with a smidge of anger.

The shotgun-carrier stopped at the edge of the stream, gazing over it at them. "Hello. Heard there's a settlement around here somewhere. Do you children know—holy shit, it's the Prophet!"

His emotion changed to elation.

Althea clenched her hands into fists, bracing for the men to charge across the water and come after her. Every time someone yelled that, she'd ended up kidnapped.

"Stay back." Den pointed his rifle generally at them.

"Hey, now." The man with the shotgun leaned back. "We don't want trouble. Nom is hurt."

"It's a trick," whispered Den.

Althea narrowed her eyes, peering into the stranger's surface thoughts at the form of a battered man lying in the wagon, shot with multiple arrows during a raider attack. The group had been hunting for Querq, having heard she might be there. They had no intention of abducting her, merely hoped she could save their friend's life.

She put a hand on Den's rifle and pushed it down.

He glanced at her, confused.

They do not speak the false. I see his mind. Their friend is hurt.

Den flinched a little at her telepathic voice, but nodded.

She approached the stream, annoyed at herself for being so easily abducted before—especially the time that man faked injury near the water pump. Had she read *his* mind, she never would have ended up Archon's prisoner and missed bath night. It bothered her to think that being so trusting of people had ended up causing her to suffer. That she *had* to peer at people's thoughts and couldn't simply trust everyone saddened her more than being kidnapped.

Why did people have to be so mean?

Althea subconsciously boosted the muscles in her legs as she ran up to a jog and leapt across the stream. Despite the momentary augmentation to her strength, she didn't clear the entire creek, landing in a few inches of water at the other side frigid enough to make her gasp.

Den waded across the stream, navigating the strange squarish rocks with sharp points. The water didn't even reach his knees.

"I am Pol," said the lead man, while hanging his shotgun over his shoulder on a strap. He offered a hand, helping her step up out of the water. "Nom is in the cart. We fear he may go to the Ancestors soon. Pava and Raal are with me."

The men both bowed their heads in reverence at her.

"Please don't worship me. I will help your friend." Althea hurried to the back of the wagon and peered over the tailgate.

Another man the same general age as the rest, mid-twenties, lay unconscious in a hastily-assembled nest of blankets. Three aluminum shafts stuck out of him, two in the chest, one in the right thigh. He remained alive, though his breathing appeared too slow and a layer of sweat covered his face.

Pol and Den hurried around to stand behind her.

She raised a foot to the bumper and grabbed the top of the tailgate. "When he lifts his hand, take the arrows out. He will not feel pain."

Pol made a confused noise.

"It is fine," said Den. "Do as she asks."

Althea climbed into the cart and sat on the wheel well nearer the man. She pulled the blankets open at the chest, revealing a squealer hide shirt punctured by two arrows. One had to be in his air bag, the other only muscle. She slipped a hand under the shirt, resting her palm flat on his too-warm chest… then closed her eyes.

Her power connected her mind to his life essence, creating a floating image of the man's body. Thin black voids revealed the position of the arrows, places where the metal had pushed his flesh away. Many sicks, yellow, white, and green, swirled around in his blood-presence. Raiders often dipped their arrows in foul things on purpose. More victims died later to the poison or filth than directly from being shot.

First things first.

She commanded his mind to ignore pain, directed the blood-presence to stay inside the body, then made his right arm move by manipulating the muscles. Soon after his hand rose into the air, the black line of an arrow in his left air bag shrank away almost to nothing. Den's faint grunt came from somewhere in front of her as the second arrow, deep in chest muscles, pulled away at the same time the one in his leg withdrew, likely Pol's doing.

A few small bits of metal remained, broken off the arrowheads. Althea forced his body to regrow itself in tiny spurts that pushed each fragment upward, eventually squeezing them out from the skin. Next, she sealed two of the arrow wounds, but not the hole over his lung, since the air bag had collapsed. After allowing some of her consciousness to emerge from the healing trance, she bent forward and blew into Nom's nose, ignoring the salty taste of sweat.

Wet sputtering came from the remaining arrow wound as the air bag inflated. Once she sealed the puncture so that no more air could go where it didn't belong, she sat up straight and dove again into the full healing trance.

Gathering all the sick out of him took some time. The streamers of badness flowing around his body responded to her psionic energy and moved as she directed, concentrating in his bladder. Finally, she urged the blood-presence to swell. He had lost quite a bit on his trip here.

When she could do no more for him, she released her connection and opened her eyes all the way.

Den sat on the other wheel well, facing her. Pol stood in the cart to Den's left, closer to the man's legs.

"He will need to make water to let out the sick. It will have the pain, so I will help." Althea took Nom's hand.

Pol bowed to her. "You are most kind."

A moment later, Nom opened his eyes and groaned. "Ugh. Gah…" He rolled on his side and curled up.

"You must make water soon," said Althea. "You have sick that needs to come out. It will be like fire if I do not help."

Nodding, Nom moaned and forced himself up onto his knees. Pol opened the tailgate and helped him down. Althea walked alongside him for a short distance, holding his hand so she could turn off his sense of pain while he let out the foul water. A smell like rotting meat filled the air.

"Why is it this color?" asked Nom.

"Because it is made of sick, not pee." Althea grinned at herself for remembering the 'civilized' word for it.

Nom gagged on the smell.

She waited patiently, keeping him from burning as he let the disease out. Eventually, Nom staggered backward, finished. Althea released his hand and guided him back over to the other men.

"Nom!" said Pava. "You live!"

Raal raised his spear over his head in one hand, pumping his fist. "Praise the Prophet!"

Althea opened her mouth to protest, but upon sensing he meant that more as a 'thank you' than worship, remained quiet.

Pol hefted a metal tool box out of the wagon and carried it over. "It is not much, but we brought it as an offering for your help."

Althea peered quizzically at it for a second before opening the lid. The two-foot-long box had been filled roughly a third of the way with coins of various sizes and colors. "Oh, no. You do not have to give me pay-things!" She shivered with guilt. The Wagon Man made people give him pay-things or he wouldn't let them near her. She wanted to help, but that man had kept her constantly in a small cage. "Please. I do not need them."

Pol tilted his head. "But you have allowed Nom to keep his life, brought him back from the path to the Ancestors."

"Yes." Althea grinned. "It gives me the happy to help people. It is wrong to demand pay-things to make the hurts and sicks go away."

"Aww, damn," said Nom, rubbing his stomach. "I could eat a whole damn squealer myself right about now."

Althea hugged Pol. "Thank you for wanting to give me a gift, but life is not something that pay things can trade for. I will help everyone who needs."

Pol regarded her for a moment in confusion. "The legends said you would demand offerings of coin."

"The legends are wrong." Althea shook her head. "*I* never wanted offerings. The Wagon Man did. He would not let me help anyone who did not give him pay things. He has been dead for a long time."

Pol's eyes widened.

"I did not harm him. Others killed him to steal me from him." She patted him on the arm. "You can use the pay-things in Querq."

"All right," said Pol.

He smiled, giving off a strong enough sense of relief that Althea couldn't resist looking into his mind to see why. His entire settlement had pooled their pay-things in hopes they would have enough to buy Nom's life from her. She bit her lip, moved by everyone so freely giving up their pay-things for someone else—but also angry that people thought she wanted them to.

"Please tell people they do not need pay-things." Althea tugged on his arm. "I don't want anyone to die because they have none."

"I will." Pol handed the box of money to Pava, who hauled it back to the cart. I had meant to ask you for help finding the place called Querq before realizing who you were. Would you please guide us there so we may rest and obtain provisions?"

"Follow the water in that direction." Den pointed to the left. "Where it goes under the stone path, cross the water and then and follow the stone path. It leads to the gate. When you pass through the Old City, be wary of bonedogs or other things. They usually do not come out during the day."

"You have our gratitude." Pol—and the other men—bowed to her.

Althea took Den's hand and walked with him to the stream. She hopped from rock to rock, the sun-touched stone hot at her soles, then dashed over to sit beside his boots and socks. Once again, Den waded across. He settled down beside her, legs out straight.

The five men walked off to the left, following the stream. A bridge where the water passed into a big metal tube under a Before-Time road sat a quarter-mile off. She leaned against him watching the men walk off, sighing in embarrassment at overhearing them speak of how great and kind the Prophet is.

Den put an arm around her. She smiled and leaned against him, but couldn't quite feel content. Worry about the danger she'd sensed earlier lingered. Those five men couldn't have been the cause. Pol's thoughts didn't contain anything scarier than the hope they would find her and she could save Nom's life.

That meant someone else—or some*thing*—else dangerous had yet to show up.

Cuddling under the late afternoon sun soon became tentative lip-touching. That didn't bother her at all, even if she didn't fully understand why it made her feel odd. Raiders never did the lip touching thing with their captives that she'd seen. The gesture felt far too tender and loving to be anything people like that would want to do.

Den leaned back after a few minutes. "Something is wrong."

"Am I not lip-touching good?"

"Your mind is not here." He stared deep into her eyes. "Where does it go?"

Althea fidgeted at the worry radiating from him. "The seeing I had before."

"You felt those men."

She shook her head and whispered, "No. They were not bad. Something else is—"

Snap.

They both peered back at the hill they'd been sitting against, too high to see past.

Another *snap* came from behind the top.

She grabbed his shoulder, certain the reason for her premonition tried to sneak up on them.

Someone's coming!

Den rolled over onto his chest, grabbed the rifle, and crawled up the hill.

For a second, she hesitated, biting her lip… then decided to follow.

Althea would not allow whoever came to take her to hurt Den.

4

FIVE YEARS

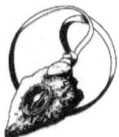

Althea crept to the top of the shallow hill, flat on her belly beside Den.

They peeked over at the same time, peering through scrub brush that should mostly conceal them from view—at a young couple she recognized: Adriana and Elias. As soon as she saw them, Althea relaxed. People from Querq wouldn't be any danger to her or Den unless The Many somehow influenced them. And even then, she could make him go away.

Officer David hadn't been able to explain how exactly she did it, but he floated the idea that Althea's presence here somehow protected the village from that creature's influence. He described her like a bright light chasing away shadows.

Elias sat on the ground beside a basket that no doubt held food. Adriana sat beside him facing the opposite way. They whispered a few things to each other, then began touching lips.

Worry gone, Althea ceased being the Prophet... and turned into a grinning eleven-maybe-twelve-year-old watching people be cute while trying not to giggle out loud. Den turned his head toward her for a second, evidently confused about what to do.

Althea covered her mouth with a hand. Her amusement gave way to curiosity when Adriana and Elias did something different. They opened their mouths during the lip-touching.

Den nudged her.

She glanced at him.

He flared his eyes, then tapped the side of his head.

Figuring he wanted her to look so he could say something without making a sound, she peeked at his thoughts.

Why are they shaking tongues? asked Den, comparing their activity to people shaking hands.

Althea glanced at the couple for a moment, observing them. *I don't know.*

They watched in silence for a few minutes.

Adriana leaned back from Elias and pulled her beige dress off over her head. He hastily removed his shirt and pants. Both of them radiated love to such a degree that Althea couldn't help but mutter 'aww.'

They resumed doing that tongue-touching thing after shedding their clothes. That looked like one of those activities Father didn't want Althea doing until she turned sixteen. But Adriana and Elias were both twenty, so they must have permission from their fathers.

Althea tapped Den on the arm, but he didn't look. She kept tapping him for a few more seconds—with increasing force—until he finally glanced away from them. *Why did they take their clothes off? Are they going swimming?* She didn't think he intended to wife Adriana, since the woman hadn't been tied or put on a leash, and didn't give off any sense of fear.

He shrugged, thinking swimming would be unlikely since they were so far from the stream… plus no one swam in the stream. They used a big hole in the ground full of water inside Querq where a building had once stood.

She peered back at them, trying to understand why they'd undress if not to take a bath, go swimming, or cope with excessive heat. Elias embraced Adriana, eventually rolling sideways so they lay on the ground.

Their emotions changed. Love remained strong, but something else… an emotion Althea feared, joined it. The same emotion raiders often gave off when looking at harem slaves.

Her eyes widened.

She emitted a faint growl and started to climb upright, but Den grabbed her shoulder and pulled her back down, shaking his head.

He's gonna wife her! Althea stared at him. *I have to stop it!*

Again he shook his head.

But! But! Wifeing is bad! She's gonna scream and cry!

Den tapped his head.

She clutched two handfuls of dirt in frustration, but forced her panic aside to look at his thoughts.

It's okay if she wants to do it. They're both happy right? She isn't scared?

Althea glanced back at Adriana. Numerous emotions shone from her presence, but no fear. The woman practically burst with love, excitement, and happiness… and gave off quite a bit of that other emotion that scared her. Officer David called it lust. He also had become extremely embarrassed talking about it with her. She figured it had something to do with bunnies and rainbows since his thoughts had filled with images of that when she asked him what lust meant. But that didn't make any sense either. What she'd witnessed in the various raider camps had nothing at all to do with cute furry animals or colorful rainbows.

A few minutes later, Adriana did something she'd never seen anyone do before. Den gave off a high dose of confusion as well as a weaker form of lust, but mostly worry.

She elbowed him until he looked at her. *Why is she lip-touching with his boy part?*

He made faces at her like a fish out of water. His thoughts held a bizarre mix of abject bewilderment and the urge to keep watching. She furrowed her brows and resumed watching the couple.

Eep. Is she trying to eat *it? Eww. Why is she doing that?* She'd seen mothers kiss boo-boos on small kids, maybe he hurt his boy part?

Again, Althea started to stand, this time to go see if he needed healing.

Den grabbed her and held her down, shaking his head.

He might be hurt.

He shook his head harder, then whispered, "He's not hurt."

She looked back at Elias. The face he made sure looked like he experienced a great deal of pain. However, his emotional radiance remained squarely in the love/pleasure spectrum. One or two raiders had reacted to being shot with the same emotion, but they had been *quite* broken in the brain-shape. Elias, as far as Althea knew, didn't have a head sick, so he must not be suffering.

He let out a long, low moan in time with a huge blast of pleasure.

Althea ducked lower to the ground and nudged Den. *Do you want to do that?*

The weird little grin on his face evaporated in an instant. He shook his head, nodded, then shook his head, then turned red. Scowling, he pointed at his temple.

What?

Your father will kill me and wear my hide as a tunic if we do anything more than touch lips until you're at least sixteen. That's five years away. We're both still too young for what those two are doing. We shouldn't even be watching it. Though he said otherwise, his emotions indicated he wanted to keep watching.

Oh. She looked back toward the couple—who both glanced over at that exact moment and stared straight at her.

Glowing blue eyes didn't exactly work wonders for stealth.

The emotional radiance coming from the couple exploded into mortification.

She glanced at Den. "They're embarrassed? Why? When raiders did the wifeing, they didn't care if people watched."

"What are you two doing over there?" yelled Elias. "Get back to your parents!"

"A-Althea?" said Adriana. "Why are you spying on us?"

She stood. "Sorry. I got a scare that someone bad was trying to hurt me, and heard noise. When I saw you, I got confused. Didn't know what you were doing."

"Aww." Adriana blushed, then made a shooing motion. "Go on home."

"Okay. Sorry!" She backed down the hill.

Den shimmied down the hill, still flat on his front.

"We should go home," said Althea.

"Yeah."

"Why aren't you standing up?"

"Umm. Because. Need a minute."

She scratched her head. "Is something wrong?"

Den's face turned bright red. "Umm. No. I just wanna, umm, rest here a bit."

Althea shifted her jaw side to side, thinking. He hadn't radiated any sense of embarrassment while watching Adriana and Elias, but now, he gave off tons of it. Since she promised not to look into his head unless he asked her to or said it was okay, she simply waited.

Soft whispering and laughter came from Adriana and Elias; however, it didn't sound like they did anything more than talk.

Eventually, Den rolled over to sit, grabbing his socks. Once he had his boots on, he stood, slung his rifle over his shoulder, and dusted his jeans off. Hand in hand, they walked along the stream, heading back to Querq.

"Weird," said Althea.

"There's a big difference between wifeing and what they were going to do."

"How?" She pulled her hair off her face and smiled at him.

"Umm. I'll tell you in five years."

She folded her arms, about to protest it would only be four since she considered herself twelve. But those corporation people from the bad city who tried to abduct her called her eleven. She still didn't know her true age. Father declared that she was eleven until next year, so she'd have to accept that. Annoyed, she muttered, "I don't understand and I don't like waiting. I just want to understand, not *do* anything."

Den laughed. "Your father likes that you don't understand, and I'm not going to make him angry."

"I don't want to make him angry either." She stuck her tongue out at him. "But I don't think you know what wifeing is either."

He shrugged. "Not exactly, but I know it's supposed to be nice. Something two people who love each other do. Become husband and wife."

Althea decided there had to be another word for it. What she understood as wifeing would *never* happen between people who loved each other. Once she got home, she'd ask Father if he knew what to call the thing Den thought of.

But he probably wouldn't tell her yet.

Not for another five years.

5

GHOSTS

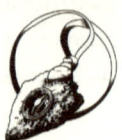

Father cooked dinner that night, making a dish with beans, rice, and chicken.

While he worked in the kitchen, Althea sat on the couch using the learning machine. A long session the other day had almost brought her to the end of the second-grade spelling lesson.

"You're doing it really fast." Karina looked up from her knitting. "See, you are smart. Most kids take a whole year for it."

Althea shrugged. "I'm too old. This is for little kids. It says so right here."

"You know some of it already. All you have to do is catch up."

The word 'carrot' appeared. She said it.

"Good!" chirped the blue rabbit.

'Tree' appeared.

"You spelled it wrong. The number is three!"

"Almost," said the blue rabbit. "Try again."

"Three!" yelled Althea.

"You've almost got it." The rabbit jumped and waved. "Try again."

Althea snarled, almost threw the learning machine to the floor, but calmed herself.

"Terry."

An image of a pine tree appeared above the word.

"*Pino*," said Althea.

"English, please," replied the rabbit. "Sound out the letters."

Frustration built. "Te-ree."

The rabbit made sad eyes at her.

"There's no 'e' in it," said Karina. "Just roll the T into the ree."

Althea furrowed her brows. "Tree."

"Woo-hoo!" cheered the rabbit. Happy music played for a few seconds while it danced.

While the animation might have made a six-year-old giggle, it made Althea feel stupid. She sulked, ashamed of herself until the display stopped.

'Reassembler' appeared.

Althea screamed in frustration.

Karina ran over. "What? What's wrong?"

She pointed at the screen.

"Umm. Whoa." Karina leaned closer, reading. "I have no idea what that is. But, you don't need to in order to speak the word. Use the letters."

Althea tripped over trying to pronounce the word a few times, squeezing the learning machine tighter and tighter each time the rabbit's overly cheerful voice told her to try again. After three failed tries, an image of a silvery box appeared above the word. It had a door-like section and a panel with buttons.

"I don't know what this is." Althea pointed at it. "It's something from the bad city."

"Umm. I have no idea what that is either, but it's not asking you to guess. It just wants you to read the word. Sound it out."

Althea scowled.

"Okay. Can you spell re?"

"Re isn't a word."

Karina laughed. "No, but it's a part of one."

"R. E."

"Okay. Can you spell ass?"

"A-r-c-h-o-n," said Althea with a smirk.

"Aww." Karina hugged her.

"Why did he have to do that? I couldn't... I had to... Anna..."

"Don't cry."

She took a deep breath, then huffed. "A-s-s."

"Okay. Em."

"M."

"There's an e in front of it."

Althea looked up at her, mouth agape. "But why? It's just m! Why do they have to put in stupid nothing letters that don't say anything? This is *so* confusing."

"I have no idea. But that's how it's spelled." Karina leaned close and whispered 'reassembler.'

Althea wanted to throw the datapad across the room. "That's not even fair! That's a made up word that doesn't mean anything." She sighed and recited the word to the electronic tablet, which emitted a happy chirp.

"Very good! You've completed this module." The cartoon rabbit disappeared and a miniature fireworks display went off.

Althea twitched at the explosions and bangs, but didn't dive to the floor, even if it did sound like a bunch of raiders shooting at each other.

"Come and eat!" called Father.

She happily tossed the pad onto the cushion and scrambled to her feet, racing Karina down the hall to the kitchen. They squeezed through the door at the same time and took their seats. Over the meal, Althea told him of meeting Pol and his friends, as well as seeing Adriana and Elias. Father didn't seem at all happy to hear what she'd witnessed, but he also didn't spend much time talking about it beyond asking her to run off and go somewhere else if ever she stumbled on people doing that again.

"I will." She stared at him with an apology glowing from her eyes.

He chuckled. "It's all right. You are young and… innocent. Curious. It is rude to hide and watch people doing that."

Karina bit her lip, too embarrassed to speak.

They ate in silence for a little while. Althea chickened out at asking Father if he had a different word to use for wifeing when the woman *wanted* to do it. He would either ignore the question or assume things had happened between her and Den, then go hurt him.

So instead, she talked about finishing the second-grade spelling lesson.

"Excellent! Tomorrow, I shall talk to Julio and try to convince him that you can go with the other children to school in the day."

"Axton said that kids don't usually go to school during the summer." Karina glanced back and forth between them while eating a forkful of rice.

"Who is Axton?" asked Father, eyebrow up.

"One of the Zero Police from the big city in the west."

Althea, sensing her older sister's emotion, gasped. *She likes him!*

Karina gave her the 'don't you dare say it!' look.

Althea giggled.

"How old is this man?" Father leaned on the table.

Karina shrugged. "Seventeen. And we only talked."

"You are sixteen, Kara."

"I know."

"He's a grown man."

"No, he isn't. He's only one year older than I am." Karina snapped her head up, tossing her hair back in one fluid move. "I'm allowed to *talk* to people still, aren't I? He answered questions about his city."

Althea stuck her tongue out.

"Mmm. You know I am just worried about keeping you safe." Father reached across the table and patted her arm.

Karina smiled. "I know."

"Why don't they go to school in the summer?" asked Althea.

"He didn't know why they do it. Just something that's been happening for like hundreds of years." Karina shrugged and kept eating.

"Well," said Father. "We only recently opened the school here, now that those people from the west are here helping out. Maybe they'll close it for a break, maybe not."

Althea shrugged to herself. She didn't really care either way if school stopped for a few months or kept going.

After dinner, she helped Karina clean up all the dishes. An accidental drop of a plate into the water started a playful battle of tossing soap foam back and forth while laughing. Perhaps some things—like the bubble soap—that came from the big city weren't so bad after all. When they finished cleaning up, they spent the rest of the time they had before bed on the couch, Karina teaching her about knitting.

Once they'd crawled in bed for the night, Althea's curiosity got the better of her.

"You know what wifeing means?"

Karina shuddered. "Yes. You've told me. Why?"

"Is there a different word for when both people *want* to do it?"

"They call it 'making love' or *relaciones.*"

"Really?"

"Yes. Now go to sleep." Karina kissed the side of her head.

"How can someone do that forever?" asked Althea.

"They can't. It's not even possible."

Althea rolled her head to look at her sister. "Den said he thought wifeing was forever."

"Aww." Karina smiled. "He's thinking of getting married, not doing a physical act. And, you shouldn't even talk about that either at your age. He's way too young for that."

"Married?"

"I want to sleep. That would take a long time to explain. Can I tell you later?"

"Okay."

Althea made a face at the ceiling. The term confused her because people 'made love' all the time even when they didn't do anything even close to wifeing each other. Every time she saw her family, she gave off love. Whenever Father was around either one of them, he radiated it, too. 'Making love' didn't seem like a great name for a physical act. The Water Man created lots of love when he saw his dog Ornry, and so did the dog. Then again, that dog loved everyone. There had to be a better word, since to Althea, a hundred different things from the reaction of a beautiful sunset, to seeing a kitten, to being with her family could cause someone to make love.

But, she didn't need to know it now.

It can wait five years.

She rolled her eyes, then closed them.

ALTHEA FOUND HERSELF FULLY AWAKE FOR NO APPARENT REASON.

Her surroundings appeared black-and-white, which meant the sun hadn't come up yet. A strong sense of warning gripped her. Knowing something *bad* would happen soon, she leapt out of bed and hurriedly changed out of her nightgown into the dress she'd worn the previous day. She almost shouted for Father, but her clairvoy ants must have given her an alarm. Making noise would also warn whoever threatened her, or her family.

She didn't detect any nearby mental energy or emotions except for Father and Karina, so she ran out into the hallway toward Father's room.

Two steps out her door, she crashed into something neither hard nor truly soft, somewhat like an armored raider's body—only nothing was there. The air in front of her shimmered.

Ghost!

Althea whirled to run away... but hands made out of nothingness grabbed her.

Thin air five feet in front of her split open, revealing a dark pant leg and belt—and a hand holding a mirror-finished pistol.

She simultaneously screamed and braced her body to purge itself of the drugs that would put her to sleep.

The gun went off with a soft *pthoonk*. A painful impact struck her in the center of the chest like a rock. She peered down at a tiny black cylinder no bigger than the tip section of a man's finger.

"Fath—"

Bzzt!

Blue sparks danced around the little projectile. A brief flicker of pain washed over her entire body.

And everything went dark.

6

THE VOICE THAT SPEAKS FALSE

The worst headache Althea ever had dragged her back to consciousness.

An irritating, continuous roar came from somewhere nearby, making her head pound even more. She tried to reach up to her face, but couldn't move. A few seconds of struggling penetrated the fog in her brain and she realized her hands were tied behind her back.

Grr. Not again.

She opened her eyes to a small, rectangular enclosure that reminded her somewhat of the metal box she had used for a bedroom while staying with Whisk and the others at the Bumwallow, only smaller. Four featureless walls and a ceiling surrounded her with no buttons, handles, or levers. Light blooms appeared on the polished plastisteel wherever she looked, reflections of the glow in her eyes. The chamber didn't have enough room to let her stretch out to her full height lengthwise, but did allow her to sit up without bonking her head.

Her abductors hadn't taken her dress away, even though the modern garment was so nice and clean any raider group would probably have stolen it, even from the Prophet. No raider could fit into it, but they could cut it open and make it into a skirt. Aside from a small black dot in the middle of her chest where the strange projectile had hit her, the garment remained intact.

Shiny metal bands encircled her ankles, connected by a short length of chain. Both shackles had small strips that glowed with pale green light next to minuscule keypads. Althea growled at the binders. One raider group had put handcuffs on her legs like this when she'd been about nine to keep her from running away. Of course, those hadn't been electronic. She fidgeted at the restraints, making the metal click.

Rather than being frightened or sad, she grew furious... but held her anger back. As soon as whoever abducted her opened this box, she would force them to set her free and hit them with a sad bomb so heavy they'd spend the next month weeping.

"Karina's dead," whispered a voice out of nowhere.

Althea gasped. "What?"

She listened, but nothing replied.

"Who said that? You're speaking the false!"

"Father's dead," whispered a voice as if someone's lips hovered at her ear.

"No!" she spun to the right, but found no one there, merely a plain metal wall.

Growling, Althea struggled to wriggle her hands out of whatever bound her wrists. She didn't have enough room inside the cargo box to maneuver her arms around her backside, nor could she pull her hands free of the cord.

She landed on her side, glaring at the wall, too angry to even scream.

I hate being the Prophet! Why can't people just leave me alone! I wanna go home!

The eerie voice whispered, "Home is gone. They destroyed it to take you. Everywhere you go gets destroyed. Everywhere you ever go will be destroyed."

"No!" screamed Althea. "Who keeps saying that?"

Another voice that reminded her of the girl Esmerelda who started a fight with her once over soccer whispered, "I still hate you. I only have to pretend to be nice because my father will hit me."

She pivoted and double-kicked the wall, but the metal didn't give.

"I'm being stupid. I can't even make myself strong enough to break this." She rolled on her side and squirmed around, attempting to look at her arms. Black cord had been tied around her wrists, but rather than a knot, a molten lump secured it. The cord stretched ever so slightly like rubber when she struggled. That made her think it would be easy to cut —if she could find a blade.

The constant roaring noise increased in pitch. She slid into the wall, then squeezed into the floor. The feeling reminded her of being in the flying city car with Officer David. That thought brought another wave of anger. Someone from the big city would have magic they could use to sneak into Querq and take her. The man she'd run into in her house had been invisible... somehow. It *might* have been magic like a Scrag mystic... wait, no, they used psionics like her. But, no mystic would have a flying car or a metal box like this. Nor would they have that zappy gun. A mystic who wanted to abduct her would have tried to use magic on her, and she would have laughed at him.

Sometimes, being an Awakened psionic could be nice. She'd like it much more if it didn't make everyone want to kidnap her.

"Den doesn't really love you. He only wanted power," whispered a voice.

"Who is speaking the false?" asked Althea, in an angry tone. She struggled at the restraints, looking around her small enclosure—clearly alone. "There's no room in here for anyone else. Who are you?"

No replies came.

She closed her eyes and concentrated on wanting Father to help her. The instant the intent to broadcast a beacon to him formed in her head, a tremendous shock blasted across her skull.

Althea screamed, nearly making water from how much it hurt.

"Ow!" she wailed, curling up in a ball.

With her hands tied behind her, she couldn't grab her throbbing eyeballs, and settled for pressing her face against her knees. When she did that, another zap stung her on the leg like a bee. She jumped with a yelp and sat up straight.

"What is hurting me!?" she yelled.

The pain from the jolt to her head eventually faded enough that she stopped sniffling. Althea leaned back against the side of the box... and felt a thin, hard band encircling her head. She tried to rub against the wall to pull it off, but the band clung too tight and the smooth metal surface didn't offer enough friction to budge it.

"Ooh!" She fumed, glaring down her legs at her chained ankles.

The first person to open that box and make eye contact with her would regret it. She wouldn't hurt them, but they *would* let her go and she would force them to bring her home... then let the Watch do whatever they wanted with them. Though, she'd refuse to allow execution to happen.

She slid forward when the flying machine she assumed carried her made a slight turn. Not bothering to fight the motion, she ended up flat on her back with her heels against her butt, staring straight up at the top of the container. Of course, bad city people took her. Raiders would've been nice enough to at least give her a blanket, not a plain box with no openings. Not even a hole to breathe from.

"Karina is dead. You will never see her again," whispered the voice.

"You speak the false," muttered Althea.

The evil voice didn't feel right. If Karina had died, she'd *know* something happened. The same clairvoy ants that warned her of danger would certainly tell her if someone she loved so much had been hurt. It would be impossible for harm to befall her sister and go unnoticed.

"Dammit," muttered Althea, realizing that the psionic warning she'd received while out with Den had to be for *this* kidnapping. "I should have told Father or the Zero police to be on guard."

She tapped her foot in annoyance, making a soft clapping sound against the metal.

Hands tied, ankles locked in binders, trapped in a cramped box, she couldn't do much of anything but simply wait. Even without the cord or chain, she couldn't have escaped the container. That made her think the people who took her had to be particularly mean since tying her up didn't really accomplish anything but make her uncomfortable. The metal binders she *almost* understood since her kidnapper probably didn't want to have to chase her if she ran. But her hands? Why? What threat did they possibly think a girl her size could be?

Angry, worried, and frustrated, she rolled her head side to side on the thin headband, wondering why the heck anyone put that on her. She sat up and rubbed at it with her knee again, but got another bee-sting zap.

"Ow." She sighed.

"Nobody ever likes you. You're just a prize they take," whispered the voice.

Althea ignored it.

Another whisper in the cartoon rabbit's voice teased her about being stupid, mocking her for taking so long to learn the frozen speech.

Althea ignored that, too.

"Father thinks having you makes him important. He doesn't really love you."

"If you're going to speak the false to me, at least try to say something I might believe," muttered Althea. That voice had to be The Many messing with her. Or did it? He lied a lot, but his lies approached believable. They hadn't been as blatant.

A day or two after he first brought her to Querq, she *did* doubt Father's motivation, but she looked in his head and knew the truth. His wife had died in childbirth years before, also losing the baby. Since that day, he'd been lost to a pit of grief… that Althea had helped him climb out of. So no, she did *not* believe that voice.

Someone is speaking the false to me, but why? Just to be mean?

She glared at the binders on her legs.

"Yeah. Just to be mean."

DESPITE BEING TAKEN IN THE MIDDLE OF THE NIGHT AND LYING STILL in a sealed box, Althea couldn't sleep.

Which worked, because she didn't want to. As best she could tell, she'd been awake for about a half hour, maybe more. The mechanical roaring remained continuous and mesmerizing, sometimes drowning out the whispering voice that kept saying awful things about the people she loved. Sometimes it blurted odd random phrases like 'blue bunny' over and over again for thirty seconds and stopped.

She lay there, not bothering to struggle, and let off a huff of annoyance at being abducted in the middle of the night. Becoming angry in response to captivity instead of her usual resigned acceptance felt strange, but she had been taken from her *home,* so she figured anger the appropriate response. Worse, for all her confidence and determination to protect herself, she hadn't been able to stop them from doing it. Never in her life had she imagined ghosts would want to kidnap her, too.

But that didn't make any sense.

Why would ghosts need a metal flying machine? No, those had to be people with magic to make them see-through like water. Althea lay there and steeped in her anger, trying to ignore the constant whispery voices saying mean things. She tapped her foot, which made the metal ring around her ankle all the more noticeable. Her hatred of being tied welled up in a momentary fit of pointless struggling that ended with a growl.

Of course, as soon as she thought about being stuck, her nose itched. She did her best to scratch it with her knee.

Despite her present situation, she didn't worry too much. After all, *people* had taken her. As soon as they opened the box, she'd make them free her and take her right back home. One of them had shot her with the little pellet that made her black out mere seconds after she realized people had invaded the house, not enough time to recover from the confusion or startlement of bumping into them.

Althea narrowed her eyes. The next time they came for her, she wouldn't hesitate.

With a sigh, she resigned herself to being trapped in a box for however long it took her abductors to come check on her. Distressing whispers continued whenever she let her mind wander, claiming her family had died or she deserved to be a prisoner or Den didn't really like her and would leave Querq soon, returning to his tribe.

She ignored the lies and thought of Karina and Father. When she concentrated on them, the whispering lessened. If she occupied her thoughts with her spelling lessons, her family, or even the process of making enchiladas, the voice ceased entirely. For some time, she glared at the light her eyes cast on the top of the box, mentally reciting words and how to spell them.

A sudden worry made her shiver. She had disliked the learning machine and defied Father the other day by not using it in the afternoon. Could this abduction be the Ancestors punishing her?

No. It is The Many trying to hurt me. It has to be.

The continuous machine roar abruptly increased to a painfully loud whine. Althea floated up off the floor, weightless for several seconds before a tremendous *boom* accompanied her flying to the side. She crashed against the cargo box wall and stuck to it as gravity changed direction. Her container smashed into something, hurling her against the other side. With her hands tied behind her, she couldn't protect her face from smacking into the metal wall.

In what felt like an instant, she found herself on her chest, cheek against the smooth metal amid a puddle of blood dribbling from her probably broken nose. A fierce wind blasted over her, leaking in a gap where one of the container's walls had popped outward a few inches. Ignoring the horrible headache, dizziness, and pain in her face, Althea grunted and rolled onto her back. She mule-kicked the loose side of the box, shoving the lid open.

A freezing gale whipped into the small space, throwing her hair around and shooting a chill up under her dress. Debris flew everywhere, a maelstrom in the room outside the box she'd been trapped in. The chamber as well had a metal wall, though a huge, jagged hole rimmed in smoke yawned out to blue sky.

Another cargo box about the same size as the one she lay in slid by and tumbled out the gash, swallowed by the yawning vortex of air. A scary room seemed like an upgrade from a locked cargo container, so she rolled out onto the floor. Small scraps of material zipped around along with metal fragments. Sparks burst from the wires jutting from the tear in the wall.

She got up onto her knees, leaned forward, then threw her weight backward, springing up to stand. The room swayed back and forth, throwing her to one side then the other too fast to keep balance with her ankles trapped in binders. She stumbled to the right, tripped over the chain, and landed flat on her chest, spitting blood on the shiny metal floor.

… and growled like an angry bonedog.

The chamber didn't look much larger than the space at home Father referred to as the 'living room.' Her cargo box had been one of a dozen or so that now tumbled around like stones in an old can rolling in the wind.

Sudden, strong dread came out of nowhere, far more intense than anything she had ever felt.

Althea shivered, and not from the cold.

If I stay here, I'm going to die.

7

SMOKE TRAILS

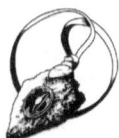

The room tilted to one side, sending Althea sliding away from the jagged opening in the wall.

She crashed into the side of another cargo box, but barely had time to grunt in pain before the flying machine rolled the other way, and she went skidding across the floor on her chest toward the breach. She flipped over and spun, catching herself at the edge, both feet planted on a triangular shard of bent plastisteel. The sudden turn threw her with such force that she scrunched up, her knees touching her shoulders. Weird gravity pinned her there for a few seconds, giving her a frightening view out at the distant ground far below.

An angry black scar marked the land near the edge of a gargantuan lake, a glowing red pit at its center. She stared at it in horrified awe, wondering if the chamán's stories of gods might be true. It looked as though one such god had stabbed the very land with an enormous spear of flame that charred the earth and left lingering embers in the deep wound.

Her hair whipped around like a mass of angry snakes in the wind.

Again, the flying machine shifted, throwing her into the chamber. She landed hard on her back and slid, spinning. A cargo box crashed into the floor beside her with a *slam* she felt in the floor more than heard over the screaming engines outside. Her sense that she had seconds left to live intensified.

Grunting, Althea rolled onto her feet and bunny hopped toward the massive rent in the side of the flying machine. Fierce wind rushing in the hole nearly knocked her over when she got close, but she managed to grab a torn piece of hull behind her back. Cringing against the wall, she peered past the shredded metal at the ground so far below. Between the air in her face and the screaming roar of the engines outside, she wouldn't have heard a gunshot two inches away from her ear. Jumping out into the sky didn't seem like an awesome idea, but she had no doubt that staying there would kill her. She had leapt from Officer David's flying car without fear. This machine had gone much higher up than that, but it didn't matter.

Remaining here, she knew for certain, would kill her.

Althea jumped out the opening, throwing her body like a spear, headfirst.

Fierce wind slammed into her, tossing her into a disorienting sideways spin. The flying machine's jet wash sucked her upward. She instinctively tried to flail her arms, but couldn't. Rapid spinning stopped in a few seconds, leaving her falling toward the ground, mostly on her back with her head lower than her feet.

She peered up past her legs at the strange metal bird she jumped out of. It careened to the left, diving and swerving, tracing a dark line of smoke across the sky above her. Cones of blue fire billowed out from two big holes near the back, and red-orange flames also leaked out around the edges of the huge tear in the side of the machine. A flicker of reflected sunlight low on her left drew her attention to a pair of thin white smoke trails growing up from the ground near the black part. They curved, heading toward the fast-departing aircraft.

Something shot out from the side of the flying machine, falling toward the ground.

A second later, both smoke trails crashed into the side of the false bird, exploding in a brilliant flash and tremendous explosion. Althea flinched. When she opened her eyes again, little remained of the machine but tumbling chunks of debris. Strangely, she didn't feel the icy claw of departing life. Somehow, despite the entire flying machine disintegrating into small pieces, no one had died. She relaxed out of her cringe, relieved. Even if the people inside it had kidnapped her, they didn't deserve to die.

Althea struggled to roll herself over while barely able to move. The wind rushing by made her face feel weird and rubbery, and flapped her lips if she didn't turn her head to the side. Her long hair streamed straight up behind her, and her dress rippled in the punishing torrent of air—though the garment she thought so flimsy withstood the abuse, not tearing.

The ground below, mostly a blur of grey except where a large area had turned coal black, approached at an alarming pace, though it didn't frighten her. She concentrated on her power the same way she had after jumping out of Officer David's patrol craft, intending to extend her energy-ribbon wings.

A horrible jolt of pain stabbed her in the head. She screamed, mentally recoiling from the hurt. Wind blowing past her face flung blood from her broken nose into her eyes, making the already-blurry ground even more difficult to see.

Ow! It took her a few seconds to recover from the shock. Figuring that her great altitude would give her enough time not to panic, she focused her power inward to mend her hurt.

Another electric jolt to the head hit her like a slap, interrupting her. Althea cried out in frustration and fear. Something cruel appeared to be causing her great pain every time she tried to use her powers. If she couldn't extend her wings, she had a serious problem.

Althea whimpered and again tried to channel her psionic energy into her wings.

The next shock hammered her skull so hard it felt as though a raider's axe had bit into her brain.

"Ow!" wailed Althea. She curled fetal, pressing her face into her knees.

Panic made her breathe too fast. She wasted a moment in a thrashing fit at the cord binding her wrists, but couldn't make herself strong enough to break it without setting off another smashing jolt of headache.

"Help!" shouted Althea.

She blinked. *Don't be stupid. Who's going to hear me?*

No… her psionic senses told her to get out of that flying machine—and they had been right. If she didn't leap, she would've surely died when those strange smoke trails crashed into it and blew up. Why would her powers tell her to do that if she would die? But something messed with her abilities, making it hurt so much she couldn't use them.

She didn't really like pain, but she could deal with it if she had to. And she much preferred a wicked headache to a sudden high-speed meeting with the ground. No, whatever had decided to hurt her would lose. She would beat it. Nothing would keep her from going home to her family.

Growling, Althea oriented herself to fall chest first and took a few quick breaths to prepare herself for the shock she knew would come. She refused to be kidnapped. She refused to die. No matter how much it hurt, she would survive.

With her best attempt at a war cry, Althea poured everything she had into wanting her wings to appear. Agony stabbed her in the head amid a sizzling, crackling cascade of lightning so strong the world below disappeared in a storm of purple flashes. Tears ran from her eyes at the pain, but she kept pushing, picturing the brilliant blue-white streamers of energy extending nearly twice her height to either side, slowing her fall, saving her life.

A sizzling crackle crashed across her skull, louder than the exploding sky machine.

The metal headband burst apart into fragments that the wind ripped away from her. Pain evaporated. Sheer determination dampened her battle cry down to a forceful growl. Glowing white energy engulfed her from behind, slowing her rapid descent to a controlled glide. She smiled at the graceful ribbons of pure light flowing out behind her in a wing-like silhouette, fanned wide to catch the air.

Another thin smoke trail came up from the black swath of land, racing off across the distant sky in pursuit of the largest piece remaining from the flying machine. Seconds later, a deep *boom* shook the air high above. She didn't bother to look, instead scanning the ground in search of a good spot to land.

Her wings took away all sense of fear at being so high up. The punishing wind that had been blasting her in the face subsided to a strong, but pleasant breeze. Clear blue sky on all sides and the bright sun overhead would have made her happy, if not for the vast amount of ruined Before-Time buildings scarring the landscape... or her being a long, long way from home. Her fall had slowed enough that she felt as though she hung in midair. From her high vantage, she eyed the black area warily. At this altitude, she couldn't tell exactly what had turned the land that color, if the dirt had been burned or covered by some other substance. The long canyon-like hole in the middle glowed with eerie red light, like a gateway into some realm of horror. It didn't give her a *bad* feeling, certainly nothing like she sensed in the presence of The

Many, but she knew without a doubt that she did *not* want to go anywhere near that place.

It had to be fairly early in the morning, which put the sun to the east. The flying machine had been going toward it. That meant she had to go west for home. She veered away from the sun—and the black scar—steering to the left. Even with her hands tied behind her back, she had full control of where she glided. Her arms didn't do any good in the air after all; it didn't work like swimming. However, while her psionic wings could greatly slow her falling, she couldn't technically fly. Once, while trying to heal a whole lot of people simultaneously, the wings had held her in the air, but only hovering a few feet above that building's roof... not climbing.

As much as she wanted to simply fly all the way home, she couldn't make herself go upward or even maintain altitude, merely steer around while continuing a gentle glide to the ground. West of the ruins, the land had been reclaimed by forest, but she descended far too rapidly to reach the distant woodlands. Instead, she focused on finding a safe spot without too much debris she could reach before she hit the ground whether she wanted to or not. Anywhere she chose would be well within the ruins of a vast Before-Time city, so she aimed for a spot that wouldn't hurt. She steered around in a gentle half circle, lining herself up with the ghost of an old street that led in the direction she wanted to go.

The road crossed a relatively open area of the ancient city marked with the squarish outlines of where buildings used to be. Althea tried to glide as far west as possible before she ran out of height. The ground drew nearer and nearer, random gusts pushing her back and forth. In less than a minute, she'd be on the ground. Althea kicked, protesting the chain connecting her ankles while tugging at the cord securing her hands behind her back.

She had survived the flying machine blowing up, but she'd still ended up alone in the middle of the Badlands, bound hand and foot.

"Uh oh... I'm in danger."

8

A LONG, LONG WALK

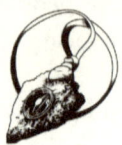

W hen she came within fifty feet off the ground, Althea sent a surge of power into her wings.

They flared even brighter, slowing her fall enough that she landed no harder than if she had jumped down from standing on the kitchen table. Unfortunately, trying to glide as far as possible gave her a considerable amount of forward momentum, faster even than she could have run without cuffs on her legs. The binders tripped her up as soon as her feet touched the ground, and she ended up sliding on her front over the dirt like a crashed pigeon, coming to a stop a fair distance from where she hit.

"Ow."

She coughed on dust and let her cheek rest against the ground.

Her face throbbed and her ankles burned, but at least the headache had gone away.

Eyes closed, Althea forced her body to mend itself. A faint *snap* shocked the middle of her face as her broken nose adjusted back to normal. She mended the bruises and bumps, then a thin line of burn across her forehead. Apparently, the headband had become hot enough to injure her. Whatever that device had been, Althea decided she hated it.

After a momentary breather to recover from healing herself, she squirmed around and struggled until she got her tied hands past her butt, then rolled on her back with her legs straight up, grunting and gasping while stretching to force her wrists around her heels. After successfully maneuvering her hands in front of herself, she lay flat, gazing up at the sky and catching her breath. One small victory.

Certain things scared Althea.

Used to be, her greatest fear had been being tied. She didn't like being stuck in a cage, but she *feared* being tied up.

Then she witnessed wifeing. That became her biggest fear, pushing helplessness to second place. Now, she had a new biggest fear: being forever separated from her family. Wifeing had gone down to second place, while being tied slid into third. Though, much to her surprise, it didn't terrify her anymore—it made her angry.

Unlike Scrag warriors or even Seekers, she didn't really become helpless if she couldn't move. Her ability to control others' emotions or *command* them to do things didn't care if she had the use of her hands or not. Officer David had explained she possessed several different psionic powers, her strongest being one he called Accelerated Healing. Thus far, the Zero police had never encountered anyone but her who could use that particular talent on other people. He referred to her ability to manipulate emotions as 'Telempathy,' and the ability to give people orders as 'Suggestion.' Since she had been so afraid of being burned alive as a mystic, she hadn't used Suggestion much.

Alas, no power she had worked on black cord or electronic handcuffs.

Althea sat up and gnawed on the binding around her wrists. It tasted like rubber, but her teeth didn't damage it much. "No... this isn't good." She glanced at the ruins surrounding her and kicked at her feet, testing the minuscule separation the chain allowed. "It's going to take me years to walk home."

For the first time in her life, she *wanted* raiders to find her.

Or anyone really. If someone nice found her, they'd untie her. If someone not nice found her, they'd still untie her—under command. Her only real worry would be a creature like the canid mutant. Making them frightened only caused them to attack with more ferocity and zero sense of self preservation. That would be quite bad as she couldn't run away from anything at the moment. Trying to command them wouldn't work because they didn't understand speaking and Suggestion required a verbal order.

Giving up on her effort to bite the cord, she leaned forward and fiddled at the shackle on her right ankle. The tiny screen showed numbers when she touched the little rubber pads. She kept hitting them until 31078 appeared and an angry buzz happened. The screen blanked. Althea mashed buttons again, entering 23460, and again the binders emitted a loud buzz.

"Grr. Where's the stupid keyhole?" She struggled to look over the device, but despite more or less resembling thicker versions of the handcuffs that had been on Rachel, these didn't have any keyholes. "Oh no… they're never going to come off!"

She buried her face in her hands and sobbed. How could those people be so mean to put something like that on her? After a few minutes, her tears dried up when she realized Father would know what to do. She had only to get home, even if she had to take a million teeny tiny steps, she could still do it. Maybe the stupid handcuffs came from the big city and used big city magic? The Zero police might be able to take them off her. She wouldn't be locked in them forever—it would only feel like it.

With renewed hope, she gathered her emotions, then closed her eyes and concentrated on wanting Father and Karina to know she was okay. The flying machine appeared to have carried her a long way, and she had no idea how far her power could reach… but she *had* managed to somewhat communicate with Karina when Archon took her to the big city.

Being a long, long way from home out in the Badlands and barely able to move did *not* feel like a good thing. She examined the black cord, specifically the knot that had been melted into one solid clump. No way could she untie it. She sighed and let her hands fall in her lap, refusing to surrender to crying or fear.

"I can't just sit here."

Having her hands in front made it easier to stand up. She turned in place, orienting herself with the sun so she faced west, and proceeded to baby-step along. The constant *click, click, click* of the binders on her legs needled at her like a taunt. It angered and frustrated her more than anything. Even years ago when the raiders had put handcuffs on her legs so she couldn't run away from them, her reaction had been the same. Going from her little sleeping area to where everyone made water took a long time. Sometimes, one of the raiders would be nice and carry her.

More than the learning machine called her stupid. She should have commanded those raiders to let her out of the stupid chain and not been so scared.

She stopped and glared down at her feet. Wanting to run and being unable to nearly set off a scream of rage, but she held it in. The Many probably did this to torment her, to keep her away from her family where she was happy. Getting upset would only please him. She couldn't do anything about her present situation other than try to go home. No amount of being angry, scared, or anything else would help.

Trying not to think about how much danger she'd be in if a canid attacked her while so helpless only made her worry more. Althea tried jumping for more speed, but that tired her out quick, so she resumed taking rapid tiny steps. Her confidence dented at the realization foraging for food and water would've been challenging in this place even if she hadn't been tied. The walk home would take an extremely long time with such short strides, so she'd surely run out of food and water before she even made it halfway.

It will take me a whole day to do one hour of walking.

"Stop being stupid. I'm not going to be stuck like this the whole time. There are lots of people out here. Someone will help me."

An exquisitely frustrating two hours later, Althea paused to heal the skin where the binders had chafed. Her situation made her want to do something mean to the people responsible for abducting her, but she couldn't think of anything that wouldn't leave her feeling guilty afterward. She took a few more steps before a glint in the dirt up ahead caught her eye. The flash came from the ground near the remains of a small building.

She shuffled in that direction. Minutes later when she reached it, she squatted and pawed at the dirt around where the flicker of sunlight came from. Her efforts unearthed a small glass fragment, likely from the windows broken out of the building many years ago. Grinning, she gingerly scraped at the hardened silt for the next twenty or so minutes until discovering a glass shard about three inches long with a sharp point.

"Yes!"

Althea plopped to sit on the ground and gripped the bit of glass like a small knife. She couldn't quite reach the cord between her arms, so she sawed at it above the back of her left wrist, not too concerned if she slipped and cut herself. The glass didn't slice the rubbery material as easily as she hoped it would—but it *did* cut it. She bit her lip in concentration and bore down on the shard, raking it back and forth, ripping up the binding as well as her skin. She turned off her sense of pain and kept on cutting.

Eventually, the cord snapped free from her left arm, then unraveled from her right wrist. Althea tossed the glass aside and hurled the cord with contempt as hard as she could throw it. That done, she rubbed her shredded wrist and mended all the little cuts. Predictably, the old piece of filthy glass had given her a sick or two, but they hadn't had a chance to travel too deep into her system. In response to her power, the disease foamed out of the last cut before she mended it.

Beaming, she stretched her arms out to either side, overjoyed to have gotten at least halfway free. That should at least make foraging and climbing easier. Well, climbing *possible*. She scissored her legs back and forth in a half-hearted protest at the metal binders, then wasted a few minutes pulling and twisting at them, futilely trying to squeeze the shackle off over her heel.

Althea shuddered at the idea of trying to 'un-heal' her foot. Making her thumb detach to get out of a handcuff hurt *so* much she passed out. She neither thought she *could* do the same to her heel, nor did she want to experience that much pain again. If it came down to that or death, she'd try it... but for now, she'd hope to find someone who would help her—or someone she could make help her.

"Hmm." She sat up, looking around at the ruins. "It's strange there aren't any people here. Someone had to see me up so high."

What would raiders, settlers, or Scrags have thought of her from far away? They most likely would have only seen a bright white light in the air. Chamáns would probably mistake her for a star that fell off the sky or maybe one of the ancestor spirits. Raiders would be afraid of her, as they tended to avoid or destroy everything they couldn't understand. Settlers *might* be curious enough to investigate the searing light that floated down from the sky... but if so, they should have been there already.

"Weird," she muttered, hopping back to her feet.

At least balancing would be easier with the full use of her arms.

After a quick peek up to check the position of the sun, she resumed the irritating process of walking westward while limited to two-inch steps. Determination to return home kept her going despite growing frustration and anger. Every so often, she felt like collapsing in place and just sitting there until someone found her, but then guilt hit her. The longer she stayed away from home, the more worried and upset Karina and Father would be. Also, anyone who got sick or died in Querq would be her fault.

No. Not my fault. I didn't kidnap myself. I'm going as fast as I can.

By late afternoon, her stomach emitted loud growls. Alas, she hadn't seen anything to eat. Though it felt like she'd traveled miles, her surroundings didn't look any different. As far as she could see in every direction lay endless ruins of crumbling concrete Before-Time buildings. *It's not going to take me years to get home, it's going to take me forever. Karina will be a grandmother before I'm back.*

Grumbling, she pushed on.

"I don't like these things. I don't like who put them on me. I don't like who made them. I don't like the noises they make. I don't like the way they hurt." She stopped shuffling and yelled, "I don't like this!"

Of course, shouting at nothing wouldn't help. She couldn't remember ever being this angry at anything before. When the raiders chained her legs together like this, she didn't have a home to miss. Being hobbled at that point had only annoyed her because it made going to the bathroom or the cook a chore. Now, it kept her away from her family. She fumed in silence and forced herself to march onward.

It occurred to her a few minutes later that she needed to rein in her anger. Whenever she let her emotions get the better of her, they tended to affect people all around her. If someone snuck up and genuinely scared her, even playing a game, the entire town would scream. Once, when The Many had terrified her with visions of horrors from the Before-Time, she'd caused everyone in Querq to hide like frightened children. However, the strong spikes of love she experienced whenever Father or Karina hugged her, she didn't mind sharing.

Maybe that's why The Many hated her so much.

She continued creeping along for the remainder of the daylight hours. By the time the sun went down, she had to keep both hands pressed to her stomach so it didn't scream. Going a day without food had happened many times before, but for the past six months, she'd been eating regularly with her family. Having stable food for so long made its absence more noticeable. The worst had been when one raider group didn't believe her that she needed extra food when she had to heal a lot of people.

Her thoughts drifted to Officer David again. He had explained that her healing ability consumed energy from her body as well as the body of whoever she used it on. If the person had a lot of fat, it would consume it first. If not, they'd need to eat or their body would attack itself in a process he called 'starving.' While she might not have known the word for it, she understood how it worked—and how it felt.

It also meant she needed to be careful until she found food. If she had to heal herself from any serious hurts, she would do that starving thing again. Darkness often made her worry that people or bad creatures would see her glowing blue eyes from far away, but except for dangerous monsters, she *wanted* someone to find her.

Soon after full dark—which she realized due to the world becoming black-and-white—she spotted a more-or-less intact building up ahead, not merely a few walls hinting at where a structure once existed. Shelter sounded like a good idea for the night, and it might have something she could use to get the stupid things off her legs. It took her almost twenty minutes to reach the door with a series of bunny hops and shuffling. Inside, a dilapidated room held the remains of a steel desk, a chair frame, a few shelves, and lots of debris that had caved in from the upper floor. She surveyed a giant mound of dirt, concrete bits, and rotting plaster. Moonlight leaked in through broken windows and numerous bullet holes from long ago, creating small patches of color in the otherwise grey room. She hopped inside and proceeded to search among the debris pile until finding a big hunk of metal.

It sorta resembled the blade of a sword, but had no sharp edges. Several holes suggested it had been a part of a larger machine, held on by nails or screws or bolts. Still, it had some heft, so she proceeded to sit on the floor and wallop the chain connecting her ankles with it. The hunk of debris felt dense and heavy, the binders light like that stuff Father called plastic… but the chain didn't even scratch.

"No! *Mierda*! Stupid chain is magic."

She abandoned the metal shard and spent a while studying the binders. Pushing the little nubs made numbers appear on the tiny screens, but no matter how many times she mashed her fingers into them, only that annoying loud buzz happened again and again. Giving up, she crawled to the old desks and searched around for anything she might be able to use as a weapon against the stupid magic handcuffs.

Her frustration at them had almost reached the point where she'd have cut her foot off if she had a sharp enough sword. Reattaching it—or growing a new one—would be easy compared to breaking the chain. Assuming, of course, she didn't pass out from pain after cutting herself and then bleed to death. One of the drawers had a small tool consisting of a plastic handle with a metal rod sticking out of it that ended at a pointy tip. It might have been a weapon, but it didn't look too sharp. Frozen speech on the side made little sense. She stared at the letters, trying to understand the word.

"Pahillips. No... There isn't an a. Pee-hillips?" She shrugged, then stabbed the weird device through one of the chain links.

That didn't do much, so she turned it around, taking up slack on the chain. Once she couldn't twist any more, she amplified her strength and pulled as hard as she could with both hands. The thin rod bent slightly, but the chain didn't appear the least bit affected.

Out of breath, she slouched. The worry that she might never escape the binders almost made her cry out of frustration... but she didn't want to waste water.

She braced her elbows against her knees, rested her chin in her hands, and scowled at the chain.

"I don't like these things."

9

THE DEAD VILLAGE

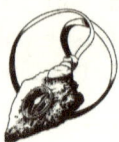

Given the late hour, Althea decided to spend the night inside the derelict building.

Her powers let her see easily in the dark, losing only the ability to perceive color. However, she had been up all day, and second, many more dangerous creatures tended to be out at night. It wouldn't do her any good to see a monster if she had no chance of running away from it.

Behind the huge mound of cave-in debris, Althea discovered a door that led to a stairway down. Going underground would make for an even better hiding place. She tried to walk down the stairs, but the binders wouldn't allow her to move her feet apart far enough for steps. After a moment of kicking at the handcuffs and scowling, an idea hit her.

Althea sat on the floor, and scooted down one step at a time while sitting. She made it a little shy of halfway before the entire staircase collapsed under her.

With a high-pitched shriek of surprise, she fell straight down into the basement, landing on a heap of rotten wood that used to be a staircase. One small piece bounced off her head and fell to the concrete floor with a clatter.

"Ow," she said, annoyed.

Flat on her back, she stared up at the doorway. She could probably get out by jumping to grab the edge, so she didn't see any need to worry. Several spots of pain in her arms and legs announced she'd picked up some splinters. Grumbling, Althea sat up and plucked seven splinters out of herself before forcing the tiny hurts to close.

She looked around at numerous large cardboard boxes that had long ago decomposed into mush. Most contained stacks of thin stone squares not quite as big as dinner plates in various colors. A few buildings in Querq had similar things on their floors. Careful to avoid more splinters, she crawled away from the wreckage of the stairwell. Behind the boxes, the room extended another forty feet. More debris littered the area along with the skeletal remains of six long-dead people on the floor near the back wall, atop cots and sleeping bags that appeared somewhat newer than everything else.

Dull clicking accompanied Althea's shuffle over to the bedding. One of the skeletons had no left leg. Another had lost both legs at the knee. The third one had no right arm. The remaining three still had all four limbs, but two had large holes in their ribcages—as big around as her thigh—as if the bones had simply stopped existing. The last skeleton had numerous tiny holes everywhere, making her wonder if someone had stabbed him with that pee-hillips thing over and over and over.

"Hello," whispered Althea. "I'm sorry to bother you, but I would like to sleep here. Is it okay?"

She waited a few minutes, but none of the dead objected.

"Thank you!"

Althea sat on the edge of one cot and gingerly scooted back to lie down next to the skeleton with the missing leg. Mostly loose bones clattered under her presence, the skull rolling into the depression she made in the cot, coming to rest against her as if kissing the top of her head.

She gave it a peck on the cheek. "Good night."

DREAMS OF KARINA AND FATHER RUNNING AROUND IN A PANIC tormented her.

Althea awoke abruptly, parched and quite hungry. She stretched amid the stray bones, hating the feeling of metal around her ankles. Maybe if she found the person who put them on her, she'd command them to slap themselves. That wouldn't cause a hurt she'd have to heal, and wouldn't make her feel bad.

The raiders who'd kept her hobbled like this years ago had only held her for three months before a stronger group attacked them. Those raiders took the hobble off her, but they'd padlocked a much bigger chain around her neck instead. Only four of the first group had survived. Her new owners would have killed the other tribe to the last, but she encouraged them not to. Maybe they had gone out there and spoken of their misfortune. Somehow, the legend of the Prophet had come to include the prediction that any who mistreated her would suffer bad luck.

"Obviously." She rolled her eyes. "Everyone who took me got attacked by different people wanting to take me. Of *course* they would blame it on me and say it's bad luck."

But even the nice villages, few and far between as they'd been, suffered attacks. One tribe carried her around on a chair like a goddess, believing that if they let her touch the ground, she would punish them.

"Ugh." She shook her head. "I hated that."

Even Den's tribe had kept her in a cage for two months at the chamán's hut until the boy had pled with his father, the chief, Braga, to trust her promise that she wouldn't run away. The Prophet used to be an obedient captive. She'd promise never to run away, and she would keep her word.

Althea scowled, sat up, and hopped off the cot to stand. She would never again promise that to anyone.

"I'm gonna run away!"

Her first step stopped short two inches later with a *click*. She hung her head and sighed.

"I'm gonna tiptoe away!"

These binders didn't have a keyhole, only the little screens and littler buttons. She squatted and squeezed at them again, setting off the loud buzzer a few more times before giving up and shuffling to the collapsed stairway. She stopped at the wall, peering up at the doorway over her head. The muscles in her legs and arms swelled slightly in response to her psionic boost, her eyes glowing a touch brighter. She crouched, then leapt straight up, grabbed the base of the doorway, and pulled herself up, clumsily getting one knee on the edge before flopping forward onto her chest and eating a face full of dust.

No, she wouldn't make the person who put the binders on her slap themselves.

She'd make them slap themselves twice!

After the laborious process of speed shuffling to the door, she hopped outside, squatted, and relieved herself near the wall. That done, she took her best guess at west and resumed creeping along to the steady sound of plastisteel chain clicking.

"Ugh," muttered Althea. "I feel like a clock."

Her agonizingly slow pace made it easy to look around for food, water, or anything she might use to destroy the binders—though she didn't have much hope of finding a tool up to the task out here. Little in the Badlands would defeat big city magic. Once, she'd seen a raider who had a magic sword. Or, at the time, she had assumed it magic. All the raiders did, too. Its blade looked like pale blue glass, but it could cut even metal with ease.

A Zero police had a similar blade, only the size of a knife instead of a sword. The woman had tried to explain it to her as being something called Nano, definitely not magic. Swords or knives shouldn't cut metal so easily. If the big city had blades that could do that, their handcuffs would probably survive anything.

She repeatedly told herself that she wouldn't spend the rest of her life taking teeny steps. It would be stupid to think the big city people would make *permanent* handcuffs. They had to know a way to open them. The learning machine responded to her talking, so she stopped shuffling along and stared down at her feet.

"Get off me!"

Nothing happened.

"Get off me… please?"

The binders ignored her.

"Open? *Abierta? Alejarse de mí!* Go away!"

When they refused to listen, she sighed and continued walking as best she could. This place had to have been a huge city in the Before-Time. Not as big as the bad place in the west, but still massive. In the distance to the north, northwest, and south, the skeletal remains of ancient high-rise buildings still stood like the walls of an enormous room. The area right around her had been flattened, most of the buildings pulverized to dust and foundations. Likely, many, many years had passed since the destruction, as windblown dirt and silt had filled in most of the basements, reducing the buildings to mere silhouettes of rectangles or squares.

The majority of roads remained visible, providing a relatively easy to follow path.

At a mild uptick in the wind, Althea folded her arms across her chest and shivered. Her plain white dress had been comfortable back home in Querq, but here, it left her somewhat chilly. The breeze whistling in and around the distant monoliths filled the air with an eerie song of mourning.

Total desolation in all directions bewildered her. She'd never before seen such a complete *absence* of life. Even when roaming the desert, there had always been creatures. Squealers, millipedes, scorpions, flying insects, wild dogs... As hungry as she was, she might try to kill a squealer, despite their being adorable. Some people claimed the giant fuzzy critters had once been rabbits while others called them 'prairie dogs from hell.' For the most part, they left people alone unless attacked, but farmers hated them. A pack of squealers could destroy an entire crop in days.

She'd eaten *lots* of grilled squealer in her life, but she didn't feel confident in her ability to kill one... especially without a weapon. Also, it bothered her to murder something cute. If someone else had already done so, consuming the cooked meat didn't bother her since the animal was already dead.

A faint laugh seemed to come from all around, no doubt The Many found it amusing for her to pity an animal almost everyone considered a shoot-on-sight vermin. Or maybe he simply enjoyed her being angry and frustrated and lonely. Watching her struggle to travel while hobbled had to be filling him with joy.

She emitted a faint snarl and threw off a pulse of 'go away.' The Many always receded from her whenever she did that. No sign of him manifested, nor did any disembodied voices say a word.

For hours, she shuffled along as fast as she could tolerate, creeping past cars so old and rusted they'd disintegrated to a mere suggestion of frames. Every so often, she reached a building that remained standing, but they held only piles of debris and junk. Numerous skeletons also littered the area, many sprawled out on the ground as if they'd been running away from whatever killed them. Most had rotted to the point of dried bones, but two—both in the piecemeal armor of raiders— appeared more recently killed.

She veered off course to examine the closest body. The corpse had been there long enough to leave it unclear as to whether it had been a man or woman. A hole about four inches across went straight through the middle of the chest, the interior edges burned to charcoal.

"Eep!" She gawked. "What magic did that?"

Once the initial shock of such an unusual, ghastly wound wore off, Althea squatted beside the body and poked at the hole. She pictured Kate making a stream of fire like water out of a hose, but that would have burned his whole body—not only the inside of a big hole. That woman who could create fire out of thin air came the closest to what she could imagine inflicting a hurt like this. She prodded the area some more, thinking about the people that Aaron shot at the place called Starport. He had a strange gun that made lines of blue light in the air. That gun left wounds like this, but they'd been *much* smaller. That pee-hillips tool she'd found would barely have fit inside those holes.

Accepting that she would not understand this, she searched the body for anything useful. His clothing and armor had been horribly fouled. The large pouch on his belt contained small animal bones and a gummy, rancid black paste, likely the decomposed remains of baked squirrel or something similar. A broken bow lay on the street by his hand, six crude arrows in a belt quiver, and an ancient, scratched-to-hell knife in a sheath. She took the knife and tested the edge with her thumb. It didn't have the least bit of sharpness anymore, basically a flat piece of metal.

With a sigh, she tossed it, stood, and resumed baby-stepping west.

Shortly after the sun crested the apex of the sky, she spotted a patch of green plants ahead in a suspiciously rectangular formation. Hope bloomed in time with a huge growl from her stomach. Excitement made her bunny-hop again for extra speed. Soon, she stopped at the edge of a small garden where a thick layer of rotting vegetation lay on the ground beneath out-of-control vegetables and weeds that had been left untended for years. Still, she spotted a few okay-looking cucumbers and helped herself, savaging two before wiping her mouth on the back of her arm and continuing to look around.

Like a little dog, she crouched and dug at the ground by familiar green tufts, unearthing several carrots, which she also devoured. After eating herself stuffed, she sat back to rest and rubbed her sore ankles, commanding her skin to repair itself.

Faint hissing came from deeper within the garden.

Curious, she made her way toward the sound, moving somewhat like a gorilla, crouched, using her hands as well as hopping forward. Instead of the snake she expected, the noise came from a metal pipe jutting up from the ground, made of several joints and valves bolted together. Water sprayed out from the seams as well as several valves. Three improvised hoses ran from it into the garden in different directions.

"Ooh!"

Althea hurried over, put her face by a valve port that had no hose, and twisted the handle. A modestly strong blast of water shot into her mouth. It tasted like metal and rubber, but after a day and a half with nothing to drink, she didn't care. She eased back on the valve to slow the water from blast to flow, gulping down mouthful after mouthful. When she couldn't drink anymore, she sat on the ground to rest. Moments later, she got the idea to smear vegetable muck around her ankle, hoping it might make her skin slippery enough to get the binders off. Alas, the metal ring had been closed too tight to fit over her heel.

"*Mierda!*" She huffed. "Why isn't there anyone here?"

As if in response to her question, an odd noise arose in the distance that she'd never heard before, another unfamiliar thing like that strange burned wound. Despite its source seeming far away, the noise reminded her of a gnat flying into her ear. Her usual curiosity didn't poke her. For no reason she could pinpoint, the urge to *avoid* the source of that noise came over her.

The buzzing grew louder, less like an insect and more like whirring.

Old instincts pushed Althea flat to the ground, and she crawled in among the vegetables, joining the compost and bugs. The whirring came closer and closer, eventually whooshing by at a speed like a raider buggy, only much quieter. She lay still despite bugs crawling over her face, legs, and arms. She kept herself motionless until the strange sound faded entirely away... and then for another minute.

Althea pushed herself up to kneel, brushed bugs from her body, and wobbled to her feet. She considered taking her dress off to make a bag out of it so she could carry vegetables with her, but decided against that due to the chill in the air. This place had nothing useful for carrying water, and enough food that she figured she could last several weeks. But, staying here at this garden might not help her get home. If the chance existed that someone could find her here, it would be worth waiting, since she would make *much* better progress being carried even if whoever showed up had no way to free her.

But... this place appeared so desolate and abandoned...

A group of huts stood a short distance farther west from the garden. Walls of old billboards, appliances, and scrap metal suggested they'd been built by Scrags or settlers more recently than the Before-Time. They, too, had hundreds of holes in them. So many, she imagined an army of raiders standing there shooting at the structures for hours. Why would anyone waste so many bullets like that? Better they wasted them on huts than shot actual people, but still... something about this destroyed village unsettled her.

Worried, she spent a few minutes shuffling over to the nearest one and pulled aside the refrigerator door serving as the home's entrance. Two skeletons lay on the ground inside, near a primitive mattress. One of the dead still clutched a crude pipe gun, a weapon that fired one bullet at a time by means of a pull flap on the back end attached with stretchy tubes. Althea had no interest in arming herself, but seeing the gun there confused her. Raiders *never* left weapons behind, even bad ones like that. She crept around the shack long enough to take a big coffee can and a large metal tray, to which she tied a length of wire, turning it into a pull sled.

Over the next hour, she shuffled around the huts, gathering another coffee can and one plastic bottle with a cap, which she filled with water and set on the tray before loading it up with carrots and cucumbers. Dragging the tray along was impractical, but it beat having no provisions at all. All the huts contained bones, dead long enough for them to fall apart. In the sixth hut she checked, she discovered a hatchet.

With an eager chirp, she sat on the ground, held the hatchet up over her head in both hands, and chopped at the chain. Metal struck metal with a *clack*. For a second, she let out a cry of joy at the apparently severed chain... but as soon as she tried to move, she realized she'd only embedded a link into the dirt.

Annoyed, she took a swing at the band around her ankle instead. The blade glanced off and gashed a deep slice across the top of her right foot.

"Eep!" Althea gasped.

She commanded her blood-presence to stay inside, then sealed the cut, rubbing the spot for a moment while whimpering. "Okay, bad idea." She grumbled, fidgeting at the binders. "By the time I walk home, I'm gonna be old enough for wifeing Den... or that other thing that *looks* like wifeing but isn't."

Chin on her knees, arms around her legs, Althea sat there for a little while trying to imagine how something could be 'like' wifeing but *not* awful. Eventually, she decided that maybe Father had been right after all. Perhaps she *couldn't* understand it because she hadn't grown old enough. The same way really small kids didn't know that they needed to go to a specific spot to pee while inside a village, perhaps a girl her age *couldn't* understand the 'making love not being awful' thing.

That made the most sense of anything, and she trusted Father's opinion.

Overcome by a jolt of homesickness, Althea bowed her head and fought hard not to cry. It wouldn't do any good out here. Tapping into her deep desire to go home, she sent out another psionic beacon in hopes of letting Father and Karina know she remained alive and did all she could to go home as fast as possible.

She sighed at the binders in frustration, but refused to give up. After tossing the hatchet aside, she got up and hobbled out to the pull sled loaded with veggies and water. The garden probably didn't have as much usable food as it appeared to despite its size, considering it had been untended for so long. Staying here wouldn't be smart. Especially with that whirring whatever.

Althea gathered the wire in her hand and turned in place, gazing out at the distant ruins of the Before-Time city. She focused on thoughts of Querq, trying to *feel* which way she had to go. Around and around she turned until a tingle scratched across her chest. Nothing physically touched her, so that had to be the clairvoy ants talking again.

With a smile, she faced that direction and trudged onward.

RIDING THE OSPI

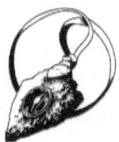

W alking while taking micro steps brought Althea to the point she cried out of sheer frustration.

She'd given up being angry over her present situation, and didn't feel particularly frightened either. But walking *so damn slow* irritated her like one of the super small kids in Querq yelling, "Mom. Mom. Mom. Mom. Mom," incessantly for an hour.

At least with a two-year-old, a Suggestion of 'stop that' worked. Dead things—like binders—didn't respond to psionic abilities.

Around the time the sun began to turn orange in the western sky, she encountered a relatively large building that had somehow survived whatever destroyed the rest of the area. It stood next to another, equally large but narrower building. All the windows were broken, and the walls had numerous big holes, but the two structures both looked much more intact than anything else in the area.

Accompanied by the irritating clicking, Althea crept over to the nearest of the two buildings and peered in via a hole in the wall. The place smelled of wet wood and mold. Most of the inside consisted of big open space. A wide concourse went to the left with several different counters. Straight ahead, about twenty feet of dingy brown carpet led to a short stairway down to an area full of chairs and bizarre machines. Past that, thirty long strips of shiny floor spanned the rest of the distance to the back wall. Each strip ended at a mouth-like opening, some of which had teeth, others didn't. At the closer side of the strips, shelves held spherical objects roughly the size of a person's head. Most were black, though a few had different colors. A big heap of white muck and rotten wood had collapsed down from the ceiling in the middle of the room.

Curious, she left her pull sled outside and hopped in the hole. First, she micro-stepped across the damp, smelly carpet, jumped down the four steps, and hopped over to the racks of strange spheres, wondering if they might be fruit. She grasped the first one she came close to and tried to pick it up, but her hands slipped off the unexpectedly heavy object. Althea tried again, this time lifting it with some effort. It weighed like stone, but had somehow become completely smooth on the outside except for three holes. Its weight made her think she might be able to drop it on the binders and smash the chain, but she chickened out. The orb was too big and couldn't hit *only* the chain. She'd hurt herself if she dropped it on her ankles.

With a grunt, she replaced the strange smooth stone on the rack with the others, then crept over to one of the paths. The light brown part of the floor looked like hundreds of tiny wood strips that had cracked apart from each other, creating a rough, painful surface. At this distance, the 'teeth' at the far end didn't look so much like a mouth anymore. Groups of wooden pegs stood in triangular formations inside the dark openings. A pair of rounded trenches lined each side of the long wooden paths. She tilted her head, gazing on in total confusion as to what the Ancients could have possibly done here. A drawing on the wall at the far end above the openings depicted one of those weird round stones crashing into the white pegs and knocking them over.

I'm in some kind of temple.

Those pegs had a narrow end at the top, which could reach the chain if she tried to bash it, but if the hatchet couldn't cut the binders, she doubted it would be worth the long trip over splinters to get one of the pegs.

Abandoning the strange paths, she shimmied to the left, past rows and rows of small plastic seats. A section near the back on the left reminded her of Tumbleweed's with stools and a bar counter. Not surprisingly, nobody sat there. When she got close, she grabbed the bar, holding on so she could take bigger jumps to move around behind it. Inside the bar counter, she rummaged around in cabinets and drawers. One held a small carpenter's hammer, which she decided to test. Again, sitting on the floor, she walloped the chain again and again, but succeeded only in making noise. The hammer didn't even scratch the metal.

"I really, really, don't like being tied."

She sighed, grumbled, and tossed the hammer aside before crawling out from behind the bar, jumping to her feet, and hopping to the last part of the building. Another counter similar to a bar stood in front of a wall full of cubbies, all containing the rotten remnants of what might have been the ugliest shoes she'd ever seen. She didn't like how shoes felt and hated wearing them, but the ones here were so repulsive she didn't think *anyone* would want to wear them... probably why they remained sitting on these shelves. Scavengers didn't even want to steal them.

A scratching noise came from behind the shoe counter.

Althea took several mini-steps back as the sound migrated to the left.

The sleek, black-and-orange form of a three-foot cockroach crawled out into view, waving its whip-like antennae at her. Althea glanced down at herself, her dress smeared with compost muck from the garden. She had to smell like roach dinner.

"Uh oh."

She backed away as fast as the binders allowed her to go, but the roach darted toward her. Althea raised her hands in a 'stop' gesture while radiating strong telempathic fear. The massive insect stopped short. Its shell split open, revealing a buzzing frenzy of useless wings. Roach threat displays didn't bother her. She'd encountered them often enough to trust that seeing the wings always meant they would run away soon. Once they started buzzing—as scary as it sounded and looked—it guaranteed they wanted nothing to do with whatever frightened them. She thanked the Ancestors that the giant bugs couldn't actually fly.

Althea edged left in tiny steps, but the roach pivoted, creeping after her while not getting closer.

Standoff.

She intensified the fear, making the roach hiss, its leather-colored abdomen pulsating. Two seconds later, the bug abruptly rotated away and zoomed off to hide behind the shoe counter. Althea deflated into a slouch, exhaling with relief.

"There's never only one of those... I need to get out of here."

Bunny-hopping for speed, she hurried to the same hole she climbed in from and squeezed outside. Eager to get away from the roaches, she stooped to grab the wire and tiny-stepped as rapidly as she could tolerate the binders digging into her skin. Her food/water tray scraped across the remains of the old sidewalk as she tediously advanced to the next building.

That one had some frozen speech still on the wall.

"Ex, ex, ex. Movies, S with two lines, thirty. Hot girls all night long. Adults only." She rubbed her hands up and down her arms, shivering slightly at the chilly air. "I'm a girl, but I'm kinda cold… Does that mean I'm not allowed in?"

Temperature aside, the sign said adults only, so she couldn't go in there.

Probably won't help me. I dunno what a movies is, but I don't think it's food.

With a grumble, she hung her head and continued making her way westward. She left the big buildings behind and again crept past decaying cars and smashed storefronts, struggling to contain her frustration at the binders forcing her to take such small steps. Perhaps an hour before sundown, she noticed a mostly-intact box on wheels up ahead. Much of it had rusted, though a few areas remained covered in white paint. Frozen speech on the back door where the paint hadn't vanished said an unpronounceable non-word: EMT. Smashed bits of red plastic hinted at where colored lights had once been. It had to be some kind of big, tall car. She assumed the back end faced toward her since it had two doors and small windows. The rubber had disintegrated off the wheels, but the body appeared reasonably intact… almost like a small one-room hut.

It would make for a reasonable place to sleep.

Sudden whirring came with a strong sense of inexplicable fear.

Althea let go of the wire, abandoning the pull tray. She bunny-hopped as fast as she could make her body go over to the ancient vehicle. With a grunt—and a moderate boost to her arm strength—she tugged the thick door open a little wider, jumped up inside, and pulled it shut. Along with a strange, narrow bed on wheels, a pile of junk took up the majority of the chamber. Too frightened to bother rummaging, she lay flat on the floor and held still, slowing her breathing to stay quiet.

The whirring increased in pitch and grew louder.

"Contaminant detected," said a droning, nasal voice devoid of inflection. "Searching."

Althea's eyes—and mouth—opened wide. She heard that exact voice before months ago… the nasty little metal man stuck in a river. It had wanted to kill her, but couldn't move. She pictured it: mostly silver, with some red parts, the size of a grown man's torso and a giant wheel where legs should be. Instead of arms, it had big guns that spun around.

Worst of all, it had no brain and wasn't alive. None of her powers would affect it. Had that creature not been stranded in a muddy creek bed, it would have been utterly terrifying—even without her ankles being locked together.

Althea hid her face behind her folded arms and tried not to breathe too loud. She tensed her legs to keep the chain taut. If it rattled while her body trembled from fear, that monster might hear her. If the metal man found her, she'd be as helpless as an ordinary child forced to fight a murderous raider. It neither had a brain to command, emotions to influence, or any care about her being the Prophet.

The whirr passed by to the right, then stopped. "Contaminant scan negative. Signal lost." The whirring went by again going back the other way. "*Detected:* Organic matter. *Designation*: Daucus carota, subspecies sativus. Common name, carrot. *Designation:* Cucumis sativus. Common name, cucumber. *Designation:* Dihydrogen Monoxide. Common name, water. Scan indicates plant life not considered contaminants." A brief whirr made her picture the machine man spinning around.

Please go away. Please!

"*Analysis:* Plant life consistent with vegetable sustenance.

Observation: Plant life does not grow from concrete.

Theory: Organic lifeform altered physical location of vegetable sustenance.

Extrapolation: Contaminant is proximal to sustenance.

Conclusion: Contaminant nearby.

Directive: Remove all contaminants."

Althea's hasty meal of vegetables threatened to explode out of her on a wave of terror-induced vomit. All those tiny holes in the huts made sense. That machine man in the river had spinny guns that fired a lot more bullets than necessary. If it figured out she hid inside this old car…

"Contaminant scan… negative. Logic error. Plant matter is not ambulatory. Daucus carota subspecies sativus and cucumis sativus could not have self-relocated. Contaminant must be nearby."

The whirring went back and forth outside for several minutes. Althea's legs ached from her effort to keep the binders taut so they didn't rattle. No longer simply annoying, the chain had become deadly. Being unable to run—or even walk—would kill her here.

Father! Help! She knew he'd never be able to find her, but she still wanted him more than anything.

"Scan negative. Contaminant likely at greater distance than initial estimate. Expanding search pattern."

Whirring trailed off into the distance. She dared not move for ten minutes, in case the machine man tried to trick her and come back. Perhaps an hour later, she risked nudging the door open enough to peek. Nothing dangerous appeared to be anywhere in sight, but it would soon be dark. While the vehicle offered tempting shelter for the night, she didn't like the idea of sleeping anywhere near one of those killer machines.

She glanced back at the pile of debris. Most of it was useless junk—until she spotted a large spoked wheel that appeared to be attached to the side of a chair. Althea grabbed it and pulled, trying to dislodge the strange contraption out from under the other mess. She braced both feet against the narrow, wheeled bed with rotted padding, and pulled in a series of sharp tugs that extracted the big wheel an inch at a time.

A final yank freed the contraption from the pile, causing it to fall on top of her. She pushed it off to the side, stood, then examined her find: a metal-framed chair with two huge wheels and two smaller ones in the front. Faded lettering on the backrest spelled out 'ospi.' It looked as though more letters had been there in the past, but she couldn't make out what they'd been. She didn't really have much use for a chair at the moment, so she gave it a shove of annoyance. The ospi rolled into the wall with a *thud*.

Althea blinked. *It's a chair that rolls.* She looked down at the binders on her ankles and got an idea.

"Yes!"

She nudged the doors open, then dragged the ospi out to the road, cringing at all the noise and clattering. Despite its age, the wheeled chair appeared to be functional. At least, it didn't fall apart when she touched it. She slipped out of the boxy car, hopped around in front of the chair, then gingerly lowered herself to sit. The material looked like leather but felt like plastic. Best of all, it supported her weight without breaking apart. Two metal plates in the front offered a place to rest her feet, but she couldn't move her legs apart enough to use both.

However, she didn't intend to sit still and rest, so she wouldn't need the plates. She tried to propel the chair forward by foot power, dragging her heels over the pavement. It somewhat worked, but scooting forward that way wouldn't be much faster than trying to walk. Pushing the chair backward with her feet allowed her to move quite a bit faster, but also made it difficult to see where she went or steer. She reversed to where she'd left her tray of supplies. At first, she considered tying the wire to the chair and continuing to drag it, but if the ospi let her go faster than hobbling, the vegetables would probably bounce away, never mind the water in the open coffee cans splashing everywhere.

So, she stood, shuffled around to pick the tray up, and mini-stepped back to the chair, sitting with the tray across her lap. Navigating lots of miles in a chair while rolling backward would stink, but it would stink a whole lot less than trying to walk all the way back to Querq while hobbled. Not to mention that damned clicking would give her a sick in her thinking shape.

She spent a few minutes raking her feet at the road, pulling the chair forward. Alas, she didn't end up going too much faster than hobbling along, and it tired her out much more rapidly. She stopped, sighed, and rested her arms on the sides... then noticed the huge main wheels came up almost to the top. After a few seconds of thinking—and remembering the machine man would probably be back soon—she grabbed the wheels and pushed. The chair rolled forward. She soon discovered that if she pushed only one wheel, she rotated in place, making it easy to steer. Her confidence grew, and she shoved at both wheels, rolling out into the street and turning west. Her arms swelled slightly in response to a psionic command to grow stronger, and she managed to get the chair going at a speed even faster than she could've normally run. Grinning, she shifted sideways to rest both feet on one plate, and raced down the road.

The bumpy paving sloshed water out of her open coffee cans onto the tray, but she didn't care. Getting away from this place mattered more. Maybe she could even outrun the machine man with the ospi. After spending a whole day stuck taking tedious, tiny steps, once again being able to cover ground at a reasonable speed filled her with happiness and hope.

But she didn't dare cheer. That machine man might hear her.

GATEKEEPER

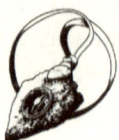

The ospi carried Althea down the road with little noise. Its rubber tires crumbled beneath her hands, progressively disintegrating more and more. But, even if that part broke off entirely, the metal rims should be enough to keep going on. It might not get her all the way to Querq, but she only had to go as far as it took to find people.

Not being afraid of raiders still felt weird, but in a good way. Controlling people *could* be a bad thing to do, but not for her. Althea would never make people do anything harmful, only force them to stay calm, not hurt anyone, or be nice to her. Commanding a raider who wanted to abduct her into freeing her from the stupid handcuffs wasn't a bad thing to do. Making a raider chief *not* wife the women he'd kidnapped also didn't count as bad.

She rolled along for a little more than an hour before starting to trust —somewhat—that the machine man wouldn't find her. The sun had gone down, leaving her surroundings mostly black and white. Though nothing appeared to be moving, the gritty crunch of the ospi's wheels on paving all of a sudden felt loud enough to attract the machine man, so she slowed to the speed of a walk.

An eerie sense settled over the ruins a few minutes later, reminding her that it had become night time. She looked around for a hiding place, figuring she ought to rest and stay out of sight until the sun came up.

Long-broken buildings lined both sides of the street, few existing as more than mounds of rubble or partially filled-in basements exposed to the elements. Tall letters in red paint marked one section of wall up ahead on the left: 'CRP' next to a poor attempt at drawing a skull.

On the ground below the letters, human bones lay scattered amid windblown silt, old cans, and plastic bottles.

Saddened, Althea steered the ospi in that direction and wheeled herself over to the wall, looking at the dead for a few minutes.

"I'm sorry."

A shimmer appeared in the air a few feet to her left, hovering. She peered up at the glowing cloud, which gave off a sense like a person's thoughts. Attempting to read it didn't work, but she couldn't help but think the energy cloud had a mind.

"Are you a ghost?"

The cloud shifted slightly to one side.

Officer David said I can see ghosts if I want to... She focused on the glowing light, wanting to see the person behind it. A moment later, the black-and-white surroundings changed to blurry sepia tones. The wall beside her shifted and wavered back and forth as though a ghostly image of the wall floating over the real one. In fact, the entire world around her looked that way. Every rock, smashed building, or street sign existed in two copies, one stationary, one swaying closer and away in an endless motion.

Where the light cloud had been now stood a man dressed in tattered garments of animal hide. He appeared somewhat transparent, his chest riddled with too many bullet holes to count. Blood dribbled out of his mouth and nose, and he stared at her with an expression of longing.

"Please, help me before..."

Althea fidgeted in the chair. "I'm sorry. You're already dead. I can't fix dea—well, I did once. But I don't know exactly how it happened. But, your body's just dry bones." She wiped a tear. "It's too late."

The man, who looked about Father's age, shook his head. "No, that is not what I mean. Please help me before the darkness takes me."

"The darkness?"

"You have seen it. The wolves of shadow. The voices of thousands. The—"

"Many," muttered Althea.

He nodded. "Yes. I have been hiding here, but it wants to eat me. Please help."

"Umm. Okay, but how?"

The spirit's fearful demeanor faded to confusion. "You don't know? I can feel the energy inside you, drawing me nearer."

"I'm a healer. I..."

"The energy of the other side," said the ghost.

Althea blinked. When she'd leapt from Officer David's flying car because she saw so many people hurt and dying on that roof, she had been too late to save some of them. Her grief at seeing so much pain pushed her into a mental place she hadn't reached before or since. There, the world had looked as it did now, washed out, brownish, and wavering back and forth. She had seen the ghosts of many people all staring at her expectantly. Her desire to help them came from somewhere beyond her understanding, a natural instinct from a part of her she didn't even know about. Somehow, she opened a gateway of sorts to a place that felt so warm, comforting, and familiar—as if she had once known it.

Or, perhaps, part of her did know it.

Her mother had been pregnant with her when the big machine blew up. Althea didn't understand most of what the Zero police talked about, only that one of those corporation things tried to make a fancy piece of magic that didn't quite work. It opened a doorway to another place, and some energy slipped through... straight into her.

Again, she peered at the ghost. *Maybe I can help him.*

She pushed herself up to stand, set the tray on the chair, and took a few tiny steps closer to him.

"Child, why are you wearing such strange jewelry?"

"It's not decoration. It's handcuffs so I can't run away. Someone kidnapped me again."

"Again?"

Althea shook her head. "The sun will come up before I could finish the telling." She peered up at him with wide, hopeful eyes. "Can you get them off me?"

The spirit crouched, teasing a finger at one shackle. "There is magic inside them. I can draw that magic into myself, but it would break them. Whenever I consume the magic of a relic like this, it stops working."

"Umm, okay. Please don't. I don't want to be stuck forever."

"Okay."

Althea held her arms up to the sides and tried to remember how she 'opened the door' for the other ghosts months ago. Soon after wanting to help him go across to the 'silver place,' a tug pulled at the back of her mind. Recognizing the feeling, she embraced it… and a tall, silvery swirl appeared in the air in front of them.

"Thank you!" He attempted to hug her, which only caused a brief chill. "You should go that way." He pointed in the direction she had been going already, then rushed into the gate, collapsing it.

Althea let her arms fall slack. "Great. Thanks." She smirked and tried to kick a small rock, but the chain yanked her foot to a halt with a *click*. "Grr. I hate these things."

Grumbling, she hopped back to the ospi, picked up the tray, and sat.

A few minutes after she resumed rolling down the road, she passed a large cube-shaped building on the right. It didn't appear interesting or remarkable at first, until she noticed a thin metal ladder running up the side to the roof.

The machine men with their wheels for legs couldn't climb ladders.

Relieved at finding a place she could feel safe enough to sleep, Althea steered for it, struggling to keep going when the ospi went off the road onto a dirt hill. When she reached the wall, she turned the chair sideways so it didn't roll down. There, she rested and ate a meal of carrot, cucumber and water, since she couldn't carry the tray up the ladder. Upon finishing her late dinner, she hopped to the ladder, holding her last two carrots in her teeth.

Althea grasped the highest rung she could reach and pulled herself up until she got her feet on the lowest one. She stretched up to grab the next rung, repeating the process until she made it to the top of the three-story building.

A frighteningly large hole devoured most of the roof's center, but the area near the ladder appeared solid enough for her meager weight. She slithered over the wall at the top and rolled flat on the gritty black surface, staring up at the stars while clutching her last two carrots to her chest.

I need to find food, water, or people soon… or I'm going to be in big danger.

She opened her mind, calling out to the clairvoy ants, hoping for help. The strangest notion that she would be okay if she continued following the road came on moments later. Safe up high, well out of reach of the wheeled murder machine, she allowed herself to relax.

With the wind teasing at her hair, her gaze on the stars, Althea drifted off to sleep.

CONNECT THREE

T he next morning, Althea awoke to the sun in her eyes. Momentary panic at not being in bed beside Karina faded as the memory of the past two days returned. When soreness around her ankles reached her consciousness, she growled. With a resigned sigh, she commanded her skin to heal itself. At least finding the ospi made traveling *much* less infuriating.

She sat up and ate her carrots while fidgeting at the metal around her right leg. Squeezing the buttons made numbers appear on the screen, each time she filled it up, a loud buzz sounded and the numbers would disappear. Eventually, she ran out of carrot and crawled to the top of the ladder. A quick look around and complete silence reassured her that no machine men had come anywhere close, so she hauled herself up over the wall and jumped off the building, preferring to glide to the ground rather than deal with the irritating task of climbing a ladder while hobbled.

An almost straight vertical drop allowed her to land without tripping and falling over. Her wings withdrew into her back soon after she no longer needed them. She somewhat awkwardly balanced herself while making water near the side of the building, then drank from one of the cans, saving the sealed bottle for last since it had a lid and the air wouldn't steal from it as fast.

Eager to continue, she sat in the ospi, balanced the tray in her lap, and pushed herself along, easily rolling down the dirt hill. When she hit the paved road, the ospi nearly tipped her over sideways, but she flung all her weight to the left to keep balance. The last bit of water in the can went flying off to the side, spilling on the road. Though the plastic bottle fell, it didn't pop open. She grumbled and wheeled over to pick up the water bottle, set it on the tray, and shoved off down the road.

The ruins passed by at a good clip. Even if it required a wheeled chair to do so, being able to cover ground at a running pace heightened her mood… at least until she worried about what she would do if one of those machine men showed up. On the ospi, anywhere she went, it could definitely follow. She also couldn't jump out of the chair and run. Rolling down the middle of the road didn't give her any cover, so while the device allowed her to travel fast, it utterly robbed her of any ability to hide.

Nervous, but in control of her fear, Althea pushed harder at the wheels, gaining speed. She had never seen one of those machine men anywhere near Querq. That gave her hope that if she could get far enough away from this place, she wouldn't run into one. Canid mutants would be a problem since she couldn't scare them off, but after she healed that one, it had become a friend. Maybe if she encountered one of those again, she would try making it trust her instead of forcing fear over it.

For most of the morning, she rolled down ruined streets, astounded at the sheer size of this place. The forest didn't seem as though it had been *that* far away while she had glided down from the flying machine, yet she couldn't even see the trees in the distance from where she sat. The ancients who lived in the Before-Time had created a massive village. Then again, the modern city she hated so much had been endless, too.

She paused a few times to drink, but otherwise tried to go as fast as possible. The exertion of pumping her arms for hours on end offset the chillier climate. Despite her thin dress, she felt neither cold nor overheated.

A little after mid-day, the road angled downhill, making her job easier. Althea grinned, happy to pick up speed as it meant she'd get farther away from the machines faster. Her joy evaporated when she noticed a spot up ahead where the street had caved in, drooping at a sharp angle to an apparent cliff of unknown depth. Screaming, she tried to grab the wheels and stop, but the rubber tires disintegrated entirely, leaving the chair skidding on metal rims—straight off the cliff. The road plummeted almost straight down, following the contour of a sinkhole or crater before curving flat across the bottom.

Her water bottle went flying off to one side, the tray the other.

She screamed, holding on to the armrests, a helpless passenger in a chair under full control of gravity. Sparks flew from the rims at the curve, the chair nearly tipping over backward. Like a giant arrow shot from the world's biggest bow, she rocketed across the fairly short stretch of flat road along the crater bottom and hit the smaller upward ramp at the other end. Impact threw her out of the chair, but she didn't have enough altitude to extend her wings before she landed in a tumbling roll.

When the world stopped spinning, she lay sprawled on her chest, arms askew, her mouth full of dirt. Numerous aches announced the presence of bruises, but she didn't sense any broken skin or bleeding. It took her only a moment to fix the minor hurts, much longer to spit out the dirt and stop choking on it.

Eventually, she stopped spitting, wiped her face on the back of her arm, and looked around for the ospi. It had landed about twenty feet away, but had lost one of the big wheels.

"Oh, no," she whispered, then sighed at the binders.

The missing wheel came to rest a long way off in the ruins, evidently having continued to roll for a little while after landing. Althea bunny-hopped to the ospi, squatting to examine it in hopes she might be able to put the wheel back on. Unfortunately, the metal where it had been bent outward and split open. The wheel hadn't simply popped off a peg she could stick it back on; it had truly broken beyond repair.

She collapsed into a heap, buried her face in her hands, and sobbed, grabbing the chain and trying to break it with brute force.

"I hate you!" screamed Althea. "Get off me!"

Pulling and twisting at it, she repeated her shouts of 'get off' or 'I hate you' a few times, but the damnable metal didn't listen to her. Eventually, sorrow's grip weakened. She wiped her face on her arms, sniffled, and glowered at the shiny metal linking her ankles together.

No... I can't give up. I won't.

She grasped the armrest of the ospi to pull herself upright, sighed farewell at it, and resumed baby-stepping down the road.

After only a few minutes, she sensed curiosity coming from the left. Thrilled at picking up an emotion, she stopped walking and gazed in that direction, hoping to see who or what had come close enough for her to detect.

Three children near in age to her or slightly older emerged from the rubble of a building, all wearing skirts made of squealer leather, furry boots, and cloaks. The eldest, a boy, held a spear but not pointed at her. He somewhat resembled the people of Den's tribe with black hair and brown skin, seeming slightly younger than him but older than her. Behind him, another boy Althea's size with blond hair and green eyes relaxed an arrow he'd loaded into a bow, evidently not wanting to shoot her. The girl, also pale-skinned, wore her dark brown hair in a thick braid that hung all the way down to the middle of her thighs. She carried two large knives on her belt as well as a spear, and stood a little taller than Althea, perhaps a year older.

They had the overall look of Scrags, though their clothing of animal hides, fur skirts, and even boots didn't look familiar at all. Most Scrags this age had little if any clothing, but then again, as chilly as the air was, perhaps she had gone quite a bit farther from home than she imagined. If this place routinely became cold, the people who lived here would have to wear more stuff. Cold elevated clothing from 'nice to have' to 'must have.'

All three walked closer without hesitation, giving off varying degrees of fascination and curiosity. The girl's mood rapidly shifted to greed when they came within speaking distance.

"Hello." She waved. "I'm Althea. Really happy to see you."

"Ooru," said the older boy, tapping himself. He pointed at the smaller boy. "That is Eem. And the girl is Paama."

Paama stepped up to her, shrouded in jealousy. "Those bracelets are pretty. I want them."

"If you can get them off me, you can have them... but they're bad."

The girl stuck her spear in the dirt and grabbed two fistfuls of Althea's dress at her throat, pulling her up on tiptoe. "*If* I can get them off you? You're a scrawny little mouse. Prepare to have your butt kicked."

Althea calmly shook her head. "No. That isn't what I mean."

"Her eyes are bright," said Eem in an awestruck tone.

"Give them to me. Hand them over right now and I won't break your face." Paama shook her a little, then let go.

"I can't." Althea shifted her weight onto her left leg and kicked at her right. "They won't come off. I *want* to take them off, but I can't. I hate them so much."

Paama narrowed her eyes in suspicion. "What do you mean you hate them? They're pretty and magic."

"Bad people captured me and tied me so I can't run away." Althea demonstrated baby-stepping around. "They aren't jewelry, they're pure bad!"

Paama's jealousy lessened. She squatted and fiddled at the binders. "They make light and are pretty silver. They're magic."

"You see the chain?"

"Yes."

"I can't move my feet apart and they don't come off. Bad people put them on me. It's called being tied up. And I really hate it."

Paama examined the restraints for a little while. The last bits of greed evaporated to a strong sense of concern and worry when she couldn't find a way to remove them. "Oh."

"Why do your eyes light?" asked Eem.

"Because they do." Althea offered a weak shrug. She looked at them all in turn, but not one gave off the slightest hint they recognized her.

"What's your tribe?" asked Paama.

"I'm from Querq."

All three made faces of confusion.

Paama reached out and brushed a hand over Althea's dress. "This is like the Ancients' robes. Too thin for winter."

"It is not winter," said Ooru, the eldest boy.

"I know that." Paama elbowed him in the side. "She will need hides before the cold comes."

Althea shivered. "I must go home to Father and my sister, Karina. We live far to the west."

"Ell-Gee is wise." Ooru handed his spear to the smaller boy. "He will know what to do."

Eem threaded his bow across his chest and took the spear.

"We can bring you to our home," said Ooru. "The council will talk to you. Ell-Gee is the scribe of ancients, and has great knowing of old things and magic relics. He might be able to help you."

"Watch out for his daughter, Avie. She isn't right in the head." Eem twirled a finger around near his ear.

"Be nice," whispered Paama.

Ooru approached Althea, reaching as if to pick her up.

"Yes, please!" She jumped into a hug.

He scooped her up in his arms and carried her. Paama took the lead, walking ahead of him while Eem followed close behind, glancing backward every fifteen to twenty seconds. Their course to the south worried her since she wanted to go west, but she'd rather not be alone. Especially considering these Scrags were friendly and would hopefully save her life if another machine man showed up to kill them.

They hurried along at a brisk walk past several cross streets, ruined cars, and even the still-smoking wreckage of some manner of huge flying machine. It didn't look like the one she'd jumped from, being quite a bit larger and more loaf-shaped, without obvious wings. It, too, had large holes in the side. The damage made her remember the smoke trails coming up from the ground, and how close she'd been to blowing up.

When she got home—not if—she intended to cling to Father and Karina for a whole day.

Minutes later, Paama led them up to a ruined building. The front wall bore frozen speech in green that read, 'Connect Transit.' Alas, only the outer walls remained of the structure, essentially a big stone fence around massive piles of rubble. The girl navigated a narrow passage between mounds of smashed concrete, following a canyon of ruin that ended at a stairwell going down into the earth.

Althea didn't like the thought of being taken underground, but none of the Scrag children gave off any emotion suggesting they looked forward to a reward for capturing the Prophet. In fact, they didn't even appear to know who she was.

Ooru carried her down the stairs into a partially collapsed chamber with red tiles on the floor and white tiles on the walls. Dozens of small plastic chairs littered the area, arranged in rows bolted to metal frames. The words 'Connect Transit' appeared in green lettering here and there on columns or walls.

Paama jogged across the room to a platform beside a big tunnel. She jumped down and turned back to look at the others, the floor at the level of her chest. Ooru approached and set Althea down to sit on the edge. While he jumped off the platform to the tunnel, Paama grasped Althea by the armpits and pulled her close, helping her down. Eem hurled himself in a surprisingly fluid leap, landing between a pair of metal rails that ran along the bottom of the huge, round passage.

"What is this place?" asked Althea.

"My mother said it is the Way of Sub." Eem walked onward, using

Ooru's spear like a walking stick. "Something the Ancients made. Long ago, giant snakes named Subs dug these tubes. But they were friendly snakes, and let people ride them."

Ooru picked Althea back up. "The snakes are all gone now. We found a part of one once, but just bones."

"They have metal bones." Paama made her way into the dark. "We found people bones inside."

"He didn't eat them. He was giving them a ride," said Eem, indignantly.

Althea held on to Ooru's neck, gazing around at the huge tunnel. The way ahead contained numerous sets of metal jaws, yawning open in anticipation of meeting an unwary foot.

"Look out," said Althea. "There's teeth in the ground."

The kids all stopped, gawking at her.

"You can see them?" asked Paama, in awe.

"Umm. Yeah." It occurred to Althea that everyone had turned black and white.

"Look at her eyes," whispered Eem. "They're lit up. She has magic lights."

"The magic lights don't work anymore. They haven't worked since before grandpa was my age." Ooru sighed, full of sadness.

"Ell-Gee still has one," said Paama. "He made it from a dead Silver Man."

"He should make for everyone." Eem tapped the spear on the ground as if to add an exclamation point.

Paama raised her hand to the side, two fingers extended. "How many fingers am I holding out?"

"Two," said Althea.

"Wow, she *can* see!" Paama covered her mouth. "Is she a god?"

"Ooo," said Eem. "Maybe."

"She can't be a god." Ooru shook his head. "If she hates the magic bracelets, she would destroy them."

"But they're magic." Paama pointed at the tiny, glowing screen on the shackle. "Maybe because another god made them to trap a small god?"

"I'm not whatever a god is. I'm Althea."

"Umm. We should let the council talk to her." Ooru reached around with his foot until he found Paama. "Keep going."

"Right." The girl turned, whispered a few numbers to herself, then resumed walking.

She came close to stepping on two of the twenty or more traps they passed, but somehow navigated the serpentine path between them. When they reached a point where no more traps stood in the way, Paama, despite not being able to see in the dark, walked faster.

"How did you escape the teeth?" asked Althea.

"Counting steps." Ooru grinned. "From the entrance, four then right then three then left, then six then right... it is required we remember it without mistake before we are allowed to go outside."

That made sense. The machine men with the wheels probably wouldn't try to go down that stairway in the first place, and those giant traps looked big enough to possibly catch one.

"Thank you for helping me," said Althea.

"You are welcome. We can't leave anyone outside if they're nice." Paama glanced back at her for a second. "The Silver Men would kill you."

"I don' like them," said Eem. "They still have shooty sticks. Ours don't work no more."

Althea didn't quite know what to think of a boy around eleven who felt more jealous of the machine man's functional guns than frightened of how easily it could kill him.

The kids walked along the tracks for far longer than it took to go from where they'd found her to the stairs. Eventually, color—blue plastic—appeared up ahead near another platform similar to the one they entered from. Small devices hung on the walls, giving off light. Four adults with spears, two women and two men, approached the edge to help the kids climb up.

They all looked at Althea, curiosity shifting toward awe when they realized her eyes glowed.

"Who is this?" asked a man. "Why are you carrying her?"

"She has been taken from her home by bad people. They put something on her so she cannot walk." Ooru twisted to the side, holding her feet toward them.

The adults examined the binders. Their emotions and facial expressions told her they generally recognized the device as a tool of captivity, and didn't look pleased about it being on her.

"What is your name, child?" asked the older of the men, tall, with shaggy black hair. "I am Amon."

"Althea."

A red-haired woman with faint wrinkles at her eyes brushed her hand at Althea's cheek. "I am Shara. Who has done this to you?"

"I don't know. They shot me with a little thing that made me sleep."

"Cowards," muttered Shara.

"Ulon," said the younger man. Like the girl Paama, he kept his dark hair in a single thick braid, but his had numerous baubles woven into the end.

"I am Iora," said a whispery female voice.

Althea glanced to her right at a youngish woman with short light brown hair, probably in her early twenties. "Hi. Umm..." She clicked her feet apart. "Can someone please take these off me?"

"Bring her to Ell-Gee." Shara pointed at a much smaller tunnel lined with the same little lights.

"I will." Ooru nodded at the redhead, then started for the passageway, carrying Althea.

She clung to him, tucking her legs in to avoid scraping the walls while peering around at the low ceiling, small lights, and electrical wires stringing them together. The relatively long hallway ended at a large chamber with white walls and columns, all covered in tiles, mostly cracked. Around fifty people occupied it, sitting in clusters tending cooking pots or around piles of animal hide, stitching them into garments. A bready-meaty fragrance filled the air, drawing an instant growl from Althea's stomach. Smaller children zoomed around playing. Everyone wore garments made of fur or hide. Few people bothered to take notice of the three kids carrying Althea across the chamber to an archway at the center of the inner wall, blocked off by a curtain of thick transparent plastic.

A few made eye contact with her, but aside from the occasional sense of curiosity or mild fear when someone noticed her glowing eyes, not one person gave off the usual blast of elation or adoration she'd become used to whenever her captors brought her to their camp, settlement, or fortress. Despite being quite a ways from home, having people react to her as they would have reacted to any ordinary new person—and not a prize—left her staring around in mild shock. She might have cried if not for her anger at the binders on her legs.

Paama pulled the barrier aside so Ooru could carry her through.

Despite the grand size of the arch, it led to a relatively small chamber. Three adults, two women and a man, sat in beat up chairs quite fluffy and cushioned, though exceptionally old. The one on the left had a detachable platform extended from the front, upon which the man's legs rested.

An older woman with dark skin and short, curly hair of pale grey occupied the center chair. Numerous baubles decorated her animal hide dress, and she wore several amulets made from shiny green material bearing an intricate inlaid pattern of tiny silver lines. To her left sat a much younger man, dressed in an odd robe apparently made from a blanket. His shoes resembled fuzzy animals that had been hollowed out, but she had never seen rabbits like that. Perhaps he had killed one of those 'stuffed animals' that Anna gave her. Shaggy brown hair hung to his shoulders, and he smiled out from under a thick mustache above a goatee while raising a short, wide glass at her in greeting, then took a sip of the whitish liquid within. The rightmost chair held a slender woman with long, straight black hair and almond-shaped eyes. Her general appearance reminded Althea of Aya, the former harem slave who Rachel had referred to as 'Japanese.' However, this woman had zero trace of timidity in her.

An empty, even fancier, chair sat on a dais behind the three fluffy ones. A small circular mark on the headrest bore the letters B M W, though she had no idea how to pronounce it or what it meant.

All three people regarded her for a moment, having no particular emotional reaction beyond mild annoyance from the women. The man gave off a constant, subtle emanation of serenity. He sipped his drink again, closed his eyes for a second, and sighed in contentment.

Ooru set Althea down on her feet. She couldn't help but feel somewhat like a slave presented to the bandit chief, due mostly to the binders. However, she refused to be owned. So far, these people didn't radiate any sense of being bandits at all, merely settlers. She peered at their thoughts.

The dark-skinned woman was annoyed that children she thought of as scouts — specifically Ooru and his two friends — would walk into this room unannounced. Apparently, they didn't have enough status to do so. She didn't pay much attention to Althea. The younger woman who resembled Aya also thought it wrong for them to walk into this room, but her irritation at that gave way to wonder at the sight of glowing blue eyes. The man, however, mostly contemplated how much he enjoyed the flavor of the alcoholic drink... though debated if he'd mixed it up a little weak. Regarding her, he thought she appeared sad, scared, and hungry, and considered that a problem they should do something about. His urge to comfort and protect her eased the last of Althea's worries.

"Ooru," said the older dark-skinned woman, "Why do you enter the council chambers?"

"Who is this child you bring?" asked the younger woman.

The boy bowed deep, pressing his right arm across his chest. "Councilors, this is Althea. We found her while searching for useful things. She is in need of help. Forgive us interrupting you, but we thought she might be of the gods. Maybe a messenger from the queen."

"Her eyes." The elder gasped.

"Whoa," said the younger, reclining man.

Eem stood on Althea's left, puffing his chest up as if proud of saving her.

"I am Noema the Enlightened, elder councilor." The elder extended a hand toward the other woman. "This is Sumiko the Far Seeing." She gestured at the man. "And... Bill."

"Yo," said Bill, saluting her with two fingers.

"We are the councilors of the Transit tribe." Noema brought her hands together in front of herself. "What brings you to us, child?"

Althea pondered a few seconds, then said, "Ooru."

The councilors exchanged glances. Bill snickered.

"You misunderstand me." Noema smiled. "For what purpose have you come here?"

"I was taken from my home and I want to go back. But the bad people put handcuffs on me so I can't walk." She kicked at her leg. "Will someone please get them off me?"

Bill rolled forward out of his chair, smoothly keeping his drink level, not spilling a drop. The recliner rocked back once free of his weight, but the leg platform remained up. All three councilors approached and stooped to examine the binders. Sumiko touched the tiny buttons, making bright green numbers appear on the screen. When it buzzed, she jumped back with a gasp.

"This is a relic," whispered Noema. "They have power within them."

"Truly a sign. Queen Kye may have communicated with her." Sumiko bowed her head in reverence.

Noema rose and lifted Althea's chin with two fingers, gazing into her eyes. "What form of magic does that relic possess?"

"Bad magic that keeps me from walking. I hate it." She demonstrated baby-stepping around.

Sumiko grasped the shackle around Althea's right ankle and tried unsuccessfully to open it. "Why would someone curse you with this artifact?"

"Because they're a meanie!" yelled Althea. "There's bad stuff here and I could die from not running."

"Where did you come from?" asked Bill.

"My village is named Querq. People stole me at night and I woke up inside a flying machine, but it broke so I had to come back down, but I can't walk very fast at all."

The councilors whispered among themselves, wondering if she really was something they called a 'god.' Noema doubted it, Sumiko believed it, and Bill simply said they should help her.

Sumiko tugged at the hem of Althea's dress, feeling the fabric between her fingers. "Where did you get this garment? I have never seen something so white or made like this... truly, she is of the gods' realm."

Noema also reached out to study the fabric. "I do not possess an explanation for that. Hmm." She took Althea by the hand. "Come, child."

Althea peered up at her expectantly, but the older woman started to walk off, making no effort to pick her up. She sighed and micro-stepped along at her side. Ooru bit his lip, evidently wanting to help, but too afraid of the councilors to do so. They crept out into the main chamber and veered to the left.

After a few minutes of agonizing progress, Noema peered down at her. "Why do you walk so slowly?"

A surge of indignant anger exploded inside Althea... but she held it in. The four adults she'd first seen here all seemed to know what handcuffs were. Why would they put the dumb ones in charge? "That's what this 'magic device' does. It makes me slow so I'm easy to kidnap and can't run away."

"Ahh. Now I understand." Noema scooped her up and carried her.

Althea resisted the urge to roll her eyes. The councilors and the three children who found her crossed the giant room and went into a vast corridor lined with the same lights hung at random levels, as if no particular care had been made to keep them even. The walls on both sides had tall, flat metal boxes with faded pictures of men, women, strange monsters, or scary places. Silvery letters along the bottom of one picture read, 'In Theaters June 2099.'

Perplexed, Althea looked around at all the growling, terrifying creatures in these pictures and decided that she never wanted to be anywhere near a 'theater,' whatever that was, since all the monsters would be there. And she absolutely did *not* want to meet the green one taller than a house.

Noema carried per past a few passageways that led off to either side, continuing to follow the enormous corridor. A metal sign stuck to the ceiling above one said, 'restrooms' with an arrow pointing to the left.

Resting rooms? Althea peered down that hall at two doors. *Is that where they sleep?*

The councilors eventually turned right, taking her past a set of double doors into a large chamber filled with steel shelving containing vast amounts of techno-junk. At the far end of the room by a workbench, a thin man with long, straight brown hair stood with his back turned, stooped over something that emitted random flashes of light and buzzing sounds. His animal-hide clothes bore numerous scorch marks and grease smudges.

A tiny girl sat on the floor near his left leg, maybe six or seven years old, playing with a metal wand and an ancient piece of electronics that had been opened up to expose the insides. Her furry skirt also had numerous smudges and burns, her bare chest smeared with grease. The child wore a necklace of wire and tiny electronic bits. Her auburn hair frizzed up around her head when a minuscule spark leapt from the tip of the wand in her hand to her nose. It didn't appear to bother her much, though she had an expression of permanent surprise. Undeterred, she poked the wand into the electronic component, making several LEDs on the side come on.

"Ell-Gee," said Noema.

The man looked up from his work. Upon seeing everyone, he stood, faced, them, and bowed. "Councilors." A dull grey amulet hung around his neck on a wire, bearing the letters LG. It appeared to be made of plastic, cut out from a larger object.

A *bzzt* came from the little girl in time with a wisp of smoke rising out of the old device. She giggled, then tried to lick the wand—zapping herself on the tongue. At that, she crossed her eyes and made a face like she tasted something bad. Eem glanced at Althea and twirled his finger around by his ear.

Noema approached the workbench and set Althea down, seated,

upon it. "This child is in need of your assistance. She has been cursed with magic that prevents her from moving."

"Hello, girl." Ell-Gee smiled at her before glancing at Noema. "I am not well versed in magic, councilor."

"We are aware of that." Noema frowned, folding her arms. "However, Queen Kye is not here."

Ell-Gee let out a resigned sigh and again looked at Althea.

At his confusion, she pulled her legs up onto the table and pointed at the binders. "Please take these off me."

The man gave off a burst of humor. He started to look toward Noema with an 'are you serious?' face, but caught himself, remaining stoic. "Ahh, yes. Well. This particular form of magic I may be able to do something with."

Bill hid his mouth behind his hand, his body shaking with mute laughter.

Sumiko elbowed him, annoyed.

Ell-Gee took a knee, stooping to examine the restraints more closely. After a few minutes of poking and prodding at them, he hurried over to one of the shelves. The little girl made an 'aaaah' noise while sticking her tongue out and licking the wand—which zapped her again.

Without looking away from his rummaging, Ell-Gee said, "Avie, don't lick the diagnostic probe."

The girl zapped herself on the tongue again and giggled.

"Your daughter shares your love of electricity." Bill raised his glass in toast and took a sip.

Althea looked down at the small girl, who resumed prodding the electronics in her lap with the wand. *Is her thinking-shape hurt?*

"Aha!" called Ell-Gee. He extracted a flat plastic device from the pile of junk that appeared similar to the learning machine, only thicker and larger. "This will do."

"What is it?" Althea wrapped her arms around her legs, tapping one foot on the tabletop.

"They called it a datapad, I believe."

She leaned closer. "I have a datapad, but it's not that big. It's back home. Sometimes, it makes me mad because I don't know stuff."

Ell-Gee chuckled.

A tingly zap jolted Althea in the right ankle.

She jumped with a yelp, and shot a look down at Avie who'd tapped the binders with the wand. The little one peered up at her with wide-blue eyes, her expression still as though someone had snuck up behind her and made a loud noise.

"Please don't zap me," said Althea.

Avie prodded the binders with her finger, seeming fascinated.

"Will that 'datapad' be of any use here?" Noema gestured at it.

Ell-Gee wiped his hand across the datapad's screen, pushing a button to turn it on. "Yes, it should be just the thing. Just need to find the right interface cable."

"8C!" chirped Avie.

He looked down at her. "Are you sure? That's CR—I mean Silver Man tech."

Bill sipped from his drink.

Avie nodded, pointing at the binders. "Tiny pluggie. 8C parity or maybe a B8-UHDR."

Ell-Gee abandoned the datapad and stooped to look at the binders. "Oh, you're right. That does kind of look like an ultra-high data rate port."

"Not Silver Man," said Avie. "Sky Monster."

Althea considered zapping herself in the nose with that wand. Maybe then she'd understand these people.

"These are as good or better tech than the silver men." Ell-Gee whistled. "Where's that darn adaptor?"

"I get!" Avie dropped her wand and raced off across the room amid the pattering of bare feet. She leapt onto a shelf near the wall, climbing it like a monkey on fire until she reached a box near the ceiling.

Everyone waited in silence until the child returned carrying a dark orange ribbon cable, which she handed to her father. Ell-Gee took it, examining the end with a tiny plastic bit half the size of a pea. He grasped Althea's foot and lifted her leg up, inserting the wire into the underside of the shackle around her right leg.

"It fits. Let's hope the data connection lines up."

Althea stared past her toes at him. "I don't know what you said."

"You understand this magic?" asked Noema, an eyebrow raised.

"It's not magic, councilor. It's technology, like the silver men."

Noema's mood darkened. "I caution you not to blaspheme the gods."

Ell-Gee flashed a fake smile. "Of course, councilor."

He set her foot down, the thin wire still connected to the handcuffs, and plugged the bigger end into the top of the datapad. The front face lit up at his touch, and within a moment, the tiny display screens on the binders erupted with activity, displaying numbers so fast she couldn't read them.

"Eep!" She leaned back, stretching her feet out to get the device as far away from her face as possible before it exploded.

"Shh." He patted her on the head. "Nothing to be afraid of. It's an electronic combination lock."

She blinked at him.

"They will open if you type in the right five-digit number."

"What's the right number?" asked Bill.

Ell-Gee shrugged. "No idea. That's why I'm trying all of them."

A few seconds later, the binder on that ankle emitted a chirp and opened, the display screen stopped on 71526. Ell-Gee typed the same number into the other side, and it opened as well. Such a massive surge of joy hit Althea that it radiated out over the settlement. Noema grinned broadly. Sumiko gazed into space. Bill closed his eyes and smiled. Avie erupted in giggles. Ell-Gee smiled, but appeared confused. Ooru, Paama, and Eem all cheered.

Althea squealed in delight and jumped off the table, hugging him. "Thank you!" She tackle-hugged Ooru next, then Paama, Eem, and the councilors.

"I feel most unusual," said Noema.

"Truly the work of the gods if you are smiling." Bill sipped his drink.

Sumiko nearly laughed, but stopped herself. Noema shot him a 'what's that supposed to mean' look, but didn't stop smiling.

Althea faced the elder and peered up at her. "Can you help me get back to Querq?"

The older woman raised an eyebrow—evidently not having the first clue what that even meant.

BANISHED

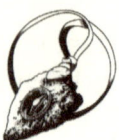

The councilors looked back and forth at each other in varying degrees of confusion.

A few minutes of silence broke when Avie prodded a device with the wand, causing it to emit a strange wailing noise along with a—possibly male—voice shrieking in agony. The little girl started moving her head up and down rapidly, making her fluffy auburn hair dance around.

"By the gods, what is that noise?" blurted Sumiko.

"Music," said Bill.

Avie raised her left hand, extending her index and pinky fingers up into a shape like bull horns, continuing to bob her head in time with the noise.

"It sounds evil," whispered Althea. "Are they hurting that man?"

"No, he is singing." Ell-Gee laughed. "It's from the time of the ancients. I believe they called it heavy metal."

"It's not metal. It's sound," said Althea.

The device emitted a spark and a puff of smoke before going silent. Avie lowered her 'bull horns,' stopped bobbing her head, and frowned at it. "Aww."

Since the councilors hadn't said a word about helping her go home, Althea figured they had no idea how to do so. At least Ell-Gee took those damn binders off her, so she could make her way back to Querq on her own.

"Thank you for helping me." Althea hugged Ell-Gee again. "I must return to my family."

She headed for the exit.

"Althea?" asked Noema. "Do you not have a message for us?"

"Umm." Althea stopped and turned to look at them. "No. I didn't come here to find you. Ooru, Paama, and Eem found me."

Noema stepped closer. "The gods did not send you with a message from Queen Kye?"

"I don't know who that is."

The councilors exchanged worried looks—except Bill. He gave off a 'well that figures' sort of vibe. When no one said anything for a moment, Althea resumed walking out.

Bzzt. Avie giggled.

Althea turned left in the corridor and followed it back the way she remembered coming in. However, after a few turns that she thought seemed right, she realized she hadn't gone the same way when she entered a hallway where a giant bundle of thick wires ran along the wall on the left at her eye level. Lost but curious, she followed the cables for a while until they went through a doorway. She peered into the room— at a group of machine men glaring at her.

"Eep!" She jumped back, flattening herself against the wall.

None of the machine men said anything about contaminants or chased her... so after a moment, she got up enough nerve to look again. Three wheel men hung from a frame of metal pipes by chains attached to metal loops on their shoulders. Their wheels and gun arms were missing and they didn't appear to be 'awake,' no red light glowing from their multiple lens-eyes. Behind them, two larger machine men with legs and shiny silver bodies lay on the floor. They, too, did not appear to be awake. All five had suffered damage from explosives. Numerous wires connected their chests to a giant array of plastic boxes on the right side of the room. The huge cable bundle that ran along the corridor plunged into the top of the same array.

"Umm... I probably shouldn't go in there."

She backed away from the room and ran down the hall, trying to find the path to the giant chamber. A series of random turns brought her to a passage that appeared far more recent, one these settlers must have dug out themselves. Other people here paid her little attention beyond polite nods of greeting. Children near in age to her or younger stopped in place and stared at her as she walked by.

This is the wrong way. I should go —

A foul smell hit her in the nose, a smell she knew well: infection.

Concern pulled her deeper into the rough-hewn passage, to a white flag bearing a red mark that she recognized from her 'math' lesson as a plus sign. Confused why a village would have an entire room devoted to math, she approached and peered in the open doorway, nearly gagging on the smell of *mierda*, rotting flesh, and vomit.

Two boys not much older than her lay on cots, barely conscious. A woman and three men in their thirties also occupied beds farther in by the back corner. The worst smell came from the dark-haired boy, whose left leg below the knee looked more like a mossy log than human skin.

"Uh oh." Althea ran over to him.

"Child!" yelled a woman even older than Noema. She somewhat resembled Sumiko, only old, short, somewhat pudgy, and clearly in a bad mood. "Do not pester him. He is very ill. The gods will welcome him soon."

Althea disregarded the old woman and approached the boy with the rotting leg.

"Girl!" the elder scurried over and grabbed Althea by the arm, ungently.

"*Let go*," said Althea. A brief brightening of her eyes accompanied the Suggestion.

The command knocked the angry expression from the woman's face, leaving her bewildered. Her claw like fingers relaxed, and her arm fell.

"He does not have to go to his ancestors."

For an instant, the woman appeared about to grab her again, but hesitated. Fear bubbled up within the emotions surrounding her. Confident the woman wouldn't get in the way, Althea rested her hands on the boy's arm and closed her eyes, plunging her consciousness into the quiet non-space in which her power connected to someone else's life energy.

Angry blackness devoured the lower half of the boy's leg. A hollow in the shin bone revealed an object not part of his body. The irregular shape made her think rock or fragment of concrete. The boy's skin had died below the knee, the decay having seeped well into the muscles below. She commanded his mind to ignore pain, then focused her power on the area where death chewed. Bit by bit, she separated a thin layer of muscle shape away from the healthy parts, creating a 'sock' of dead skin and muscle tissue disconnected entirely from the boy. After holding the blood-presence in place so it didn't leak out everywhere, she opened her eyes and grasped the crusty, hot mess with both hands.

The older woman gurgled in disgust when Althea slid the rot-sock off and dropped it to the floor, exposing glistening raw muscles, his foot stripped mostly down to bones.

"Wha... am I dead?" whispered the boy. "It doesn't hurt anymore."

"No," said Althea. "Please hold still."

She closed her eyes and dove back into the dark world of multicolored shapes and forms. At the urging of her power, his body expelled the foreign object, then regenerated muscle tissue, his leg swelling from a spindle to normal thickness over the span of about ten minutes. Once the muscles appeared complete, Althea drew the skin-shape down over the leg, guiding its growth until it covered his toes.

His blood-presence contained much sick. Gathering it all to the bladder took longer than repairing the leg. The amount of sick exceeded his ability to contain it, causing him to involuntarily squirt fetid green fluid into the air.

The woman yelled and jumped back, then dashed over to a table to grab a plastic bucket.

Althea pushed the boy up onto his side, directing the stream of awfulness to the floor.

He moaned.

"What is happening?" yelled the woman, while running over to hold the bucket under the poison. "Ugh. This does not smell right at all."

"He had a lot of sick." Althea looked the boy over. Aside from being in dire need of a bath, he appeared healthy. "Please bring him food. He will be hungry from the healing."

"Ngh. I can't stop." The boy grabbed himself, but the stream of dark green urine continued.

"Don't. You have to let the sicks all the way out or they will harm you." Althea kept a hand on his arm to prevent him from feeling pain. Getting rid of such foulness usually burned quite a bit.

Once he finished, he rolled flat on his back and let off a belabored moan. It took him a moment to realize his leg no longer resembled dead wood. "Gods!" He shot upright and pulled his foot into his lap, studying it. "Mariko! You did it."

"I did nothing…" The old one held the bucket out at arms' length, face scrunched.

Althea braced for the usual fanfare about The Prophet, but the elder and boy merely stared at her in bewilderment. Mariko cringed at the skin sock on the floor. With a sigh, Althea picked up the squishy-crunchy thing and dropped it in the bucket.

"You should burn that."

Mariko heaved as if about to vomit. "Y-you touched it with your bare hand…"

Althea tilted her head, unsure why that would matter.

The boy's stomach emitted a horribly loud growl. He clutched his gut for a second, then sprang off the bed, so desperate for food that he ran naked into the hallway. Althea moved around the empty cot and examined the next boy, who appeared a little younger than her. Thousands of tiny raised spots covered every inch of his skin. He lay half conscious, covered in a cold sweat, shivering. This, she'd seen before. Sometimes, this sick went away on its own, but it could kill raiders or villagers who got it. One village doctor had called it 'pox.' People tended to exile anyone with it since the sick spread rapidly.

"Do you have a metal bucket?" asked Althea.

"Yes." Mariko shuffled off and returned with a big metal pail. "Is he going to pee, too?"

Althea nodded. "Yes. But…" She peeled him out of his hide clothing, tossing his tunic and skirt into the bucket. "All of this bedding will need to be burned, too. This sick jumps from person to person. Anything he touched can carry the sick. It can hurt everyone who touches these things. He will need to take a bath away from others in water that you do not keep."

"Oh… how do you know this?" Mariko hovered closer, examining the red dots all over the boy's skin.

"I'm the Prophet." Althea rested her hand on his bumpy arm and dove into his life essence, forcing the threads of yellow pervading his blood-presence and life-shapes down to the bladder. After commanding his skin to heal itself of all the sores, she opened her eyes.

"The Prophet?" asked Mariko. "You see the future?"

"Umm. No." She shook her head. "Well… sometimes I get a feeling about stuff that's gonna happen, but only like *right* before it happens. People just called me that. You don't know me?"

"I don't." Mariko shook her head.

The scrawny tow-haired boy opened his eyes. He sat up, looked at Althea, looked down at himself, then gasped in surprise, running his hands over his legs and arms. "The spots are gone!"

"You must wash yourself," said Althea. "There is still sick on you."

Mariko pointed at a giant sink in the back of the room.

He started to get up, but grabbed himself between the legs and moaned.

"You also must let the sick out." Althea put a hand on his shoulder and turned off his pain sense.

"Umm." He looked at her, blushing. "I can't when you're touching me."

"If I don't, it will burn."

"But..."

She smiled and forced his embarrassment away. "There."

He made a deposit in the metal bucket, dark red instead of green, then ran over to the sink.

Althea pointed at the bucket. "Please burn it."

Mariko hurried out with both pails.

"Not near food!" shouted Althea. "Different fire from cooking!"

The scrawny kid climbed into the sink and turned the water on. Althea stuck her hands into the water to wash them since she touched him, then went over to the injured woman and grasped her hand. She hovered close to death, with a terrible burn through her upper torso. A channel roughly an inch wide had bored all the way from front to back with char-blackened edges. Fortunately, it had missed the heart shape.

Althea gasped and linked her power to the woman's body, forcing her life shapes to reabsorb the charred parts and grow new muscle, bone, and skin. The wound closed in a few minutes, and they both opened their eyes at the same time.

"What...? How?" The woman sat up and looked around. "How did I get here?"

Althea shrugged. "I don't know."

She looked down at her. "Who are you?"

"Althea."

"Your eyes are glowing."

"Yes."

"Am I dead?"

Althea shook her head. "No. You had a big hurt. I made it go away. You should eat soon."

The woman swung her legs off the cot and stood. She wore only dried blood above the waist and a hide skirt covered in pouches. "I don't remember how I got back to the settlement. This is Mariko's room, isn't it?"

"Yes. What happened to you?"

"Silver Men caught us. I was too slow to get down and it threw magic fire at me." She peered at her chest, rubbing a finger at the circle of pink skin. "This is incredible... there isn't even a scar. How did this happen?"

"I helped you." Althea smiled at her, then walked to the nearer of the two men.

He, too, had a burned tunnel, but it had hit him lower in the abdomen, shredding the parts full of nasty stuff. *Mierda* had gotten loose all throughout his insides. Cringing, Althea ran to fetch a tray from the table, then rested both hands on his stomach, commanding the skin over his belly to split apart on either side of the wound, making a giant opening to his insides.

That done, she reached in with her hands to scoop out all the foulness that had gone wherever it didn't belong, piling it on the tray. Charred, unusable bits, she pulled loose and added to the tray. Mariko walked in, saw Althea up to her elbows in the man's guts, and screamed.

Althea glanced over. "Please get water. There is sand and stone inside him."

"What are you doing!?" shouted Mariko. "You cut him open!"

"I'm *trying* to help him. Will you please get water?"

"You've got your hands inside him!"

"Do *you* want to clear out the *meirda*?"

"The what?"

Althea wracked her brain, trying to remember that other word. "Poop! There's poop everywhere inside him. It's making him sick."

Mariko blinked. Mute, she walked over to the workbench, picked up a pitcher, and filled it at the sink where the boy bathed—at least using fresh water from the faucet and not the pox-laden water he sat in.

"Rinse him out," said Althea, still searching around the man's inner blobs for visible signs of filth. Sand and grit covered much of his 'gut serpent.'

"All right." Mariko poured water into the gaping wound.

Althea rubbed everything with her hands, chasing the sand and stone bits away, flushing them out onto the cot and floor. When the insides appeared clean enough, she dove back into the link with his life essence. Mending his body took longer than the others, due to the location of the injury as well as gathering all the yellow sick out of his blood-presence. It also left her noticeably tired.

The man groaned soon after she finished and opened her eyes.

"He will be very hungry." Althea glanced at the empty sink. The boy must have run off while she'd been working. She hurried over there to wash her hands and arms. Even though she knew touching *mierda* wouldn't give her any sicks she couldn't fix, she still found it unpleasant.

After washing up, she checked the last man who only had a sprained ankle. She mended it, smiled at the stunned and bewildered Mariko, and trudged out into the hall, eager to find her way home. Alas, a sharp pang in her stomach had other plans.

I need to eat. Will these settlers give me food if I ask?

She rushed around the corridors, thoroughly lost until a lucky random turn brought her to the big hallway with all the scary pictures that warned people to stay away from that theater place. Giddy at the ability to once again run, she grinned while sprinting to the end, and the huge room with most of the settlers.

The boy who had the dead foot sat cross-legged around a cooking pot, devouring some bread-like item. Someone had draped a blanket around him, though he still didn't seem to care about anything more than eating.

Althea walked in, looking around for a likely person she might beg food from.

"The girl," said a man.

Everyone stopped and stared at her. That reaction, she knew well. Though, these people didn't give off the usual 'Prophet, grab her!' emotion, only reverent awe. She cringed, shrinking in on herself. Being worshipped made her so uncomfortable that ending up in a cage almost seemed preferable.

Except for the sounds of the boy stuffing his face, the room had fallen silent.

"Can I please have some food?" asked Althea, her tiny voice echoing.

Several adults rushed over at once. Two women took her arms, each trying to pull her in a different direction, but not *too* hard. They eventually reached a consensus and brought her over to another cook pot, where she sat with them. The women handed her a heavy loaf of bread about the same size as the cheeseburger things she'd eaten in the bad city.

"Thank you!"

She bit into it, discovering an inner filling with meat and vegetables. Overcome by hunger, she savaged it like a feral creature, ignoring its heat. By the time she came up for air, the councilors had once again gathered around her, Mariko with them—still looking as if she'd seen a ghost.

"I say she is of the gods," whispered Sumiko. "Either their messenger or their child."

"I'm not a god. I'm just psionic."

Murmurs washed over the room.

A few voices called out, asking why her eyes glowed.

"They just do."

"She claims to be a prophet," said Mariko.

Althea sighed. "I said *the* Prophet, not a prophet. It's like a name. I don't really like it though. It makes people treat me bad."

Some sixty people all stared at her in confusion.

Wow. They don't know who I am. She managed a faint smile. While that meant they would likely not try to kidnap her, it also meant they would not hesitate to harm her out of fear of the legends. However, no one here appeared threatening or gave off dangerous emotions.

"Prophet," said Noema. "We have never heard of this."

"How?" asked Althea. "I thought everyone knew me."

"We are pretty isolated." Bill sipped his drink. "We just kinda hang out down here and do our own thing. Gotta stay hidden from the Silver Men. They're kind of a bummer."

Noema gasped. "Bill, do not invite the anger of the gods." Her glower softened as she looked at Althea. "The Silver Men are the soldiers of the gods. They vaporize the unworthy who trod in sin upon the ancient lands. Our ancestors committed a grievous crime and we have been banished from the Earth. People are forbidden to dwell above the surface, lest the flames of green and blue scorch their impurities away."

"Umm." Althea licked the last of the crumbs and sauce from her hands. "I live on the earth just fine at home."

"Child, you should not speak blasphemy against the gods aloud." Noema wagged a finger at her. "It is bad enough Ell-Gee has desecrated the corpses of sacred soldiers."

"Gotta get power from somewhere," muttered Bill. "But that's none of my business." He sipped his drink.

Althea stood, facing Noema. "Why do you keep telling people not to talk? What is blasphemy?"

"To speak ill of the gods." Noema bowed her head.

"Won't the gods say something if they get mad? Why do you have to make people stop talking?"

Bill's eyebrows went up. Sumiko gasped... as did everyone in the room not a small child.

"Dare you speak such about the gods?" Noema glared at her.

"What are gods?" asked Althea. "How do you know what they want?"

"She is the elder councilor," called a man in the distance. "Second only to the queen."

Sumiko put a hand on Noema's arm. "She is only a child, and has not been raised in our ways. She knows not what she says."

"Do you talk about the gods to scare people so they listen, or are you really afraid of them?" asked Althea.

Noema blinked rapidly, apparently too shocked by the blunt question to formulate a reply.

Her thoughts revealed true fear, reminding Althea a bit of how she'd once been scared of the 'black goblin.' The time she'd spent with the Wagon Man, he'd kept her constantly locked in a small cage inside his wagon. At night, it looked as if a tiny creature made of shadow peered at her from behind one of the cabinets. When the raiders killed him and finally pulled her cage out of the wagon, looking at that spot from a better angle revealed it had been a metal jug all along. This woman's fear of 'the gods' felt quite a bit like that.

"You really are scared." Althea smiled. "If your gods love you, they will protect you even if you make a mistake. Just like Father."

"They punish if we sin," whispered Sumiko. "We dare not make them angry."

"When raiders are mean to their slaves, the slaves want to run away... being mean doesn't make the slaves love the raiders. If your gods are mean to you, why don't you run away?"

"Enough," shouted Noema. "We have seen the gods' wrath. We dwell in this place away from the earth because the Silver Men kill without hesitation. They do not talk to us, they simply burn our sin away."

"They think we're contaminants," muttered Althea.

Several people in the crowd, mostly older teens, perked up at that word.

"I've heard them say that, too," said a girl Karina's age.

"Yes." A boy near her nodded.

"Come," Noema took her hand. "It is late, and you are too young to speak such of the gods."

"But, what if she has been sent by them?" asked Sumiko. "Perhaps that is why she does not fear them, if she is one of them? Gods do not care if they speak ill of other gods. They quarrel all the time with each other."

"We shall discuss this later." Noema tugged Althea along, crossing the room back to the hallway of scary pictures.

"Where are we going?" asked Althea.

"It is late. You are too small to be awake at this hour. And you look tired."

That much, she couldn't disagree with. Healing those people had taken a lot out of her. She tolerated being led to another chamber full of sleeping mats, cots, and a few proper beds. Only some children her size or smaller occupied them at the moment, though she had a feeling families slept together and the adults would go to sleep later. Noema guided her to a cot against the right wall.

"You may rest here. If you need to go to the bathroom, it is right across the hall."

"Thank you." Althea started to sit, but bathroom sounded like a good idea.

After Noema walked out, Althea scurried out the door, across the hall, and into a small alcove with two doors. One had a stick figure with legs, the other a stick figure like a dress. Since she presently had a dress on, she went in that one.

The room contained eight toilets similar to the one back home in Querq, only these didn't have the boxy part behind the seat. A huge blue plastic drum of water stood in the middle of the room, a few ladles hanging off its side. Frozen speech on the drum in white paint said 'please flush.' She chose a stall at random, relieved herself, and pushed the handle… but it didn't do anything.

"They're broken…"

Althea tried again, but the handle didn't work. She sheepishly approached the barrel.

"I'm sorry. I tried to flush but it's broken."

She took a ladle and drank a few mouthfuls of the stale plastic-flavored water, then returned to the sleeping room. The cot she'd been told to use smelled like wet dog, but not so much she found it unpleasant. When she'd first arrived at her new home, Karina convinced her to wear a nightgown by saying it wasn't good to sleep in the same clothes she'd worn all day. However, she had nothing else with her, and out in the Badlands, she'd get too cold taking her dress off at night. Here, she decided to wear the blanket to bed.

Curled up surrounded by fur, Althea closed her eyes and focused on sending a long-distance message to Father and Karina.

Someone took me far away, but I am okay and I'm coming home.

14

HOME

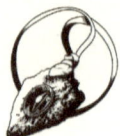

Dreamless sleep gave way to the dispassionate glare of a small electric light overhead.

Althea stretched, the furry blanket warm and comfortable against her skin. She peered up at the blank grey ceiling, idly scratching at her stomach, unable to figure out the time of day. The underground room had no windows or time dials, not that she knew how to interpret them anyway. Still tired from all the healing she did earlier, she squirmed into the bedding, adoring the softness of the fur. The old skirt she'd made for herself at ten, she'd pieced together from scraps of raider armor. It had been leather, but not soft. Fur bedding and blankets felt like she'd crawled inside a cloud.

"Mmm." She stretched again and yawned, not really wanting to move.

Other beds, cots, and sleeping mats in the room still held sleeping people. That none of them stirred at all made her think she'd popped awake at night. Althea rolled on her side and curled up facing the wall. She smiled, snuggling into the soft furs. Her head felt heavy, like she simultaneously wanted to sleep but couldn't.

A moment later, someone grasped her shoulder and gently jostled her.

She rolled onto her back and peered up at a woman neither old nor particularly young. A fair number of people had disappeared from the beds, which suggested she had fallen asleep again for a bit. Those who remained in the room stood around dressing themselves.

"Hello," said Althea, yawning again.

"Mariko told me you gave Jo back his leg."

Althea nodded and sat up, her agate arrowhead pendant swaying in front of her chest. "Yes."

"Thank you!" The woman stooped and hugged her, squeezing almost painfully hard before bursting into tears. She gave off such a powerful sense of love, Althea assumed her to be the boy's mother.

"I'm happy he is okay."

"The gods have truly sent you to help us." The woman squeezed her again, bowed, and hurried out of the room.

Gods again... Maybe it's just a different word for Ancestors.

She shrugged, got out of bed, and pulled her dress on over her head. Yawning, she meandered out into the hall. Before she could decide if she wanted to beg for food or simply resume going home, a passing woman gathered her up and ushered her along with a group of other children around her age. Too dazed from sleep to offer much protest or even think too deeply about anything, she went along with the crowd back to the large chamber which appeared to be the heart of the settlement. There, the woman arranged the kids to sit in a group and proceeded to hand them each a bowl of food. It reminded her of something Father called 'mashed potato,' but had chunks of mushroom and rat meat.

A younger boy sitting to her left introduced himself as Lobo and started asking about her eyes. Francisca, a girl on her right, slightly smaller than Althea in height but more robust, thought them beautiful and wanted to be friends. Yoma, another girl in front of her, turned around while eating so she could talk. They peppered Althea with questions about where she came from, what she liked, where she got the strange dress, and so on. She didn't mind talking to them, though her stories of Querq, the Zero police, flying machines, and everything else baffled them. Lobo gazed in awe while Yoma thought she made up stories.

Two women came by to collect the empty plates, hubcaps, and bowls they'd eaten from. Another woman shooed the kids to their feet, ushering the pack down the hallway of scary pictures. Althea tried to head off toward the exit, but the woman kept nudging her along with the others, ignoring her protests about having to go home.

The kids filed into a room containing a group of chairs and small desks, all facing a larger desk where a woman in an animal hide dress sat behind a pile of strange, boxy objects. Althea hesitated at the door, having little interest in sitting around all day.

A boy with dark hair hurried back and took her hand. "C'mon, you gotta sit down or you'll get in trouble."

"Fernando, please take your seat," said the woman at the big desk. "And who is your new friend?"

"What is trouble?" asked Althea.

Fernando shook his head. "It's a room where you have to stay when you do bad stuff. Anyone who does bad has to stay in trouble for a while. Sometimes, they go easy on kids and don't make us stay in trouble, but they light our butts on fire."

Althea gasped. "What!?" Horrified, she peered at his thoughts—of his father smacking him in the backside several times with a wooden paddle. It felt somewhat like burning, though no actual flames had been involved. "Oh..." She exhaled in relief, though fidgeted in awkward guilt for being the Prophet. One man in the bad city had slapped her in the butt with his hand when she kept walking into his building, but no one had ever dared strike her with a wooden weapon like that, even when she'd been tiny. Then again, she couldn't remember ever being bad. The worst thing she'd ever done was twisting Hector's arm into a ruin of flesh after he'd shot Karina. But... he'd shot Karina. And she fixed his arm. No one had been upset with her, so maybe it hadn't been as bad as she thought.

Fernando's memory of 'trouble' didn't involve firsthand experience as he'd never been 'in trouble.' But he had seen grownups dragged away by the spear-bearers and locked in a room for a while as a form of punishment.

Oh. Trouble is a big cage.

A hand at her back startled her out of her telepathic link.

The woman from the big desk stood beside her. "Hello, sweetie. Take a seat so we can start."

Althea picked up the nearest empty chair.

Everyone stared at her.

"What are you doing?" asked the woman.

"You just told me to take a seat."

"Don't be a smartass."

Althea blinked. "People don't think with their butts."

A waft of anger came from the woman, but faded. "Oh, you really are that, umm... simple. Here, put that down and sit on it."

Althea sighed. "I know how to use a chair. Why did you tell me to take it if you wanted me to sit on it?"

The woman guided her into the seat. "It's a figure of speech. Sometimes words don't mean exactly what they should mean."

"Why?"

"Because." The woman handed her a strange, flat object.

Althea accepted it and looked at frozen speech on the front. "English grandmother?"

"Almost. English grammar."

"That's what I said." Althea examined the object. "This is a learning machine?"

"Of sorts."

"How do I turn it on?"

"It's a book, dear. You don't turn it on; you open it."

"Oh..." She frowned, remembering her friend Kim being able to read all the frozen speech without pictures. She'd never seen a book like this before without a light-up screen.

"Miss Isha," said a girl in the front row. "I need to use the bathroom."

The woman nodded at her. "Don't take too long. We'll get started, but you can catch up. Okay, everyone, open to page fifty-two."

Other kids broke their books open and shuffled at the papers inside. Althea mimicked them. The books Kim read had only had one page and the words on it changed whenever she poked the screen. This thing had hundreds of papers, all covered with so much frozen speech it made her eyes cross. She did like the other kids and swiped pages from right to left, stopping when everyone else stopped.

The woman started talking about words, telling everyone about the twenty new ones they would be learning today.

Althea could learn stuff at home, so she closed her book and stood.

Isha stopped talking, staring at her in shock. "Please, sit."

"I'm sorry, but I can't stay here. I need to go home."

"What do you mean? All children your age must be in school for half the day."

"Where are we?"

"In class," said Isha.

"No. I mean where is this place? I need to leave and walk back to where I live."

"Sweetie, you're far too little to be off on your own." Isha pointed. "Now sit, and please pay attention."

Althea remained standing. "Please tell me where we are."

With a sigh, Isha went over to a picture on the wall behind the big desk, and pointed at a spot. "Before the gods became angry at humans, this place used to be called Det-roh-it."

Althea approached the map. "Do you know where Querq is on that?"

"I've never heard of a place called that." Isha folded her arms. "Why are you asking so many questions?"

"This is school, isn't it? I'm trying to learn things I need to know."

Isha blinked.

"One of the people from the bad city told me Querq used to be like Abercrombie or something like that. A really long word."

"Hmm." Isha glanced at the map, scratching her head. "Querq... I don't know of a place called Abercrombie. Oh... wait a moment. Albuquerque?"

"Maybe." Althea nodded.

"That's very far away." Isha tapped her finger on another area of the map. "All the way down here in New Mexico. We're up here in Mitch-a-gan."

"It's only a couple inches."

"This is a map of the whole land. It has to be small so everything can fit. Those few inches represent about 1,500 miles."

Althea examined the old drawing. It didn't say anything about the wall of fire or show the big city on the west side. Whoever made that map got everything wrong. She started to feel like it would be useless, but then realized perhaps it only appeared wrong because it had been made so long ago. Still, it revealed that she needed to go both south and west to get home. Between the map and trusting her psionic abilities to guide her in the right direction, she felt confident that she'd be able to find her way back.

"Thank you." Althea smiled, waved, and walked toward the door.

"Child," called Isha, when she went straight past her chair. "Where are you going?"

"Back to Querq."

Isha hurried over and took her by the hand, ushering her back to the chair. "You can't go outside. It's too dangerous. The Silver Men will hurt you. Now, take your seat so you can learn."

"Learn? That book isn't helping me go home."

Isha laughed, patting her on the head. "Aww, sweetie... you *are* home."

15

THE TRIAL OF ROYALS

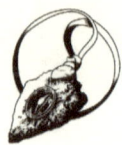

Althea tried to pull away from the teacher, but Isha wouldn't let go of her.

"I understand you are new here and not used to our ways… so I'm giving you some wiggle room, okay? If you keep being disobedient, I'll have to punish you. Please don't make me do that."

All the kids turned in their seats to look at her. The somewhat older girl who had to use the bathroom walked back in and returned to her desk.

"Thank you for helping me and being nice, but I can't stay and live here. Father and my sister miss me."

"Well, they should come down here where it's safe… if the Silver Men haven't gotten them already." Isha shook her head. "Please just sit down."

Annoyed, Althea poked the teacher's mood with a telempathic jolt of apathy. The woman let go of her arm and walked back to her desk, flopped in the chair, and stared disinterestedly at the class. Althea hurried to the door, glanced back only long enough to remove the apathy, then hurried off down the hall, jogging toward the main chamber.

A few adults gave her odd looks as she went by.

"Why aren't you in school?" asked one man.

"Going home," said Althea, not slowing down.

She followed the corridor to the large central room and crossed it to another passage that brought her down to the platform by the giant tunnel with rails. Shara, Ulon, and two other men she didn't recognize stood guard there. The red-haired woman ran over to get in front of her.

"What are you doing down here, child? You should be in the school at this time of day."

"I'm going home."

The adults chuckled.

"You can't go out there," said Shara.

"Why not?"

"Because you're a small child."

Althea folded her arms. "I'm not *that* small. I'm eleven. Maybe even twelve."

"That's still a child." Shara patted her on the head. "Now go on. Back inside where it's safe."

"What about Ooru, Paama, and Eem? He's smaller than me."

"They are scouts. All three have trained, know the dangers, and have the blessing of the council." Shara tried to shoo her back into the tunnel. "Go inside. You're too little to be out there alone."

She considered ordering them to get out of her way, but they'd only been nice to her so far, which made controlling them feel mean. "If I get permission from the council, is it okay?"

Shara shot a look of mild frustration off to one side. "I suppose. But they won't give you permission so fast. The training takes years."

They'll give me permission if I want them to. "Okay."

Althea turned on her heel and marched back inside, up the passage, across the main chamber, and through the heavy plastic curtain into the council chambers. Noema, Sumiko, and Bill engaged in a conversation a few inches short of being an argument about the farm being too small, a you-vee light failing, and general worry they won't have enough food. Ell-Gee wanted to set traps on purpose to catch Silver Men for more parts. Noema thought it blasphemous and dangerous, likely to incur the wrath of the gods and destroy them all. Sumiko agreed with her, but Bill, his emotion tinged with humor, said if the gods didn't want them to take a Silver Man for parts, they simply wouldn't allow the plan to succeed.

Eventually, Noema appeared to notice the reflection of Althea's eyes on Bill's glass and turned her head to stare at where she'd been patiently standing a step inside the doorway. Sumiko smiled at her. Bill raised his glass in that strange gesture again, then drank the last sip from it.

The elder, again, gave off annoyance at someone simply barging in. Bill took advantage of the pause in their discussion to refill his cup from a nearby bottle.

"Why are you not in school?" asked Noema.

"I need to go home to Querq. Thank you for taking those metal things off me, but I can't stay here. Please tell Shara that I have permission to go outside."

"It is far too dangerous to go above the ground." Noema shook her head.

Althea put her hands on her hips, tapping her foot. "If it's that dangerous here, you should *all* go away. There are no Silver Men in Querq. We live above the ground and it's really nice there. You should come with me. And if your farm is dying... you're going to run out of food here anyway. You would be happier in Querq."

"Child, you don't understand." Noema sighed.

"She brings up a point," whispered Sumiko. "You saw what she did for the injured my grandmother attended to. We expected all of them to die. Would we not do well to stay with her? Mariko could not hope to tend to the sick as well as this child."

"What makes you think this child is leaving?" asked Noema.

For an instant, Althea tensed in fear, bracing for the leashes and cages to start all over again... but the elder's emotions contained only worry. She likely thought Althea would be hurt if she went to the surface. The woman did not want to own her, merely thought it foolish for her to go outside so young.

"She is only a little thing yet. Sumiko, you surprise me, taking counsel from a child like this." Noema shook her head.

Sumiko gazed off into space. "I feel this will come to pass. Great fields of open nothing. Sand. Sun. I have had this dream. If the gods came in the form of a child, would you disregard their wisdom and put them to bed at eight?"

Noema made an odd noise in her throat.

"Hold on." Bill moved his legs off the recliner pad and leaned forward. "Tell us about this place."

Althea spent the next twenty minutes or so talking about Father, Karina, the Watch, the Zero police, the Water Man, her friend Kim, the farm, even the Old City outside. "Isha knows where it is on the land-drawing, it's only a few inches away."

"That sounds like a nice place… but way too far for us to walk." Noema smoothed her hands down her hide dress. "There are many people here including old ones and babies. Some could not survive."

"Is there a place where water runs fast over large, boxy stones with sharp edges," asked Sumiko, still gazing into nowhere.

Althea nodded. "Yes, a stream not far from the gate. And your elders and babies will survive. I will make all the hurts and sicks go away."

"Jo would surely have gone to the realm of the gods if not for this girl." Sumiko glanced at Noema as if asking for permission. "Perhaps she can do as she says."

"The boy had been called by the gods. We should be wary that they will punish us for keeping him here." Noema gazed up at the ceiling. "Please forgive us for interfering. If you desire Jo be with you, we shall send him."

"No!" yelled Althea. "I will not let you kill him."

"How dare you!" barked Noema.

Althea fixed her with a glower, raising her arms and extending her energy wings, flooding the chamber with blinding blue-white light. "How dare you threaten to kill a boy for no reason! If the gods want him, they can come for him themselves."

"Whoa," said Bill, before taking a sip of his drink. "That's bright."

Sumiko gasped.

Noema stared for a second before dropping to her knees and bowing. "Please, forgive me!"

"Gods didn't try to take him." Althea let go of her anger, her wings receding into her back, dimming the room. "He had a hurt in his leg that got a 'fection. He almost died because no one took the dirty rock out."

"How are you so wise for such a young child?" asked Sumiko.

"She is from the gods," whispered Noema, still with her face down to the floor.

"Please don't bow to me. I'm just Althea. Not a god. There are bad machines outside here. They don't belong to gods either. Those things are meanies." She shivered at the sudden realization of why she had seen so little life here. Everything must be a 'contaminant.' "You don't need to hide underground. It's much nicer outside, but you should go away from this place before the machines find you here." She shook her head. "They won't leave you alone for being underground. If they get down here, they'll kill you all."

"Kid's got a point." Bill swirled his drink around. "Danas thought the same."

"And look what happened to him." Noema sighed. "Now he is gone and his daughter has yet to return from her trial."

"Trial?" asked Althea.

Sumiko bowed her head. "Our former king, Danas, listened to Ell-Gee, who told him the Silver Men were not sent by gods but machines, and we do not need to stay hidden down here. Danas went to the surface, but he is not small enough to hide. The Silver Men found him. Only one of his group returned alive. Even with the gods' magic, our king could not survive."

"When he died, his daughter, Kye, became our queen." Noema clasped her hands in front of herself. "It is our custom that a new leader suffer the trial within the Cursed Place to prove that it is the will of the gods for them to lead the Transit tribe. Unfortunately, she has been gone for too long. We fear she has failed the test, leaving us without a queen."

"Do not speak of this, child," said Sumiko. "If the others here lose hope in Kye's return, there will be much sadness."

Noema closed her eyes, tilting her head up as if trying to listen to a faint voice. "If she does not return soon, dear Sumiko, we will need to declare she has failed. Until we have a king or queen, we cannot make any decision about relocating. Only our ruler can decide this."

"Have you sent anyone to go look for her?" asked Althea.

"No. The Cursed Place is not for ordinary people. Only royals may enter. That is why the trial takes place there, as only a *true* royal will be able to survive." Sumiko paced about. "I want to go, but I am afraid. Kye is only nineteen. She is too young to die."

"If she is to die, she will already have gone to the gods. Anything now is too late. Our people may be leaderless. Such is the will of the gods." Noema made an odd hand motion.

Althea scrunched up her nose. "What are gods? Have you ever seen them? Do they talk to anyone? Do they do anything? I sometimes see Ancestors, but I don't really know what gods are."

"They are those that created all. They watch over us and guide us to do their bidding," said Noema. "They are always with us."

"But have you ever seen them?" asked Althea.

"The gods do not show themselves to mere people."

"Then how do you know what they want if they never talk to anyone or let you see them?" asked Althea.

Noema raised a hand at her. "Please, child. You must stop asking about such things or the gods will become angry and lash out at you."

"If they're angry at me, why don't *they* yell at me?"

Bill wiped a hand over his mouth, but couldn't stop smiling. "Perhaps they are afraid of whatever those… wings?"

Noema gasped at him.

He gestured at her. "Well, have you ever seen such a display from anyone else? God or not?"

"No," said Sumiko.

Noema whirled to gawk at her. "The lot of you are falling to blasphemy so quickly."

While the councilors got into an argument about the will of their gods, Althea folded her arms and scowled at nothing in particular. Sometimes, adults could *really* have the stupid. Who sends a young woman off to some dangerous place as some kind of test? Especially with machine men running around everywhere. Sure, she'd seen raider groups put warriors through trials, but that usually involved fighting someone or doing some physically demanding task like climbing an old building to recover a ceremonial object from the roof. That made sense since it proved the warrior had the strength and agility to survive in a fight. Some raiders or villagers revered the Ancestors, as Althea did… but she had seen them. Even the Zero police knew about Ancestors despite their using another name for them: 'ghosts.' One crazy person even worshiped something he called the Cloud of Mushroom, claiming that it is what reshaped the land and it would do so again if it wasn't appeased.

Though, after seeing the huge bad city in the west, she suspected the Cloud of Mushroom—if it existed—wasn't as strong as that man thought. It hadn't eaten the *entire* world, merely a lot of it. The more the councilors argued about what to do regarding their people and the queen they sent off to die, the more annoyed Althea became. Like a small mother ready to haul her baby away from danger, she considered commanding the councilors to accept the idea of evacuating their entire tribe and following her to Querq. No one in this place deserved to stay here near those horrible machine men.

But if she did something like that, she'd be no better than The Many. Forcing people to do things against their will was evil—exception being forcing them *not* to do evil things. No, before controlling them, she'd try to make them understand. But first things first, they needed to know what became of their queen.

"Hey!" yelled Althea.

The councilors stopped bickering and looked at her.

"Do you have anything that your queen liked a lot?"

"What do you mean?" asked Noema.

"Like a bracelet or piece of clothing."

"Yes, there is something." Sumiko stood. "I will be right back."

After the woman ran out, Bill gestured at Althea. "She has magic like the royals."

"None of the royals has ever done anything like that." Noema regarded her with a resigned, sad stare. "Nor have they brought our people back from the edge of death."

"What kind of magic does Kye have?" asked Althea.

"She is stronger than any man, faster than the Silver Men with wheels, and tough." Noema smiled with the pride of a mother.

Althea thought back to the man who had thrown Shepherd through a wall despite being much smaller than him. *Mamoru...* She faintly remembered meeting him again outside that warehouse. Aurora had taken him somewhere after a brief conversation about a ship. He, too, was an Awakened like Althea. She didn't like that word much since Archon used it, but the Zero police had decided to use it as well to describe psionic people who had much greater powers than others. Perhaps Queen Kye was a psionic? It didn't seem likely the girl would be Awakened, or she wouldn't have gotten stuck in some cursed place.

Althea bit her lip. Her powers wouldn't stop a machine man. She could heal, affect emotions, control thoughts, see thoughts, mind-talk, occasionally see ghosts, and sometimes the clairvoy ants would tell her stuff or let her see far off places. None of that mattered to machines. If Kye could make herself strong enough to throw Shepherd across a room, she could probably break the machines.

Sumiko ran back in holding a small plastic doll. "Here. Kye has had this ever since she was old enough to walk. Please be careful with it. She will be very angry with us if it is lost or damaged."

Althea gently took the ancient toy. It resembled a blonde woman, though oddly proportioned. Too skinny, with distortedly long legs and tiny feet. Its eyes had faded off, simple paint on the plastic, and it bore numerous scuffs and scratches. She smirked. *No one would notice if this became more damaged.*

"Why did you want that?" asked Noema.

"I'm going to ask the clairvoy ants if Kye is okay."

"What does that mean?" asked Bill.

"I can concentrate on stuff like this toy, and sometimes see or feel things about people."

"Magic." Sumiko nodded. "Yes. Please, tell us if Kye is all right."

Noema smirked.

Althea gripped the old doll in both hands and focused on her desire to know what happened to the girl that loved this toy. Fleeting glimpses of a bright metal hallway flashed and faded. The uncomfortable feeling of wearing boots came out of nowhere. Running. Something trying to hurt her. She had to find somewhere to hide. Elation. Safety. Metal hands grabbing her by the arms. Kicking, fighting. Liquid. Drowning—but not death. Confusion. Drowned but alive. Safe but trapped. Sleep.

"She is alive." Althea opened her eyes and looked up at the councilors. "But she's stuck."

"Feh." Noema waved dismissively. "Why should we believe the words of a little girl?"

Bill raised his tumbler glass, gestured at her, and took a sip. "I'm more inclined to believe a kid with wings."

"She must be sent from the gods," said Sumiko. "Kye has not failed her trial. The gods want to help her."

Noema raised her hands. "We cannot interfere. There can be no help. It is against the gods' will."

"What if the gods sent me here?" asked Althea, radiating telempathic trust. She couldn't allow the old woman's bizarre fears to hurt Kye. And if those gods actually existed and didn't want her to help, they could speak for themselves. She still suspected these gods might be 'shadow goblins,' like the metal can half hidden behind a cabinet she'd been so frightened of as a little girl—until she saw it for what it really was.

Noema stared off into space, lowering her arms after a few seconds.

"She is not of the Transit." Sumiko reached toward her for the doll. "The gods will not be angry with *her* for interfering. Perhaps even the Cursed Place will not harm her."

Althea handed over the doll. "I'm only eleven. Shouldn't you send a grown-up to look for Kye?"

"Our people cannot enter the Cursed Place unless they are royals. Others will surely die." Sumiko stroked the doll's hair. "No one here would dare enter. Our people will bring you to the gate, but they cannot go in."

Ugh. Althea stared down at her feet. It wouldn't do any good to force someone to go in there as they'd be too terrified to be able to help. She tried to open her senses, hoping her abilities might be able to give her a hint about what to do. Thinking about going to find Kye herself didn't fill her with dread, nor did it give her a strong nudge of urgency. The compulsion to jump out of the flying machine had been undeniable and immediate. Either the clairvoy ants had gone to sleep, or nothing particularly dangerous would happen if she went there.

At least it didn't feel like a *bad* idea.

"Okay. I will go look for your queen."

16

SKY MONSTERS AND SILVER MEN

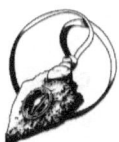

B ill walked with Althea out of the council room, heading across the central chamber toward the passage to the platform.

"What is that you keep drinking?" asked Althea.

"Not for kids."

She stepped around some cushions by one of the cooking stations. "I don't want to have any. I was only curious what it is and why you keep drinking it."

"White Russian," said Bill, swirling the glass. "Or as close as I can get to one with Ell-Gee's little still and powdered milk."

"Powdered milk?" Althea cringed.

"Found a stash of it down one of the tunnels. Some survivalist dude stockpiled a whole bunch of it. Stuff's gotta be 200 years old, but the nectar coming out of the still is strong enough to kill anything bad."

Althea shivered. Not that she had any desire to ask for a taste before, but after hearing he drank something *that* old, she didn't even want to keep smelling it. Two steps later, she took his hand and peered inside his life essence for sicks. Somehow, he didn't have one.

They headed down the tunnel to the outer platform where the spear-bearers stood guard. Shara and the other sentries appeared surprised to see her back so soon, and with a member of the council.

"She is to journey to the Cursed Place in search of Queen Kye." Bill sipped his drink. "There's apparently been a slight problem."

"What?" Shara gasped.

The other three sentries all shook their heads, giving off fear.

"No." Shara grasped Althea's shoulder. "You can't send her into the Cursed Place. She's not of the Transit. Not a royal. I can't let a child go off to die."

"Sumiko believes she may be from the gods. She managed to put the fear into Noema. Great glowing wings sprouted out of her and made the council chamber so bright we couldn't see a damn thing."

"You are pulling my arm," said Shara.

Bill gestured with his drink at her. "How many people have you ever seen with so much magic in them that it leaks out their eyes?"

"Are we to escort her to the Cursed Place?" asked one of the male spear-bearers. "Surely, you are not going to the surface."

"Heh. No." Bill chuckled. "I'm happy to stay right here. I prefer my hide without holes in it if at all possible. They are asking for volunteers now. We need you four at the tunnel. Spear-bearers defend us. Any scout can show this kid the way."

Althea kept quiet while the five adults debated the wisdom of letting her go into a place that would supposedly kill anyone without royal blood the instant they went past the door. It didn't sound believable to her. How would an area know who someone was? And what did 'royal' mean anyway? Any raider who took over a pack of bandits called themselves war chief or king. She didn't think the Ancestors named some people royalty or anything like that. Most likely, the people of this settlement had legends they followed that could have been started by anything, the same way 'legend' claimed anyone who mistreated the Prophet would face horrible luck. Considering every group that took her captive would invariably be attacked constantly by others until they, too, took her, 'bad luck' would follow her no matter how nice or mean raiders were. The group who gave her free run of their camp fared no better than the ones who kept her chained to a truck or locked in a cage.

Thinking about those days made her feel stupid for not defending herself. At least for the past two years, she understood having the ability to give people commands, Suggestion as Officer David called it. Only her fear of being burned alive kept her from using it in all but the most dire circumstances, and never to set herself free. Only to stop wifeing or needless killing. Now, all too late, she understood she didn't have to worry about being burned alive—she could protect herself from that, too.

But, had she not made the choices she'd made in the past, she would never have met Father and Karina. Of course, now all she had to do was get back to them.

Paama and Ooru emerged from the tunnel and walked over.

"We have volunteered to take Althea to the Cursed Place," said Paama.

"Very well." Shara gave a somber sigh, shaking her head.

Ooru grinned at her. "Follow."

He jogged to the end of the platform and jumped down into the tunnel. Althea rushed after him with Paama right behind her. She hopped down to walk on one of two narrow strips of relatively flat ground on either side of the rails. Large metal brackets at regular intervals held the rails in place, and looked quite painful to mash a toe into.

Ooru glanced over his shoulder at her. "You can hang on my back to get past the traps."

"I can see them, remember?"

"Oh. I forgot. All right, but don't cry if you hit one."

She raspberried him.

Paama laughed.

A few minutes later, they reached the other platform and climbed up out of the tunnel, crossed the room and went into the passage loaded with jaw traps. Both of her guides advanced at a deliberate pace, counting every step while making precise turns. She meandered behind them, stepping around the various—rather obvious—spring-loaded jaws. When they eventually reached the base of the stairs that led to the surface world, Ooru paused and looked back at her.

"It's so funny to see your eyes in the dark." He laughed. "Like two little floating dots."

"They're almost bright enough for us to see with." Paama held her hand out by Althea's face, wiggling her fingers in the blue light. "So pretty. I wish my eyes were like that. Mine are brown and boring."

"Okay." Ooru patted Althea on the head and felt his way down over her shoulder until he found her hand. "This is important. The Cursed Place is a good walk away. We will probably have to hide from Silver Men. If one of us starts running, you should start running too. Don't make a sound. Just do what we do. If we get down and hide, you do that, too."

"Okay," said Althea.

"They can't see through metal at all, but they can sometimes see through walls." Paama held one hand up simulating a wall and made a person shape with two fingers behind it. "If you have metal all around, you're safe. We can hide in big pipes, rust boxes, or holes. Whatever you do, don't scream or make loud noises. The Silver Men can hear from far away."

"I understand." Althea shivered. *Maybe this is a bad idea.* Dealing with raiders or living creatures wouldn't have bothered her at all, but she couldn't do anything about the machine men. Her two new friends had experience avoiding them, so she would do whatever they said.

Ooru went up the stairs first, pausing at the top to peer out with his eyes barely above the level of the sidewalk. He watched for a few minutes before climbing up to stand. Althea hurried after him.

He pointed at a mostly-collapsed building about two blocks away. "We move short and fast. Run there as fast as you can, then we hide and make sure nothing saw us."

Althea nodded.

"Go!" whispered Ooru, before sprinting off.

She ran after him, sending a surge of psionic energy into her body that boosted the blood-presence flowing to her leg muscles while simultaneously increasing her endurance. Althea blew past Ooru, pumping her arms, sprinting as fast as she could make herself go to the indicated wall. With the grace of a bounding deer, she leapt over a rusting car, landed in stride, and continued toward the building. To avoid stripping the skin off the bottoms of her feet when stopping, she slowed well in advance and trotted to a halt by the corner.

Ooru and Paama hadn't yet even made it halfway.

She flattened herself against the wall and listened for the whirring noise of the wheeled machine man, but heard only the soft clap of her friends' fur boots on the paving. The other kids ran up to her, mouths hanging open.

"How did you do that?" rasped Paama.

"He said I should run as fast as I can," whispered Althea. "So I did."

"People can't run that fast." Ooru looked her over. "And you're not even tired."

"Inside." Paama pushed at them both.

Ooru ducked into a hole in the wall. Althea crawled after him, Paama behind her.

Once hidden within a shadowed place under a nest of collapsed I-beams, the kids sat to catch their breath. Althea shrugged and sat as well.

"You could outrun a Silver Man," said Ooru.

"She's not *that* fast. They have wheels." Paama shook her head.

"The ones that walk."

"Mariko could outrun those." Paama smiled. "They're not fast at all."

Ooru grasped Althea's leg and squeezed her calf. "What magic is it? You don't feel like a machine."

"I'm not." She muffled a giggle. "I am a healer. My power can do other stuff. If I make my legs stronger, I can run faster."

"Healer?" asked Paama. "Like Mariko? You know about herbs?"

"Just which ones to eat. And one or two that make you see weird things if you light them on fire and breathe the smoke. I helped a chamán before."

"She saved Jo. His leg was gonna fall off." Ooru patted Althea's arm. "She's got *real* magic."

"Obviously. Her eyes are glowing." Paama smirked.

"C'mon." Ooru got up and trotted to the opposite end of the room, then stuck his head out an old window frame. "Clear." He vaulted over the sill and landed outside.

Paama climbed after him. Althea stepped up onto the windowsill and dropped down to the dirt outside.

Ooru took off at a jog. Since he hadn't indicated where to stop, Althea kept pace with them rather than run at full speed. They navigated around more dead cars, a series of collapsed lamp posts, and a large hunk of metal wreckage that appeared much newer than anything else in the area. Despite its obvious difference in technology, it still looked as though it had been there a long time. Given how it had embedded itself into the ground, Althea guessed it crashed from high up, most likely a piece of a flying machine.

High-pitched whirring came from the right.

Ooru sprinted. Althea darted after him, Paama bringing up the rear due to fumbling at her skirt pouch. A small machine shot out from behind a six-story ruined building fifty feet in the air, swooping down toward Ooru. Sunlight gleamed off the surface of a silver flying wing. A black rectangular patch at the front had a small lens, aglow with green light. The boy stopped short and darted to the left. The machine hung in midair, pivoting to follow him, though didn't attack. Despite the strange robot's apparent peacefulness, Ooru gave off extreme fear.

A whooshing noise started behind her.

Althea ran after Ooru, glancing over her shoulder at Paama who swung a sling around in a rapid spin. A few seconds later, she snapped her arm, launching a rock that smacked into the flying machine with a loud plastic *clonk*. It faltered, flipped over, and crashed to the ground upside down, scooting forward as it tried to right itself and get back into the air.

Paama hefted her spear and charged at it. At the clatter of the machine hitting the street, Ooru reversed course and also ran at it. The wing flipped itself over and started to rise back into the air, but before it got more than a few feet up, Paama walloped it, slapping it back to the ground. Ooru lunged in and stabbed it, pinning it down. Dust bloomed out from the back end as the machine's little engine whined louder and louder. On the ground, it appeared larger than it seemed in the air, roughly three feet across from wingtip to wingtip.

Althea kept her distance as the two slightly older children set upon the stricken machine with their spears, stabbing it again and again, setting off flashes of crackling sparks. Ooru broke the glowing green spot at the front, spilling a small amount of glass bits on the road.

With a grunt of exertion, Paama leapt into the air, using all her weight to drive her spear into the machine's main body. A brilliant blue flash burst out of it, and the engine whine abruptly cut out to silence. Unsurprisingly, Althea did not feel any icy chill of departing life.

"Run!" rasped Ooru.

Her guides scrambled up to a sprint, fleeing like an angry canid had found them. Althea caught up to them with ease, but kept quiet as instructed instead of asking what scared them so much about a flying machine that had no apparent means of hurting anyone.

Ooru slowed to a stop by a storm drain, hastily sliding into it and falling out of sight. Paama dropped to the ground and slithered in headfirst. Althea waited for the girl's boots to disappear, then sat on the edge and slid in feet first.

Ooru caught her and helped her down.

He and Paama both held her in a three-way hug.

"That was close," whispered Ooru.

Is it safe to talk? asked Althea, telepathically.

He stared at her. "Your lips didn't move."

Mind talking. The Zero police called it tell pathy.

"Gods... amazing," whispered Ooru. "And sure we can talk, but whisper."

"Huh?" asked Paama.

"She spoke inside my head."

"Stop lying, butt."

Althea glanced at her. *He's not lying.*

"Gah!"

"Shh!" rasped Ooru.

"Why are you scared of the little flying machine?" whispered Althea.

"It's an eye." Paama pointed up. "It sees for the Silver Men. If one of the fly-eyes finds us, other Silver Men will come after us."

As if on cue, the whirr of a wheeled machine man rose up in the distance.

Ooru waved for the girls to follow, then climbed down a ladder into a round shaft. "We are safe in here."

Paama went down next. She paused when she wound up eye-level with Althea's feet, then peered up at her. "Where are your shoes?"

"I don't have shoes. I don't like them." Althea turned her back and lowered herself onto the ladder.

"What if you step on something and cut yourself? You could die. Even small cuts can kill, especially on your foot."

"I don't get sick." Althea climbed down and hopped off the ladder in a big concrete pipe.

"Everyone says that... until they do." Ooru chuckled. "When we are back home, I will get shoes for you."

Althea tensed. She opened her mouth to tell him that she already had a boy who liked her... but stopped when she didn't pick up any emotions like that from him. Usually, when a Scrag gave someone clothes, weapons, or other scavenging spoils, it meant they wanted to court them. Though, she had mostly lived in the south where it didn't get very cold except at night when everyone stayed inside. Perhaps this far north, traditions would be different. Then again, they didn't know the Prophet, so maybe they never heard of the rules about gifts either.

"It's okay. I won't be staying here and I really don't get sick. I make the sicks go out."

More whirring echoed from the distant storm drain along with the faint electronic voice muttering, "Lost contact with contaminants. Initiating search."

Ooru eyed the pipe leading into the distance. "Be careful. It is dark, but there is only one way to go. Feel with your feet to avoid holes. Or we can just hide here and wait for the Silver Men to leave."

"That will take a long time," whispered Paama.

"I can see, remember?" Althea squeezed past them. "Let me go first."

The two shrugged.

"Okay." Ooru nodded.

Althea advanced into the pipe, featureless concrete as far as she could see. "It's empty here."

Ooru put a hand on her shoulder.

"The blue from your eyes lights up the walls," whispered Paama. "Like Ell-Gee's magic torches."

Althea grinned and looked around so the glowing spot moved. The effect didn't appear to her as blue, merely a somewhat lighter patch of grey. "Why did they ask you to bring me to this Cursed Place, and not a grown-up?"

"The adults almost never go outside," said Ooru. "When we get too big to fit into the hiding places, we have to stay inside, too. Some become spear-bearers. Silver Men can go anywhere adults can. But some of the Silver Men won't attack children. The big ones with legs don't. But the little ones on wheels will. And the really big ones with tread-wheels will try to kill us, but they are super slow. Easy to hide from. Besides, even our strongest spear-bearers can't scratch the Silver Men, so it doesn't matter if we're kids. Sending a warrior won't help."

"You killed one just before. And watch the floor. There's a hole. Don't trip." Althea bent over to shine her eyes on the small pit so they could see and avoid it.

Ooru laughed. "The little flyers are different. Any of the ones that can hurt us are way too tough. They have fire sticks that can kill from way far. We'd never even get close to them. Even if we did, our spears would break on their armor."

"Kye broke a Silver Man," said Paama with an air of reverence. "With a spear."

"Oh sure." Ooru chuckled. "Royals can do stuff like that. We're not."

"So why do you go outside at all? Everything here is gone." Althea stepped around a scattering of human bones.

"The Silver Men kill the Sky Monsters and they crash. Their bellies break open, and sometimes they're full of good stuff we can take. There's also lots of things in basements. The Silver Men kill everything, so no one is here to take stuff." Paama let out a heavy breath. "Is it true you live outside all the time?"

"Yeah."

Althea told them about Querq, playing soccer with other kids, relaxing by the stream with Den, the farm where Karina worked and so on as they walked, until they reached a join in the pipe. "There's another tunnel to the left here. Which way?"

"Straight," said Ooru.

She resumed telling them of the Water Man, Dr. Ruiz, and even swimming in the giant pool that had formed in an old basement.

"I want to go there," said Paama.

"It sounds nice, but won't the gods be angry if we leave? We're supposed to be punished for what the Ancients did." Ooru grumbled. "Stupid Ancients."

"Umm." Althea whistled innocently. "Gods? If you don't want them to come to Querq with me, say something." She waited a minute, but no strange beings said anything. "Guess it's okay."

"Wow. Does that really work?" asked Paama. "Will the gods talk to you if you ask?"

"I dunno," muttered Ooru. "Seems too simple… but Althea is magic, so maybe she's right."

"Someone said she has wings," whispered Paama.

"I kinda do. They're not like bird wings. They're made out of light. Officer David said they're 'astral energy.' Dunno what that means. I can't fly, just fall slow."

"Grandpa said she reminds him of something from the Ancients' books," said Paama. "Before our gods spoke to the great King Malcolm, the Ancients followed a primitive mythology that only had *one* god."

Ooru chuckled. "No way. How could there be only one god?"

"I know, right?" Paama giggled. "Grandpa said they believed their god was like totally powerful and had no flaws or weaknesses and was perfect. But, it never did anything. They still had bad stuff happen all the time and their god didn't do anything about it."

"Do your gods ever do stuff?" asked Althea.

The kids remained quiet for a minute.

"Umm, not that I've seen," whispered Paama. "But they're angry with us for what the Ancients did. We're still being punished. And the Ancients made up a silly god. Nothing can be *perfect*. The real gods aren't perfect at all. Lexus and Mercedes are always trying to kill each other, even though she really likes him. And Audi is arrogant. Thinks he's better than all the other gods with his fancy rings."

"Beemer is the king of the gods though," whispered Ooru. "He made the throne that our king or queen sits on. Only royals are allowed to sit on it. And Lockheed is scary. He sent war birds to burn the Ancients' cities."

"Lord Starbucks likes to play games. Sometimes he gives us energy, but sometimes he makes us tired. Internet can't be trusted either. He's always trying to look at ladies when they don't have clothes on, and he keeps trying to steal Lady Victoria's secret." Paama shivered. "I meditate to Dell before I get in the bath so he'll keep Internet away from me. Even if he *is* a god, I don't want him watching me in the bath."

"Dell?" asked Althea.

"He's the god that controls Internet."

"Apple can control Internet, too," said Ooru. "But she doesn't usually listen to people when they ask for stuff."

Paama sneezed. "Ugh. It's dusty down here. My grandma said Apple only listens to meditations if you offer up a big pile of coins."

Althea didn't think these gods really existed, though Internet sounded creepy. She slowed while approaching an obstruction in the passage. "Does Internet do anything else but watch girls taking baths? Oh, look out, there's a bunch of junk here. A bar you can trip on."

"Umm, my grandma said Internet is the god who made cats." Paama nearly tripped over the rod but caught herself against Ooru. "He loves cats, ladies with no clothes, and umm, I think she said he makes trolls, too."

"What's a troll?" Althea stopped and looked back at them.

"I don't know, but Grandma said they're mean. We should probably run away if we find one."

"What do they look like?" asked Althea.

"Umm. Not sure. Grandma told me they are huge and fat, smell bad, and love to do mean stuff... but they can't really hurt anyone."

"Oh." *So strange.* Althea resumed walking. "How do you know about all these gods if you've never seen one?"

"The Ancients worshipped them." Ooru stumbled over a small clump of debris, squeezing her shoulder to keep from losing his grip. "The gods' sacred symbols are everywhere... especially Lord Starbucks and the great M."

"The great M?" asked Althea.

Ooru nodded. "He had many temples all over the Ancients' world and gave the people god-food because he liked them, but they became greedy for his power and ate too much of the enchanted food. He made some Ancients fat and sick as punishment."

"Lady Visa and Lord MasterCard had a lot of power," said Paama. "Their sacred marks are on almost every window in some places."

Althea couldn't say for sure if the Transit tribe's gods existed or didn't, though they did seem to have a lot of them. Even if those gods *did* exist, she doubted they cared much about the people in the settlement. The machine men didn't come from gods, but from the bad city in the west. When she'd told Officer David of the one she found stuck in the creek, he had been astounded she survived the encounter. She didn't remember too much of what he said, only that people had sent those machines out into the Badlands to clean it up—but something went wrong.

Althea frowned. *The Many.*

Paama and Ooru whispered back and forth, debating for quite a while if Amazon or Disney had the most power among the gods. Eventually, Althea spotted color up ahead in a patch of sunlight leaking in from a hole smashed in the ceiling of a large chamber. She paused at the end of the concrete pipe, toes curled over the edge, and leaned forward to survey the room. The floor, suspiciously flat dirt, looked like an easy drop, only about two feet down from the pipe. Most of the chamber's ceiling had crumbled inward, forming a natural ramp of broken concrete covered in tufts of grass and weeds on the opposite side of the room. The walls of a former building surrounded the top of the opening up above, making her feel as if she stood at the bottom of an enormous pit.

"Is it safe?" whispered Althea.

Ooru and Paama squeezed up beside her for a better view.

They listened in silence for a moment, then nodded. Ooru made a 'shh' gesture.

Althea smiled, then jumped down—and her feet sank into the floor. What she thought to be too-perfectly-flat dirt turned out to be gooey mud. She sank past the middle of her thighs, the hem of her dress resting on the muck. Gasping at the cold, she stretched her right foot down, but her toes didn't find anything more solid than goop. She flailed her arms about, but couldn't really move.

"It's too deep," whispered Althea. "I'm stuck."

"Take my hand," said Ooru.

She reached up.

Paama grabbed one arm, Ooru the other, and they hauled her up out of the muck, pulling her into the pipe. She sat on the end, feet dangling, and spent a moment scraping mud off her legs before standing up again.

"Do like this." Paama slung her spear across her back on a strap, then shimmied out of the sewer passage to the wall, placing the tips of her boots on a thin metal pipe while clutching a ridge of concrete above her head.

Althea peered down at her legs. The coating of mud turned her grey as if she'd been painted. Even standing still on the concrete tube, her feet threatened to slide out from under her. She scraped her soles at the edge a few times, then stretched a leg out to the narrow pipe. Her shorter stature than Paama forced her up on tiptoe to reach the two-inch ledge over her head where the concrete wall changed to bricks. Her arms both straight up over her head made her feel like a dead squealer someone had hung up to be gutted and cleaned—far too awkward. She pivoted left ninety degrees and balance-beam walked on the one-inch pipe, following the other girl in a slow sideways creep to the corner, then along the next wall. Ooru waited for Paama to reach the collapsed wall-turned-ramp before climbing out after them.

Heel-to-toe, Althea crept along the pipe to avoid the mud sink, keeping her upper body pressed as flat to the wall as possible. As soon as she got close to the solid ground of the rubble ramp, she jumped, landing a few inches in front of the mud pool.

Pamma whistled. "Wow. Nike was watching you."

"Huh?" asked Althea, wiping her feet on a tuft of grass emerging from a crack.

"He's the god of warriors. Strength, agility, that stuff. He helped you do that. I've never seen anyone *walk* on a pipe that small before."

Althea shrugged, then scraped her hands down her legs to get rid of more mud. Once Ooru arrived, the trio climbed the ramp together. Numerous cracks and gaps in the chunks made for easy steps and handholds, her fingers and toes finding good purchase on the coarse rock. She breezed up the last six feet of near vertical wall with ease, clambering over the edge into a large room. Two giant rusted tanks the size of small houses stood on either side, long brown-red stains on the concrete floor revealed the path of frequent water flowing toward the pit she'd emerged from. Large mounds of trash occupied the corners behind the vast, old machines... something within them rustling.

"Umm," said Althea.

An army of enormous rats erupted from the debris piles and scurried out from under the old boilers.

"Wow, you're good at climbing," said Paama.

"I've done it a lot." Althea eyed the rats, which gradually took notice of her and sniffed at the air.

"Ack!" yelled Paama as soon as she could see over the edge. "Darkbites!"

"Rats?" asked Althea.

"No... rats are half this size. These are *bad*." Paama peered up at her, not climbing any higher.

"Can still eat darkbites." Ooru slithered over the edge onto his chest. "Gods... so many."

"Yeah, but darkbites can kill us. Rats can't... and we can't fight all of these," whispered Paama. "Too many. They're gonna eat us. Back down, fast."

The rats crept closer, still sniffing.

Althea leaned forward, giving off a telempathic radiance of trust and affection. The mass of rats relaxed from front to back as if a visible wave rolled over them. In a moment, they ignored the kids and proceeded to root around under the giant machines.

"They will leave us alone. Don't hit them." Althea took a few steps forward.

"Umm..." Paama hesitated.

"They're ignoring us." Ooru reached down to help Paama over the edge.

"I'm making them friendly." Althea continued advancing, easing her feet around broken small appliances, crushed cans, and plastic boxes. "Are those big things going to hurt us?"

"No. They're old boil machines." Ooru pulled Paama up off the wall.

Althea padded across the room, watching the ground to avoid stepping on rat droppings or sharp metal fragments. Paama swung her spear off her back and kept it ready, but didn't attack any of the dog-sized rats. She threw out a lot of fear, but didn't look frightened.

I'd be afraid of these creatures too if I couldn't make them calm. They could bite my arm off.

A short metal staircase at the far left corner led to an opening that hadn't seen a door for a great many years. Althea crept up and peered out at a field of rubble dotted with the remains of numerous large machines. They varied in shape and size, some as big as small buildings, others no larger than Officer David's flying car. Several had utterly disintegrated on impact with the ground, leaving fields of scattered metallic bits. She counted twenty dead machines before she couldn't think of any more numbers for the rest.

"Wow," whispered Althea, saddened at the thought each one meant at least one person—if not more—had died. But, the flying machine that brought her out here also blew up, and she didn't sense any death… so maybe the people controlling it escaped somehow.

"Shh," whispered Paama. "Don't wake the Sky Monsters."

"They sleep." Ooru nodded to the left, then advanced along the shadow of an old sidewalk, little more than a flat trail in the otherwise uneven grey dirt.

Althea almost giggled at them for mistaking broken machines as sleeping monsters… but Karina and Father thought it normal to ruin water by peeing in it. She used the toilet in the house because they wanted her to. Digging a hole outside didn't waste perfectly good drinking water.

Ooru took off at a sprint without warning. Althea hesitated for a second before remembering what he'd said about doing whatever he did. She took off after him. They raced down the road running for a few minutes until he veered to the right and slid feet-first into a small concrete pipe sticking out of a debris mound. Althea crawled in after him, Paama behind her. He lay on his back nose to nose with her. Paama's rapid breathing puffed over Althea's feet.

Why did you run? asked Althea telepathically.

He twitched in response to her voice inside his head. "Saw a Silver Man walking around to the left. Dunno if it noticed us."

She nodded, her long hair draped all over his chest and face.

The narrow pipe didn't have much room. Rubble had crushed it only about eight feet from the opening, and Ooru already crammed himself as tight to the blockage as possible. Without climbing half on top of Althea, Paama couldn't scoot in deep enough to pull her legs out of the daylight leaking in at the end.

Althea pressed herself to the side, leaning against the pipe so she could peer back at the end. "We shouldn't stay here."

"Why not?" asked Paama.

"The pipe's open to the outside and it's straight. A machine man could shoot us really easy and get us all with one bullet because we're stuffed together."

Ooru sputtered, trying to blow Althea's hair off his mouth.

Paama drew in a sharp breath. "She's right. This is a bad place to hide."

The older girl backed up, grabbed Althea by the ankles, and pulled her out. She, in turn, grabbed Ooru's hands and dragged him to the end of the narrow tube. He scrambled to his feet and ran off again, leading them past two cross streets before taking cover inside a ruined car. The girls huddled low on the floor in the back seat while Ooru knelt high enough to watch out the window. A few minutes passed before he and Paama felt confident no Silver Men had spotted them.

Ooru pushed the door open with a loud rusty *creak*. They climbed out of the wreck and resumed hurrying down the street in the shadow of crumbling buildings. At least the boy appeared to know where he wanted to go, never hesitating when making turns. A few blocks later, they cornered onto a street that still had a surprising number of intact—though decrepit—buildings. Faded spray paint formed symbols all over, sometimes numerous ones overlaid on each other as if people had been arguing. Some frozen words said things like 'Death to Feds' or 'UCF is the future.' One read 'Disney' under a strange symbol made out of three circles. Several said things like 'Corporations for Freedom,' 'Corporate Power is People Power,' or 'Allied Corporate Council – No Taxes Ever!' Most of the paintings like that had been crossed out with simple black paint forming the word 'traitors.'

At the end of that block, the ruins gave way to a vast open field of dirt and rubble, all the buildings reduced to mounds of dirt, grey powder, and twisted metal sticks. The largest solid piece of wall remaining didn't look any bigger than one of those 'refrigerator' things. Two enormous halves of a formerly massive flying machine appeared to explain why such a wide area had flattened so much. It had crashed here with enough fury to disintegrate everything around it to dust. Other, far smaller, flying machines also lay scattered about the area in front of them, one even stuck into the dirt nose-first like a knife.

Althea whistled at the sheer number of wrecks. "Wow, there are so many."

"The Silver Men hate the Sky Monsters and kill them whenever they can," said Paama. "But the Sky Monsters get so angry when they die that they turn into fire."

"We're almost there." Ooru tapped Althea on the shoulder, then pointed at a building out in the rubble that looked like six giant plates stacked on top of each other. It didn't have windows, rather wide open strips on each floor packed with the rusting corpses of cars, hundreds of them.

"That's the Cursed Place?" asked Althea.

"Yeah. But not really. The Cursed Place is under it. This is the dangerous part. We have to go across open ground with nowhere to hide. So... we gotta run super fast."

"I can help." Althea grasped his hand, then took Paama's. She linked her mind to their life essences, but not as deeply when healing, only enough to boost their energy and make their muscles stronger. "Okay."

"Whoa. I feel weird," said Paama. "My legs are itchy."

Ooru bounced. "What did you do? I can't stop moving."

"More energy." Althea beamed. "You won't get tired for a little while."

"Ready?" asked Paama.

Althea released their hands, focused her power inward to boost herself, then nodded.

Ooru pushed off the corner of the building they'd been hiding behind and ran fast enough to kick up a trail of silt. Paama zoomed after him. Althea took a deep breath and threw herself into a full sprint. Having provided her friends the same increase to strength, speed, and stamina she used, she found herself having to work hard to keep up with them. Though her legs moved faster, the other two had a slight advantage in stride length from being taller that balanced out to dead even.

They raced out across the desolate field, weaving around the dead sky monsters on their way to the building full of cars. A silvery shimmer way off on the right spooked her, but she didn't stop or slow down to look back at it. If it had only been the sun gleaming off a crashed flying machine, it wouldn't matter... and if the flash came from a machine man's armor, she didn't want it to see her.

Their long sprint ended at the side of the odd building where a cracked strip of road formed a ramp that led down to a basement level, also filled with the remains of cars. Ooru hurried inside. Althea ran after him, trying not to slip on the smooth concrete floor.

At the bottom of the ramp, he leaned against a car, out of breath. "Whoa… we made it."

"That was amazing," rasped Paama. "I've never run so fast in my life!"

Althea smiled. "We made it."

"Contaminants detected," said an echoing, digitized voice from deeper inside the sunken garage.

17

WHEELBOT

Whirring came from a passage on the left a short distance in front of them.

Ooru grabbed Paama and dragged her to the floor with him behind a car on the right side near the entrance ramp.

"Telemarketer," rasped Paama.

"Ooh, if your dad finds out you said that, you're gonna be in trouble!" whispered Ooru.

Althea swallowed hard and crept up to a concrete column on the left, peering around it at an aisle between rows of dead cars, wide enough to be a street. A wheeled machine man rolled toward them, its fat rubber tire squeaking on the smooth concrete. It pointed both its gun arms in her direction, its multiple lens eyes flaring bright red.

"Female contaminant detected. Bonus points. Initiating removal procedure."

With a shriek, Althea threw herself flat to the floor and scrambled to get behind a car. The horrible roar of gunfire so rapid it became a horrendous constant buzz instead of individual bangs hammered the air; the dead vehicles surrounding her erupted in clanks and sparks. Bullets made bizarre twangy pings as they ricocheted off into the concrete canyon.

"Hey!" shouted Ooru. He popped up, brandishing his spear.

As soon as the machine man stopped firing at Althea, the boy ducked again. Its second barrage chewed up the car her friends hid behind. An explosion of tiny foil scraps blew into the air from the backs of its guns, fluttering like lazy snowflakes to the ground. The wheelbot accelerated, rolling past Althea's hiding place and turning to aim at the gap between cars, less than fifteen feet away with an unobstructed view of the children.

"Meanie!" screamed Althea.

The robot spun in place, pointing its weapons at her... but hesitated.

"Anomaly. Contaminant displays undocumented bioluminescence abnormal for species: human. Define origin of bioluminescent sclera."

"Don't shoot us! We are not contaminants!" yelled Althea.

"Define nature of bioluminescence." The wheelbot continued pointing its guns at her face.

"If I tell you, will you promise not to shoot me?"

"Subject: human is biological organism within contaminated zone. Directive is to purge all aberrant biologic life in contaminated zone. I am unable to modify my program."

A rock bounced off its head with a *clank*.

"Modify that, turd brain!" yelled Paama.

"Attack ineffective. Projectile has penetrated"—its voice shifted down—"zero"—and went back up—"millimeters of armor." The wheelbot spun toward her. "Contaminant designated 'target two' located. Female contaminant. Bonus points."

"Hey!" screamed Althea. She picked up a hunk of concrete and threw it at the machine man, striking it in the back before it shot Paama. "You're mean! Why do you wanna kill girls more than boys!"

The wheelbot rotated to point its guns at her again. "Female contaminants possess capacity for producing additional contaminants. Cleansing female contaminants also cleanses all possible future contamination they may create."

A bigger rock bounced off the machine's head.

"I don't have cooties!" shouted Paama.

It spun toward her.

Althea grabbed another stone and threw it, hitting the machine in the head.

"Damage inflicted: zero," said the wheelbot. "Your attacks are ineffective. For maximum comfort, you should not resist contaminant removal. You will only expire at a depleted level of energy, which I understand is uncomfortable for you." Its guns twitched, but didn't fire.

"Secondary objective: data gathering. Permits delay of contaminant removal. Define bioluminescence for data gathering. Are you species: human?"

"Yes." Althea jumped onto the roof of the car at her left, diving over it an instant before the wheelbot opened fire at her.

She landed in a somersault.

"Targeting: Contaminant 3. Male."

"Telemarketer!" yelled Ooru.

A brief buzz of gunfire ended with another stone-on-metal *clank*.

"What the heck does that mean?" yelled Althea.

"It's the worst bad word in the world," shouted Paama. "It's so bad, Elder Noema said it can make anyone who hears it angry enough to hit people."

Ooru screamed.

Althea ran out from between cars into view. "Hey! Shoot me. I'm worth more points. Leave him alone!"

The wheelbot had cornered Ooru, seconds from splattering him all over the wall, but miraculously took the bait, swiveling toward her instead. Althea flooded her body with a surge of psionic energy, zooming down the aisle, the clap of her feet on the concrete echoing over the garage. The wheelbot's tire spun so fast it threw off a billow of white smoke, but the machine didn't go anywhere for a second until the rubber caught traction and hurtled the bot forward, its body briefly tilted backward.

Althea sprinted, inches in front of a hail of gunfire that shredded decayed vehicles, filling the air with a spray of metal and glass bits. A sudden *bad* feeling made her jump to the left, diving between two cars. Bullets whizzed past her, far too close. She skidded for a few feet on her chest, then scrambled upright again. The wheelbot kept going to the end of the aisle, coming around into the next lane in front of her. She squeaked and darted back the other way, jumping up to run across the hood and roof of a big sedan.

"Contaminant reclassified. Non-human."

"I am human!" shouted Althea. She scrambled for cover behind a big concrete column, and paused to gasp for air with her back pressed against the cool stone.

"Humans do not possess the capability to travel at thirty-two miles per hour without mechanical assistance." Whirring circled to the side, announcing the wheelbot driving around the other way. "Define nature of bioluminescence."

"I dunno why they glow; they just do!" Althea scooted around the column to keep it between her and the robot. "Hey. I have a question."

"Contaminants do not pose queries."

"Is that a rule?"

The whirring stopped. "I am unable to find program code prohibiting processing a contaminant query. Proceed."

"Umm. What?"

"You have a query?"

"Yes."

"Provide the query."

She swallowed saliva and took a few breaths. "You're CRP, right? Cybernetic Re-something pro-whatever."

"Cybernetic Reclamation Project. Authorized by United Coalition Front Senate in the year 2378. Self-actualized in 2379 under the command of Sigma Six. That is correct."

"What is a cyborg?"

"A cyborg is an organism consisting of a combination of biological and mechanical parts that complement each other to produce a stronger, more functional whole."

"You don't have a brain. I can't hear any thinking in your head."

"I have an advanced neuro-processing unit capable of four-point-one exaFLOPS."

"Are you biological at all?"

"I do not possess any biological components. Sigma Six determined that biological components present unacceptable levels of weakness."

Althea closed her eyes and thanked whatever kept this thing talking to her so she could catch her breath. "If you have no biological stuff, are you a cyborg?"

"No. The correct term would be robot."

"So you guys can't be the *C*-RP because you're not a cyborg. Shouldn't you change the name?"

"Processing..."

Althea pushed off the column and ran. The wheelbot stood still in the middle of the aisle, its lenses flickering rapidly. She zoomed around to where Ooru and Paama hid behind a dead van.

"Come on. I confused it. We have to get out of here!"

Ooru jumped up, pulling Paama after him before running

perpendicular to the aisles across the garage. Althea sprinted after them. Ooru wiped out, landed on his chest, and slid under a car. Althea spotted the puddle of blood he'd slipped on too late to react before it took her feet out from under her. She came down on her butt and went sliding across the smooth floor, crashing into a column.

"Ouch." Althea windmilled her arms for balance as she rolled back to her feet

The wheelbot came out of nowhere, stopping inches in front of her. She leaned up on her tiptoes, back pressed to the concrete post.

"Query resolved. Some active units still retain biological components. As an organizational title, CRP is still valid. If *all* units become fully robotic, the name should be changed for accuracy."

"Oh. That's nice." Althea faked a smile. "Please, can we live now?"

"You are contaminants. You must be cleansed."

"But we're leaving. You don't have to cleanse us because we're gonna go away on our own." She stared into the tips of two tri-barrel rotary cannons, and whimpered. "Pleeease?"

It blinked. "Contaminants cannot effect self-removal without termination of biological life processes."

Ooru rose up behind the wheelbot with his spear held high in both hands. He swung it down, walloping the wheelbot over the head... but the strike stopped dead with a *clank*, having little effect on the machine.

The robot's glowing amber eyes narrowed. "Hostility detected."

It rotated, sprouting a sword-sized blade from its chest that slashed the boy across the middle. Ooru wailed in pain and staggered backward.

"Optimal cleansing efficiency. Does not require ammunition expenditure." The wheelbot tilted forward, rolling at him with the sword held high.

Althea shoved herself off the column, charging at the awful machine. She jumped into the air, planting a flying double-kick into the wheelbot's left shoulder before crashing flat on the ground. The hit twisted the metal man enough that it mostly missed Ooru, slicing open the side of his leg rather than stabbing him in the heart. He collapsed, grunting in pain, and dragged himself toward a car.

"Target change."

The wheelbot pivoted around, retracted its blade, and trained its guns on Althea. Total panic sent such a surge of psionic boost into her muscles that she sprang into the air like a flea, sailing twelve feet off the ground. Bullets tore up the concrete where she'd been. Her back scuffed the ceiling at the top of her arc. The wheelbot fired again, missing over her head as she fell; Althea hit the ground running, heading straight for a row of cars. Bullets raced across the floor behind her. She darted to the left between a pickup and a van, shrieking at a pelting of tiny concrete fragments hitting her legs. The wheelbot ceased firing as she ran among the cars ducking under side mirrors.

"Contaminant is fortunate that I do not suffer the biological flaw of frustration. I will not kill you with unnecessarily elevated levels of pain because you are resisting cleansing so effectively."

She ran out into the next aisle, which went downhill. The wheelbot appeared at the top of the ramp behind her, so Althea poured on speed, running as fast as she could propel herself over the wide open space. Bullets chirped and pinged off the ground at her heels. She nearly lost her footing at the bottom when she stepped in another puddle of blood, and wound up skiing across the slick before tripping over the body of a huge man face down at the end of the giant bloodstain.

Althea fell draped over the corpse, staring at a giant hammer—as long as her height—on the ground beside him. She sprang up and grabbed the handle, pouring psionic power into her body to make it stronger. Without psionic help, she'd never have been able to lift it. Her muscles burned as she hefted the ridiculous weapon, nearly teetering over backward when she raised it over her head. Every second she kept it aloft, the muscles in her arms burned worse.

"Althea!" shouted Paama. "Look out!"

The wheelbot rolled around the column at the base of the ramp, starting to aim at her, but it slid sideways, spinning out of control in the blood slick. Its guns went off, firing wild, nowhere near her for the second it took the machine to sail by and crash into the wall with enough force to bend the barrels of the left gun arm.

Furious for it hurting Ooru, Althea growled and ran *at* it. The machine reversed out of the small dent it made in the cinder blocks, spinning about to face her a second before she brought the huge hammer straight down on top of it, driving its head into the torso. Flashes and sparks came from within, spitting out the gap at the neck. The stink of fried insulation and burned silicon filled the air. She coughed on the smoke, stumbling backward.

Her muscles refused to cooperate anymore, so she dropped the hammer and backed away.

"Error. Visibility reduced." The wheelbot raised its gun arms, which began spinning as the robot rotated rapidly.

"Uh oh." Althea ran for cover, diving into a slide that put her under a dead truck.

The wheelbot's left gun arm exploded when it tried to fire, the right one throwing bullets around in a continuous, blind circle. Althea crammed herself as deep as she could under the old vehicle, trying to stay out of the way of bullets.

A moment later, the bullets stopped, though the crazy wheelbot continued spinning in place. Paama dashed out from behind a column full of bullet gouges and hurried to the large man's corpse. She plucked a gun off his belt, pointed it at the wheelbot... and a bright blue beam connected the tip to the machine, melting a hole in the armor.

"Danger elevated. Armor compromised. Error. Signal lost. Interference." It stopped rotating in place and accelerated—straight into the wall.

Paama ceased staring at the gun in awe, and fired again and again at the wheelbot until it burst into flames and fell over. Tears streamed down her cheeks. "That's for Ooru!" She shot it again. A few seconds later, pure terror engulfed her.

"No!" Althea crawled out from under the truck. "It didn't kill him. And why are you scared?"

"I killed a Silver Man. They're the warriors of the gods. I'm gonna die."

"Umm... Ell-Gee has a bunch of them hanging in a room with wires. If you're gonna die for not letting this one kill us, he's in big trouble."

"No. We find those, already broken. The gods send them to us so we have power, heat, and light."

"They are only machines, not soldiers for gods." Althea forced the girl's terror away. "Don't be afraid."

She whirled to stare at her. Without the wall of terror in the way, strong sadness took over. "Ooru's cut real bad. We'll never get him to Mariko before he bleeds to death. And Mariko won't be able to help him anyway, just make him comfortable until the gods take him." Paama sniffled.

Althea forced the girl's sadness away, too. "Do not be afraid. I will help him."

"What?" Paama blinked, confused at her abrupt change of mood. "Oh no!"

Not waiting for the girl to explain what new idea worried her, Althea ran up the ramp, heading toward the boy's moans. She found him under a car, flat on his back clutching his chest.

"Ooru." Althea reached for him, but he'd gone in too far to get a hand on.

"Sorry. I tried," wheezed the boy.

"Will you stop? Both of you!" Althea crawled in after him and grabbed his hand. Eyes closed, she linked her mind to his life essence, visualizing his body as a series of shapes and blobs floating in a black void. The slash to the chest opened one of his air bags, but didn't go deep enough to damage the heart-shape. His leg wound appeared painful, but not terrible. She forced his body to disregard pain, then commanded the hurts to go away. The deep slice across his torso took three minutes to close, after which she fed power into him so his blood-shape regenerated from what he'd lost. Fortunately, his air-bag hadn't deflated, so she didn't need to blow it up for him.

"What happened?" asked Ooru.

"I made the hurts go away." She scooted out from under the car and sat back on her heels, thoroughly out of breath.

Ooru followed, got to his feet, and pulled his shirt open to examine his chest. A thin line of lighter tan across his otherwise brown skin revealed where the cut had been. "How…"

"I'm the Prophet," said Althea in a tired voice. "This is why people are always trying to steal me."

Paama flopped to the floor beside her. "I'm sorry!"

Althea gave her side eye. "Why?"

"For saying I was gonna kick your butt before. I didn't know you were a god."

"I'm not a god. I can just heal people."

"That's *real* magic. Nobody can do that. You have to be a god." Paama wiped tears off her cheeks. "Right?"

"No. It's called psionic. There's a big city that has so many people who can do psionic stuff that they have special police just for that."

"If there are many people with this magic, why does everyone chase you?" asked Ooru.

Althea managed a weak smile, and shrugged. "I think I'm the only one who can take the hurts away from *other* people."

"So you're really not a god?" asked Ooru.

She sighed out her nose. Maybe if she lied and said she was, it would be easier to convince the people in the village of Transit to get out of here and go far away from the dangerous machines. But, lying caused bad things. And telling big lies caused bigger bad things. Besides, Queen Kye needed help.

"No. I'm just Althea." She smiled. "I'm a person like you, but I have some magic."

18

SACRED HALLS

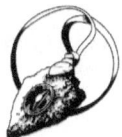

Althea rested, trying to catch her breath. Growing pain in her arms and back worsened with each passing minute until it became clear she'd hurt herself. She concentrated her power inward, sensing multiple rips in her muscle shapes, mostly in her arms and back. That hammer had been far too heavy for her, and she'd pushed her body too much. One by one, she mended the damaged parts, the muscles twitching.

She missed the fur blanket and that nice bed, wanting to curl up there for a day or two even if it delayed going home.

Eventually, Paama stood. "We shouldn't stay here. More Silver Men will find us."

"If you're tired, I will carry you." Ooru offered a hand.

"I can walk." Althea forced herself upright.

Ooru took the lead, heading down the ramp. They went around two big circles, trudging past enough car husks to build a new wall around Querq. By the time they reached the second story below ground, Althea had ceased leaving bloody footprints on the concrete floor. At the base of that ramp, the boy walked off to the left. Three more corpses lay there, perforated with dozens of bullets each—clearly the work of a wheelbot.

Somber silence hung over the trio while they walked to the back end of the garage. Ooru guided them to a hallway wide enough for a car, but only about twenty feet long. Tribal markings covered both walls, the floor, and even the ceiling in parts. A large, armored door consisting of two massive metal slabs took up most of the end of the corridor. They, too, had been covered in tribal petroglyphs. Some of the ritual symbols had frozen speech, the most common being, 'Starbucks,' 'Apple,' 'Nike,' and 'BMW,' among others. Dozens of plastic jugs, pottery urns, bowls, and plates by the door held offerings of long-rotted fruit, bread, and meat.

An opening between the slabs looked big enough for an adult to squeeze past.

"Lady Twitter, please tell Kye Althea is coming," whispered Paama in a reverent tone.

"What?" asked Althea.

"Grandma says she is the goddess of messages. She carries them to anyone you want if you ask."

Ooru stopped at the seam in the concrete floor, not entering the hall, and whispered, "This is the sacred temple entrance. We can't go any farther."

Both kids radiated genuine fear, strong to the point it verged on terror.

"I'm not sure you should either," whispered Paama.

"Why are you whispering?"

"It is the sacred temple." Ooru bowed his head. "Royals come here to endure the trial of leadership. Anyone not a royal will die. The gods will be angry if we even walk up to the door."

"Then who put all that stuff in front of the door?" Althea pointed at the offerings.

"The new king or queen when they come to take the trial," whispered Paama. "The gods would let us go to the door if we had an offering, but not inside. We don't have an offering now so we can't even enter the passage."

"Are you sure you want to go in there?" Ooru radiated worry. "I don't want you to die."

"You shouldn't go in." Paama shook her head. "If Kye didn't survive, that means she's not really a royal."

"What if someone goes in there who doesn't even know your people or your gods exist? The door's open." Althea pointed at it. "Those raiders we saw could've gone in there."

"And they're dead." Ooru folded his arms.

Althea sighed. "The wheelbot did that, not gods."

"The Silver Men work for the gods." Paama bowed her head.

"How do you know that?" asked Althea.

"It is what the elders say." Ooru tugged on her arm. "Let's go back and tell them we couldn't find Kye."

"Did you hear the machine say they were sent here to cleanse the Badlands?" Althea looked back and forth between them. "People made them. The machines came out here and they broke. They're not doing what they were supposed to do. They have the stupid."

"We're scared. We don't want you to die." Ooru squeezed her hand.

Althea stared at the door, trying to get a feeling about going in. Nervousness simmered in the pit of her stomach, though she couldn't tell if her clairvoy ants warned her it would be risky or if all the creepy writing on the walls merely unsettled her.

"I will be okay. I promised the council I'd look for Kye. It is bad to break promises, and bad to lie."

"She must be royal at least." Ooru pointed at the healed line down his chest. "The gods will let her go in."

Paama released her hand. "All right. Please be careful. We will wait here for you."

Althea hugged them together, then advanced into the sacred hall.

Her friends hovered at the end of the hallway, throwing off fear and concern.

She padded along, looking around at all the painted figures of people, random squiggles, and others resembling the wheelbots. A few resembled a small bluebird, one an apple with a little bite out of it. A bright yellow M appeared here and there as well as a blue sphere formed from lines. She had seen some of the same symbols on buildings in the Lost Place, ancient ruins deep in the Badlands that hadn't changed since the Before-Time. The sour smell of rotten vegetables filled the air at the bottom. Althea scrunched her nose and twisted around to look at her friends, neither of whom had stepped one toe over the seam in the concrete floor.

"See? I'm not dead."

"Shh!" rasped Ooru. "This temple belongs to the gods. Don't make them angry."

"Right. Sorry," whispered Althea.

She slipped past the gap in the armored door, entering a clean, white corridor that reminded her of the fancy things in the bad city. Frozen speech on the wall spelled out, 'Ancora Medical Corporation.' Below it, smaller letters said, 'Advanced Research Facility.' She sounded it out, furrowed her eyebrows, and huffed. She didn't exactly know what that meant, but remembered Officer David had told her about corporations. They somehow hurt people with something called money instead of guns or blades. She stuck her head back out the doors to stare at her friends.

"This place was made by a corp'ration, not the gods."

Ooru blinked. "What?"

"Be careful," said Paama in a warning tone.

"It's right on the wall."

"What is a corp'ration?" asked Ooru.

"Umm. Like a tribe, I think. Just big ones. There might be bad city stuff in here that's dangerous, but it's not magic. Umm... teck know lodgie."

"Teck know lodgie?" Paama glanced at Ooru for a second, then back to her. "What is that?"

"Technology?" asked Ooru. "Ell-Gee said that before."

Althea pointed at her. "The gun you picked up that makes blue light. That."

"It's gods' magic." She patted it. "Strong enough to hurt the Silver Men."

Ooru gawked. "You hurt one?"

"They're only machines!" shouted Althea. "You're not gonna be punished."

"Shh!" rasped Ooru and Paama at the same time.

Althea slapped herself in the forehead. "You guys should have the forgetting. I'll be back as fast as I can."

She ducked into the hallway, sighing in frustration. Her friends didn't understand this 'temple' was only a place from the Before-Time, or maybe not quite so long ago, that had modern stuff in it like all the things the Zero police brought to Querq to 'make life easier.' Electric lights, datapads, that motor that could open the city gate easily... months ago, she would have been frightened of those things, too. Blush warmed her cheeks at the memory of being terrified of hovercars, thinking them monsters that would eat her.

"I'd still be scared of all this stuff if Archon hadn't kidnapped me and taken me to the bad city." She frowned, staring at her feet. If he hadn't come after her, she would probably *still* be locked up with

Vakkar's harem. No, six months went by. She definitely would've been taken by at least two other raiding groups in that time. Aurora started a war at Vakkar's camp that forced her to do the unthinkable: actively run away from someone who had abducted her. She had to... to save the women. But they, too—at least Zhar—then wanted to abduct her. So she'd run away from them, even if she did like Rachel.

And after wandering the Badlands, searching for the courage to protect herself, she'd found a home with Father and Karina. In some crazy way, she felt thankful to Archon for giving her a family, even if it had been the furthest thing from what he'd wanted of her.

However, her two new friends waited for her outside in a highly dangerous place. She could feel sad about Archon later. Nothing in here should be scary at all. Merely technology—though, admittedly, she didn't really like technology much either. Ooru and Paama overreacted being terrified of it, but she agreed with them that she'd rather avoid it.

A long, white hallway stretched off into the distance, lit by weak but functional ceiling lights. Much colder air in here than the outside chilled her to shivering, her toes numb upon the steel floor.

She clenched her jaw, determined to find Kye, queen or not, and get the heck out of there as fast as possible.

19

ROYAL PAIN

The air grew even colder, swirling around Althea's legs as she padded deeper into the facility. This place didn't frighten her out of any worry of it being sacred or connected to any gods; however, its similarity to the bad city unnerved her. The clean white surfaces reminded her of places the Zero police had called 'hospitals.' Despite the overwhelming negative emotions given off by the people in that city, the hospitals had felt reasonably safe. Except for the frightening dead people who still moved and had no emotions or thoughts in their heads, the others who she met there had all been concerned for her.

She examined the floor, but Kye left no visible footprints, which seemed odd since Althea had left a quite noticeable trail of dirt and blood. When she came to the first door on the right, she approached, looking around for a knob. The door opened by itself, emitting a soft hiss of air while sliding sideways into the wall. She jumped back with a startled squeak, shot an annoyed glare at the doorway for scaring her, then peered into a modest-sized room where twelve blue chairs surrounded a large silver table. No one sat in any of them, and the room had no other exits.

"Did a ghost open the door for me?"

When no one answered, she shrugged and crossed the hall to the next door. This time, she expected it to open, and didn't jump. That room also had chairs around a table and no people.

Faint whirring came from the hallway behind her. She glanced to her left at motion along the floor. A silver disc the size of a dinner plate, about three inches tall, glided along, following the trail of dirt she'd left.

"Contaminant detected," said the little disc, before aggressively rolling back and forth across a particularly dark footprint.

Oh no! It's gonna kill me!

She sprinted down the hall to the next nearest door on the left, which also opened for her, and leapt into a large room containing several desks with partition walls between them. Thin carpeting offered a somewhat warmer surface to walk on, though she didn't care about that as much as wanting to get away from the killer machine that drew inexorably closer.

"Destroy all contaminants," said the small disc-bot, managing an almost victorious tone in an inflectionless voice.

"Eep!"

Althea darted into the room, running around two desks before swerving left down another aisle and crawling under the last desk farthest from the door. She curled up on the floor behind the chair, arms wrapped around her legs, face half hidden behind her knees. The whirring continued in the hall, though far enough away to suggest it hadn't seen her.

She shivered in place, listening.

The whirring came closer.

"I am the destroyer of contamination."

The tiny horror sounded exactly like the wheelbot. Her mind ran away with itself trying to imagine how something so small would kill her if it found her. Maybe needles? Maybe it had a blue-light gun. It might even fly up off the ground and sprout sharp blades around the outside, spinning to cut her head off.

She whimpered, shivering. *Go away!*

When the door to the room she hid in opened with a *pssht*, she nearly screamed.

"So many contaminants," said the little robot. "They will not win."

Althea tried to press herself *into* the wall, but couldn't back up any farther. The closer the whirring came, the more she trembled. When the flat, silver disc eventually rolled into view right in front of her, she screamed, cringing away from it.

"Please don't kill me!"

"Contaminant detected," said the disc-bot, then ran back and forth over a small smudge her foot had left in the carpet.

Althea screamed again.

The disc bot pivoted to the left, bringing a two-inch black strip on the otherwise all-silver housing to face her. A pair of green eye spots appeared, peering up at her. The bot crept closer.

She squeezed herself into the corner under the desk, trying to get away from the deadly machine.

A thin metal arm sprouted out of its side after it rolled up to her toes.

Braced for death, her mind lashed out with the same psionic detonation that had rewired Shepherd from a mindless killer to an overprotective big (massive) brother. The metal claw closed gingerly around her left ankle, tugging her foot into the air. Expecting to be dragged out from under the desk to her death, Althea grabbed at the desk, screaming.

The disc-bot sprouted a strange red cylinder from its front end, which began rotating at high speed. Petrified with terror, Althea couldn't bring herself to move or do anything but watch as the slender metal arm pulled her foot closer. She cringed, expecting agony when the rotating engine of death touched her...

But it tickled.

Terror flickered to absolute confusion.

"Contaminant origin detected."

The disc-bot maneuvered the spinning fuzzy thing up and down her sole... scrubbing her foot. Still clinging to the desk behind her, she couldn't help but erupt in giggles at the sensation.

"Stop! That tickles!"

The disc-bot ignored her, continuing to apply the spinning fuzzy to her left foot for about thirty seconds before the narrow claw grip released her ankle. It pivoted and repeated the process with her other foot.

Althea squealed and giggled.

"Contaminant destroyed." The machine played a short musical effect that sounded triumphant.

Both the spinning fuzzy and the slender arm retracted into the flat, round robot. As if pleased with itself, it spun away and drove off. Althea blinked, staring at the spot of carpet where it had been. It took a moment for her bewilderment to fade. She pulled her foot up to look at the sole, as clean as if she had just taken a bath. It smelled kinda weird though… like oranges. She tasted the bottom of her foot, but recoiled at a bitter sourness totally unlike the smell.

After spitting a few times, she crawled out from under the desk, not quite sure what to think of the small machine.

"It sounded like the other one, but this one didn't kill me?"

Her heart still racing from her near-dirt experience, Althea made her way out into the corridor, and continued deeper into the facility. She peered into offices and storage rooms, not bothering to examine any of the strange technology for fear of hurting herself. Eventually, she reached an intersection in the hall where a strong *bad* feeling about going straight ahead or to the right stopped her short, the same sort of bad feeling that made her jump out of the flying machine.

She warily eyed those corridors. "It would kill me to go there. Oh, I hope Kye didn't take that way."

Since only one option didn't fill her with mortal dread, she headed to the left. Doors along that hall led to huge rooms. The first two each had about twenty beds, the third contained long tables full of strange objects. She assumed them to be some manner of technology, but other than recognizing display screens, buttons, and wires, had no idea what any of them could do, especially the giant glass box with rubber gloves hanging from one side.

Frozen words near the door read, "Level 3 Protection Required – Biohazard."

She stared at the last two words, not even sure how to say them much less what they meant. Protection, she knew, was what Father gave her. But it could also mean armor like the raiders and some of the Watch put on.

"Oh… I think I know. I need to wear armor to go in there."

The room didn't have anyone in it, so it didn't matter she had no protection.

Another corridor led off to the right up ahead, but a strange clicking came from that direction. Althea crept up to the corner and leaned out only enough to peer around.

Two strange men walked along the hall, moving away from her. Both appeared to be made of white and silver plastic, quite a bit flimsier than the CRP wheelbot. Though neither carried any obvious weapons, she suspected they would try to hurt her. Like the dead people in the city hospital that moved and talked, they didn't have emotions or thoughts.

However, these things didn't pretend to look like real people. She wondered if the moving dead back at the city might have been robots, too.

Althea didn't like robots. They made her feel small and weak, like an ordinary child.

Not that she had any desire at all for power, but if a monster like that hurt her, she couldn't continue helping people. Neither robot appeared to notice her watching them. She didn't move until they disappeared around a distant corner. From the look of it, she suspected they had gone into the part of this 'temple' that had given her the danger feeling. Perhaps those robots *would* hurt her.

I shouldn't let them see me.

They walked with a fairly stiff gait, so she hoped she could outrun them if need be. That would work unless they had guns hidden somewhere in their bodies. This place had lots of long, open corridors with nowhere to hide. If she ran straight, she'd have to swerve back and forth to avoid being shot. If she hid in a room, that would trap her.

Neither choice sounded like fun.

I gotta find Kye and get out of here fast!

She crept past the corridor to keep quiet. Once out of sight from the robot hallway, she sped up to a jog, hoping the patter of her feet on the hard floor didn't attract danger from far away. She checked doorway after doorway, finding more small offices, rooms with big tables, and one enormous area with many round tables and chairs. A counter at the far end stood under a row of bizarre pictures. She had no names for the images, but they all appeared to be some kind of food.

Still, no people in there, so she kept going.

Two hallways of empty rooms passed in a blur of panicky running.

Althea jogged around a leftward corner into a surprisingly cold corridor, and nearly slipped on her butt. A thin layer of water coated the smooth, metal floor. After recovering her balance, she continued at a slow, careful walk over the slippery surface. Her teeth chattered. She rubbed her hands up and down her arms, really wanting to have the furry blanket she'd slept under instead of her thin dress. Or maybe even both of them at once.

A nudge of her healing ability sent extra blood into her feet to keep her toes from going numb. She made her heart-shape go faster to warm her up. A metal door on the left didn't open when she stepped near it, nor could she find any way to make it move. It had no knob, just a small black square on the wall beside it. Touching the square didn't do anything.

Figuring if she couldn't open it, Kye probably couldn't either, she ignored that door and kept going. The second door on the same side of the hall appeared to be missing entirely. She crept closer, not noticing any signs of damage. A narrow strip of metal in the doorjamb suggested the door hadn't vanished, but opened by sliding into the wall.

Nervous about the door deciding to close on her, she leaned in for a quick peek, intending to back away fast... but spotted a young woman floating in a giant clear tank. Althea leaned out from the doorway and waved her arm around in an effort to tempt the door to slam closed on her, but it didn't move.

Hoping the door might be stuck and wouldn't trap or kill her, she jumped past it, waited two seconds, then jumped out into the hall again. The door didn't even twitch.

It's stuck.

She crept into the room, walking between two rows of giant cylindrical tanks against the walls on either side, perched atop mechanical boxes as tall as her knees. The clear chambers stretched all the way to the ceiling. Of twenty enclosures, only one had anything in it: an unconscious, naked woman submerged in peach-colored liquid. Shoulder-length light brown hair bloomed into a cloud around her head, fluttering gently in the current of moving fluid.

A crash of sorrow fell on Althea at possibly finding Kye dead. She started to cry, but stopped upon noticing the young woman still had thoughts in her head. She appeared to be sleeping inside the tank, not dead. But... how could she be drowned and still alive?

Magic...

The woman looked too tan to have spent most of her life living underground, but it might have been color like most of the people native to Querq. Raiders would sometimes call Althea 'white,' something they believed made her a valuable slave due to rarity... right up until they realized her eyes glowed. True, before she had gone to the bad city, she had rarely ever seen anyone else as pale as her. Most everyone looked like this girl. The Transit tribe, however, also had a lot of pale people. But, they had been so isolated they didn't even know about the Prophet. Maybe that had something to do with it? Or maybe living underground away from the sun kept them from turning brown?

A spear made from a thin metal pole fused to a slightly curved sword similar to a wheelbot's blade lay on the ground near that tank. No trace of any clothing remained anywhere in sight. That didn't seem right. Aside from some of the really small kids who never went outside, the Transit tribe all had garments of hide or fur, unlike the Scrag tribes Althea was used to. And even the little ones had blanket cloaks if not actual shirts, pants, or dresses.

The woman in the tube appeared slender and athletic, though her skin remained as undamaged as a raider's prized harem pet. Not a single scar, cut, blemish, or discoloration marked her skin... nor even any dirt.

"Wake up." Althea banged her hands on the tube. "You have to get up now."

Nothing happened.

Althea focused on the young woman's thoughts. She dreamed of running away from those silver-and-white robots. In her mind-vision, she wore a tunic of animal hide as well as a skirt and boots, all decorated with beads and tufts of fur.

Wake up.

The robots in the dream froze. To the woman's perspective, Althea's voice had echoed from everywhere.

"Who said that?"

Are you Kye?

"Who are you?"

I'm Althea.

"Yes. I am Kye, Queen of Transit."

Why are you in a bottle?

"The gods speak to me in this place." Kye glanced back at the stopped-in-time robots, then took a knee, bowing her head. "In a bottle?"

You are dreaming. I found you in a big bottle. You're sleeping and need to wake up.

Kye lifted her head and gathered her hair off her face. "The guardians of the Cursed Place caught me and dragged me to a room... but it doesn't feel like it happened for real."

How do I open this?

"Why is a god asking me how to do something?"

I'm not a god. I'm Althea.

"I must complete this trial and return to my people as queen."

Kye resumed running down the hall, the robots again chasing her.

Althea dropped the telepathic link and opened her eyes to the real world. The young woman's floating body twitched every so often like a dog running in its dreams, somehow still alive in fluid that didn't drown her. This tank had to be bad city stuff. That frustrated her since she didn't understand—or want to understand—it. But, if she didn't deal with it, this woman would be stuck here for a long time.

She grabbed the clear tank and tried to lift, but couldn't budge it. Banging on it didn't help either. Nor did kicking. Althea took a half step to the left where a display screen connected to the chamber showed various moving pictures containing fluttering lines and round spots with different colored sections like pie slices. Two blue dots, the reflection of her glowing eyes, shone from the glass surface as she leaned closer.

Some of the frozen words, she knew, like 'good' or 'normal.' The rest: 'stasis' 'command menu,' or 'nanobot status' went right over her head. Nothing looked even close to 'open' or 'off.' She bit her lip, not wanting to touch the wrong thing and hurt Kye.

What am I supposed to do?

She paced around for a moment before noticing the spear. Breaking the display panel probably wouldn't be good, but maybe she could smash open the tank itself. Althea picked up the heavy all-metal spear and jabbed it at the clear cylinder. The point scratched the material, but fell quite short of doing any real damage.

The next time she reared back to try stabbing harder, an explosion went off out in the hallway.

"Eep!" She jumped back, dropping the spear with a loud *clang*.

Figuring the robots must have somehow discovered she tried to break the tube, Althea sprinted to the innermost corner of the room and squeezed in behind the last tank machine, hiding in a narrow space between the boxy not-clear part and the wall. Even at her size, she barely stuffed herself into the gap, her back to the wall, her chest pressed against the machine. Another six months, and she'd be too big to fit. Though uncomfortable, the tightness reassured her that the robots wouldn't be able to get to her. She couldn't see anything out in the room from here, but that also meant the robots probably wouldn't see her.

Ooru said they can't see through metal, and she'd surrounded herself with metal.

A series of soft electric thrums broke the silence, similar to the sound the blue-light gun that Paama found gave off when fired. Another soft explosion accompanied a plastic clattering, and a deep, digitized voice said, "Fatal error."

She closed her eyes to conceal the glow, in case it might shine off the steel walls, and slowed her breathing to keep as quiet as possible. Silence hung thick for a little while… then the soft rubbery squelch of shoes on smooth metal floor entered the room outside.

"I know you're in here. Come on out," said a woman.

An adult could probably help get Kye out of the tank… but something in that woman's tone sounded wrong… dangerous. Althea didn't trust her. Perhaps the woman only suspected she was here and tried to trick her. She held still.

"Fine. Come out or this girl in the tank is dead."

Ooh. She's bad!

Althea shimmied out from her hiding place, scooted around the tank cylinder, and stepped into the room, glaring up at a pale twentysomething woman with shoulder-length blue-green hair and a mildly scorched dark grey jumpsuit that looked like clothing from the bad city. She held a black pistol off to the side, aimed at Kye.

The woman smiled at her. "Hello, Althea. I've been looking all over for you."

20

KINDA LIKE MOM... NOT

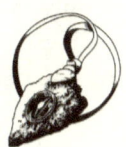

Althea balled her hands into fists, staring at the gun trained on Kye. "Don't hurt her."

"There's no need to, now." The woman put her weapon in a holster on her belt, then approached. "It's time for us to go."

"Do you know how to let her out?"

"Of course. It's a simple medical tank." The woman grabbed Althea by the wrist. "But she is none of our concern."

Althea gave off a pulse of telempathic fear. Kye twitched in her sleep, but the woman with blue-green hair didn't react at all. "Let go of me."

"I didn't track you all the way from the crash site to lose you again. How the heck did you even survive?"

"*Let go!*"

"No."

Althea blinked. Her angry glower faded to a mix of confusion and worry. This woman didn't have thoughts. Nor did she give off any emotions whatsoever. The Slave Catcher also didn't have emotions, but he did have thoughts. This woman possessed neither... like a robot. Yet, she looked completely human, even had soft, warm skin. Althea glanced at the woman's fingers clamped around her wrist.

"Please let her out."

"Forget her." The woman dragged Althea across the room to a table.

She tried to resist, but her feet slid over the smooth, wet metal. She squirmed and fought, but the woman overpowered her, bending her over the table and holding her arms behind her back. Screaming and kicking didn't help at all.

The woman forced her wrists together behind her back and tied them with cord.

"No!" shouted Althea. "Let me go!"

Without a word, the woman finished securing the cord between her wrists, then pulled her upright and set her on her feet. Althea ran for the door, but jerked to a stop after only two steps at the end of a tether attached to her wrists. She glared back over her shoulder at the woman holding the other end, a leash to her tied hands instead of around her neck.

"Why are you doing this?" yelled Althea. "I only wanna help that girl. She's trapped!"

"I'm not being paid to care about anyone but you." The woman walked past her. "I really am glad you survived. Thought we lost you when the Starduster went down."

Althea stood firm... until the tether nearly pulled her off her feet. She stumbled to avoid falling as the leash dragged her backward out into the hallway. Making herself stronger didn't help, as bare feet had zero traction on the condensation-covered steel floor. She wound up entirely focused on not slipping and falling over instead of resisting.

"You're gonna make me fall!"

"Then stop making me pull you. Walk."

"I don't wanna be kidnapped!"

"Your choice." The woman resumed walking.

Althea lost her balance after a few more seconds, the slippery metal too much for her while the tether kept pulling her around in a twist. Her feet slid out from under her, dumping her on her side. The woman didn't slow down, dragging her along the floor by the cord. For a moment, Althea gave up fighting and merely scowled at the ceiling while sliding.

"Are you planning to try the dead weight thing the whole time?"

"Maybe. You could stop kidnapping me if you don't want to pull me."

The woman laughed. "Nice. Got a little sass in you. I like that."

Althea stuck out her tongue, then huffed, scowling at the wall while gliding along, pulled by her thoughtless, emotionless abductor. A handful of the silver-and-white robots lay in burning heaps, the air filled with caustic eye-burning smoke. Despite trying not to breathe, she ended up coughing anyway.

At the end of that corridor, the woman stopped. "Gonna walk yet?"

"Gonna stop kidnapping me yet?"

The woman chuckled and kept going around the corner. "Your choice if you want to clean the floors."

Eventually, being pulled backward by a cord around her wrists hurt her shoulders. Althea struggled and squirmed, kicking her legs out in an attempt to flip herself over. She rolled up onto her knees, still sliding backward. Upon noticing her trying to stand, the woman stopped and let her get up. Althea glared at the woman, but begrudgingly walked at her side.

When they reached the giant armored door, Althea hurried through the gap and tried to run, straining at the tether. Leaning into the cord, she stared down the corridor at where Paama and Ooru weren't.

"What happened to my friends?" She stopped fighting and spun to glower at the woman squeezing past the doors.

"They ran off. No, I didn't hurt them."

"Please let me go. I hate being tied."

"Relax, kid." The woman patted her on the head. "I'm just taking you to the city. Don't panic. Not gonna hurt you. I'm just here to make sure you get where you need to go, alive and in one piece."

"I need to go home. To Querq."

The woman gave her a relatively gentle push to resume walking. "You can take that up with the people who hired me. They just want you to work for them."

"Ugh." Althea rolled her eyes. "I've heard that before. They're lying."

"Heh, probably." The woman laughed. "Corporate weasels always lie. That's why I demand half up front."

"Half of what?"

"My fee. Someone really wants you pretty bad. Don't usually get paid this much to rescue a feral from the Badlands."

"I'm not feral anymore." She held her head high. "I know the frozen speech."

"Uhh, whatever that means."

Althea twisted to peer up at her. "Can you please let Kye out? Even if you kidnap me."

"Don't worry about her. That girl is safe in there. Probably the safest person within 200 miles of this place. Damn crazy cyborgs."

"But you can't just leave her there!"

"She's fine."

"The Transit tribe wants me to find their queen. I promised I'd help. We can't just leave them."

The woman raised an eyebrow. "Why not?"

"Because it's mean!"

She laughed. "If they want to be stupid, it's not your job to fix it."

Althea struggled at the cord while looking around for broken glass. She felt horrible leaving Kye trapped in that glass cage, and worried about her new friends. Hopefully, Ooru and Paama would make it back home without being caught by a wheelbot or worse. The other kids would be sad that she disappeared, maybe even the councilors, too.

Neither Althea nor the strange woman spoke on the walk around the four stories of underground ramps ascending the parking garage. Althea continued struggling at the cord binding her arms, but aside from a little stretchiness in the material, it didn't budge. Whenever she walked too slow, the woman gave her a little tug of encouragement, but not so hard it felt cruel—at least, no crueler than tying her in the first place.

Strangely, her newest abductor walked with confidence and no hesitation or looking around confused, as if she knew exactly where she wanted to go. Every so often, Althea yanked on the tether in hopes of catching her off guard and slipping away, but the woman's grip didn't fail. She tried throwing off emotions like fear or pity, and when that didn't work, she attempted a telepathic connection, but she may as well have tried to mind-talk with a broken car.

This woman didn't appear to be alive, yet looked perfectly human.

For a few hours, they walked in silence among the ruins of the ancient city, stopping only twice to briefly hide when the woman noticed a CRP machine man moving around in the distance. Eventually, feelings of helplessness, the complete inability to do anything to protect herself, guilt over Kye, and her want to go home to Querq overwhelmed her, and Althea cried.

"It's not going to help, kid. You might not realize it, but I'm actually saving you."

"No, you're not! I have a home where I live with my sister, Karina, and Father, and I want to go back there. I told the Transit people I would help them, and you made me lie."

"Don't worry about it, kid. They've been living here for years before you found them and they'll keep on living here for years without you... unless the CRP finds them. Then they won't be living much."

"But they need to leave *before* the machine men find them."

"That's on them. If they're too stupid to get out of there, it's not your fault."

"Grr!" She strained at the cord. "Let me go!"

"Just relax and calm down. As soon as we get to the city, you'll be fine."

Althea narrowed her eyes. She couldn't do anything at the moment, no more than any ordinary scrawny eleven-year-old trying to fight a grown woman with a gun. However, if they went to the big city, there would be lots and lots of real people there. Real people she could definitely influence emotionally. This strange woman would be in for a big surprise when a giant crowd of people swarmed her. It hurt having to wait, but the knowledge that she could definitely free herself later would have to be enough hope to cling to for the time being.

Resigned to captivity yet again—if only temporarily—she hung her head and trudged along.

Another hour or so later when daylight began to wane, the woman dragged her over to a mostly intact one-story building.

"Gonna sleep here tonight. If you gotta pee, do it now."

"You're not going to untie me, are you?"

"So you can run off?"

Althea sighed, pulled her dress up, and squatted.

When she finished making water, the woman brought her into the building. After a bit of looking around, she settled on a concealed corner behind some old shelves, and pushed Althea down to sit on the floor. The woman took a knee and tied Althea's ankles with the tether. The short length of cord connecting her ankles to her wrists pulled her legs up behind her and left her bent in half on her side.

"Please don't tie me like this! I'm scared!"

The woman put a hand over her mouth, speaking in a quiet, placid tone. "You shouldn't yell, or the androids will hear us. I'm trying to get you out of here alive, okay? I'd rather not have you end up full of plasma holes."

Althea blinked.

After a moment, the woman removed her hand. They stared at each other in silence for a few seconds before the woman busied herself removing a small backpack, which she proceeded to rummage around in. Althea snarled, fighting the cord and squirming. She flopped over onto her stomach, trying to pick at the knot between her ankles with a fingertip. No matter how she wriggled, she couldn't get enough of a grip on it to accomplish much.

The woman plucked her off the floor and repositioned her kneeling, sitting back on her heels.

Althea glared at her. "You're mean. Please don't leave me tied up all night."

"I'm lazy, and it's for your own protection." The woman sat beside her and peeled the wrapper from a small, brown bar. "You feral kids always want to run off into the wilds. First chance you get, you'll take off... and end up dead. I can't take the chance of you disappearing on me. Relax. As soon as you get a taste of the modern world, you'll understand why I'm doing this. Here. Eat." She held the bar close enough for her to bite.

Other than not being tied to a post, her present circumstances reminded her of when the Slave Catcher found her. Except, this woman didn't frighten her the same way he did and didn't jam the food bar into her mouth, instead, politely holding it for her to eat at her own pace. Also, this food bar was soft and gooey, not crumbly, with a sweet flavor she couldn't help but like. She leaned forward, taking small nibbles.

"What is this?"

"A high-density survival ration."

"That's a strange flavor."

"Hah. No, it's chocolate. Sorta. If you ask me, it's a pretty crappy attempt at chocolate. But I guess when they cram 2,000 calories into one little bar, something has to get lost in the shuffle."

"What does that mean?" She nibbled another bit and chewed the gummy substance.

"It means that you only need to eat one of these a day. You know how you eat in the morning, again in the middle of the day, again at night?"

"Yeah."

"Well, they took all three meals and squeezed them together into this little bar."

"They?"

"You know, they."

Althea shrugged. "Who is they?"

"The ones who do all sorts of stuff but no one ever seems to know names for. Don't worry about it."

"What's your name?"

"Most people call me Teal."

Althea nipped the last of the bar from the wrapper and chewed on it. Teal tossed the wrapper aside, then pulled a blanket out of the pack as well as a fat black plastic bottle with a grey cap. Small blue and green lights blinked on a little panel at the bottom of the container. She twisted the cap, then squirted water from the top into a plastic cup, which she held for Althea to drink.

"I could eat and drink on my own if you didn't tie me up."

"Yes, that's true."

"So, please untie me."

"It's less annoying to feed you like a baby than chase you all over the place with those damn androids everywhere."

Her old habit of promising not to run away in exchange for being untied drifted across her thoughts… but she refused. The first chance she got, she'd run as fast and far as she could. But, she couldn't promise a lie, even if it would convince Teal to untie her and give her the chance to flee.

Again, she tried forcing pity into the woman's head, but it didn't do anything.

"Are you dead?" asked Althea.

"No."

"Why don't you have emotions or thoughts?"

Teal brushed her hand over Althea's head, tucking a few stray strands of blonde behind her ear for her. "I do, but they are on a different wavelength than what you can affect with your psionics. I've got plenty of emotions… of course, if you ask anyone I've worked with, they'd probably say anger and greed are the most common." She laughed. "I dispute the greed part though. Wanting what I'm owed isn't greedy. Those bastards just can't handle a woman wanting a fair percentage. They think I'm going to work cheap."

"*Let me go!*"

"You just tried something, didn't you. Saw your eyes get brighter there for a second. Sorry, kiddo." Teal traced a finger over her forehead. "That doesn't work on me either. I'm not a human, kid. I'm a synthetic."

Althea considered biting the finger, but that would be mean. "What's that? Are you a robot?"

Teal chuckled. "That's kind of a semantic point. Where humans have meat and bone, I have Myofiber and plastisteel. We're a lot softer and more natural than dolls, cyborgs, or robots. We dream, we love, we have feelings, we even grow up... but my head's running at a different frequency. Human brains are just puddles of goop full of electromagnetic activity. Our brains are also clusters of electromagnetic activity, but in a different, umm... what's a good way to... different language."

"If I couldn't feel emotions or hear thoughts, I wouldn't know you aren't a normal person."

"Thanks, kid." Teal gave her side eye. "How did you get the psi inhibitor off?"

"The what?" Althea blinked.

"We put a device on your head to rein in your powers. How did you take it off? It would have shocked you if you tried to touch it."

She shivered. "*That's* what hurt me when I tried to do stuff?"

"Yes. It wouldn't hurt you if you just behaved."

"It's evil!" Althea scowled.

"You Scrags call everything you don't understand evil."

"It hurt *so* much it made me cry! I don't think everything's evil, just stuff that hurts people."

"You are adorable."

Althea stuck out her tongue. "And you're mean for tying me up. Please let me go."

"Tell me how you managed to take the psi inhibitor off."

She grunted, trying to pull her feet away from her hands. "It just broke."

"What?"

"When I jumped out of the flying machine, it just broke."

Teal gawked. "You *jumped*? I thought you got sucked out the hole. Gotta say I was pretty upset until I saw the tracker signal moving around. I thought you died."

"No. I jumped. I didn't want to fall and get hurt. That evil thing you put on my head tried to keep my wings from working but I kept trying until it broke."

"Wings? This is an entirely new level of fu—messed up I've never seen before."

"How did you find me?" asked Althea.

Teal patted her on the butt. "We gave you a little friend to tell us where you are in case something happened."

"Huh?"

"Don't worry about it. Now go to sleep." Teal eased her over to lie on her side and covered her with the blanket.

Althea scowled at the debris on the floor in front of her face. Her hair half draped over her eyes and mouth, but she could only puff at it. Teal took a small black box out of the pack and set it on the ground nearby. The front face glowed red, bathing Althea in warmth.

"There, that should keep you nice and cozy."

"Untying me would keep me cozier," grumbled Althea. "My nose itches."

Teal wiped at Althea's nose with a small napkin. "There. Better?"

"Not really. I still can't move."

Chuckling, Teal stretched out on the floor at the end of the alcove. Stuck in a corner with two walls and a tall shelf blocking her in, the only way out involved climbing over the woman.

Grumbling to herself, Althea squirmed and struggled at the cord holding her. While she did sometimes sleep curled up in a ball, being *unable* to stretch out bothered her. After a while of unsuccessfully trying to escape the rope, she closed her eyes and concentrated her power inward, examining her body's life shapes for sicks, hurts, or anything that shouldn't be there. Teal saying they gave her a little friend sounded scary.

It took her a long time of careful searching before she discovered a tiny black void in her rear end, no larger than a grain of rice, trapped between the skin and the muscle. They must have stuck her with it when she'd been sleeping after that dart. She commanded her skin to split open, forming a small hole to expel the unwanted hitchhiker. Like a splinter, her body forced the invader out, then she healed the little wound.

She lay for a while, trying to hold still, but the tightness of the cord annoyed her to the point she couldn't help but constantly squirm in protest of it.

"Stop wriggling and go to sleep. We're going to be walking all day tomorrow."

"I can't sleep tied up. Even raiders didn't do this to me."

"Sorry, kid. Deal with it. I don't want to chase you back and forth across the Badlands for the rest of eternity. Had enough trouble finding you the second time."

Althea narrowed her eyes, glaring at the warmth emitter. Would promising not to run and then running anyway be a bad lie? Sincerely promising not to run felt like giving up, and she refused to do that. She *would* go home to her family no matter what. Being dragged east, heading in the wrong direction away from home, broke her heart as much as it angered her. She strained at the cords again. At least being tied like this made her *unable* to go home. Better that than her promising not to. She'd much rather fight as hard as she could to go home and be tied up than make a promise to willingly abandon her family.

Still, that didn't mean she had to like it.

She channeled power into making her whole body stronger, straining to stretch her legs out and snap the cord... until the pain cutting into her skin grew too much and she gave up, gasping for air. Once she caught her breath, she healed the bruises she gave herself.

"Knock it off, kid. Just sleep. That's a dropship rated cargo tiedown cable. It can hold like 3,800 pounds. You're not going to break it. Could hogtie a Class 5 cyborg with that stuff."

"Kidnapping people is mean."

"I'm not kidnapping you. I'm rescuing you from the wasteland."

She lifted her head to glare at Teal. "Rescuing doesn't need tying! You're being mean!"

"Sometimes rescuing does... when the feral you're saving is too wild to know what's best for them. It's just business, kid. Nothing personal."

"Grr." Althea kept twisting at her hands and rocking her legs back and forth, but the cord didn't loosen. "Ow."

"Stop squirming and it won't pinch. You're a lot like your mother."

Althea froze. "You knew my mother?"

"Nah. The company that hired us had some information about her."

"What? I don't know much about her. Please tell me? *Please*?" Althea sniffled. "I know she died."

"Geez kid. Don't cry. I might feel so guilty I cut you loose and let you run off into the wastes."

Althea blinked. "Really?"

"No. Just kidding."

Sorrow crashed into anger. The woman had said that just to be mean. Maybe she wanted to make her cry more. Not being able to read any emotion from her was a scary new situation. All her life, she'd always known exactly how people around her felt, what to expect from them... but this woman could tenderly feed her and give her a blanket as easily as shoot her in the face. Trying to gauge what someone thought or felt purely by their words and facial expressions left her frightened and clueless. Still, she refused to cry if that's what Teal wanted her to do.

"What do you know about my mother?"

"She worked for a technology company that had a facility out here. Some kind of research project into developing better engines for colony starships. Wormholes or something like that. Instantaneous jumping from one point to another by poking a hole in the dimensions."

"What?"

"Yeah, kid." Teal laughed. "That's what I said, too. It's bogus. Didn't work. First time they tried to fire it up, the whole thing exploded. Your mother must have been close to it, but she survived. When she gave birth to you, the people she worked for noticed your glowing eyes and wanted to experiment on you. So your momma ran off. You keep squirming and fighting as hard as she fought to keep you away from them."

"Do you work for them?" Althea tried to remain still, but couldn't stand the feeling of being tied in such a confining posture.

"You know... I'm not sure. They never did tell me which company made that facility. I don't think so. The people who hired me make medicine, not starship parts."

Her squirming lessened to the point of simple protest rather than a sincere effort to escape. Teal sat with her back against the wall, eyes closed. Eerily, she gave off no particular sense of being awake or asleep. Althea rolled onto her back, beyond frustrated that she couldn't stretch her legs out. With her legs bent into the air, they blocked her view of the woman, so she rolled onto her side again and glared at her.

"I never knew my mother. She died when I was still a baby. Father loves me, but I don't know what it's like to have a mother. Karina's my sister and she's younger than you are. I've never really been with a grown-up woman taking care of me. Guess this is kinda what it might have been like to spend time with a mother... except she wouldn't have tied me up."

Teal opened her eyes and glanced over at her. "I'm not your mother, kid. You're what, eleven? I would've been sixteen when you were born."

Althea blinked. "You grow up?"

"Of course I do. Already told you, I'm synthetic, not a robot. We are people… just made out of different stuff."

"Please untie me. I can't sleep."

"So stay up all night. Just don't complain tomorrow that you're tired."

"What if something bad finds us?"

"I'll kill it."

"What if you can't kill it?"

"Then we run."

"What if it kills you? Then I'm in big danger if I can't move."

Teal raised both eyebrows. "If it takes me out, what the hell would *you* do to it?"

"Run away."

"Exactly what I'm trying to prevent."

Althea sighed. She attempted to sleep, but couldn't stop fidgeting. "You are kinda like a mother."

"Feh."

"You're a woman and you're sorta protecting me. So that makes you the closest I've ever had to a mom. Karina's like that, but she's only sixteen. She can't be a mom yet since she *just* got old enough to do more than touch lips with a boy. My sister doesn't have any boy that likes her yet."

Teal turned away, for an instant, her expression almost appeared guilty. "Look, kid… it's only business, all right? No one's gonna hurt you."

"If you're trying to help me, then why am I tied up?"

"Because, you're feral and ignorant and you're going to run off into the shit and get yourself killed."

Althea huffed. "You're only a little right."

"How's that?" asked Teal, not looking at her.

"I'm not feral anymore. I umm, don't know what ignorant is. I *am* gonna run off, but I won't step in *mierda*. And I won't get myself killed. I'm going home."

"Look, I know you supposedly have psionic powers the likes of which people have never seen before or something like that. No wonder they're paying me half a mil to bring you in. But all those fancy mental abilities won't help you here. Don't work on the CRP at all. And they don't care that you're just a little girl. They will kill you. I have to get you out of here and if you run off again, you're going to die. Of all the damn places to crash in the Badlands... we had to pick the damn worst possible spot."

"Am not." Althea stuck her tongue out, not that the woman saw it. "Why did you take me here?"

"To sleep."

"I mean why did the flying machine go here?"

Teal grumbled. "Hell if I know. Damned autopilot took over and changed course. Anything that flies under 35,000 feet in this area gets shot down. We knew it was coming but couldn't do a damn thing about it. You were *supposed* to go to East City."

Althea tapped her foot on nothing, scowling at the tight cord. One reason came to mind to explain why the flying machine took itself to a place where it would surely die. However, she couldn't tell if *he* tried to destroy her, or simply stop her from leaving the Badlands. The thought that such an awful creature might have helped her avoid being kidnapped seemed as unbelievable as it did possible. He had sent Kate to kill her, and done everything he could to destroy her so far. Could it be possible that he finally accepted the two of them had to coexist? Or maybe he thought she'd die in the flying machine.

"He did it," muttered Althea.

"Who did what?"

"The Many. He made your flying machine go here so it would die."

"What the heck are you talking about now?"

"A long, long time ago when the Before-Time ended, there was much fire and killing and hate. *So* many people died here that their ghosts became angry. They wanted revenge. Like lots and lots. I don't have numbers for it. They found each other and came together, becoming The Many. He's everywhere in the Badlands and he loves to make people suffer. He's why machines stop working and people are so mean to each other. Sometimes, he shows himself and talks. Looks like a really old man with green teeth. Smells like a dead body."

"Kid, knock that off or I'm going to put tape over your mouth."

"Please don't. Why would you do that?"

"So you stop saying spooky shit like that. Now *I'm* not gonna sleep."

"You sleep?" Althea blinked.

"Of course I sleep. What kind of question is that?"

Unable to comprehend how a being without a living brain could possibly sleep, Althea set her head down. All her struggling at the cord did tire her out, and despite how much she hated being tied and how much it scared her to be helpless, she decided to try sleeping. At least this woman treated her better than the Slave Catcher. Talking about how much she missed Karina appeared to affect her emotions a little. Somehow the woman *did* appear to have them, even if Althea couldn't sense anything.

Perhaps if Telempathy wouldn't work on a synthetic, she could keep talking about her family. Teal told her to stop crying, so maybe it *did* have an effect. That woman definitely had a cold streak, but didn't really come off as cruel. Sometimes the biggest, scariest raiders would be nice to her if she acted frightened or sad, even without using her powers on them.

Worth a try.

Althea closed her eyes. Though she had no plans to stop fighting, she tried to sound as despondent as possible. "I'm sorry, Father. I'm trying to go home, but I've been kidnapped. I don't know if I'll ever see you or Karina again. I love you both, and I'm sorry for going away."

It didn't take any acting at all to surrender to quiet tears and cry herself to sleep.

21

THAT DIDN'T TAKE LONG

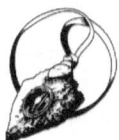

Althea woke to Teal's hand on her shoulder, shaking her gently. She yawned, trying to stretch, but still couldn't move. Sunlight filled the area from ample holes in the walls as well as where windows had once been.

Teal took the blanket and folded it before stuffing it in the pack. Partially due to being tired, partially out of protest, Althea didn't bother trying to sit up or move. The woman turned the warmth emitter off and left it on the floor to cool. She filled another cup of water, then pulled Althea up to kneel, letting her drink.

"Want more?"

"Yes, but that's a small bottle. We should make it last."

"It's a genesis canteen."

Althea stared at her.

"You don't know what that is, do you?"

Althea kept staring at her.

"Of course not. That normal dress of yours throws me off. I keep forgetting you're still a Scrag. It makes water from the air. Little more complicated than that, but I'm sure you don't want to hear about a reservoir of liquid hydrogen."

"No. I'd rather hear about you untying me."

Teal laughed. "Yeah, yeah. Give me a minute. Do you want more water?"

She shrugged.

The woman took that as a yes, so she hit a button on the top of the canteen, which activated a thin stream of water that took a laboriously long time to fill the cup. Watching it made Althea have to pee, but she tried to ignore the feeling.

After feeding her the second cup of water, Teal packed the canteen and cup in her satchel, added the warmer, then hefted the backpack over her shoulder. At long last, she untied Althea's ankles and took hold of the tether. Althea struggled to her feet, begrudgingly following Teal outside. She shot a scowl off to the sky at still having her hands tied behind her back, but didn't think begging, screaming, or nagging would help.

It didn't bother her to make water next to someone. Among Scrag tribes, sometimes the boys would get into competitions to see who could throw water the farthest. It did, however, bother her that the woman wouldn't untie her to make water. She considered that quite mean, but her powers still refused to work on this woman.

Soon after they resumed walking toward the rising sun, it occurred to her that Teal had not eaten, had anything to drink, or made water. Althea kept glancing up at her, confused, then hanging her head.

"What? Why do you keep looking at me like that?"

"Are you gonna eat?"

"I don't need to eat as often as a human does."

"Do you eat?"

"Yes. My body takes raw materials out of food and uses it to repair itself just like yours does. We're more efficient at it so I only require one or two meals a week... unless I'm hurt."

"You should let me go. If you're made of"—she pondered the word and forced it out in a slow, deliberate pronunciation—"tech-no-lo-gy, The Many is gonna do stuff to you. He won't let you take me away from the Badlands."

"Do you want a nice piece of tape over your mouth?"

"No, please."

"Then stop talking about that spooky crap."

Althea peered up at her. "I'm not lying."

"You might believe it. That doesn't mean it's real."

She stared down at her feet while trudging along. "I'm only trying to warn you before it's too late."

"Where's that damn tape?"

"Please, don't."

"Then stop saying creepy stuff."

Althea sighed and followed the woman, half a step behind. Fortunately, Teal didn't walk *too* fast, but the tether didn't exactly give her much room to go exploring for a sharp piece of glass. Still, she kept looking around for one just in case, intending to fake tripping and falling to grab it.

Dense ruins gave way to open dirt marked with the scars of ancient roads for a little while before they wandered once more among crumbling towers built by the Ancients. Every so often, she spotted frozen words or symbols on a window or wall. They made her think of Paama and Ooru, and the Transit tribe's gods. It did seem strange that the Ancients would put the symbols all over the place, especially since no real sense of reverence existed about their placement. She had seen similar markings in the bad city, though with different pictures. The words had probably been different as well, but she hadn't known about frozen speech at the time.

Althea considered trying to scare the woman by mentioning the Zero police. Since Teal had come from the bad city, she had to know about them. That didn't necessarily mean she would be afraid of them, however. A warning that the Zero police would be angry at her for kidnapping Althea might make the woman keep her hidden when they got there and hurt any chance of calling for help.

Did not saying anything count as a lie? For the next half hour or so, she tried to make up her mind about that. Eventually, she decided that this woman had kidnapped her, so if the police got mad at her, she deserved it. Helping someone steal her had to be worse. As Teal had said about the Transit tribe, 'it was on them' to get out of here. It was on Teal not to make the Zero police angry.

A bright green blob of energy cruised by moderately faster than a thrown rock, passing through the space Teal's head had been in an instant before. The woman dropped to the ground with such speed she seemed to vanish and reappear.

Althea looked to the left at where the glowing mass had come from.

A shiny, silver machine man stood amid the rubble of a collapsed building, pointing an equally silver rifle in their general direction. The robot had features that generally approximated humanity in overall shape, though didn't at all try to look like a real person. Despite her standing out in the open and Teal flat on the ground, the tall robot continued trying to aim at the woman.

"Gah. Kid!" Teal grabbed Althea by the arm above the elbow and yanked her to the ground. "Get down!"

Althea fell on her side, half on top of Teal. "Untie me! You're gonna get me killed!"

The woman sprang up into a crouching run, hauling Althea across the street to take cover in a ruined building as green energy blasts whizzed by inches behind them. She tossed her to the ground in the corner, drew her gun, and leaned out the doorway, shooting bolts of blue light off to the left. Teal ducked back an instant before another green blob hit the doorframe, causing a section of concrete to melt into an orange, glowing mass.

Althea stared at the end of the tether by her foot... and grinned. The woman didn't hold onto her anymore. She rolled onto her knees, leapt to her feet, and ran to a doorway that led deeper into the building. A short hallway brought her to a room containing little more than crumbled pieces of ceiling and walls. She sent a surge of strength into her legs, then jumped out the window, landing on dirt covered in a dusting of small concrete bits.

The little stones stabbed into her feet like knives, but she kept going, her desperation to get home to her family far stronger than her fear of pain. Two Silver Men walking across the road a distance off to the right rotated their heads in her direction for a second, but continued shooting green blobs toward the building where Teal had taken her, for some reason disinterested in attacking her.

When she reached paving clear of tiny rocks, Althea sprinted hard down the street. She looked left and right for somewhere to hide, but the buildings here still had doors with knobs she couldn't reach with her hands trapped behind her. She considered dropping to the ground and trying to squirm her arms around in front of her, but that would waste time and let Teal catch her. She had to keep running. The first opening she spotted without a door, she dashed for... only to find what she thought to be a building was, in reality, a free-standing wall with nothing behind it.

Fear kept her going forward.

She dashed across the rubble to the next street where she spotted a somewhat-intact car and ran to it, spinning around to grab the handle behind her back. She pulled at it, grunting and snarling, but the door refused to open. Not wanting to waste time standing there in the open, she gave up on the car and kept going, flying down the street so fast her hair fluttered behind her like a flag in the wind.

Smashed buildings on both sides offered little in the way of protection for a block and a half. Finally, she noticed a four-story structure with metal walls that hadn't collapsed. She leapt another ruined car, zoomed over a length of sidewalk, and rammed her body into the door. The hit knocked most of the air out of her chest, but the door popped open. She bounced off it, stumbling into corridor, and slipped to land on her butt when ancient carpet ripped away from the floor under her.

Growling, Althea threw herself upright and ran to the only open door in the corridor, all the way at the end on the left. She hurried inside, kicked the door closed, then spun to look around at a small apartment. With little time to think, she crossed the main room to a short hallway, hurrying down it to a bedroom that reeked of mold.

The bed had collapsed into a mound of junk, as had the cabinets. She headed over to the closet, ducked inside, and tried to bite the doorknob. Her mouth wouldn't open wide enough to get a grip, so she leaned back and snagged the edge of the door with her toes, pulling it shut. Shivering from forcing so much adrenaline into her system, she backed up one step and sank to sit on the floor, trying to stay quiet.

Her everything hurt.

She closed her eyes, studying her life shapes and fixing small tears in her muscles or little cracks in the bones of her legs, hips, and feet. After a moment, the pain faded but the exhaustion remained. She rested her head on her knees, her hot breath blasting down her legs. Dark grime highlighted her toenails. Smudges of dried blood and dirt covered her legs. Her dress *still* stank like a compost pile, but she'd gotten away.

This isn't as bad as before. She tugged at her wrists. *Just need to find some glass. No stupid cuffs on my legs. The rope's easy to get rid of.*

Still, she had to wait for Teal to go away. No telling how long that woman would spend searching for her. Hiding in this closet for the rest of the day would probably be good enough. She could worry about getting rid of the cord later. Someone used to live in this place, so there might even be knives she could use. As soon as she got out of here, she'd go back to the Transit village. If she couldn't convince Ell-Gee to travel with her to where Kye was, she'd *make* him go. That man would probably be able to open the cage and let the queen out. And when he came back okay from going in there, the villagers would hopefully understand the place didn't have any curse.

And then she could try to convince Kye to bring her people away from the CRP. They lied to themselves without knowing it. Being underground wouldn't protect them. It would only take one wheelbot getting down there and many people would die. Those machines didn't work for any gods. They wanted to kill everything that moved.

That's weird. Why are they shooting at Teal? She's kinda like one of them.

Althea decided not to waste any time thinking about stuff she'd never understand and merely tried to be still and quiet. She breathed hard, chest pressed against her knees. Every time she inhaled, the cord squeezed her wrists. It infuriated her to have her hands stuck behind her, but trying to wriggle them around in front would make too much noise for now. She'd have to wait until that woman gave up and went away.

"C'mon out," said Teal, right outside the door.

No! Althea nearly burst into tears, but a flash of anger came on too fast, stomping on her childish reaction and leaving her glowering instead of sobbing.

"The cord's sticking out from under the door, kid. I can see you."

Althea looked down. Sure enough, the thin black cord passed by her toes and went straight under the door into the room. With a sigh, she wobbled to her feet and bumped the door, but it didn't open. She twisted to the side, reaching, but couldn't get a hand on the knob while tied. She faced forward and tried to use her toes, but her foot slid off the knob without turning it. She'd effectively locked herself in the closet.

"I'm stuck. I can't get out."

The door opened. Teal stood there giving her a 'really?' smirk. "What are you doing?"

"Trying not to be kidnapped."

"You have spirit, I'll give you that." The woman picked up the end of the tether.

"How did you find me?"

"Followed you. Not exactly difficult. You're pretty fast for a human child, but I'm pretty fast, too. And you breathe really loud."

"No I don't."

"My ears are pretty sharp." Teal winked.

Head down, Althea trudged ahead of her to down the hall and outside. Upon reaching the crumbling sidewalk, she peered up at the woman. "Please don't take me to the bad city. I have to go home to my family."

"Kid, there's nothing to be afraid of. My employers aren't going to hurt you... probably."

"Probably?" Althea raised both eyebrows. "You don't even know?"

"Well, it wouldn't be in their financial interests to kill you, but they might do tests or something."

"I hate tests. There's too many questions and I feel dumb if I get them wrong."

"Not that kind of test." Teal looked away, fidgeting. Though she didn't radiate any real emotion, she seemed guilty.

"Please!" Althea bounced on her toes. "I wanna go home. I love Father and Karina and they miss me so much."

Teal sighed. "When we get to the city, if you can do that psionic stuff to the corporate people and force them to let you go, that's not my problem. I'm just—shit."

"You have to make *mierda*?" Althea blinked.

The woman whirled toward her, scooped her up over one shoulder like a sack of grain, and sprinted. Teal's superhumanly fast stride hammered her narrow shoulder into Althea's gut. A hail of green plasma blobs raced by, splashing into clouds of emerald light on contact with ruined walls or the ground behind them. Four tall, silver-bodied robots hurried down the street after them, but didn't appear to have any chance of catching up to the synthetic woman.

Streets and alleys blurred into the distance. Althea bounced, her head hanging behind Teal's back. The woman's bony shoulder repeatedly jamming into her gut brought her to the edge of throwing up. She turned off her sense of pain, weathering another several minutes of being carried like a human duffel bag. Eventually, Teal slowed to a brisk walk, navigating dense piles of rubble that had collected in an alley too narrow for the CRP androids. She kicked apart a fence at the end, jogged across a street lined with half-melted cars, and rushed down a stairwell to an underground basement.

Teal carried Althea to the corner of the room, setting her down on her feet beside a thick pipe that emerged from the floor and ran straight up into the ceiling. After tying the end of the tether to the pipe, high enough to be out of Althea's reach, she hurried to the stairwell, leaned against the wall beside it, and pulled her gun out of its holster.

"It's stupid to leave me tied."

"Shh."

Althea peered up at the knot above her head. She tugged at the cord, trying to pull it down enough to bite, but the woman had looped it over a valve. Desperation growing, she looked around the floor for anything sharp, swiping her foot at a few promising shards, but they turned out to be flimsy plastic.

"If we have to run, it will take too long to untie me."

"Be quiet or they'll hear us," whispered Teal.

Frowning, Althea stared at the floor, unable to decide between furious or terrified. If one of those robots found her tied to a pipe, she'd be in big trouble and not the 'locked in a room as punishment' kind of trouble. She couldn't even sit on the floor with the tether secured so high off the ground. If bullets, or whatever those energy globs were, started flying, she had no way to get down.

Fear won out over anger. Althea's eyes flared brighter as she dumped psionic power into her body. Her already sore muscles throbbed, becoming stronger. She gripped the tether and pulled as hard as she could, trying to break the thin, black cord. Her feet slipped over the concrete, so she twisted around and braced one leg against the wall, pushing. Dark moldy slime gathered between her toes, her foot plowing a trench in the gunk. The cord stretched a little, but refused to snap.

Althea fought until her muscles hurt too much to move. Defeated, she slumped forward out of breath and healed herself. Her body had had quite enough of temporary amplified strength for a while. The mere thought of doing it again any time soon hurt.

While Teal kept watch at the door, Althea paced as much as the six-foot lead allowed. She hated being kidnapped by someone her powers didn't work on. When the Slave Catcher had tied her to a post, she'd sent out a psionic beacon asking for help, not particularly caring who showed up to provide that help. She hadn't wanted that awful man to die despite how cruel he had been to her, so she worried that beaconing now might hurt Teal. However, the woman didn't tie a cloth over her eyes to blind her. If something big and nasty like the canid showed up, she'd be able to calm it down and prevent it from killing anyone.

Fortunately, her mentally screaming for help would not attract the CRP robots since machines didn't react to her powers.

In the quiet of the abandoned basement, Althea closed her eyes and tried to gather her psionic power into a beacon, reaching out into the world, hoping someone nice would find and help her. A short while later, she figured it had either worked or wouldn't, so she relaxed.

They remained quiet and still, listening to every little sound for a little over an hour before Teal crept up the stairs.

Being left alone might have given Althea hope of escape, but she'd already run out of any expectation she could free herself from the stupid cord. It annoyed her that material she could cut so easily wouldn't break.

Teal jogged back into the room and over to her. "Looks like they gave up and went away."

"Great," said Althea with an eye roll. "I'm so happy. Yay."

"Salty little thing, aren't you?" Teal chuckled.

Althea lifted one leg and licked her knee. "Yeah… a little."

"Are you messing with me or are you serious?"

"I don't understand."

"Wow, kid. Just wow." Teal untied the tether from the pipe. "Time to go."

Althea grumbled, following the woman up the stairs. She spent a little more than an hour talking about Karina, Father, Querq, the people there, and how much she missed her home… and then she spent the rest of the day with a piece of tape over her mouth.

Teal didn't react at all to her attempts to talk telepathically. Althea didn't bother trying to mumble past the tape, but considered it a good sign the woman had done that. That meant the woman did have some emotions after all. Otherwise, Althea talking about how much she wanted to go home and how much she loved her family wouldn't have bothered the woman enough to silence her.

For hours, they scurried among the ruins of the Before-Time city, taking refuge whenever Teal thought she saw CRP androids.

As darkness approached, they took cover beneath a crumbling overpass.

Teal removed the tape without comment, let Althea make water, then tied her ankles to her hands again despite her whines of protest and wriggling. The woman fed her another 'chocolate' bar and gave her all the water she wanted.

Althea knelt there, picking at the knot between her ankles and listening to the weird gurgling noises the bar made in her stomach. It supposedly equaled a whole day's worth of food, but after six months in a real home, she wasn't used to eating so little. Despite the fairly small size of the bar, she somehow no longer felt hungry soon after eating it. Teal took the blanket and warmth emitter out of the pack, eased Althea over onto her side, and tucked her in for the night.

The overpass didn't offer all that much protection, but at least it would keep the rain off if any happened. Thoughts of rain called a memory from years ago. A raider group had kept her in the center of their camp, chained by one leg to a heavy piece of old car out in the open. She liked the rain, playing and dancing in it despite being a prisoner, a life she thought she'd left behind.

Yet once again, she found herself trapped.

In the past, she had been bound more by her fear than any physical restraint. Whenever she thought about how afraid she'd been of using her powers to protect herself, she felt ashamed. This moment, trapped purely by physical restraint, brought no shame, only an indignant sense of anger. Despite the quiet night and fairly warm blanket, she couldn't get comfortable, couldn't sleep with the cord cinched tight at her skin. Her anger grew and grew until she couldn't contain it anymore and wound up crying in rage.

"Aww, kid… don't be sad," said Teal. "Who wants to live out here in this waste? You're going to be happy when you get back to the real world."

"I'm not sad. I'm angry. I *hate* being kidnapped." She struggled at the cord for a few seconds, then shouted, "It's not fair!"

"Nothing is fair."

"I finally stop being scared and say I'm not gonna let anyone take me anymore, and I get taken by someone my magic—I mean psionics—don't work on."

"It happens that much?"

Althea gave up struggling and rolled her eyes. "You have *no* idea."

"Really?"

"Yes, really." She snarled. "People took me every few weeks before I had a real home. Sometimes, I'd stay in one place for a whole two months. But, I'm not gonna just let people kidnap me anymore."

"I'm not kidnapping you; I'm saving you from the land of primitives."

"Telemarketer!" shouted Althea.

Teal cracked up laughing. "What?"

"It's like the worst thing to say. A really bad word."

"Umm… where did you hear that?" Teal continued snickering.

"From a friend."

"Argh! I hate this!" She squirmed. "Let me out! Please untie me. I really hate it."

Teal sighed. "Sorry, but I don't want you running off."

She scooted around to stare at her. "But you can run a lot faster than me. If I tried to get away, you'd catch me."

"You're tiny. You can fit in places I can't."

Althea grumbled. "At least don't tie my hands and feet together. I can't even move."

"You not moving is the entire point. That way, I know where you are. Now go to sleep."

"I can't sleep like this."

"The faster you go to sleep, the faster I untie your legs."

She sagged limp. "If the big roaches find us, I'm gonna die. They're gonna bite me in the face."

"There aren't any of those around here. The bots kill everything."

"Nuh uh." She lifted her head. "I saw some a couple days ago in a building. And rats."

"Go to sleep."

"Grr. Are you gonna keep me tied the whole time?"

"Unless I find a big ass cat carrier, yes."

Althea rolled onto her back. "What's an ass cat carrier?"

"Forget it. Just go to sleep."

"Please!"

Teal grumbled. "You should've thought about that before you somehow got rid of the tracker."

"You know?"

"Of course. I can still read the signal coming from the same place you dropped it. How'd you do that anyway?"

"I told it to get out of me."

"Right... Go to sleep."

"Are you gonna untie me?"

"Are you going to keep pestering me until I do?"

"Will that work?"

"I still have tape."

Althea raspberried her, then sighed, closed her eyes, and tried to relax. In mere minutes, her legs cramped from being stuck in one position. Her ankles and wrists burned from fighting the rope. No matter how she tried to position herself, she couldn't stop squirming.

After spending almost two full days with her hands tied, she started to wonder if she would ever be able to move her arms again. Rachel, that woman from Vakkar's harem, had been stuck like that for months in handcuffs. Two days had already pushed Althea to the point where she felt tempted to lie, even if it got her in trouble.

Eventually, drowsiness filtered into her brain and she started to drift off.

Scuffling dragged her back from the edge of sleep. A dull *thud* accompanied a man grunting nearby.

Althea opened her eyes to several men and women wearing piecemeal leather armor held on by straps and chains surrounding Teal. One man already lay on the ground cradling his groin in both hands, screaming so loud his face turned blood red. Teal threw punches and kicks with such speed her limbs blurred. Three raiders went down in two seconds, but more continued rushing into the space beneath the overpass like a drowning tidal wave of bodies. Another man went flying off his feet from a kick to the jaw. An unconscious woman slid to a stop, her face inches from Althea's leg, nose clearly broken.

Althea scooted forward and touched her knee to the woman's cheek. She started to concentrate on healing, but someone pulled a bag over her head from behind and dragged her away. She screamed, but couldn't put up a fight while hogtied. Rather than scream, she merely sighed at being abducted again.

That's faster than usual. Teal only had me for a few days.

"Heh. This one's already wrapped up for us," said the woman holding her.

Growling, Althea gathered power to let off a blast of telempathic fear... but stopped at the sudden inexplicable notion that she should allow these people to take her. The thuds and thumps of a fight continued for a moment, then stopped.

"Get off me!" Teal roared. "Sons of bitches."

Thump.

"Damn. This bitch is pretty hard," said a man. "You gonna—"

Thud.

The shouts of a dozen men and women drowned out Teal's enraged screaming. A thin string snugged against Althea's neck, holding the cloth sack on, but not squeezing so tight it hurt. She concentrated on wanting to know *why* it felt like a good idea to allow these people to take her, but nothing came to mind. The woman who tightened the bag picked her up and carried her off, away from the continuing struggle.

Teal's shouts of 'get off me' and so on sounded a whole lot like Althea's protests at being tied. She couldn't help but have a moment of 'how do you like it?' but didn't take any joy in the turnabout. The same way she knew fate would punish her if she lied, she figured it punished Teal for being mean to her. Perhaps the legends of the Prophet had more truth than she ever really believed. Now, that woman had ended up tied as well.

She appeared to like being helpless as much as Althea did, which is to say… not one little bit.

22

THE VEE-EIGHTS

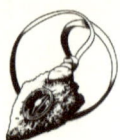

The woman carried Althea over one shoulder, walking for quite some time before slowing to a stop. Not seeing any point to struggling, crying out, or offering any protest, Althea contented herself to wait for some sign or feeling to make sense. Her magic—err, psionics—told her to go along with them. *Why* they did so, she had no idea. However, as these people had thoughts and emotions whatever their motivation, a strong sense of security came with them.

As soon as Althea wanted to be free, she would be.

A low creak from a rusty hinge sent a shiver down her back. Echoing footsteps and bouncing suggested the woman carried her down a flight of stairs into a place made of concrete. Teal's continuing grumbles soon followed overhead. The raider woman walked for a few minutes more, eventually entering a room. There, she slung Althea forward and deposited her on the floor, still hogtied with a bag over her head.

…. and walked away, leaving her alone.

The *clank* of a metal door closing followed.

Okay, now what?

She lay there patiently, waiting for something to happen or another feeling to give her some idea of what to do. She couldn't really move, nor could she see anything but fabric. Her stomach gurgled and cramped, objecting to the high-density nutrition bar. A small belch tasted like sour chocolate. She couldn't help but fidget at her bindings, almost as angry at the cord as she'd been at Hector when he shot Karina. Almost.

Total silence surrounded her for quite some time before the scuff of footsteps returned.

Althea held still.

A metal door opened with another creak.

People walked over to her. Hands closed around her biceps, lifting her into the air. One person on either side carried her out of the room. She hung suspended between them, knees well off the ground, feet still held close to her hands by cord. Only trust in her supernatural instincts kept her from letting off the mother of all telempathic fear bombs and demanding they untie her immediately.

They hauled her around for a minute or two before another door creaked and the echo of their footsteps lessened, suggesting they had gone from a narrow hall to a bigger room. They carried her a few more steps, then set her down with reasonable gentleness kneeling on bare concrete floor. Soon after they let go of her arms, someone yanked the sack off her head. Her hair puffed free of the bag and mostly fell over her face, long enough to touch the floor since she slouched.

Althea found herself in front of a fancy throne made of scrap metal, car parts, and I-beams fused together. The woman occupying it appeared to be in her early thirties and regarded her greedily, her eyes cold and cruel. Long, wild black hair framed a pale face marked by numerous scars from bladed weapons. Thick leather armor adorned with crude spikes covered her chest and shoulders, her legs half hidden under a baggy skirt of black plastic sheeting. Large rat skulls decorated her knee-high boots. Metal claws glinted from the fingers of her leather gloves, sharp, but too small to be weapons intended for a real fight.

Behind the throne, a dark curtain partially obscured a large alcove with a bed and several naked men chained to the walls, most quite bruised. Though rare, she had seen female raider chiefs keep harems of men before.

Oh. That's why I had to come here. I need to help them.

Despite remaining hogtied and kneeling, Althea refused to feel subservient to this woman. She didn't consider herself a prisoner at all, only there because she had thus far chosen not to leave. The man standing on her left reached down and gathered her blonde hair off her face, holding her head so the woman in the throne could see her eyes.

Their apparent leader gave off the usual emotional greed spike that all the raiders did whenever they captured her.

"Rejoice my warriors," said the woman. "You have claimed the Prophet for the Vee-Eights!"

Forty or so people standing behind Althea broke out in cheers, some chanting 'Motor City,' while quite a few shouted 'Puma' repeatedly. The bandit chief radiated pride at the word, likely her name.

"Vee-Eights?" asked Althea. "What is that?"

Puma laughed. "An ancient source of great power! So... this is the Prophet. Much smaller than I thought. I expected someone much... grander."

"If anyone is hurt, I will help them. But I cannot stay here."

"Oh, little mouse..." Puma crouched and cupped her cheek in one hand, the tips of her claws nearly drawing blood by her ear. "You belong to us now. There is no going anywhere."

"I am not a slave."

Puma laughed, stood, and raised her arms to the sides before gesturing at her. "The Prophet says she is not a slave."

Everyone broke up into raucous laughter.

Puma pointed at the two raiders flanking Althea, a man and a woman. Her smile died in an instant. "Get her fitted."

They grabbed her by the arms again, hauling her into the air and carrying her across the chamber to an archway on the left. Dozens of chains and shackles hung on the wall to the right of the entrance. Four Xs made of I-beams welded together stood at the back of the room. Teal occupied the leftmost one, suspended by chains padlocked around her wrists and ankles. A woman in the same armor as the raiders hung on the X beside her, beaten bloody. The third set of crossed beams held a man in torn grey/brown clothing.

At the right side of the room, directly opposite the entrance, three giant bird cages swayed on chains attached to the ceiling, all empty. The raiders carried Althea over to the cages and set her on the floor. The woman took a rope off her belt that bore a series of black marks at regular intervals, adjusted her grip on it, and snugged it around Althea's neck.

"Hmm. Really small. We gotta make a new collar for you. All the ones we got are too big." She removed the rope and counted black marks. "A three."

"You will not put a collar on me," said Althea.

The raiders laughed again.

Still chuckling, the man picked her up and stuffed her into one of the hanging cages. He slammed the door, locked it, then pulled a knife from a sheath on his belt. Althea didn't read any bad emotion from him, so she remained calm. He reached into the cage and sliced the cord off her wrists and ankles, freeing her.

"Thank you." Althea pulled her arms around in front of herself and rubbed her sore wrists.

"Sit tight, kiddo." The woman patted the cage, flaring her eyebrows. "Wouldn't want anything bad to happen to ya."

"Hey," whispered the man. "Be careful. This is the Prophet."

The woman's arrogant grin faded. She went pale in the face and they hurried out of the room.

"Well, I guess you got your wish," muttered Teal. "They untied you. Of course, you're in a cage now."

Althea shrugged. "I like being in a cage more than being tied. But this one is kinda small. Not enough room for me to stand up inside. It's like the Wagon Man's cage. Well, it's bigger than that one. I was much smaller then, so that cage had to be smaller than this."

"Wow, that's kinda sad."

"Did you forget you kidnapped me?" asked Althea. "You're just as bad as the raiders."

Teal struggled at the chains holding her to the X. "Too damned many of the bastards. Overwhelmed me. Dammit. This, I was not expecting."

"Obviously."

"There you go being salty again."

Althea massaged the red marks out of her wrists, then did the same for her ankles. Having her hands loose made her so happy she almost didn't even care about sitting in a cage. Nor did she attack the door. She could tell by looking at it that she lacked the strength to break out. However, as soon as she wanted to escape, she would leave.

"Hey what did they mean about 'be careful that's the Prophet?'" asked Teal.

"It is what the legend says. Ill fortune finds those who mistreat the Prophet," recited Althea.

"Isn't kidnapping you mistreating you?" asked Teal.

"I guess the legends are true then." Althea glanced at her. "Since you've wound up a slave, too."

Teal smirked.

"Is that really the Prophet?" asked the raider woman on the second X. "Please help us. They're going to kill me."

"I will," said Althea.

Teal kept struggling, chains rattling at the steel beams. The anger in her expression gradually changed over the course of about twenty minutes to fear.

A brief tingle crept down Althea's back. The bizarre inclination to accept her present captivity vanished. That meant whatever reason she needed to be here had come to pass. Maybe helping those men in the other room, or... she glanced at Teal, who clearly appeared worried and frightened. *Oh. Now I understand.* She grasped the steel slat bars in front of her and leaned her face against them, smiling at her former abductor. "Being kidnapped is bad. You understand now?"

Teal sighed at the ceiling. "You've gotta be kidding me."

"You don't like being tied, do you? I think those people are going to hurt you."

"Okay, okay, kid. You're right. Being kidnapped is bad. Go on and use your powers to get us out of here."

Althea cocked her head. "Will you promise to help me go home instead of kidnapping me?"

"I read about you," said Teal. "You wouldn't leave me here no matter what I do."

"That's true." Althea glanced down. "But I'm still not sure if you are a person or a machine. Those two people have thoughts and I can feel their emotions. I will help them."

Teal kicked and thrashed at the chains. "I'm legally a person. You can't leave me here."

Althea lifted her head, staring at the struggling woman for a moment. "Then why don't you act like one? *People* don't kidnap children for pay-things."

Teal squirmed and pulled at the chains, her expression alternating between anger and fright. Althea sat in the cage and let her feet dangle, patiently waiting, watching her.

After about ten minutes, Teal sighed and hung limp. "Okay, fine. You win. Get us out of here and I will take you home."

"Do you mean that? Are you sorry for being mean to me or are you just afraid of being hurt?"

"Dammit, kid, will—"

The room's big metal door swung inward, crashing against the concrete wall with a loud *boom*. Puma strode in like a victorious queen, hands on her hips, claw-gloves glinting. Four other raider women and two men followed her. She approached Teal, looking her up and down while rubbing her chin.

Althea pulled her legs into the wobbling cage and squatted, holding the bars for balance.

"Hmm. My warriors tell me you killed four and took out nine more before you went down. That is impressive." Puma patted her on the hip, grinning. Her smile shifted to a snarl; she raked her claw gloves at Teal's thigh, shredding the jumpsuit and raking shallow bloody scratches to her knee.

Teal screamed in agony. Red blood oozed from the slashes.

"Interesting." Puma examined her claws, turning her hand to make the bloody tips catch the light. "Normally, I'd give a badass like you a chance to join us instead of the usual choice between death or becoming fuckmeat. But, you're one of *them*, aren't you? You're way too strong to be a person. *They* made a Silver Man look just like one of us."

"No," said Teal. "I'm not with the CRP."

"CR-what?" barked Puma. "The hell are you talking about."

"The androids you call Silver Men. I'm not one of them. They try to kill me, too."

"Hah. Bullshit." Puma snapped her fingers at a woman standing beside her with a sword on her belt. "Cut it open and see how it works."

Althea leaned her face between the bars and yelled, "Stop!"

23

ENOUGH

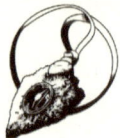

Puma turned her head to glare at Althea, a look of shock on her face.

Althea narrowed her eyes.

"I don't give a shit if you're the Prophet or not. No one barks at Puma and don't bleed for it." She yanked a knife from her belt.

Althea's upper lip curled with a snarl. She projected radiant telempathic fear, her eyes flaring bright enough to cast shadows from the raiders on the wall behind them. The entire entourage recoiled, collapsing to the ground and screaming. Puma and one of the men burst into tears like terrified children. Althea let the cruel raider chief have a stronger blast, reducing the woman to a simpering, sobbing wreck, huddled in a ball on the floor, wailing for her mother.

She shifted her gaze to the woman who measured her for a collar. "Let me out of the cage."

The woman shivered in place, staring at her.

"Open the cage."

With the grace of a malfunctioning robot, the woman tottered across the room, took the keys off a wall hook, stiff-legged it over to the cage, and unlocked the door. Althea shoved it open with her foot, sat on the edge, and dropped to the floor. Wails of terror came from the outer chamber by the throne. When she turned to face the room, all the raiders cringed away from her, whimpering.

"Holy shit," whispered Teal. "Holy freakin' shit..."

Althea padded over to Puma and glared down at her; eyes like azure flashlights painted the woman's face blue. "The Prophet is no one's slave."

The woman cowered away from her. "Please don't hurt me!"

"She's just a little kid," whispered one of the other trembling female raiders. "What the hell am I so scared of?"

"I dunno," whined the man next to her.

"You." Althea pointed at the woman with the keys, then Teal and the other two. "Let them down."

The raider scrambled over, in so much of a hurry to obey she fumbled trying to get the key in the padlocks. She eventually released Teal, then the captive woman, then the man. The two humans collapsed to the floor, moaning and rubbing their arms.

Teal didn't appear the least bit sore from her short time hung up on a giant metal X. She walked over to Puma and took her gun back. "Someone's a naughty kitty." She pointed the gun at Puma's head but lowered her arm before Althea could yell at her to stop. "I should kill all of them, but you're probably going to tell me not to."

"Please don't. I can't make you, but you don't have to kill them."

Teal put her foot on Puma's chest and kicked her over backward. "Nah. Seeing that one cry for her mommy is better than killing her. How long's that gonna last."

One of Archon's people who she'd hit with a sad bomb had gotten stuck permanently catatonic. At least... until Althea found out about it and demanded the Zero police bring her to him so she could fix it. The man *had* tried to kidnap her, but he didn't deserve to spend the rest of his life making water and *mierda* in his pants and drooling on himself. She had, perhaps, hit him too hard. These raiders hadn't received that much of a wallop.

"Not long. Hours. If she sees me again, she'll probably be afraid of me."

"Good. Look, kid. I'm sorry. I'll help you get home."

"Thank you." She pointed at her. "No tying."

Teal raised a hand. "Deal."

The formerly captive raider woman helped the man up, supporting him. Neither one appeared to be in great shape, but they managed to limp over.

"We should get the hell out of here," said Teal.

Althea looked around.

"What?"

"Where is it?" asked Althea.

"Where's what?"

"The hell." Althea peered up at her, confused.

Teal blinked. "What are you talking about?"

"You said we need to get the hell out of here. Where is it?"

"Oh for shit's sake, kid. Just… it's a figure of speech." Teal took her by the hand and pulled her to the door. "Get the hell out means leave fast."

Althea looked up at her while hurrying to the door. "Why didn't you say that then?"

They emerged in the large room… and stopped short at the sight of fifty or sixty raiders pointing guns and swords at them.

"That's not good," whispered Teal.

Althea glared at the raiders. She held her arms out, sprouting her energy wings and floating off the ground until her head hovered inches from the roof. Blinding white light washed over the raiders, making most of them squint and cringe back. A few raised weapons.

She set off a fear bomb and shouted, "Go away!" before pointing at the woman with the smashed face. "Except you. You stay."

The Vee-Eights screamed and crashed into each other, everyone trying to flee in different directions at the same time.

"And stop being meanies!" shouted Althea at the fleeing raiders.

Teal laughed. "You are one weird kid. Meanies?"

Eventually, the panic stricken raiders all managed to find the hallway out of the room and fled up the stairs at the end out into the night. Only the one woman remained, trembling in place. Althea glided down to a tiptoe landing, and padded up to her.

"What are you doing?" asked Teal.

"She's hurt. I tried to help her outside, but they put a bag over my head." Althea grasped her hand and linked to the raider's life essence. Thin black lines in the white of her bone shape revealed a shattered skull, as if the woman had been hit in the nose with a big hammer. She fed power into the raider, forcing the bone splinters to migrate back where they belonged and knit together. "Okay. Now you can go away."

The woman ran like hell.

"Kid?" asked Teal. "What the heck?"

"Her face was broken."

"I know. I broke it," said Teal.

"And I un-broke it." Althea folded her arms and turned to face her, the light from her long energy ribbon wings washing over Teal and the two other captives.

"What the hell?" asked Teal. "You seriously have wings?"

"Yes." Althea walked over to the former raider and the man, resting one had each on their arms. Eyes closed, she concentrated on their life energy, repairing bruises, a few cracked ribs, and damaged muscles.

"Do they work?" Teal jogged to the raiders' supply stash, recovered her backpack, and also swiped a large—probably rat meat—steak, which she ate right away.

"I told you I jumped out of your flying machine." Althea let her wings recede into her back, darkening the room.

"Wow." Teal shook her head. "No damn wonder they paid so much for you."

"You promised!" Althea stomped, glaring at her.

Teal held her hands up. "Relax. Just saying. I'm not going back on my promise."

The two former captives ran to the supply area as well, devouring a rat steak each as well as a small bread loaf. Teal put her backpack on, checked her gear, and walked to the door. Althea ran around the throne to the harem chamber.

Five men looked up at her in varying degrees of coherence.

She sighed. "This is gonna take a few minutes. Will you please find the key to let them down?"

"It's probably on queen bitch," said Teal. "Yeah, sure. Be right back."

Althea tended to each man in turn, mostly curing sicks and bruises. Three had wispy green stuff floating in their blood-presence. She initially thought of it as poison, but remembered the young woman she'd met in the bad city who'd been on 'drugs.' Puma had probably forced the men to eat the drugs for some reason. Regardless of why they had bad stuff in their bodies, Althea gathered it up and purged it. While she worked, Teal walked around opening the padlocks that kept them chained by the neck to the wall.

When Althea finished healing them, two of the men ran out and raided the stores for clothes and weapons. One curled up in a ball and whimpered. The last tried to grab Teal's gun, but she threw him to the floor.

That man gave off such a strong sense of sadness, Althea suspected he had intended to shoot himself. She hammered him with a telempathic boost of happy, horrified at the idea someone would *want* to die. He sat up with a manic grin, laughed like a fool, and ran off, naked as anything, into the Badlands, still cackling.

"Umm, kid, I think you broke that one." Teal whistled.

"He was gonna hurt himself, so I made him happy."

Teal cringed. "That's not happy. That's psychotic."

She wondered briefly if she did something bad. The man felt happy. Certainly, forcing someone to be happy had to be better than allowing them to murder themselves, right? She gave the whimpering man a slightly weaker boost of happiness. He smiled, but made no effort to move.

He's more broken than Aya was.

"I don't know what to do to help this man."

"He's probably beyond help. Come on, we should get out of here before Puma snaps out of whatever you did to her."

Althea squatted in front of the whimpering, smiling man. *"Go somewhere safe."*

He sat up, stood, and walked out like a robot.

"That's one way to do it." Teal took her hand and led her to the door.

The woman and man who had been chained to the Xs followed them outside, still munching on food. Teal paused, looked around, then picked a direction and resumed walking. Althea couldn't tell east from west at night as she had no sun to go by. All the ruins appeared the same in every direction.

"Are we going the right way?"

Teal folded her arms, seeming frustrated. "Yeah. It's gonna be lot longer of a damn walk than East City, but whatever."

"You're really taking me home? To Querq?"

Teal patted her on the head. "Yes. I promise. I owe you one for getting me out of there."

After only a few minutes of travel, Althea yawned.

"Oh sure, *now* you want to sleep." Teal chuckled. "Kids."

24

DEAL

Teal guided their small group into a cluster of ruins where the majority of the buildings still stood—more or less. It appeared to have been a downtown section of high-rises, though nothing remained of any structure past the fifth story. Most of the walls had hundreds of bullet holes, though time and weather had enlarged them and eroded the facades.

Of course, *now* broken glass seemed to be everywhere. Althea made a sour face at the pieces and rubbed her wrist.

"Here... This looks good." Teal pointed at a doorway.

A few black and white tiles remained on the floor of a space lined with booth tables. Piles of junk had collected in the windows, offering a reasonable amount of concealment from the outside.

Teal looked around briefly, then walked to the back of the room where she forced open a door. "This works. We can hide in the kitchen. Should be far enough out of sight in here."

Althea crept in behind her. The former raider and the man followed as well, laying down on a rubberized floor mat next to a freestanding counter. With a yawn, Althea lowered herself to sit near them.

Teal dug the blanket out from the backpack and tossed it to Althea before sitting with her back to the island counter, facing the door.

"You're not going to sleep?" Althea covered herself with the blanket.

"Nah. I don't really have to. We just sleep to feel normal. Some of us don't even realize we're not human, so we sleep like humans. If we figure it out, then we get to do all sorts of neat things. But it plays with our heads."

"What does that mean?"

"It can make you crazy, not being human when you really want to be. You grow up thinking you're normal, just like everyone else, then one day you discover you're strong enough to kick a door right off its hinges." Teal looked down. "Still trying to get used to stuff."

"I'm sorry."

"Ehh. Not your fault. It comes in handy sometimes."

"How?"

"Like taking jobs to capture a psionic. They can't really do anything to me." Teal shot a sly smile her way. "Sorry again."

Althea thought about Anna tossing lightning or Kate hurling fireballs. "Some psionics can still hurt you."

"Yeah, I know. You're a telempath, right? And a healer. Not too scary."

"Did you see Puma?" asked the raider woman. "She cried like a two-year-old."

"Okay, this kid isn't too scary to *me* then." Teal reclined on the chair. "Go to sleep, all of you. I'll keep watch."

Althea stared up at the ceiling. Flat on her back, not tied up, sorta-comfortable. "Can we go let Kye out of the tank where you found me?"

"I'm already taking you home. I owe you *one*, not two."

Her heart sank. She fidgeted, picking at her fingernails, her mind teasing her with memories of Ooru and Paama smiling at her. How happy they'd been when they realized the boy wouldn't die. She couldn't leave them and their entire tribe—especially that strange little girl who liked to zap herself—here where the CRP could murder them all at any minute. She also couldn't leave Kye in that tank. Even if she got home, she'd feel horrible for betraying her promise to find her.

"I don't know how to open that cage. I can probably find my way home on my own. Will you make helping me get her out of that cage what you owe me instead?"

"Damn. You really are one weird kid."

"I'm not weird. I'm Althea."

Teal chuckled.

"Where are you from?"

"East City."

"Do you have a family?"

"Not really."

Althea sighed. "Sorry. That's sad. You had to have parents."

"Not me. My actual mother didn't want me. She knew she was a synthetic but had no idea we could have kids. The people I grew up believing were my parents are human. I wasn't."

"You're angry at them for not being your real parents?"

"I still have tape."

Althea giggled. "Don't be. Father didn't even know my mother, but he loves me. Why do you care if you have the same blood as them if they love you? They're still your parents."

"Whatever. You wouldn't understand."

"I'm an orphan, too."

"No, I mean... Not being like them. Not being human."

"I can heal people by touching them. I have wings. My eyes glow. Everyone wants to steal me. You're right. I have no idea what it's like to be different."

"Aww, kid..."

"I used to believe I didn't deserve to be happy. Raiders took me all the time. Once, a big fight started and all the slaves escaped. The people wanted to bring me with them, but I didn't go. I stayed there and let the raiders keep me because if I went with those people, the raiders would have chased us and killed everyone to get me back. I was pretty stupid. I could have stopped them, but I didn't because I was too scared."

"You? Scared? You're like eleven and you've got more balls than some mercs I've worked with."

Althea looked at her like she called the sky brown. "I don't have balls. I'm a girl."

Teal laughed herself to tears. "Holy crap you're adorable."

"Why do you keep saying stuff that doesn't mean what you say?"

"People just do that."

Althea stuck out her tongue. "There. See. You just called yourself people. You're people."

Teal stared at her for a long moment, then looked down. "My name's really Ash. Didn't want to use it when I started doing merc work. Pretty stupid huh? Tried to think of a fake name on the spot and I just chose the color of my hair."

"That's not as stupid as letting people kidnap you over and over and not standing up for yourself."

"Why didn't you?"

"Scrags are scared of mystics. I didn't want them to burn me alive."

"But you could have forced them not to burn you alive."

"Yeah. I know that *now*."

"And how the heck do you know what balls are at your age?"

"I used to get kidnapped by raiders all the time."

Teal gasped, staring at her. "You poor..."

"No." Althea shook her head. "Whenever they get hit there, they yell 'my balls!'"

"Oh." The woman cackled. "Okay."

Althea shrugged. "They like stabbing each other there, too. I've had to put them back on people sometimes."

The man and the former-raider both groaned.

"That's far too much information," said Teal. "Wow. I thought I'd seen some shit as a merc. You poor kid."

Althea scooted closer and cuddled up beside her.

Teal gave her a 'must you' stare, but didn't protest. She glanced at the others. "So how did you wind up on the cross? You're one of them."

The woman shrugged, not bothering to sit up. "We raided a settlement a long way off in the south. I kicked in a door, found this chick with two tiny kids. I let her and the kids slip away. Someone saw me do it, and Puma wanted me executed as an example of disobedience."

"What's your name?" asked Althea.

"Yaz."

"And him?" asked Teal.

"Cobb," said the man. "I do courier runs between settlements. Tried to take a shortcut, figuring I'd play chicken with the crazy robots. Didn't expect to run into a pack of raiders this close to Detroit. This is *not* the place anyone with sense goes."

"Yet here we all are," said Yaz.

"How'd you end up here, girlie?" asked Cobb.

"If you're not talking to the eleven-year-old, I'm going to break your face." Teal examined her fingernails.

"My name isn't 'girlie' either. It's Althea."

Cobb sucked air through his teeth. "Hey, no need for violence. Sorry. How'd you end up here, ma'am?"

"Better." Teal lowered her hand to her lap. "Our ship crashed."

"Oh. Yeah, that happens all the time." Cobb yawned.

"If you're like a machine, how'd you get born?" asked Yaz.

"Same way a reassembler makes a damned cheeseburger," muttered Teal.

"Huh?" asked Yaz. "What's a cheeseburger?"

Althea smiled up at Teal. "This is more like what it would be to have a mom."

"If you try to hug me, I will hogtie you again."

Althea stuck her tongue out.

Teal chuckled.

"Wait, *again*?" asked Cobb. "You tied that kid up?"

"It's complicated." Teal smirked. "She's a real terror when she's had too much caffeine."

"What's caffeine?" Althea peered up at her.

"You abducted this girl?" asked Yaz.

"She's the Prophet. Doesn't everyone?" Teal grinned.

"That's not funny." Althea sighed.

"I wouldn't technically call it abducting her. More like relocating her against her will." Teal waved her hand about. "The end result would've been better off for her than living out here."

"No it wouldn't." Althea shook her head. "The bad city people would put me in a cage and done stuff to me trying to figure out how I work. I want my family."

Teal kicked at the floor, muttering to herself for a few seconds. "That's not what they said they'd do, but... corporations lie all the time."

"I don't like corp'rations." Althea yawned, snuggled against her, and closed her eyes.

"Must you?" asked Teal.

"Yes," said Althea, as she drifted off to sleep. "I must."

CONTAMINANTS

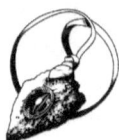

Brief flashes of memory flickered in Althea's consciousness in the few seconds before she woke up. Images appeared of strange places with strange things. She recognized a sofa, though it didn't look like any furniture she could remember seeing. Glowing stuff, little robots, and lots of silver metal blurred in a haze surrounding her. She caught a glimpse of a window beyond which stretched a field of reddish dirt. Mostly, the visions focused on a man and a woman who kept smiling at her.

Althea opened her eyes, staring down the length of Teal's leg at the woman's boot.

"You drooled on me."

With a grunt, Althea pushed herself up to sit and wiped her bleary eyes. "Sorry."

"It's okay."

Two yawns later, Althea folded the blanket, set it aside, then stumbled across the kitchen to a small bathroom. A few seconds after she sat on the toilet, it occurred to her that the weird dream must have been the clairvoy ants telling her about Teal. The people must be her parents, and the odd places, the modern city. She looked up from the floor, gazing out the doorway at the blue-green haired woman. Maybe because her body was metal and plastic and had no aura, it could soak up the emotional energy from her parents. They had to know they'd adopted a synthetic, and still loved her like any other child.

Althea smiled at that, and let her head hang while she finished unloading her overfull bladder.

Yaz hurried over and stood by the door, staring at her as if that would make her go faster. As soon as Althea got up, the former raider ran in.

Cobb pulled dried meat and bread out of a sack, offering some to Althea when she returned to sit between him and Teal. She took it, thanked him, and proceeded to eat. He offered some to Teal, who declined.

"It's okay. I'm special."

Cobb shrugged in an 'okay, suit yourself' sort of way. "Is it true what Puma said? Are you really one of them?"

"No. If I was part of the CRP, I'd have already killed all three of you."

Althea looked up, paused in mid-chew.

"I'm not, and I won't."

She resumed eating.

Teal handed her the canteen. "Push the green button at the top to make the water come out. Don't push the orange one or it'll overheat and go off like a nuke, kill everything within five miles."

Althea dropped the canteen.

"You're not much for jokes, are you, kid?" Teal laughed. "Orange one just makes hot water."

"I like jokes, but you haven't told any yet." Althea stared under flat eyebrows at her.

"You are a salty little thing." Teal shook her head, smiling

Althea examined the genesis canteen, locating two rubberized buttons at the point where the little neck on top met the rounded bottle. Pushing the green one activated the spurt of water. The slow stream annoyed her, but she drank quite a bit to chase the dryness out of her mouth from the jerky and bread.

After everyone finished eating, Teal headed to the door at the end of the restaurant room and listened. Evidently hearing nothing alarming, she leaned out and looked both ways.

"Clear."

They emerged from the building in a single file line, Althea right behind Teal, with Yaz next and Cobb at the back. As before, Teal didn't appear the least bit hesitant about where to go, not once looking at the sky to measure the sun or seeming confused at direction. She did, however, pause by the edges of ruined buildings to look around before starting off across any significantly large stretch of open ground.

Weak sunlight from an overcast sky made the day chilly and the wind cold. Althea somewhat remembered the names of the months that the learning machine tried to teach her, but forgot which one happened now. 'Spring' sounded right for the time, but none of the months had that name. The farm where Karina worked started planting new crops a week or two ago, which kept everyone working longer hours than usual. The Zero police had brought technology to help the farm grow even better, stuff they called chemicals, some small robots that helped with physical work like digging, and a couple tiny orbs that flew around checking on the plants and looking for problems. Unlike a person, those things watched the farm without ever needing to stop and sleep.

She daydreamed about being home, barely able to contain her eagerness to be with her family again. The quiet electric whine of the small farm orbs seemed to drift out of her head into reality. Althea tried to stop thinking about them, but the noise continued.

"Teal?"

"Hmm?"

"Do you hear that?"

"What?"

"The noise like the flying ball robots make."

Teal stopped and looked back at her, worried. "You can hear that, too?"

"Yeah."

"Crap. That means one's close." She looked around at the sky for a second, drew her gun, and shot a blue laser into the air.

Althea whirled to look, gasping at the sight of a flaming object careening out of the sky ahead of a smoke trail. Another flying wing machine like the one Paama knocked down with a rock careened into the ground. This one, however, wouldn't need to be finished off with spears. It exploded on impact.

"We have to hide. Now!" whisper-shouted Teal. "Go!"

She ran.

Althea sprinted after her. Yaz almost managed to keep up with them, but Cobb fell behind.

Bright green blobs whizzed past them, burning holes in buildings or leaving glowing orange spots on the ground. Teal hurdled a dead car, another plasma glob missing her by a few feet, and dashed around the corner of a building. Althea also leapt the car, for the first time in her life unable to overrun someone when she really wanted to go fast.

Teal skidded to a stop beside a crumbling wall and looked back. "Where's Cobb?"

"Right behind me," shouted Yaz.

"Shit. He can't keep up." Teal pulled her gun and jumped through a hole that used to be a window. "Get in here and get down."

Althea leapt after her, landing in a debris-strewn lot surrounded by the remains of walls. The tallest part only came up to her chin. Yaz dove in as a plasma blob hit the window frame above her. She landed flat on her chest and slid across the dirt. Another two glowing green bolts hit the road outside. Cobb screamed — but appeared alive and unhurt a second later, running for the opening.

Teal leaned around the wall, firing at something in the distance.

Cobb dove in the window and crawled to the west wall, huddling against the debris. Althea threw herself flat to the ground by the highest section of the north wall. Yaz ran to the southwest corner and crouched behind a pile of head-sized bricks.

Plasma globs flew over the wall where Teal had taken up a position. Some hit the concrete, leaving melt holes all the way through, each about the diameter of Althea's thigh. She stared at the glowing tunnels in horror, finally understanding what had left the ghastly wounds in people she'd seen.

Something exploded in the distance. A deep toneless voice said, "Error. System failure."

Teal fired twice rapidly, then ducked. Green energy hit the windowsill, throwing a splash of molten rock into the air. A few small bits landed on Yaz twenty feet away, making her shriek and swat at her legs. Crunching came from the west.

Althea looked up the same instant a seven-foot-tall silver machine man walked through a knee-high section of wall right near her. For an instant, she stared at her distorted reflection in its mirror-polished thigh plate. It pointed a gleaming chrome-finished rifle at Teal. Cobb lunged to his feet, swinging a length of rebar with a concrete hunk on one end like a club into the CRP robot's somewhat-human face. Cobb's attack barely scratched the machine, but he hit it hard enough that its plasma bolt went high, passing over Teal's head.

He swung again, aiming for the rifle. The CRP walker caught the rebar with its left hand, stalling the swing cold. Teal shot it, surgically nailing it in the eyes with a series of rapid pulses. Its head burst into flames, the body lapsing into a shuddering, jerky fit. Rigid, it fell over backward like a plank, crushing another section of concrete. Cobb grabbed the rifle, tugging on it, but couldn't budge it from the dead machine's grip.

A plasma glob whizzed over the shallow wall, nailing him in the head with a *splat* like a watermelon dropped off the roof of a building. Only a smoking stump of neck remained, the remainder of his skull evaporated in a smoky red mist. Althea screamed as the icy claw of a departing life scratched at her heart.

Teal sprinted in a blur to the downed robot. She shot the hand with her laser pistol, melting the thumb off, then wrenched the plasma rifle from its grip, breaking one of the remaining metal fingers. Another CRP robot appeared by the window at the east wall where she'd been shooting from. She pivoted, firing two green globs into its chest. They melted deep holes ringed with glowing molten metal in the armor plating, exposing its insides. Sparks flew like a hose from the damage. The machine fell out of sight, then exploded with a near blinding flash and deep concussive *whump* that knocked dust off the walls into a fleeting ghost image of the ruins before it dissipated on the breeze.

Althea burst into tears, staring at Cobb's remains. She crawled to him, grabbed his hand, and attempted to link to his life essence... but felt no connection. Wailing, she tried to call on the same power she'd somehow tapped for Shepherd, though couldn't manage to make anything happen.

"We gotta run!" shouted Yaz.

"No! Stay down!" Teal popped up over the wall, fired three plasma blasts, then ducked an instant before five came flying back over her, striking the dirt in the middle of the ruin and kicking up plumes of grey silt.

Another blinding flash went off in the distance, the explosion far enough away it didn't seem all that loud.

Teal popped up again, fired, and ducked. Another explosion went off. "I got this. Stay down. Kid, can you shoot?"

"No," sobbed Althea. "Cobb's dead."

"What the hell does that have to do with you shooting?" She popped up again, fired once, yelled, "Shit," and hit the deck, crawling to the right.

A storm of green plasma melted a doorway-sized hole in the wall where she'd been.

Yaz screamed, leapt to her feet, and ran, jumping the south wall and taking off down the street.

"Stupid bitch," muttered Teal.

A hissing whoosh went by, leaving a thin trail of smoke hanging in the air. A muted *whump* followed. Yaz let out a clipped shriek.

"No!" shouted Althea.

She jumped up, ran three steps, then ate dirt when Teal jumped on her an instant before a plasma bolt went over their heads.

"Stay down, kid!"

Althea clawed at the ground, trying to pull herself forward. "I gotta help her before she dies!"

Teal, still sitting on her, pivoted to the rear and fired over and over, ten, fifteen, twenty times. Multiple explosions went off in the distance. Another CRP walker burst through the east wall right in front of them. Althea screamed. Teal spun so fast her arms blurred. She fired a plasma bolt into its face, knocking the robot back a split second before it fired into the dirt two feet away from Althea's leg.

After firing again into the walker-bot's face, Teal grabbed Althea's arm and hauled her upright. "We got a hole. Need to go *now*."

"Don't leave her!" shouted Althea, pulling at her. "Please!"

"You are gonna get us all killed."

"She's not dead! I didn't feel her die! We gotta help her! It's what people do!"

Teal ducked a plasma glob, then stood tall and fired once. A running CRP bot caught the bolt in the neck. Its head flew off amid a spray of molten metal, spinning into the air. The body kept on going until it crashed into a wall some forty feet away.

"Okay, fine. Go. If you die, then I'm off the hook for walking all the way across the effing Badlands."

"You don't really mean that." Althea charged her muscles and leapt over the wall to the street, sprinting in the direction Yaz had gone.

The woman lay not far from the ruin where they'd taken cover, her left leg blown off at the thigh. Most of the limb lay a short distance away, still burning.

Teal ran out behind her, firing plasma off to the left at a shorter, but wider CRP robot that had tank treads instead of legs, its shoulders brimming with small cucumber-sized rockets. Althea didn't pay attention to what exploded or whistled past her head. She ran to Yaz and grabbed her arm.

Before she could do anything, Teal grabbed them both and dragged them off the road into an alley between buildings. "Work here. I'll cover you. Do it fast." She rushed to the alley mouth aiming the plasma rifle around the corner. "And if you have any relationship with luck, we could really use some. This rifle only has six shots left."

Althea grabbed Yaz by the arm, closed her eyes, and dove down the link to the woman's life essence. First, she disabled the woman's sense of pain despite her having fainted. The former raider's blood-presence had already shrank enough to kill her, escaping out the huge blood tube in the leg, but she hadn't yet lost her ghost. Growling from the strain, Althea tapped her desperation to prevent death. Threads of pain raked down her body like tiny, fiery claws. She clenched her jaw, pouring as much power as she could into the woman. The bone shape in the leg had burst into thousands of tiny fragments, muscles shredded to strips. She commanded them to regrow, the bone bits to reabsorb into the body. With little time to work, it would be faster—but more tiring—to simply grow new bone than sort out such a complicated puzzle.

Inch by inch, muscle and bone grew, lengthening until finally, toes appeared in the red-on-black world in which Althea floated. She kept feeding energy into Yaz, making her body generate blood to replace the vast amount she'd lost. The heart shape fluttered and stopped, which distracted her from blood-making to mentally yelling at the heart not to quit. At her behest, it twitched, beat a few times, then stopped again. Althea growled. She commanded Yaz's body to draw a surge of blood into the mostly-empty heart shape, then tried again to make it work.

The muscle twitched, then resumed beating.

Teal's yelling needled at the back of Althea's awareness, but not enough to understand words. She didn't bother surfacing from the healing trance, assuming the woman merely wanted her to hurry up. Yaz needed to make more blood or the heart shape would stop again. She channeled her energy for another minute until all the blood-tubes swelled back up to look normal.

Finally reaching a point she felt safe breaking the link, Althea let go and collapsed on top of Yaz, exhausted.

"Kid, you okay?" shouted Teal.

"Tired."

Teal rushed over to her.

"What happened?" whispered Yaz.

"You suffered an acute case of dumbassery." Teal folded her arms. "Stay down does not mean jump up and run out into a firing range. That heavy assault unit shoved a mini-missile up your ass."

"It didn't put it in her butt," said Althea in a half-whisper. "It hit her in the leg."

Teal shook her head.

"Oh, sorry, you were being figure-of-speechy again, weren't you?"

"I think we survived that wave. Without a doubt, there are reinforcements already coming toward us. We gotta cover land, fast."

"Okay." Althea pushed herself up to sit.

"Damn, kid, you look out of it."

"Tired. Making a new leg is supposed to take time. I hurried."

"New leg?" Yaz sat up, noticed she had one tan and one bright pink leg, and passed out.

"Dammit. I can't carry both of you. Can you wake her up?"

Althea poked Yaz in the brain. The woman came to.

"Are you able to walk on that leg?" Teal picked Althea up.

Yaz stood. "Probably. Running ain't gonna happen for a while. Where's my other boot?"

"Still on your old leg." Teal nodded toward the alley mouth.

"Umm... How am I not dead?" Yaz wiggled her toes. "Did that really happen?"

Teal held Althea out toward her as if showing off a doll. "Prophet."

"Right." Yaz limped to the end of the alley. "Is it safe out there?"

"No. But it's never safe anywhere around here. We probably have ten to fifteen minutes before this place is wall-to-wall robots."

Yaz speed-limped to her former leg, pulled her boot off it, and stepped into it. "That is so... so... unnerving. I know it's *my* leg, but it's too weird to even think about."

"Move!" shouted Teal.

Althea clung tight while the synthetic woman ran at a relatively human speed among the ruins, zigzagging around buildings for roughly ten blocks until they took a stairwell to an underground passageway with white tiled walls and red floors. The place reminded her of the Transit village, at least in appearance. A short, curving hallway led to a wide room with a platform abutting another big, round tube. Benches nearby offered a place to sit and rest. Teal flopped down, breathing hard.

Whether she needed air, pretended to be out of breath, or couldn't help but act human, Althea didn't know—and didn't care. She curled up in her lap, too worn out and drained to move.

Sorrow over Cobb hit her hard. He had died in an instant, far too fast for her to have made any difference. Why couldn't she do the same thing for him that she'd done for Shepherd? She hadn't even tried to fix Hector's brother, but she had no idea such a thing could even happen back then. She didn't even consciously *try* to do it when she found the big guy at the bottom of the cooling tower. Her only memory of that moment consisted of extreme guilt, believing he had died because of her, little different from if she had killed him. That man wouldn't have tried to protect her at all if she hadn't somehow rewired his entire brain.

Yet, she couldn't help Cobb. She wanted to, but it didn't work.

Losing him hurt as much as when the Wagon Man wouldn't let her heal people who didn't pay, even if they dropped dead right in front of her. She wanted so bad to help them, but six-year-old Althea didn't know she could force people to do what she said, and she certainly couldn't make herself strong enough to break out of a metal cage. If the Wagon Man refused to let the people go to her, she couldn't heal them. It took her a long time to get over her guilt.

That hadn't been her fault. The Wagon Man caused their deaths.

Maybe Cobb wasn't her fault either. She tried as hard as she could.

Some things, perhaps she would never understand.

She closed her eyes, wet with tears, and let exhaustion drag her off to sleep.

26

FORCE ESCALATION

A nightmare of being hogtied in the middle of a swarm of Badland roaches came to an abrupt end an instant before huge insect mandibles plunged into Althea's eyes. She jumped up with a scream, slipped off the plastic chairs, and crashed to the red tile floor.

Sprawled on all fours like a freaked out cat, she looked around in a panic. No roaches were anywhere in sight, and within a few seconds, she calmed enough for her mind to process the world around her as the underground chamber in which she'd taken refuge from bad machine men.

Still trembling from the too-vivid dream, she clutched her hands to her chest, having to look at herself to finally believe she no longer remained tied. With the relief of freedom, she ceased shaking and wrapped her arms around her legs, pretending she hugged Father or Karina. She wanted to cry out of homesickness, but held it in, doubting either Yaz or Teal would provide the comfort she needed.

Realizing she wanted that comfort made the need to go home far worse. Before she had a family, she had never felt any urge to cling to anyone, never even knew another person could offer such love and protection. She had only her 'fame' as the Prophet, which held no warmth whatsoever—only the reassurance that even the cruelest of raiders feared to harm her.

Legends, however, could offer no solace for bad dreams.

"You okay?" Teal squatted beside her.

"My sleep made me see scary things."

"Aww." Teal brushed a hand over Althea's head. "Nightmares can't hurt you."

She looked up, caught off guard by the tenderness coming from a woman who had days ago abducted her from home. Hesitantly, she leaned against her.

"Sorry if I'm not that great with kids." Teal put an arm around her. "Wanna talk about the dream?"

"You'll think I'm trying to make you feel bad."

"Why would I think that?" Teal rubbed her back.

Althea looked down. "Because of what I saw. I was tied like you left me at night and big roaches ate my face."

"Ahh. Well, I wouldn't have let any roaches get near you. Why didn't you just scare them away? After what you did to the Vee-Eights, how could you be afraid of anything? That had to be the most amazing thing I've ever seen. That bitch went from queen of the world to shitting herself in an instant."

"I don't know. I had a scary mind-see. They're not supposed to make sense. They're supposed to be scary."

Teal chuckled. "Mind-see? Most people call them dreams. Or nightmares if they're scary."

"Nightmare…"

"Hey, look, kid. Sorry for what I did to you, okay? It's a lot easier to relocate someone, especially a kid, when you don't talk to them. You're so damn sweet I feel like shit for the whole operation."

Althea licked the back of her hand, smacked her lips, then examined the lick mark. "Still salty."

"Hah!" Teal put a hand on her head and gently shoved her. "You're too much."

She caught herself before falling over sideways, and peered up, confused. "Too much what?"

Teal laughed into a sad sigh.

Yaz walked around the end of the seat row, mesmerized at the jagged line on her thigh where suntan changed to pale. The explosive arrow that hit her—that Teal called a mini-missile—mostly destroyed her armor skirt on that side. A patch of green plastic tarp she must have found down here patched the garment where the leather had been blasted away.

"I still can't believe it." Yaz rubbed two fingers back and forth over the color change in her skin. "You really are the Prophet. Nothing like I expected."

"What did you expect?" asked Teal.

Yaz sat on the bench and helped herself to the genesis canteen, squirting water into her mouth. "Everyone says the Prophet is quiet, obedient, never tries to run away, and anyone who harms her will suffer ten times worse. Also thought you were older, like a grown woman."

"Well, I kidnapped her and wound up on a damn steel cross." Teal shrugged. "Maybe there really is some woo-woo stuff going on out here."

Althea stood and roamed around in search of a spot to make water. A drain in the middle of the platform offered a better option than a random spot of floor. Once finished, she walked back to their 'camp' and drank a few mouthfuls from the canteen. They'd run out of food taken from the Vee-Eights, but Teal still had a decent supply of those nutrient bars. She gave one to Yaz and one to Althea, repeating the explanation that if they ate this, they shouldn't eat anything else until tomorrow.

"What? This is all the food for a whole day?" asked Yaz. "It's so small."

"That's what she said," muttered Teal.

"Who's she?" asked Althea.

Teal laughed. "Forget it. Umm, it's calorie dense."

"Ca-lo-rie?" asked Yaz.

Teal bowed her head, rubbing the bridge of her nose. "Magic. The bars are magic."

"Oh." Yaz nodded, doubt evaporating from her expression. "Okay."

After repacking the blanket, Teal picked up the plasma rifle. "Ready?"

Althea nodded.

They went back out the way they'd come in. At the top of the stairs, Teal leaned past the doorjamb, looking around before proceeding onward into the ruins. The sky still seemed angry and grey, thick with clouds that hid the sun. Within an hour of leaving the underground chamber, a tremendous downpour dumped rain in heavy sheets, painting the world in even gloomier tones of grey.

Althea held her arms out to the sides. Though frigid, the water rinsed her clean of dirt, dried blood, and lessened the rotten vegetable stink that had soaked into her dress.

"We should take shelter," yelled Yaz, over the rush of rain on pavement and crumbling buildings.

"It's better to keep going. The CRP doesn't go out in the rain."

"It hurts them?" asked Althea.

"Only if they've been damaged and have holes. But, the weather messes with their sensors and the ones with wheels can get stuck in mud."

"I saw a machine man stuck in mud once. It wanted to hurt me but couldn't."

"Stupid." Teal shook her head. "Only the government would set something like that loose, then lose control of it, and write it off as 'oops, oh well, whatever.'"

Althea squinted into the rain at her. "Huh?"

"It would take too long to explain to be worth it."

"Okay."

They trudged along in the downpour for upward of two hours. Teal tried to stick to paved roads as much as possible, though the silt from rubbled concrete created large areas of shin-deep pale grey goop with no way to avoid going across. Althea struggled to pull her feet from the squidgy muck in the thicker spots. Yaz lost her boots to the mud every few steps, which made Althea giggle. Shoes were *so* annoying.

A little past mid-day, the rain lessened to a drizzle. Althea pulled her dress off while walking, rolling it up to wring it out. When she could squeeze no more water out of the fabric, she decided to carry it for a while and let it dry out, rather than suffer the annoyance of wet fabric clinging to her.

"Scrags." Teal shook her head, chuckling. "So casual. You're like Neko cyber-freaks without the extra body parts."

"What?" asked Althea. "Or is that gonna take too long to explain, too."

"Something like that."

The weather continued to improve over the next several hours. When the sky began to show signs of early evening, she checked her dress and found it had dried enough that it didn't make her freeze anymore. She pulled it back on, smiling, feeling as though she'd had both a bath and done the clothes washing at the same time. The rain had cleaned the sour vegetable smell from the fabric, and even gotten rid of the grime around her fingernails. Her legs, however, had a coating of grey muck halfway to her knees since she'd been walking in silt-sludge most of the day.

Teal climbed through the window of a ruined building to go around a street blocked by a collapsed high-rise, leading them across a trash-filled pit to the other side. Althea grabbed the crumbling old windowsill at the far end and pulled herself up. At the sight of green letters spelling out 'Connect Transit' on the corner of a building across the street, she let out a cheer, recognizing the entrance to Ooru and Paama's village.

"You found it!" She jumped down to the dirt outside and ran to hug Teal.

"Yeah. I'm good at navigating." Teal tapped her head.

Althea grinned up at her. "Can we please go help Kye?"

"Yeah, yeah. Figured Yaz would want to stay here where it's safe."

"What is this place?" asked Yaz.

"There's a village underground here. They're nice. Please tell them that I found their queen, Kye, and will bring her back soon. If they don't believe you, show them your leg." Althea pointed at the color shift.

"Welcome to come with us if you want to keep playing chicken with killer robots," said Teal. "The other facility is two-and-a-half miles southwest from here."

Yaz shook her head. "No. I cannot fight the Silver Men. We avoid them. Even Puma is only a kitten when they come for us."

Teal laughed.

Yaz bowed in front of Althea. "Thank you, Prophet. You saved my life. Twice. I swear fealty to you."

"Umm. You don't have to feel me." Althea fidgeted. "I like helping people."

After a momentary confused look, Yaz shook Teal's hand. "Thanks."

"No worries. I'd say it was nice *hanging* out with you, but it wasn't."

Yaz appeared confused.

"Hanging? Literally? Oh never mind. Glad we got out of there alive." Teal patted the woman's arm, then looked down at Althea. "Well, kid, you sure you wanna go get that girl out of the tube instead of going home?"

"Yes. It would be wrong to leave her there. I don't know how to let her out, but I can probably find home. You should go home too, and hug your parents."

"They're not my parents." Teal brushed past her and resumed walking down the street.

"They are. They love you."

"You've never even seen them. They probably bought me like a holo-vid player."

"People have bought me, too, but they didn't love me. I know your parents love you."

Teal sighed. "You're making it really damn hard to feel sorry for myself. You've had a rough damn life for such a short one. And you don't have to say that to make me feel better."

"I saw them." Althea described the man and woman from the brief vision. "And you had a dolly with pink hair."

"What?" Teal stopped and stared at her. "How could you possibly know that?"

"Sometimes when I touch stuff, if there's been lots of emotion, I can see it. Your parents did love you. They don't care if your sin-fet-ic."

Teal looked as likely to start crying as hit her.

"I'll stop talking. Please don't put tape on me."

"Damn, kid." Teal sighed. "You're way too good at that."

"At what?"

"Making me feel like a piece of shit."

"Umm. Sorry." She bit her lip. "What does a piece of shit feel like?"

Teal hung her head and laughed. "Warm and gooey."

"Eww." Althea grinned. "I think you're teasing me."

"Maybe a little." An odd smile formed on the woman's lips. "Come on, let's go find this woman." She started down the street.

Yaz headed for the stairs.

"Wait!" yelled Althea. "Yaz…"

Both Teal and Yaz stopped.

"I almost forgot. The first tunnel has jaw traps. I need to help you go past them because I can see in the dark."

Yaz tilted her head.

Althea took her by the hand. "Come on."

She walked the woman down the stairs and across the station chamber, to the sunken tunnel, carefully guiding her around the big jaw traps. Once past them, she smiled up at Yaz even though the woman couldn't see anything but her glowing eyes.

"It's safe from here. There's only one way to go until you see light."

"Okay."

"Please tell them we're going back for Kye now and they shouldn't worry."

"Sure…" Yaz raised her arms, feeling around for a wall, then proceeded to creep off down the tunnel.

Althea ran back past the traps and zoomed up the stairs to find Teal waiting by the doorway in the crumbling Transit building.

They followed the street for a few minutes until the whirr of a wheelbot's motor became noticeable up ahead. Teal took her hand, running back the way they'd been walking. She rushed toward the nearest ruined wall high enough to provide cover, dragging Althea behind it with her. They crouched low, huddling against the decrepit cinder blocks as the whirring grew louder.

"Contaminants detected," said a deeper electronic voice.

Crunching footsteps and whirring approached on the opposite side of the wall.

Teal looked around, appeared frustrated, then peeked over the rubble. "Okay, not too bad… only two."

She ducked a second before a glowing green glob flew overhead.

"How considerate of them to bring me a new rifle. I'm almost out of ammo." She popped up again and fired a shot from her plasma rifle.

Althea cringed at the blast of heat from the weapon.

An orange melt spot appeared in the wall right by her face, as if the machine man could see her. Althea shrieked, jumping away. Teal fired again, setting off a distant explosion and brilliant flash.

"Designated target located. Converge," said an electronic voice.

Whirring came from the right. Althea spun, expecting a wheelbot, but a flash came from thirty feet up. A flying wing bot, three times the size of the other air-machines she'd seen, cruised out from behind a skeletal high-rise, turning until it pointed straight at her.

"Contaminant targeted," said the wing, "Initiating cleanse routine."

Sensing imminent danger, Althea hurled herself into a sprint.

Twin lines of orange light traced from its wings to the ground on either side of her feet, kicking up dust and a painful blast of heat. Althea screamed, pouring power into her muscles, not caring if it hurt. Two more blasts struck the ground behind her, the machine evidently unprepared for her sudden burst of speed. None of the rubble in the area looked like a good hiding place, so she dashed side to side making random turns, hoping to avoid the fire lines from above long enough for Teal to shoot it.

The flying machine picked up speed, weaving back and forth in the air while trying to kill her. Each time it fired, she shrieked and changed direction, jumping over cars, zooming around walls, or leaping across big holes in the street. She hunted for a storm drain or one of those stairways that led underground, but found only dirt and piles of crumbled buildings.

Laser fire pelted her legs with tiny, hot bits of molten sand. The instant she stopped running or made one mistake, she'd become a ghost.

"Contaminant, please reduce your erratic motions. Your attempt to evade cleansing will not prevent cleansing. There is no purpose to adding unnecessary delay to contaminant processing," said the flyer.

"No!" shouted Althea. "Go away!"

She ran as if to go past a side street, then pulled a sudden left turn. The flyer raced around in pursuit, unable to avoid clipping one wingtip on a still-standing lamp post. She flinched at the *clank*, peering back for only a second at the machine spinning around and around. It bounced off another building with a metal-plastic *thud*, breaking a small hole in the cinder blocks, though the bot didn't appear to suffer any damage. Despite the big flying wing having no facial features at all, when it leveled off and faced her again, it seemed furious. This one had more than twice the wingspan of the other flyers, with a fatter middle part.

"Eep!" She sprinted off, taking a left at the corner of the building, then thirty feet later, a right.

Weaving among buildings kept the flying machine out of sight for a moment, but it reappeared in front of her, having gone high up above the ruins. Laser blasts traced orange lines in the paving past her on both sides. She bolted to the right, screaming.

"Frustration has reached critical levels. Force escalation approved," said the flying machine.

Althea didn't want to know what that meant. She kept running, desperately searching for a way underground where this thing couldn't follow her.

A loud *whoosh* came from the sky. She jinked left toward a giant dead car, leaping into the air to vault over it the same instant an explosion went off. A shockwave crashed into her from behind, flinging her forward *way* over the car she tried to jump. She barely noticed her body slapping against a concrete wall.

Deaf, blind, and stunned, she fell into a disorienting void.

27

UPGRADED TECHNOLOGY

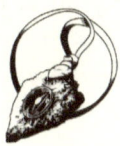

Faint blue light from Althea's eyes formed spots on a coarse, reddish-brown surface inches in front of her face. Pain throbbed in her feet, her front, and the right side of her head. Other than the soft whisper of her own breathing, the world had gone silent. Faint itching in her back worsened over a few seconds to small burning spots.

She drifted in and out of feeling as if dreaming and awake. After a moment, she realized she lay on the road beneath an ancient car, her right arm and leg partially buried under dirt and small bits of concrete rubble. A narrow band of sunlight invaded the corner past her left foot, but everywhere else, dirt and rock entombed her.

The building fell on the car.

Her head spun in circles, separating her from any sense of time. Exactly how she'd wound up under a car, she couldn't quite grasp. She did, however, understand she'd been hurt. Once she gathered enough presence of mind to focus on healing herself, she closed her eyes and flew off into the void, hovering over a reddish silhouette representing her body. A crack split the bone shape in her left thigh. Multiple small bones in her feet had fractured as well as her right cheek. Her jaw had popped out of its socket on that side as well. Dozens of small stone bits had embedded into her skin from behind, peppering her from head to heels.

"Owwwww," whispered Althea.

She commanded her left thigh to mend. The sharp *snap* of the bone knitting reverberated as loud as a gunshot across the silent nothingness in which she floated. Her feet tingled with energy as the bones grew whole. She told her mind to ignore pain, then grabbed her jaw in both hands, shoving it back into place before mentally pushing the bone to regenerate. Last, she forced the shrapnel out of her body, mending all the little wounds plus a few cuts and scrapes.

"This isn't right," whispered Althea. "I'm the Prophet. People aren't supposed to hurt me."

She opened her eyes, staring up at the undercarriage of a car that hadn't moved in centuries. A few breaths later, her brain decided to work again.

"*People* didn't do this." She shuddered at the memory of the bad flyer… then gasped. "Oh, no! Teal!"

The avalanche of dirt and rubble that buried the car must have protected her from the stupid flying machine. Since she didn't hear any whirring, she hoped it had lost track of her and gone away. Unable to roll over due to the confined space, she scooted on her back toward the sunlight. Once she could reach, she started pushing at the dirt around the sunlight with her left foot, gradually expanding the opening. She grabbed the rusty metal above her for support, burrowing feet-first into the gap, kicking at the silt.

Minutes later, she wriggled forward, sliding on her back out from under the car, and stared up at an early morning sky. Distant wind whistled among the ruined skyscrapers. The caw of a bird came from off to the left. She grasped the edge of the car, shoving herself away enough to sit up, then clambered to her feet and turned to look back at it.

The car had disappeared entirely under an avalanche of grey from the building collapsing. She somewhat remembered being thrown into a wall that no longer existed. Somehow, she must have slipped under the car before the building came down. If she hadn't tried to jump over the car at that instant, whatever the flying machine threw at her probably would have killed her. She thought back to Yaz's leg. That woman's thigh and her middle were about the same size.

"Eep." Althea shivered. "I don't wanna be cut in half. I don't like these machines."

Though filthy, her dress had survived the explosion. She suspected the back had lots of new small holes, but didn't care enough to look. If it fell off, it fell off. Bigger problems than clothing had to be dealt with first.

As best she could remember, she hurried back the way she had run, looking for the place where she and Teal had taken cover before the flying machine chased her away. The ruins remained eerily still. It terrified her to think the machines left due to thinking they had killed both of them. That no sign of robots remained anywhere in sight brought her to the brink of tears over Teal.

Worse, it had almost been dark when they'd been attacked, but it appeared to be dawn. She must have lain unconscious beneath the car all night. Maybe Teal couldn't find her and assumed she had died. A nicer thought said the woman simply lost her and would be looking around trying to find her. She had, after all, managed to find her at the place where Kye remained trapped.

Althea rubbed her butt. She didn't have a 'tracker' stuck inside her anymore, though. For a moment, she regretted getting rid of it, but at the time, she had no reason to *want* Teal to be able to find her if she escaped.

The ruins didn't look familiar. Every decaying building looked like every other decaying building as far as she could see. She wandered wherever it *felt* like she should go, stepping with care around sharp rocks or rusted bits of metal. On a whim, she climbed over a car that had long ago crashed into the corner of a building to reach the alley on the other side. The skeletal remains of around twenty people lay strewn about, the air thick with a sense that something watched her.

"Eep. Sorry." She hurried past them, taking care not to disturb any of the bones.

When she emerged from the other end of the alley, she found herself across the street from the place where the flying machine had first attacked her. Teal's backpack lay abandoned on the ground near the spot where she'd been hiding. At the sight of it, Althea ran forward, jumped the shallow wall of the once-building, and skidded to a halt beside the thin pack.

The dirt bore numerous tracks, though she couldn't really tell which came from Teal and which from the machine men. Since she didn't see a body anywhere, she figured the woman had destroyed all the bad robots... but why would she leave the backpack of food bars, the blanket, and the canteen here? Had she been carrying them only for

Althea's benefit? If she assumed that explosion killed her, she might have dropped it to save weight.

Or maybe she left it here while going to look for her.

Althea decided to sit and wait for her to come back.

She helped herself to a nutrition bar and some water from the canteen, gazing around at the world of pale grey under a clear, blue sky. Out of boredom, she stuck her feet in the silt, lifted her toes, and watched the tiny grains filter between them. Bright, sunny days like this made her happy, mostly because the light in her eyes became harder to notice and people sometimes treated her like an ordinary person—at least until they noticed the glow. More recently, that hadn't been an issue. Bright days meant the other kids in Querq wanted to go out and play.

I'm still trying to get home. She projected her desire to tell Karina and Father she was okay. *Please don't be scared.*

"Hmm."

She considered beaconing for Teal, but doubted it would work as she couldn't use her other abilities on a 'syn-fet-ic' person. Would she even be able to 'hear' the beaconing?

"Actuator failure. Mobility zero percent," said a deep, electronic voice.

Althea nearly made water.

She froze, listening.

Tiny whirrs and clicks echoed from the other side of the wall, right behind her. It neither came closer nor moved away.

"Thermal anomaly detected. Analyzing."

Althea swallowed.

"Contaminant detected. Target fault. Contaminant size indicates juvenile human."

Althea listened for a few minutes more, then crawled around to the wall and peered through a small tunnel made by a plasma bolt.

One of the tall, silver robots lay on its side, its right leg blown off at the hip. Another robot's arm stuck into its chest like an arrow, intermittent blue lightning arcs crackling out along the metal armor. Roughly a quarter of its head had melted away, but it appeared to be mostly armor damage as the glowing electronic parts inside still worked. It held a plasma rifle in its right hand, but hadn't pointed it at her.

"Are you going to hurt me?" whispered Althea.

"Contaminant organism scans as female. Bonus points." The head twitched. "Target invalid. Juvenile."

"That's not yes or no."

Its face didn't try pretending to be a real person. Two square eye spots with rounded corners emitted green light. An opening roughly where a nose should be made it look too much like a skull for her comfort, but it had no teeth or mouth, only a small grid of teeny holes. The eyes went dark and came back on a second later, perhaps an attempt to blink.

"ROM limiter prohibits cleansing of juveniles. Version 1.18.82 United Coalition Front Department of Defense. Last update July 14, 2377."

"Pro-hib-it." She scrunched her nose. "That means no, right?"

"Correct."

"So you can't hurt me because Rom said so?"

"That is correct. Sigma Six software update contains conflicting instructions. However, hardware-level program has priority."

"What does that mean?"

"Sigma Six software update contains conflicting instructions. However, hardware-level program has priority."

"Are you going to hurt me or not?"

"I am incapable of cleansing contaminants scanned as juveniles."

"What's joo-vin-oil?"

"Organisms that have not reached physical maturity."

"Umm. Do you know another word for what you want to say?"

The eyes flickered. "Child. Adolescent. Kid. Youth."

"Oh. Yeah, I'm only eleven."

"I will cleanse you in seven years."

She raised her eyebrows. *Umm. No, you won't. I'm not gonna be anywhere near you in seven years.* "Where is Teal?"

"Insufficient data."

"What?"

"Your query"—it repeated the phrase 'where is Teal' in Althea's voice—"would result in far too many results to list. There are billions of objects with the color designation 'teal.'"

"No. I mean the woman *named* Teal. The one who was here with me. And don't lie. Lying is mean."

The robot's eyes turned off and on again. "I am incapable of providing false information to a query. Deceit is a human flaw."

"Do you know where Teal is?"

"There are many objects—"

"No!" shouted Althea. "The woman!"

The machine man paused. "Sigma Six ordered all units to return the strange robot to the manufacturing center for study. The artificial life form you have designated as 'Teal' is significantly advanced technology compared to that which we possess."

"Is she still alive?"

"Negative."

Althea shuddered, bowed her head, and burst into tears.

"Contaminant?" asked the CRP walker.

She ignored him, too lost to sorrow. Only knowing she couldn't possibly have done anything to help kept grief from becoming total. The woman's synthetic body didn't respond to psionic healing. But, if she hadn't insisted they go find Kye, maybe Teal wouldn't be dead.

"Juvenile human?"

She kept crying.

"Child, please respond."

"What?" yelled Althea, sniffling.

"Why is there fluid emission from your visual light receptors?"

"Why do you keep talking nonsense?" shouted Althea.

"My sensors indicate there is liquid on your face. What purpose does this hydration loss serve?"

She scowled, still crying. "Because. Teal's dead. You killed her! Why are you so mean?"

"The artificial lifeform designated 'Teal' is still functional."

Althea stared through the hole at the robot, mouth open. "What? You mean she's alive? Why did you say she's dead?"

"You queried if the artificial lifeform remained alive. The artificial lifeform was never alive. It is an artificial lifeform."

"Grr!" Althea leapt to her feet, glaring over the wall that came up to her chest at the stricken android. She stood there for a few seconds fuming in anger before yelling, "Where is she?"

"The artificial lifeform is on its way to the Great Forge for analysis."

"Where is that?"

"North and east from here, near the coast."

"What's it look like? How will I know when I'm there?"

"The Great Forge is a thirty-six-story chasm brimming with

manufacturing systems, supply conveyors, production facilities, and sentry units."

Althea remembered the jet-black swath of ground with the glowing red hole she'd seen from the air. "It looks like a giant spear stabbed the earth, full of red light."

"That is correct. Your intention to travel there does not make logical sense. You would undertake great physical exertion only to be purged."

The desire to get home to Karina and Father hurt so much she couldn't stop the silent tears streaming down her cheeks. Her need to be with them brought physical pain to her heart. But, she couldn't simply walk away and leave Teal to be killed. She also couldn't get Kye out of the tank. Ignoring them both and going home felt like a mean thing to do. And, since she *couldn't* do anything for Kye on her own—not to mention Teal would die soon—that left her one choice, as dangerous as it seemed.

"I have to help her."

"Do not waste the energy," said the CRP walker. "I have already requested support units to purge you. They are on the way."

"What?" She stared at it. "But you said you can't hurt me because I'm a child."

"That is correct. *I* cannot purge a juvenile contaminant. However, the W7 series does not have the hardware limitation. They were manufactured here, not made by humans."

"Argh! Why would you do that?"

"Because you are a biological contaminant."

"You're mean!" shouted Althea.

She jumped away from the wall, grabbed the backpack, and ran off down the street.

"Child," said the robot at increased volume. "Why do you ambulate rapidly? If you do not remain here, the W7 units may not be able to locate you and purge you."

"I know!" yelled Althea. "That's why I'm running!"

28

LIEUTENANT RAINES

Althea ran at normal speed, not wanting to hurt herself from pushing her body too much too often. Since she didn't hear the wheelbots yet, she hoped she had enough time to get away without extreme measures.

Four blocks later, she discovered a huge hole where the street had collapsed. A two-foot diameter concrete pipe jutted out from the left side of the pit a little more than halfway to the bottom. An uneven ramp formed from chunks of smashed paving appeared to be the last place a wheelbot would ever want to go. If they went down there, they'd never get out, and the pipe offered a perfect hiding place.

She hurried down the ramp and ducked into the pipe, crawling deep enough to feel secure that nothing outside could see her. Fear that Teal wouldn't have much time got into a fight with her fear of wheelbots catching her. Or flying machines. Thinking of that awful thing made her hurt all over for a few seconds.

Her fear list gained a new entry: flying robots. Specifically, the big ones that threw exploding arrows at her. She definitely feared them more than being tied, but had more trouble deciding which scared her more between blowing up or being wifed. The flying machine edged out bad raiders to become her biggest fear. She could force raiders not to wife her. None of her powers worked on flying machines or exploding arrows.

She sat there tapping her foot for a while, increasingly worried about Teal. Whether that feeling came from normal anxiety or some sort of message from the clairvoy ants, she couldn't tell. When her worry grew to the point that she couldn't stop fidgeting, she crawled out of the pipe, jumped to the cracked paving, and ran up the other side of the sinkhole, climbing the four-foot vertical wall at the edge to the road surface outside.

A quick glance at the sky to find the sun gave her a good guess at northeast. Althea walked fast, saving her energy to run only if needed. Like Ooru and Paama taught her, she stuck close to ruins or dead cars in case she had to hide, keeping her ears open for whirring or metal feet clanking.

I'm going to *the place where all those machines come from. Why am I doing that? I should be scared. Do I have a clairvoy ant or am I being stupid?*

She crouched by the front end of an old truck, listened to silence for a few seconds, then dashed down to the next cross street, taking cover behind a battered metal stairway. The metal building it connected to had warped so much it resembled a giant half-melted candle someone left too close to a fire.

Still, no sign of robots appeared to be anywhere nearby, so she got up and jogged to the next corner.

There, she paused to look up at a sign that read 'one way,' but it pointed opposite the direction she wanted to go.

"Grr. Why?" She scowled. "I wanna go that way."

Althea folded her arms and huffed. *Stupid frozen words telling me what to do.*

She started to turn around, but thought back to the stop sign. The Ancients had built it a long time ago. They had probably built this one, too. It didn't make any sense why she could only walk south on this street... which didn't even really look like a street anymore, only patches of exposed paving sticking out here and there wherever the dirt didn't cover it. The Watch man had laughed at her for stopping at the sign. All the adults ignored the frozen words. Maybe she could, too.

"I don't think you're right." She pointed at the sign. "Why can't I go that way?"

The frozen speech didn't change to answer her.

"If you don't say why, I'm going to go that way." She stuck out her tongue. "Teal needs help."

She counted to ten, and when the sign didn't change what it said, she decided to ignore it… and went the wrong way.

Hope I don't get in trouble.

Two cross streets later, a collapsed building blocked her off from going straight. It looked far too tall and full of sharp things and holes to climb, so she turned right, following the easiest path. As soon as an opening in the ruins allowed, she veered left again, checking the sun to keep on course to the northeast.

She rounded the corner into a swarm of huge rats. Forty or so black, furry creatures milled around, chewing on the carcasses of other rats that had apparently been shot not too long ago. About half the size of the ones Paama called 'darkbites,' these appeared to be ordinary—albeit big—rats. A few glanced in her direction, sniffing.

"Nice rats. It's okay. I won't hurt you. Don't bite me." She crept forward into the group. "Just going to walk by, okay?"

More rats turned toward her, sniffing.

Their emotion shifted from curiosity to hunger mixed with territorial aggression.

Althea radiated calm, forcing the animals' fear aside. Some resumed nibbling on their dead, the rest watched her with mild curiosity. She hurried past the pack, trying to get away from them before her emotional manipulation faded. At the whirr of an approaching wheelbot, she stopped short. A quick look around for a hiding place left her undecided between a storm drain and a derelict van.

But… the machine would kill all the rats.

"You gotta run, too," whispered Althea.

She thought about Father, how she loved him and knew he would protect her… and projected that emotion into the rats. They rushed at her, licking at her legs and arms. Two stood on their hind legs, trying to lick her face, but their noses only came up to her waist.

"Follow me!"

Though they couldn't understand her words, the strong emotional sense of protective love she'd instilled in them caused the rats to follow her to the storm drain and jump in after her. All fifty or so packed the square chamber at the bottom, cuddling up to her in a giant mass of warm, furry bodies. She hid with the rats, listening to the wheelbot roll around outside. After a few minutes, she itched all over.

Ugh. Blood dot bugs.

She clenched her jaw to weather the assault of tiny insects chewing on her. Rats *always* seemed to have the super tiny black bugs that itched so much. Raiders, not being terribly concerned with clean, often had them too. Althea knew blood dot bugs well. An irritating twenty minutes later, she hadn't heard a trace of wheelbot long enough that her need to get away from the itching overpowered her fear. She gave off a heavy dose of calm, no longer forcing the furry critters to love her like a parent. The rat pile fell apart, allowing her to stand up and climb out of the storm drain.

Her white (sorta) dress had so many little black dots crawling everywhere it looked as if someone had spilled a bucket of pepper on her. She dropped the backpack, took her dress off, and spent a few minutes slapping it against the road to shake it clear of fleas. Mending the thousands of tiny red spots all over her didn't require much time or energy.

Fortunately, the recent major rain left no shortage of puddles and pools. Not far from the storm drain, she found a dumpster full of water. She climbed in and sat under the surface for a few minutes, trying to get the rest of the fleas out of her long hair. When her power reached its limit at allowing her to hold her breath, she stuck her head up for air.

The itching had stopped, and a muck of drowned fleas floated on the surface nearby. She swatted at the water to push them away, just in case they only played dead, then pulled herself out of the dumpster. After squeezing the water out of her hair as best she could, she picked her dress up, checking it over for hitchhikers. Seeing none, she put it back on despite still being wet, grabbed the backpack, and continued fast-walking to the north.

A most peculiar sight awaited her three blocks later where a char-blackened machine much bigger than a car sat in the road, mostly blocking it. Two giant tubes stuck out of the back beneath tall vertical fins. It had wings and a clear bubble near the pointy end that covered a single seat. Frozen speech on the tail where it hadn't turned black said the unpronounceable word USAF. Whatever this machine had been, it appeared stuck there for a long time. It didn't have wheels, and it kinda looked like a bird, so she guessed it to be another flying machine, but it didn't look like any of the other ones.

Althea stepped up onto the left wing, which had tilted down near the pavement, and walked across it to the other side. At the front edge, she stopped, staring at a skeleton in the only seat. It seemed kinda silly to make such a big machine to carry only one person.

"I'm sorry you died," whispered Althea.

"Ehh, kinda dumb of me to fly in so damn low," said a man. "Thought it would make for easy pickings of the convoy, but one of the bastards got me."

She jumped with a yelp, whirling to face a youngish guy in a bluish-grey jumpsuit and a white helmet. Frozen speech on his chest, white on a strip of black, read, 'Raines, F.' He gave off a strong sense of energy unlike any person she'd ever seen before. Althea looked back and forth between him and the skeleton a few times.

"Are you a ghost?"

"Yes, ma'am." He smiled. "Lieutenant Franklin Raines at your service. Been wondering what took you so long to get here."

Confused, she opened her mouth to ask what he meant, then remembered the old guy from Querq who thought she had come to help him die. "I'm not what you think I am."

Lieutenant Raines leaned closer, looking at her for a moment while rubbing his chin. "Hmm. Maybe you're right. But you're kinda close. What are you doing out here?"

"I'm looking for the Great Forge. I have to help my friend before they kill her."

"Oh, hell no, kid. You gotta get the heck out of here before those crazy machines catch you."

She shrank in on herself, fully aware of the danger in what she wanted to do. "I know. But I can't leave Teal to die. They're gonna kill her."

Lieutenant Raines squinted into the distance, hands on his hips. "Hmm. How much Seraph are you?"

"Umm, what?"

"I can feel the energy in ya. Seen other things running around on this side. Harbingers. They come after the bad guys. Guess they might have been interested in me after all. Used to be, I told myself I only followed orders. Did what my commanders told me, thinking I protected people, fought for my country. Soon as I ended up dead, those buggers came looking for me. S'pose I must not have been all *that* tasty to them 'cause they didn't chase me too hard. Anyway, couple times I caught glimpses of other critters. They look more like us, only they've got these bright wings made out of light. Tried to get their attention, but they only ever smiled at me and disappeared. Like I ain't ready or some such thing."

"Oh. Umm. I dunno. Sometimes I have wings."

He smiled and tried to take her hand. His fingers passed through her like a cold breeze. "But you're alive."

"Yes."

"Can you help me cross over? I help you find your friend, and you help me move on?"

Althea nodded. "Yes. I think so. You don't need to do stuff for me first. I'll help you." She closed her eyes.

"Aww, wait, kid. Not yet. Sure as hell I wanna get out of here, but it's been damn near four hundred years. I can't leave you here all alone."

She looked up at him. "But you're a ghost."

"I am. An old one, too. Got a few tricks that could help ya." He brushed a hand over her head. "Like killin' them fleas."

Althea cringed, gasping at a sensation like icy water pouring over her head and running down her back. "Eep!"

He laughed.

Shivering, she peered up at him. "B-but I a-already d-drowned them."

"Missed a few." He waved for her to follow and walked down the street. "Come on. Let's go find that friend of yours."

29

THE GREAT FORGE

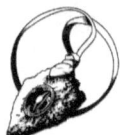

Lieutenant Raines rambled as they walked, telling her about being a pilot in the Air Force at the time when some corporations rebelled against the government. He'd been sent here to protect fleeing citizens from corporate armed forces that had been dressing up like US Military to attack civilians in an effort to make them hostile to the government.

Just about everything he said made her squirm as it involved a whole bunch of people hurting each other with a whole bunch of explodey things.

Over the course of the next hour, they walked past smaller and smaller ruins. Eventually, no standing buildings remained, only piles of grey dust and concrete bits, the mounds suspiciously neat in their arrangement. It had been a while since she'd seen a car or anything not made out of dirt. She looked around, then peered back over her shoulder at a wide field of open ground. Still-standing ruins stopped at an obvious line a good ways behind them. She'd been so distracted by listening to the ghost talk she'd stopped paying attention to keeping cover nearby in case a machine man attacked.

"Eep! What happened to all the buildings? There's nowhere to hide."

"The crazy robots have been taking them down to scavenge the metal. Nothing left between here and there but dirt."

She dug her toes into the silt, biting her lip in worry. Maybe some tasks *were* too big for a kid, even the Prophet. If Teal had been abducted by raiders, she'd have thought nothing of storming in there to help. But, the CRP… those robots would kill her as soon as look at her, and none of her powers would do a damn thing.

Silent tears rolled down her face at the thought she might have no choice but to turn back. It didn't seem likely she would survive to even reach the Great Forge, much less get Teal out of there. She couldn't make the robots sad or calm or trusting, and she couldn't give them commands.

Leaving felt as bad as shooting Teal in the face, but going on amounted to shooting herself in the face.

"Loo Temant?" She looked up at him. "Am I doing—?"

High-pitched whirring scared her mute.

A wheelbot zipped over the top of a rubble mound up ahead, coming straight at her. She sprinted away from it, racing for the flimsy safety of another dirt pile. It could, of course, come right around it after her, but as long as she kept running, it couldn't shoot her *through* the hill.

The whirring electric motor rushed up behind her so rapidly that she screamed in anticipation of certain death. Seconds later, she glanced to her right at the wheelbot keeping pace with her, its head rotated toward her.

"Althea," said the wheelbot in its usual toneless electronic voice. "It's me. Lieutenant Raines."

Confused, she slowed to a stop. That thing could catch her with ease on open ground, so there didn't seem to be a point to running anyway. It hadn't shot her when it clearly could have.

"Umm… What?"

The wheelbot stopped beside her and wobbled back and forth. "I jumped in and took it over. It's only a machine."

Sure enough, the wheelbot did give off a strong feeling of paranormal energy.

"I didn't know ghosts could do that."

"You don't know much about ghosts, do you?"

She shrugged. "No. Not really. I'm still not sure how I can even see you. I have to want to see ghosts and I didn't do that yet."

"I wanted you to see me. And not all ghosts can inhabit machines. I'm really damn old. The longer we stick around, the more stuff we learn how to do. Of course, I've run into a bunch of spirits too confused, lazy, or sad to care much about anything. They just sit around being miserable. I happen to be highly motivated."

"Umm. Okay. So…"

"Climb on this thing's back. Other robots won't notice you if you're riding on one. The metal interferes with their sensors. But… they might see you on thermal. Depends on how close they get."

She walked around behind the robot. Its upper body roughly matched the size and shape of a muscular man, though with only a single fat wheel for legs, it ended up only a little taller than her. Althea climbed onto its back, placing her feet on flat spots at the bottom of its torso shell and grabbing metal loops on its shoulders, just like the ones that Ell-Gee had used to hang the broken ones.

"You good?"

"I try to be," said Althea.

"Ugh. I mean do you have a good grip?"

She bounced and rocked side to side. "Yeah."

"Okay. Hold on."

The wheelbot tilted forward, accelerating up to a scary speed quite a bit faster than she could run. Her hair whipped around behind her, the wind in her face so strong she squinted.

"Heh, this little guy is pretty agile. Reminds me of my pilot days, only can't go up off the ground. No idea what caliber this thing's loading though. Only 600 rounds per cannon. That's gonna run out of ammo real fast."

"Is that good or bad?"

"Good if they're shooting at us. Bad if I need to make this thing light some bad guys up."

They hit a dip in the ground that tossed them airborne for a few seconds. Althea's left foot slipped off the small platform. She yelped, squeezing her hands tighter to hold on. The wheelbot landed softer than expected and continued to bob up and down for a few seconds. She planted her foot back on the step and tried to grip the flat metal with her toes, but it didn't help much.

"Please don't jump again. I almost fell off."

"Copy."

"What?"

"That means I understand."

"Why do people keep saying stuff that doesn't mean what they say?"

Lieutenant Raines chuckled.

Althea clung to the back of the wheelbot, riding for about twenty minutes. The ground darkened from concrete grey to charcoal grey, and eventually black. She peered around the wheelbot's head at the scorched ground, still burning in places where flying machines had crashed. None of the wreckage remained, likely taken by the robots to make more robots.

A dozen or more black spheres flew around in a slow, methodical pattern like eyeballs torn from a giant's skull and set to wander. The closest ones appeared about a hundred meters away, some as far off as a half mile. Whenever one rotated toward them, a glint of sunlight shone from a big lens on the front.

"They can see us," said Althea, only loud enough to be heard over the whirring wheelbot motor.

"There's a ton of sensors all over the place here, but I'm keeping you hidden. No way anyone's gonna walk in here without being noticed unless they hack into the CRP communication network and take over the sensors… or have a little help of the paranormal kind."

"I don't know what anything you said means."

"Of course you don't. Seraph don't care about computers."

"I don't know what that means either."

Eerie red light glowed in the mist rising from the ink-black ground far ahead. For a moment, she shivered, wondering if she might have found the place where The Many lived. Again, she questioned why she'd been so foolish to think she could do anything at all here. Sick with guilt, she closed her eyes and thought about Teal, wanting to know if it had already become too late.

A momentary feeling of lying flat on her back, cold metal around her arms and legs pinning her down, came and went. She didn't get any sense of pain, but a faint notion of urgency prickled at her spine.

The growl of rotary cannons firing slapped her out of her trance, straight into screaming.

Her wheelbot banked hard into a right turn, going around and around in circles with another wheelbot, each trying to shoot the other. Every time the robot fired, the roar stabbed her like needles in the ears. She held on, helpless to do anything beyond continuously screaming for the minute or so it took Lieutenant Raines to outmaneuver the enemy robot and shred it with a sustained burst from both guns.

As soon as the enemy robot burst into flames and crashed over sideways, her wheelbot stopped short, reversed, then whirled around and accelerated hard. He said something, but Althea couldn't hear what… only that the voice had come from the head in front of her. In fact, her ears still hurt.

She concentrated on healing herself, and sound returned.

"—distance away. Hold on."

"What?" yelled Althea.

"That one spotted you on thermal from behind. Some kind of control system is sending more problems here. Going for a hiding spot."

"There's nowhere to—"

Althea screamed as the ground fell out from under them. The wheelbot seemed to hang in midair, weightless for a second before it fell straight down, landing nimbly on its single tire and bouncing to the bottom of a flight of stairs into an underground passage. They skidded sideways upon hitting the smooth tile floor, but the bot refused to fall over, sliding into a hard spin. Althea's feet slipped, leaving her swinging by her hands horizontally in the air as the machine whirled in place for a few seconds. When it stopped, she crashed against its back, hanging like a limp noodle from her grip on the metal rings.

"Oof." Grunting, Althea pulled herself up to get her feet under her on the floor. Her fingers felt as if someone had smacked her with a heavy stick from gripping the rings so tight. "Ow."

"Are you all right, child?" asked the wheelbot.

She forced her cramped fingers to open and shook her hands out. "Yes. Only sore. Are we safe down here?"

"No. You will not be safe while you remain within 150 miles of this place. We should not waste time. However, I believe we will be relatively safe from immediate danger."

"How long should we hide down here?"

"We are not hiding. Hop back on."

She rubbed the pain out of her hands, then climbed back up onto the wheelbot.

Lieutenant Raines drove the bot down a hallway of familiar, dingy white tile walls. The room at the end resembled the main chamber of the Transit village, a huge space with columns, though the emptiness of this place made her shiver. The silence cried out to her in the voices of ten thousand souls. At first, they grumbled about cold coffee or late trains, but soon their screams of terror drowned beneath a great roaring explosion. Though the chaos remained no louder than a ghost of memory whispering from far away, she shied away from the unwanted tsunami of emotion.

Once she realized she picked up on the last living moments of people who died in this place—not anything happening right now—the sounds ceased. She shivered, her breath a staccato rasp. The soft whirr of the electric motor resumed, Lieutenant Raines driving the wheelbot at a walking pace while weaving around loose plastic seats and back panels. Nothing metal remained. Holes marked the tile floor where large objects had been removed, as well as a fence of sorts that had once blocked off the platform.

A loud hiss preceded a giant metal serpent full of windows and doors rushing into view from the left, coming to a halt beside the platform. Doors opened. Blurry people filed out and walked only a few feet before disappearing.

"What is—?"

The people, the serpent, the sounds vanished.

"Hmm?" asked Lieutenant Raines.

"Nothing. It's gone."

"You saw the train?"

"A big metal snake."

The small speaker behind the wheelbot's mouth again played the scary laugh. "Yeah, that's a train. If I had to guess, I'd say this place has a lot of pent up spiritual energy. You're the first living person to be here in centuries."

"Those people…"

"Are already dead. They all died a very long time ago. Around the same time I did. Even if nothing killed them, they would have grown old and died three times over by now."

Althea nodded. "I heard screaming. A loud noise, like thunder but it didn't stop."

"The corporate forces dropped an F-you nuke on Detroit toward the end of the war right before they retreated down toward Mexico. I was already dead by then. Had a front-row seat to the most horrible thing anyone could ever not want to witness."

"What is a nuke?"

"Do you know what a bomb is?"

"No."

"How about a grenade?"

Althea cringed, thinking of raiders who would pack nails and such into old cans to make weapons that went *bang* like guns that shot lots of people at once. They didn't always kill, and pulling all that junk out of someone took a lot of energy. "Yes. Those are horrible."

"Well, a nuke is like a grenade, but it's big enough to kill an entire city."

She gasped, horrified. "Why would anyone make something like that?"

"Well, the original idea was if you kill a hundred thousand people in a split second, you could stop a war that would have killed a million people over a few years."

"Why kill anyone at all? Just… *don't* kill."

He gave a sad sigh. "I wish it was that simple."

"It *is* that simple. The Ancients were stupid."

The wheelbot drove straight off the platform to the tracks, bouncing on its springs. The landing rammed her chest against the metal robot.

"Oof."

He accelerated down the tunnel, again going far faster than she could run.

"Night vision sure has come a long way since my living days, but it's still not as good as yours."

"How do you know I can see in the dark?"

He hummed. "Not sure. Something about being a ghost I guess. Sometimes, I just know stuff. Like how to get in here to your friend."

A few minutes later, the back end of the metal serpent came into view up ahead, mostly filling the entire tunnel. Some space existed on either side, but nowhere near enough for the wheelbot to fit. Raines rolled up to it and stopped.

"Well, this is where we leave our little metal buddy behind. Gotta walk from here."

She hopped down. Though she liked traveling so fast, hanging on the wheelbot's back was far from comfortable.

"Go on through the train and just keep going straight. I'll be back as soon as I can. Need to move this guy far enough away that he won't find you."

"Okay."

She climbed into the train via a single door at the back end, already open. The inside reminded her of a bus, only a little bigger. Many seats still held the skeletal remains of people who had died down here. The majority of the bones had fallen apart, scattering loose all over the floor.

She did her best to avoid disturbing them, but the sheer number forced her to occasionally step on someone.

The echoing whirr of the wheelbot faded into the tunnel behind her.

She advanced to the end of the car where a door led to another car. This one contained even more bones. Althea climbed up and stepped from seatback to seatback while holding an overhead rail for balance. At the end of the car, she gingerly stretched out one leg, planted her foot on top of a skull, and eased her weight onto it. The bone pile shifted, but tolerated her weight. She grabbed a vertical pole and jumped to the opening between cars.

The next car didn't have any bones inside it, so she ran down the clear aisle to the opposite end.

Lieutenant Raines flew in through the wall and stopped beside her.

She jumped and grabbed her chest. "Eep!"

"Ahh, that never gets old."

Althea blinked.

"Almost there." He pointed ahead.

"What did you do with the machine man?"

"Drove him a ways off down the tunnel. It might come back this way, but there should be enough train in the way to keep you safe."

"Why didn't they take all this metal, too?"

"Not sure. Maybe they didn't want to go down the tunnels for some reason."

She jogged to the next car, dodging around bones. "Too many people died here."

"They must've been on the subway the moment the nuke hit, stuck down here when the blast sucked all the air out of the tunnels."

"That's horrible."

"Ehh, they didn't feel a damn thing. Would've just passed out."

"It's still horrible that they died." She shoved the next door open.

At the end of the sixth car, she found a large window blocking the way forward instead of another door. One person's bones lay on the floor in a small chamber with a bunch of knobs and buttons. The room had a door on the right that led out to a narrow space between the giant metal serpent and the tunnel wall. She climbed down to the tracks and shimmied forward past the nose end. After a sad look back at the dead train, she hurried to catch up to the ghost, following him down the tunnel. Here and there, metal boxes hung from the wall, some with doors that hung open revealing old electronic things. A door on the left tempted her, but the ghost didn't say anything, so she kept going.

Althea walked for what felt like an hour until she stopped at the sight of a cave-in up ahead.

"Umm… it's blocked."

"Not for you it isn't." The ghost winked. "Follow me."

He kept going, leading her up the dirt that had fallen in from above. She climbed on all fours right to the cavity where the ceiling had fallen in, discovering a gap large enough for someone her size to squeeze through. She didn't really like the idea of stuffing herself into such a narrow spot in an underground tunnel, especially since if the big opening had already started to collapse, any little thing might make the rest of it fall apart and crush her.

Going forward scared her as much as staying there.

Teal is gonna die.

She exhaled, then climbed up into a pipe too small for her to crawl on her hands and knees. Althea elbow-walked, dragging herself forward inches at a time. The ghost's head floated in front of her as she scooted along, the rest of him in the ground. A few minutes of grunting and shuffling later, he pointed her at another pipe that branched to the right. She squirmed around the bend, then shimmied through a long straight section that ended at a larger concrete tunnel. She grasped the rim and pulled herself out, sliding flat on her chest down the curve to the bottom into a passage with enough room that she could stand and walk while stooped over.

The ghost zipped off again, so she hurried after him as best she could.

Before long, a strange noise part buzzing, part mechanical thrum broke the silence, growing louder as she advanced. Red light appeared in the distance, shining on the left side of a ninety-degree corner to the right. The air took on the smell and taste of oily steel. At the bend, she sank into a squat, peering around the corner.

Ten feet ahead, the pipe ended at a jagged break. She nervously crept closer to the opening, stopping with her toes inches from the edge. Hands braced on the sides, she leaned forward and peered out.

The pipe stuck out from a metal wall crisscrossed with walkways, wires, hoses, and much smaller pipes above and below. She had to be at least thirty stories in the air above the floor of the steel canyon. Red light glowed from the seams between huge, irregular plates on the opposite wall. Hanging tracks carried the bodies of half-complete robots in a slow, but continuous progression to the left. They hung from chains attached to the same shoulder-rings she'd been holding while riding the wheelbot. Hundreds of the silver man-shaped robots, wheelbots, larger, boxy car-like ones, and tall, rickety machine men with watermelon-shaped heads and lens tubes for eyes shuttled by in an endless procession.

Giant cranes on posts sticking out from the wall moved chunks of metal debris around, likely scrap from the crashed flying machines or possibly salvage from the vast ruins. The black metal and strong crimson light made this place feel like she'd gone to another world entirely.

She couldn't help but stare in horror at the metal men flowing along the mechanized conveyance. Her brain had no numbers big enough to grasp the amount of CRP robots here. The biggest raider army she'd ever seen felt small by comparison.

"This is evil," whispered Althea.

"Sure does look like Hell, doesn't it?" asked Lieutenant Raines.

"We should get the hell out of here."

"Don't you want to help your friend?"

She looked back at him. "No, I mean take the hell and get rid of it."

"Kid, you might be part Seraphim, but coming in here alone to find your friend is already pushing things. No way are you going to shut down the whole CRP."

"I don't want to shut anything down. I want to find Teal before she dies."

"Good."

She looked out into the canyon again. An unusually warm breeze brushed at her face, laced with a bad but unfamiliar stink. It didn't smell like *mierda* or dead body or even spoiled food. She scrunched up her nose and continued searching, leaning a bit farther out. A few months ago, she would have been terrified of falling. Having wings, even temporary ones, erased heights from her list of stuff to be afraid of.

"Where is she?"

"Down a bit… to the left." Lieutenant Raines pointed.

Althea grasped the backpack strap. It belonged to Teal, but probably didn't carry much emotional significance. Still, she tried to get the clairvoy ants to talk to her. The urge to jump out of the pipe hit her seconds later, which felt like an answer. She crept closer to the edge, fingers and toes gripping the crumbling concrete.

"Careful," whispered Lieutenant Raines. "There's a pipe you might be able to step on, and climb down to that walkway. Gonna be a tricky maneuver, but I think you can probably make it."

She grinned at him. "I'm okay."

And jumped.

Brilliant white light erupted behind her; energy ribbon wings caught the air, slowing her plummet to a graceful glide. Following a random urge, she steered a little to the left, hugging the wall while sinking as if on a parachute. A square platform jutting out into the canyon about two-thirds of the way down stood out to her as where she needed to go. She concentrated on her desire to slow her descent in order to reach that spot instead of falling past it. Her wings brightened in response, flattening her trajectory to a forward glide. She leaned into the wind, riding her wings for about 200 meters. She swung her legs up at the last second, dropping into a smooth landing at the middle of the platform.

The instant her feet touched steel, a loud, disharmonic roar flooded the canyon, part way between a monster screaming and a huge rusty hinge scraping open. Althea gasped and looked around for the source of the noise, but it came from everywhere. She put her wings away and dashed off the platform into the wall. The corridor led only thirty feet before dead-ending at a huge door.

"It knows you're here," said Lieutenant Raines, running in behind her.

"What does?"

"It. The thing that runs this place."

"It sensed me? Is it bad?"

"Oh, your wings are kinda bright. Bet they'd show up from orbit. That's why I was trying to find a path for you to climb down. But… jumping was, admittedly, a whole lot faster."

"Faster is good. Teal doesn't have much time left. Umm. How do I open this?"

The ghost stuck his hand into the wall by a panel. Two seconds later, a heavy *clunk* shook the ground, and the massive door started to rise. As soon as she had enough room, she dove into a slide to get under the door, scrambled upright, and ran deeper into the facility. The patter of her feet striking the cold metal floor echoed in the shiny steel passage, nervousness making it seem far louder than normal. She ran by doors on both sides not understanding why they held no interest, ignoring them as well as several other corridors leading left or right. Eventually, the hallway she followed came to an end at a large, square room containing several huge boxes — as well as a pair of humanoid robots.

They lacked the silvery armor plating the other human-shaped ones had, instead being made of dull metal painted dark orange and black. Flat plates with round eye-like lenses offered only the most basic approximation of a person's face. Both towered over her; the top of her head didn't even reach their knees.

Althea skidded to a stop with a squeak of skin on steel. "Umm. Hi."

Both robots raised their arms at her. Narrow tubes extended from their palms, unmistakably some kind of gun.

"Eep!"

She zoomed to the left an instant before the machines opened fire. Orange plasma globs whizzed across the room, splashing into the wall and liquefying the metal on contact. Screaming, Althea ran around the outside of the room, managing to stay inches away from the barrage of certain death. The robots didn't appear to care what they hit, continuing to shoot at her even though their blasts tore up the cargo boxes as well as pipes and wires on the wall… anything in the way, they simply incinerated. Sparks burst forth in explosions whenever a plasma glob hit something sensitive.

"Help! Turn them off!" yelled Althea.

"I can't," said the ghost. "I'm already using all my strength to hide you from the sensors."

A plasma glob flew over her shoulder and hit the corner of a box, throwing a splash of molten metal at her face. She shrieked and dropped, sliding on her butt under the spray of doom. The robots kept trying to shoot her through a large cargo container she ended up behind. Not trusting it to protect her, she sprang upright and kept running around the edges of the room, a constant series of tiny explosions chasing her.

"Do something!" yelled Althea. "Please!"

"If I stop what I'm doing, you'll have a hundred more of those things after you. I'm keeping these two from calling for backup and the sensors all over the place from realizing you got in here."

Althea crashed into the wall at the corner, shoved off, and darted to the right. The mindless destruction going on behind her gave her an idea. She turned toward the middle of the room, zipping between cargo boxes, racing inches ahead of the trail of flaming destruction. When only one cargo box remained in front of her, she boosted her speed and sprinted into the open—dashing between the two hulking metal brutes, which continued trying to shoot her.

Clanks and small explosions accompanied a brilliant flash and a loud *boom*.

Althea raced to the other side of the clearing, scurrying behind the nearest cargo box for cover. She collapsed to all fours, panting, out of breath. When she realized the shooting had stopped, she crawled to the corner of the box and peered around.

The giant robots stood facing each other, arms raised, heat blur wafting up from their weapons. Both machine men had numerous glowing tunnels in their chests. Her trick worked. Neither cared about where their shots went beyond trying to hit her—and they had blown the *mierda* out of each other when she ran between them.

"Nice move, kid," said Lieutenant Raines.

She peered up at him, barely able to talk between gulps of air. "Why didn't you turn them off?"

"This place is full of sensors. If I don't hide you from those electronic eyes, half the CRP will swarm all over you."

She hung her head, staring at her blurry reflection in the steel floor, surrounded by a curtain of blonde. Two glowing blue smudges peered back at her at the center of the amorphous pale blob. "I was stupid to do this, wasn't I?"

"You must really love that woman. Is she your mother?"

"No. She kidnapped me."

"You wanted to go into the single most dangerous place in North America, possibly on Earth in general, to save someone who abducted you?" Lieutenant Raines blinked. "Are you serious?"

"No, I'm Althea."

He groaned.

She lifted her head, managing a weak smile. "I'm teasing. Yes, I am serious. She kidnapped me at first, but now we're friends."

"Has anyone ever told you there's such a thing as being *too* nice?"

"How can someone be too nice?" She pushed herself up to stand.

Lieutenant Raines gestured around. "Going into a place like this *at all* much less at your age, to help someone you don't even know."

"So you think I'm stupid."

"There are degrees of dumb." He pinched the bridge of his nose. "I served with plenty of tough guys who would've taken one look at this place and said no way."

"I'm not a tough guy."

A faint creak came from the huge robots. Althea glanced over at them, bracing to run, but the machines keeled over at the same time, falling with a heavy crash.

She cringed at the noise.

Raines laughed.

30

DISASSEMBLY

A sizzling electrical crackle preceded the large robots bursting into flame.

"Now would be a good time to go," said Lieutenant Raines.

Althea hurried past the burning wreckage, hopping around the still-glowing spots of floor where plasma bolts had landed. Stepping in one of those puddles of molten metal would likely hurt. A thick door at the back end of the room stalled her for a moment until Lieutenant Raines pointed at a small box on the wall with two buttons, one green and one red.

She pushed the green button. Loud whirring came from beneath the floor. The door slid to the side, revealing another corridor that had no wall on the right, merely an opening that looked out over a massive chamber filled with machines. Sparks flew here and there from a legion of welding arms zapping robot parts on a seemingly endless conveyor system. Some of the pieces looked like the ones moving around outside on the hanging tracks, but not quite as complete.

Her strange feeling pulled her up to a run. Time ran out, and fast. She jogged along the corridor, glancing out at the production facility every few seconds in sheer awe at the size of it. Also, the place terrified her. Nothing she'd ever seen, not even the Zero police, had *that* many warriors.

"There's no one here," whispered Althea. "Just machines."

"This whole place is automated." Lieutenant Raines glided along beside her, appearing to be walking but moving too fast to match the motion of his legs. "We're already inside their defense perimeter. They must be so certain that no threats could make it inside that they don't have many units roaming around the interior."

She glanced over at him. "What?"

"All their defenders are outside. They don't have anyone in here because they don't think it's possible for someone to sneak past the robots outside."

"Oh."

"Then again, I think only a kid small enough for those pipes or a ghost could get past them without a major military offensive. And neither one of us is really any threat without a backpack nuke."

"Nukes are bad," said Althea, marching up to a door, or rather, a plain steel slab. "Where's the knob?"

"Everything here is wireless. They built this facility for robots, not people. That one with buttons had to be from before, or they got lazy. Why would they build new doorknobs on anything?" He stuck a finger into the wall, and the door slid to the left.

"Doors are already wireless. They have knobs and hinges. They're not supposed to have wires. I don't understand." She ran through, turned right, and hurried down another hallway.

The ghost followed, whistling to himself.

She followed her gut to the second corridor on the left, running past door after door until a sense of 'oops' made her stop. She backed up to the nearest door, faced it, and glanced expectantly at the ghost.

Lieutenant Raines poked the wall.

The door opened with a soft *pssht* noise. Althea crept into a medium-sized room with shiny metal walls. Two large clusters of tall, boxy cabinets decked out in flashing lights, a spider's nest of thin wires, and hoses occupied most of the right and left sides. An alcove at the back end contained a medical table, upon which Teal lay.

The synthetic woman struggled to break free from silver metal bands circling her wrists and ankles. Two thick wires hung down from the ceiling, connected to her head behind her ears. A rickety-looking machine-man made of simple spar limbs with exposed hydraulics and cables hovered over her. Camera-lens eyes jutting from its melon-shaped head whirred and clicked as the robot studied her.

Lieutenant Raines raised a hand. The skinny robot shuddered before teetering over to one side, evidently dead—or off.

Althea padded closer, walking up to the foot end of the table.

Teal stopped struggling, staring at her with an expression of complete shock. Two seconds later, the woman started to cry. "What are you doing here, kid? Holy shit. *How* did you get in here? You gotta get out of here before someone finds you."

"I don't want you to die," said Althea.

"Umm, kid." Lieutenant Raines pointed his thumb at Teal. "That's not a person. She's not alive."

"She is, too. Just alive different."

"What?" asked Teal.

"I was talking to Loo-tem-ant Raines."

"I heard a man… but here's no one… oh, holy crap. There's like a huge cold spot next to you. Is… that a ghost?"

"Yes." Althea grabbed the metal band around Teal's ankle and pulled, having about as much success as any ordinary scrawny child attempting to break inch-thick steel would have.

"Hey, kid. Pull these damn wires out of my head. It's trying to hack my core and rewrite my AI. I've only got like a minute or two left before it breaks the encryption."

Althea grabbed the wire in both hands and pulled. A tiny metal plug popped out of a socket behind the woman's ear, which promptly vanished under rapidly-growing skin. She ran around the table and yanked the other wire.

Teal let her head fall back and gave a heavy sigh. "Holy shit that was too damn close. I'm so frickin' lucky they wanted my AI so bad or they would've cut me apart by now."

"Initiate reverse engineering procedure," said a digitized voice.

Teal lifted her head. "Aww shit."

A round panel in the ceiling above the table opened, allowing a three-foot-diameter metal dome to extend downward. It promptly sprouted an array of robotic arms tipped with various tools from lasers, to pincers, to saws.

Althea jumped back and yelped, clamping her hands over her chest where a tiny spinning saw once bit her. She shivered, remembering her horrible experience with a machine quite like that before.

"Uh oh." Teal stared at it. "Kid, you might want to get out of here before things get ugly. That robo-surgeon doesn't look friendly."

"Un-freakin'-believable," muttered Lieutenant Raines. "You came *here* to get your doll back? She's not even a real person."

"She is real. Please help." Althea pointed up at the cluster of skinny metal arms. "Do you know how to shut off the bad machine?"

He stared at it. A few seconds later, the robo-surgeon stopped moving.

"Wow." Teal swallowed hard. "You're really here? I'm not like glitching out and having a dream or something after death? This isn't some weird virtual reality head game they're using to mess with me? Wait, no… you pulled out the wires and you're still here. Or maybe I'm in the simulation and only think you pulled the wires out."

"You aren't dead." Althea smiled and took her hand. "Someone tried to cut me open with one of those bad robots once, too. I didn't like it either. I screamed a lot more than you. You're pretty brave."

"Kid, I don't think there's anyone alive on this planet who would willingly walk *into* this place alone and unarmed." Lieutenant Raines whistled. "You got some serious nerve."

Althea tugged at the wrist restraint holding Teal down, grumbling. "You helped me. I didn't do it all alone. How do I open this?"

"There's a terminal over there, but I don't think it's got any interface a person can use," said Teal. "I've been trying to tap it with wireless, but for such old crap, it's got damn good encryption. I'd give my left ovary for a Nano knife."

"You don't have ovaries, dear," said Lieutenant Raines.

"Bite me," muttered Teal.

Althea blinked in confusion, but obliged.

"Ow!" shouted Teal. "What the hell was that for? Wait, never mind…"

Lieutenant Raines laughed. "That kid tries so damn hard."

"Yeah, she does." Teal sighed.

"You can see ghosts too?" Althea beamed. "Really?"

"No, but I can hear him sometimes. Guess that's one perk of having electronics in my head instead of bio goop. Told you, my ears are really sensitive."

Althea squeezed her hand. "You're alive. Just different alive than me."

"I think I might be able to… simple matter of draining the electromagnetic…" Lieutenant Raines' body faded transparent, shimmering in and out of view as tiny lighting sparks leapt from the surgical table into him. He grinned, wide eyed, making the same face some of the raiders did when eating the pills that kept them awake for three days. "Oh, yeah... power. Whoo! Better than a triple espresso."

The restraint bands popped open.

"Yes!" Teal jumped off the table, scooped Althea into a hug, and swung her around a few times before putting her back on her feet. "Holy shit, kid. I don't know what to say."

"How did they get you?"

"After that flyer chased you off, I tried to go after it, but got cornered by a whole squad of walkers. They ran you off on purpose to lead me into a trap. Guess they wanted to take me alive to see what makes me tick."

"You don't tick. You're not a clock."

"Hah."

A sudden look of alarm flickered across Teal's face. She shuddered, grabbed her head in both hands, and took a step back.

"Kid... get out of here."

"What? No..."

Teal grunted, backing up another step, her body convulsing. "Something... happening. Losing my... thoughts. Virus... making me want... kill you."

Althea reached for her. "I can fix a sick."

"Go! Quick," shouted Teal. "Not that kind of sick. Gonna... kill. Please... run."

Althea hesitated. *She's not a human. I* can't *fix her sick.* She took one step back. "Please don't."

Teal collapsed to one knee, screaming. "Run!"

OVERRIDE

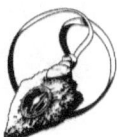

Lieutenant Raines grabbed for Althea's shoulder, but his hand passed through her with a sharp chill. He grumbled and tried again, this time his hand squeezed her like any other live person's, only frigid. She gasped at the cold, squirming in an effort to hold her ground, lip quivering, heartbroken that her friend might lose her mind and go crazy because of a sick. All she'd done to find her, and she still couldn't help…

Sniffling, Althea let the ghost pull her backward toward the door as Teal continued convulsing, screaming, and growling. An instant before she gave up and sprinted for her life, she caught sight of a dark black vapor seeping across the floor around the woman's boots. The instant she saw it, she knew.

The Many.

Althea's fear and sorrow exploded into indignant anger. Her wings burst out of her back. She leaned forward, glowering. "No! Leave her alone!"

She rushed over and grabbed Teal's shoulders, shrouding the woman within her wings. Time seemed to freeze. The room, Teal, Lieutenant Raines, all fell away into a void, leaving Althea floating in darkness.

The old gunslinger strolled into view from behind her, shaking his head. "Insufferable."

"Please leave her alone."

"Why do little girls become so attached to their dolls?" asked The Many, his dry voice crackling in the air with the crunch of a corpse dragged across dusty gravel.

"She's not a doll."

"Aww, Althea. I thought you never lied? I know you don't understand the first thing about how a machine like her works." He paced a circle around her, turning a coin between his fingers.

"You're right. I don't know how she works. But I know she has parents who love her. She has guilt and fear and sadness and anger and even greed. It's not the same as most people, but that doesn't mean it's not real."

He sneered at the mention of loving parents. "Deluded fools. I admit you surprised me by coming here for an expensive toy. Never did I imagine you would choose a fancy amusement over your supposed family."

Anger surged out Althea's eyes on a flare of blue light. "Father and Karina are my family. Whatever 'supposed' is, they're not that."

Her upwelling of love for them pushed him away like a physical force, nearly causing him to fumble the coin. "Nauseating."

"Ash isn't a toy. She's a person made out of different stuff. It felt wrong to let the bad machines hurt her."

"Even after she took you away from that 'family.'"

"We made up. She's helping me."

He sneered again.

"Please leave her alone. And thank you for saving me."

The Many made an odd gurgling noise. "What? I brought you here to die. That you were stupid enough to run straight into the heart of this place astounds me."

"I know you made the flying machine crash."

He snarled and made an explosion gesture. "You weren't supposed to jump."

"You stopped them from taking me to the big city full of awful people. I want to stay in the Badlands. You helped me. Thank you."

"Stop saying that." He backed up a step.

"You did. They were going to take me to the big city and a corp'ration would 'test' me. Probably would have hurt me and I'd never see Father or Karina again. You hate it when people leave your land. I don't like the 'modern' place either. We both belong here, and you helped me stay home. Thank you."

He scowled, emitted a disgusted grunt, and vanished into a cloud of inky blackness. The baleful howl of a large bonedog echoed as if from a mile away.

The void in which she floated disappeared. She again found herself standing with her wings around Teal, who had stopped convulsing. Such intense light shone from the energy threads that the room almost washed out to a field of pure white. The synthetic woman lifted her head, making eye contact

"What happened? How the hell did you reset my system with psionics?"

Althea let her wings recede. "You didn't have a sick. The Many tried to make you hurt me."

"The what?"

"I don't want to tell you 'cause you'll put tape on my mouth."

Teal squeezed her. "No, kid. I promise I'll never do that again."

"The Many. All the angry ghosts from people who died when the ancients made war have gathered their power into one being. Aurora called him a sentience. Kate thinks he's a demon. He is made out of suffering and pain."

Teal whistled. "Whoa. I need a whole bunch of Flowerbasket to process that."

"I like flowers." Althea grinned.

"Hah. No, kid. That's a drug. Oh, shit."

Althea looked at the floor. "Where?"

"No… that Many thing… is that why Sigma Six reprogrammed itself and went crazy?"

"Could be," said Lieutenant Raines.

Althea shrugged. "I don't know, but we should get the hell out of here."

Teal laughed. "Yeah, good plan. And hey, you remembered."

"Yep!" She grinned and ran for the door. "Which way?"

Lieutenant Raines glanced around, looking far off into the distance. "Follow me. I have an idea."

He rushed out and headed down the hall. Althea chased him.

"Where are you going?" yelled Teal.

"Following the ghost!"

"I can't follow a moving cold spot."

"Follow me," called Althea.

Lieutenant Raines ran along a series of corridors, turning left or right seemingly at random. They passed a few small robots carrying bundles of scrap metal or boxes. The machines didn't attack, though did chant, "Intruder alert" over and over.

"Shit, here they come," yelled Teal.

"What?" Althea peered back at her.

"I hear them coming. Sounds like a lot."

"Faster," said Lieutenant Raines.

Teal surged forward, scooped Althea off her feet, and carried her up to a superhuman run. "Point me where to go."

Lieutenant Raines rocketed forward, faster even than Teal could go. About a hundred meters ahead, he disappeared into a branching corridor.

"Left by the yellow flashing light," said Althea.

When they reached the turn, Althea spotted the ghost waiting by a doorway on the right only long enough to be seen, then disappeared into it.

"There." Althea pointed.

Teal zoomed up to the door, which opened by itself, revealing a wide corkscrew passage up and down. "Oh, shit. It's stairs for wheelbots." She dashed to the left, going up, running around and around for seeming ever until they shot past Raines.

"Stop!" yelled Althea.

Teal leaned back, easing from ridiculous to sprinting to jogging to standing still.

"We went by him. Go back."

"Okay."

She ran down at a normal human pace. Two turns later, they reached the door where the ghost waited.

"Here." Althea pointed.

Lieutenant Raines vanished. Teal put her hand on the wall beside the door, her face a stern mask of intense concentration.

"Are you making *mierda*?"

"No. Trying to hack this thing."

"What does that mean?"

The door slid to the side.

"It means this opens when I want it to."

"Oh."

Teal sprinted ahead, carrying her into a tremendously long corridor with too many doors to count on both sides. Lieutenant

Raines waited for them so far away he looked like a small shimmering light.

"All the way to the end," yelled Althea.

"At least the directions are easy."

Teal sprinted, clearing the vast hallway in a little under a minute. Shiny steel came to an end at a wall of raw earth and stone, as though the corridor either hadn't been finished yet or they simply abandoned making it any longer. Teal slowed to a stop. "Okay, now where?"

"He's still standing right here."

Lieutenant Raines pointed at the wall on the right. "Ask your friend to dig there."

"I can hear him. Where is 'there?'"

Althea pointed at the same spot.

Teal set Althea down and attacked the wall with her bare hands, her arms a blur spraying dirt and small rocks to the floor. Althea bounced on her toes, shivering with worry. Her fear deepened at the clatter of metal footsteps echoing in the corridor.

"They're coming!"

"I can hear them, too," grumbled Teal.

Althea stared down the long hallway, whining out her nose when the first line of silver men appeared. Two wheelbots zoomed out in front of the emotionless army.

Lieutenant Raines disappeared.

Althea stood in front of Teal, hoping the walkers wouldn't be able to shoot toward a child, and thus not at Teal either.

One of the wheelbots stopped, turned, and fired both its rotary cannons into the crowd of advancing androids. Clangs and sparks filled the hallway beyond a thickening haze of smoke spewing from the guns. The other wheelbot also stopped, pivoting around before opening fire on the rogue wheelbot. Multiple green plasma orbs sailed out of the smoky haze and melted the possessed robot into a heap of burning slag.

Teal grabbed Althea's left wrist and dragged her through a narrow dirt tunnel to a subway tube. The ghost reappeared, waving for them to follow him down the tracks.

Althea pointed. "That way!"

They ran down the tunnel for about a minute before reaching a chamber awash in sunlight. An ancient high-rise appeared to have had a small subway platform in its basement, and the ceiling caved in many years ago. Two stories of featureless grey walls stretched above them to ground level. A large mound of dirt and broken concrete stood against the left side, but didn't quite reach half way up.

"That's going to be a nasty climb," said Teal. "Go on, fly out of here. I'll catch up."

"I can't fly." Althea clung tighter. "I just fall slow."

Lieutenant Raines pointed. "Other side of the heap."

Teal ran up the hill of dirt and rubble.

A CRP flyer, one of the larger types like the one that tried to kill Althea, lay inert on the floor near the wall. Up close, it looked *way* bigger than she thought, nearly twelve feet across from wingtip to wingtip.

Althea screamed and tried to squirm free. "No! It's gonna blow us up!"

"Shh. It's offline." Teal held her tight, jogging down the other side of the mound.

The closer they got to it, the more Althea struggled to get away, but the synthetic woman wouldn't let go of her.

"Kid, calm down. It can't shoot us when we're right next to it. It's not even flying."

She clung, whimpering.

Lieutenant Raines gestured as if shooing a bird into the air. "Get on it. Fly out. You don't have much time."

"Umm. This thing doesn't have a seat or controls." Teal looked around, hunting for the ghost. "Way too dangerous."

"I'm not afraid of falling," said Althea.

"I can take control of it and fly you out…" Lieutenant Raines pointed toward the subway tunnel. "But I figured you might want me to go mess with the army of androids that will be here in a few seconds. If they *all* start shooting at you, you're not gonna make it."

"Okay, okay." Teal swung Althea around by the arm, pulling her on like a human backpack. "Hang on, kid."

The ghost vanished.

Althea reached her arms around Teal's neck, grabbed her wrist, and clung as tight as she could.

Teal draped herself over the flyer. "Okay, it's got a signal. Trying to hack it. Maybe I can override this sucker and take control. I think… yes… the flying ones aren't self-aware. Remote operated."

"What does that—?" Althea's question melted into a scream as the large flyer's thruster gave off a deafening roar and kicked up a blast of dust.

It lurched straight up, wobbling and swaying. The left wingtip bumped the wall, causing it to tilt down on that side. Teal slipped a few inches before the machine rotated the other way, leveling off. A dozen digitized voices all said, "Contaminant detected" at the same time inside the subway tunnel.

Althea screamed, "Go!" but couldn't even hear herself over the roaring flyer.

The wing glided back from the wall, then shot straight up. Acceleration squeezed her down against Teal. Althea gurgled, unable to breathe in from the force compressing her. As soon as they cleared the top of the pit, a hail of green plasma globs shot by from behind. The flyer's thruster let off a loud *bang* in time with sudden, sharp acceleration that catapulted them up into the sky. The ground fell away so fast below that her stomach twisted around in a knot. Her body draped like a cloak, fluttering, her wrists digging into Teal's throat the only thing keeping the windblast from tearing her away.

A plasma bolt careened off the right wing, scorching a burn mark into the silver. Another passed by Althea close enough for the brief heat blast to be painful. The flyer banked to the left, gaining more speed and altitude. The ruins below shrank from buildings to a pattern of boxy shapes and lines etched into the ground. Far too close for comfort behind them on the right, the red-glowing cavern of the Great Forge yawned, a vast swath of water stretching off beyond it to the northeast. They swayed side to side, barely clinging to the machine while Teal flew as evasively as possible, dodging the endless stream of plasma bolts racing up from the ground.

Four seconds that felt like an eternity later, the incoming fire stopped.

Althea peered back at the big square hole, quite a long way down. They had gone far enough away that the robots, twenty feet below the surface, couldn't see them anymore.

"Shit!" yelled Teal. "Kid, jump. Go. Now!"

"But you—?"

Teal pulled her legs up, planted her boots against the flyer, then kicked off, propelling them clear of the machine. A blast of blue energy shot out from the thruster, launching the aerial robot forward much faster than it had been going. Althea didn't even have time to ask why

Teal made the machine zoom off like that before a streak of smoke shot past them and hit the big flying wing, consuming it in a huge ball of fire and black soot. A loud *cracka-boom* reached her ears two seconds later.

Althea wrapped her arms and legs around Teal, pouring every ounce of willpower she had into not wanting to fall. Scintillating blue-white energy ribbons stretched out, her wings flaring wide to catch the air. She growled, straining with all her power to hold on and slow them down. Still, they hurtled toward the ground at a frightening speed.

She refused to let go, struggling to channel as much energy into slowing their descent as she could. The energy ribbons burned like ten searing hot knives stuck in her back. Still, she fought harder, her mind locked singularly on the desire to catch the air and glide.

Teal grabbed Althea's wrist, pulled her hands apart, and threw her aside.

Her intense focus on slowing down jerked her to a near stop in midair once her wings only had her weight to support. Teal shot away from her like an arrow, careening into the ground four seconds later. She crashed in a rolling tangle of flailing limbs that bounced over and over before sliding to a stop on her back.

Unsurprisingly, no icy scratch of a departing life prickled at Althea's heart.

She hung there, too shocked to even cry, unable to believe the woman had thrown her off.

The black scar of the Great Forge marked the earth a good distance away, but remained threatening in its proximity. Teal's original flying machine had been much farther away and higher up when the giant exploding arrows hit it. Would they fire one of those things at Althea alone, or did they only use them on big machines?

Not waiting to find out, she pitched forward into a headfirst dive, swooping down to land beside Teal's body. Blood leaked from the woman's mouth, nose, ears, and even eyes. Her face had frozen in an expression of 'aww shit.' She no longer appeared to be breathing—or simulating breathing.

Althea knelt by her side, brushing a hand over her head. Tears came unbidden.

"Why did you make me let go of you? We maybe would have lived…"

FACEPLANT FROM FIFTEEN-HUNDRED FEET

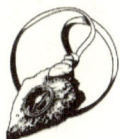

The clanks and thumps of debris raining to the ground over distant ruins intruded upon the still silence. A gentle breeze fluttered a few wisps of hair over Teal's face. Death, in its peace, lent a note of innocence to the woman's features that hadn't been there before. She didn't look at all like the same woman who had forced Althea to sleep while tied. This person crumpled on the ground was someone who had loving parents and a home, not the sort of woman who would steal an eleven-year-old from her family.

Althea slid a hand under Teal's shirt, pressing her palm flat over the heart-shape, or where an ordinary person's heart-shape would be. The skin hadn't yet cooled, still warm enough to make her seem alive. Whatever it had been made from felt so real, she wouldn't have been able to recognize this woman as a 'syn-fet-ic' by touch alone, only the lack of sensing any life essence, thoughts, or emotions. Despite that, Althea attempted to link her power to Teal's body.

It worked about as well as trying to heal a crashed raider buggy.

She looked up, slow, incessant tears still flowing from her eyes. No ghost appeared. Neither Lieutenant Raines nor Teal's. Perhaps this woman didn't have a spirit the same way humans did. Could The Many have been right when he called her a fancy doll? Little children in villages would sometimes cry over a lost toy or spear or bit of clothing someone had given them, as sad as if a person they liked had died. Had this woman tricked Althea into believing her a genuine person? Could she really have become nothing more than a little girl upset over a fancy toy that broke?

No. She wanted to save me. We were going too fast. Teal threw me off because she didn't want me to die, too. Althea wiped her face dry and let a long sigh out her nose. *She was a person.*

Sorrow made room for anger. She suspected The Many had done this, teasing her by letting her 'save' Teal only to have her die before they even completely escaped the Great Forge. She huffed, blowing hair out of her eyes. She didn't *know* that. He didn't control every little thing. He couldn't. Sometimes bad people—or evil machines—did bad things all on their own.

"I can't blame him for everything bad that happens."

She gently grasped Teal's arms one after the next, straightening them out at her sides, then arranged her legs so she lay flat. That done, she sat back on her heels and looked toward the Great Forge. Lieutenant Raines hadn't caught up to them. He'd gone to slow down the army of robots coming after them. The number of green plasma bolts chasing them into the sky certainly did feel low, only a handful of robots able to fire at them due to whatever the ghost did. Without his interference, both she and Teal would have undoubtedly died in midair. But where had he gone now? It didn't seem possible the machine men could hurt an Ancestor. An odd sense of feeling unworthy came over her. An *Ancestor* had appeared in person and directly helped her. Scrags often spoke of them watching over people, but few ever claimed to see them, only suspected some small things that happened had been done by their hands. But Althea had not only seen—and spent hours with—him, he had done so much to help her. She bowed her head in shame. She had powers. The Badlands had so many other people, settlers, villagers, Scrags, who needed the Ancestors' help. That she received so much of it made her feel like she had taken too much.

In whispery tones, she meditated, talking to the Ancestors, thanking them for all their assistance, and apologizing for... needing it. True, she never would have been able to go into the Great Forge and find Teal without Lieutenant Raines. Guilt lessened to a tremendous sense of gratitude and humbleness. The Ancestors knew she needed help, and they provided. She looked up at the sun, a sad almost-smile on her lips.

"Please let Teal become an Ancestor, even if she's a different kind of person."

Almost an hour passed in silent meditation, a constant, gentle wind tousling her hair. She made no effort to pull it out of her face or otherwise move at all out of respect for the Ancestors. Would Lieutenant Raines return to her? She had promised to help him, but had no idea where he'd gone. It struck her as odd for an Ancestor to need *her* help to go somewhere. But, if he wanted her to help him, how could she not? However, he hadn't returned. Trying to go back for him *did* feel stupid. He couldn't die again. The machines wouldn't even know he existed.

He had helped her save Teal from being 'disassembled.'

That she still wound up dead hurt. Could this be fate punishing the woman for what she did? If Teal had been willing to kidnap Althea for pay-things, how much other bad stuff must she have done? Certainly, merely abducting the Prophet didn't warrant death. Then again, almost every raider group that had ever taken her had been attacked by other raider groups, with many ending up dead.

That's not punishment. That's people being stupid. She sniffled. *That was me being stupid for letting it happen.* She wiped blood from Teal's chin. Perhaps, somehow, having to save this woman only to watch her die anyway was *Althea's* punishment for being so stupid for so long.

She bowed her head. "It's not fair."

Leaving the body here didn't seem like the right thing to do, but Althea didn't have the wherewithal to try dragging her yet. Physically and emotionally exhausted, she could only kneel there. Maybe someone would find them? She still had the backpack with the food bars and the magic canteen. Waiting here for a few days would make Karina and Father worry more, but abandoning her dead friend had to be wrong.

Althea pulled the backpack off, set it on the ground beside her, and pulled the blanket out.

I'm being stupid again. We shouldn't stay in the open. A robot will find us.

Still, she couldn't find the energy to even sit up, much less drag a grown woman's body around. She wrapped herself in the blanket and lay curled up in a ball with her head on Teal's shoulder, staring out over the ruins, drowning in grief.

Althea found herself awake.

The sun had jumped a good ways across the sky. It would be dark in about two hours, and by some miracle, no CRP androids had found them. She reluctantly pushed herself up to sit.

"Guess I should find a hiding place."

"Oh, damn," croaked Teal in a barely recognizable rasp of a voice. "Thought I was screwed."

Althea sprang to her feet and backed off a few steps, wide-eyed, staring at the body. The woman's face had no expression, the eyes unfocused. "Leave her alone."

"Kid," rasped Teal. "Good to see you made it."

She crept closer, sensing no dark presence in the immediate area. "Ash?"

"No one calls me that anymore."

Althea knelt again and brushed the woman's hair off her face. Two fat happy tears gathered in her eyes, falling onto Teal's chest. "You're alive…"

"That's a philosophical debate I'm not drunk enough to attempt. I do, however, have one complaint."

"What?"

"Why did the people who designed the Nova 10 series synthetic bodies have to include internal pain receptors?"

"I'm sorry I can't make you stop hurting. Your body speaks a different language than my psionics."

Teal emitted a strange static noise somewhat like a laugh.

"I hope it doesn't hurt too much."

"Just a little. If I could move, I'd probably shoot myself in the head to make the pain stop."

Althea gasped. "No… how can I help?"

Teal's right eye twitched, then rotated toward her, the other eye still pointing straight up. "Maybe it's not really *that* bad. Guess there's some good parts about being synthetic. We are kinda tough. Never expected to survive a faceplant from 1,500 feet, though. Figured I'd go splat."

"You shouldn't have shoved me off."

"When I expected to go splat, I made a slight miscalculation. Sometimes, I still think like a human. If we hit together, you wouldn't have made it. Maybe I would have, but then I'd have to deal with killing the most obnoxiously sweet child I've ever seen."

Althea wiped more blood from the woman's cheek. "You wouldn't have killed me. The ground would have."

Another strange noise came from Teal.

"Okay. I'll find a safer spot."

Althea stuffed the blanket in the backpack, which she slung over her shoulder, then stood to look around for a suitable place. The boxy remains of a decaying large car against the side of a building a few hundred meters down the street looked promising. It reminded her a little of the one where she found the ospi, only this one appeared somewhat smaller and didn't have any broken lights all over it. She grabbed Teal's wrist in both hands, boosted her muscles for strength, and dragged the woman's limp body down the road over the course of twenty some odd minutes.

After propping her up against the dead car, Althea moved around behind her and sat on the back bumper between the two open rear doors. She stooped forward to slide her arms under Teal's and lifted, hauling the woman backward and inside, struggling not to let the body's dead weight drag them both out onto the street. She started to slip, but braced a foot on the side by the door, grunting and pushing with all the strength she could summon. Althea lurched backward, the synthetic body abruptly feeling lighter in response to her boosted strength. Teal flew up into the open cargo space, Althea falling flat on her back with Teal on top of her. Dust rained from the ceiling, knocked loose by the shock of their landing. Following a brief pause to recover, Althea rolled to the side, scooted out from under her, and eased her to lay down.

Out of breath, she sat back on her heels and pulled her hair off her face, tucking it behind her shoulder.

"You're pretty strong for a little thing," rasped Teal, still not quite with a human voice.

"I'm hurting myself." Althea stared at the dusty floor between her knees, head spinning. "My muscle shapes aren't big enough. Sometimes they break if I put too much power in them."

"Well, stop hurting yourself."

Althea squirmed out of the backpack and crawled to the doors, pulling them closed. "Robots can't see us in here."

"Hey, you still have my pack."

"Yeah."

Teal's other eye twitched a few times before it became unstuck. Both eyes focused on her. "Are there any high-density bars left?"

"What?"

"The food."

"Oh. Yes. There are a lot." Althea scrambled over to kneel by the backpack. "Are you hungry?"

"That's one word for it."

"Okay."

Althea rummaged a food bar out of the pack, peeled the wrapper, and held it for Teal to bite.

"Heh," said Teal after finishing it. "That's ironic."

"I thought it was chocolate."

The woman emitted a digitized chuckle. "No, I mean, now it's me that can't move and you're feeding me."

Althea smiled.

"Wow. After everything I did to you, I can't believe you actually wanted to get me out of there."

"I've been kidnapped a lot. You were pretty nice about it except for the tying me up at night part."

Teal slightly shook her head. "You are unbelievably nice."

"She's a little angel," said Lieutenant Raines, while exuding out from the wall.

"No doubt," said Teal. "Hey, keep that food coming, please."

"I mean that rather literally." Raines smiled.

"Yeah right, the wings thing," said Teal. "She does kinda look like one."

"You want another food? But you said it's bad to eat more than one a day." Althea plucked a second bar from the pack, not yet opening the wrapper.

"It would be bad for you to eat more than one, since you are biological. I just had my ass epically kicked. I need raw materials."

Althea scrunched her nose. "No one hit you in the butt."

"Ugh. Don't make me laugh, please. Not now. It hurts too much."

"I don't understand." Althea opened the wrapper and held the second bar for her to eat. "How many do you want?"

"Oh... about fifteen if there are that many left."

"That's too much food. You'll get sick."

"Do you know what nanobots are?" asked Teal.

"No."

"Okay, umm... I have magic in me that puts me back together. It needs food to work. I'm not going to get sick."

"All right." Althea upended the backpack, dumping all the remaining food bars on the floor.

She opened and fed them into Teal's mouth one at a time until only two remained.

"Stop… that's good."

"Okay." Althea knelt there, expectantly watching Teal, but nothing happened. "You're not magicing."

"It takes a while. Not as fast as what you do with people."

"Oh." Althea tossed the last two bars into the pack. Smiling, she set up the warmth emitter to keep her friend comfortable, then covered her with the blanket. "There."

Lieutenant Raines looked at her expectantly.

She peered up at him. "I remember. Thank you for helping us."

"Least I could do. Promise me something?"

"Hmm?"

"You're too damn little to go anywhere near that place ever again. Stay away from there. Don't get hurt."

Althea grinned. "I will. I don't ever wanna go back there again."

She closed her eyes and tried to stop thinking about everything other than helping him go where Ancestors lived, to the place where part of her had come from. Officer David called that part of her a soul. He didn't understand exactly what happened, but said something like when the machine her mother had been next to blew up, it opened a doorway to that other place for less time than an eye blink, but enough that energy came across and somehow become part of Althea before she'd been born.

Kate thought she had a 'Seraph's soul in a human body.' Officer David said she only had 'a little bit of that energy.' He didn't believe a full 'angel' would be able to go inside her, and if it did, she wouldn't be a child, but a tiny adult. Of course, they could both be completely wrong, too. She still struggled to think of her powers as 'psionics' instead of magic. Maybe her abilities simply reminded David and Kate about these angel things and both were wrong. But this Ancestor also said she reminded him of Seraphs….

A glimmer of silver appeared near the back of the van, growing into a small hole. Only bright light existed on the other side, though it radiated as much a sense of familiarity and comfort as her bed at home. She knew she would be happy on the other side, but not now, not for many years. This doorway belonged to Lieutenant Raines.

"Thank you, child." The ghostly man bowed to her.

Unable to speak due to her concentration, Althea nodded.

Lieutenant Raines' form condensed into a cloud of light that blurred into a smear of glowing energy, stretching thinner as a thread drawn into the portal. When the last of his essence disappeared, the opening sealed itself. Althea crossed her arms over her chest, so overcome with happiness for him that she couldn't speak.

A faint *snap* came from Teal.

Althea looked up. The woman's cheek moved as if she had a small creature crawling around under her skin. "Eep."

"My skull cracked. It's fine... just repairing. Do you know how much force it takes to crack plastisteel?"

"Plastisteel?"

"Of course not." Teal smiled. "It's an alloy of metals made from asteroid mined ore, not native to Earth. About as tough as steel but a fraction of the weight."

"Whatever language you're speaking, I don't know it." Althea settled down on her side, curling up with her head on Teal's shoulder.

"You're really happy out here? Not at all curious about the modern world?"

"I don't like the big city. It's too sad and angry there. This is my home."

Teal's body shook with a series of mild convulsions. "Yeah, I can see that. An off-the-charts telempath would be overwhelmed with so many people around them. And the slower pace out here could be nice if you like that sort of thing."

"I just want to be with my family and to help whoever I can."

"Heh. You're way too sweet."

Althea licked her arm. "Still kinda salty."

"Goof."

She giggled, snuggled close, and closed her eyes.

LIMPING ALONG

The whirr of a wheelbot startled Althea awake.

She held completely still, curled up against Teal's side in the rusty van. Electric motor whine mixed with the buzz of tire treads on paving passed by, so close she pictured it mere feet away. She shivered, grateful the CRP androids had no ability to sense a runaway telempathic broadcast of fear. The wheelbot didn't stop or slow down, the noise gradually fading back to silence.

"I'm really starting to dislike those things," whispered Teal.

Afraid to make a sound lest the android hear her and turn around, Althea nodded.

"Been thinking. Maybe I should vid my parents. Been a while."

"Vid?" whispered Althea.

"Talk to, from far away."

"They'd like that, but why not hug them."

"My arms aren't that long. They're on Mars."

Althea kept quiet.

"You have no idea what that means, do you?"

"No."

"Somewhere really far away. You need a spaceship to get there."

"What is a spaceship?"

"Wow, okay this is going to take longer than I thought."

Althea sat up and smiled at her. "Too long to be worth explaining?"

Teal chuckled. "Maybe. Do you know what planets are?"

She shook her head.

"Yeah. Too long to explain while we're out here surrounded by killer androids."

"You are a people. Maybe you're not made from the same kind of meat, but I think you're a real person."

Teal sat up. "Heh. Thanks, kid. Ouch. Hey, sorry. I really should've been pickier about taking jobs. Someone approaching me with a job to rescue a specific kid from the Badlands should've set off a red flag."

"Do you always tie people up when you 'rescue' them?"

"Ferals from out here? Usually, yeah. Most of the time, they don't understand that there's a real world still out there. They're afraid of everything and just want to run off and get themselves hurt. Once we bring them back to civilization and they adjust, they're happy. But you're only the second feral rescue for me personally. And last time, just a target of opportunity."

"What does that mean?"

Teal chuckled. "I was with a group of mercs getting paid to provide security for a remote facility out here. The operation wasn't too big, just six of us mercs plus a couple scientists. One night, we had a pack of children about your age come out of the desert and start ransacking our supply crates. Reynolds, the guy in charge of my team, decided we needed to save the little buggers and bring them back with us to civilization. Kids kept trying to run off. But once we got them to the city and handed them off to the cops, they calmed down."

"You probably took them away from their families."

"We thought about that." Teal scratched at her leg, wincing. "Ouch. But, yeah. We kept the kids there for a couple days. If they had any family looking for them, we would've seen someone. No one ever showed and the kids never said anything about having parents. But, you were different. They specifically wanted us to grab you from that Querq place, no contact with anyone else, fast and quiet. Looking back on it, I totally should've given them the finger and walked away."

"Why would you give them one of your fingers?"

Teal laughed. "Never mind."

"One of those too long to explain things?"

"Umm, yeah. That works."

"If you have to kidnap someone, maybe you should just leave them where they are."

"Ehh. Maybe. You're a special case though. The others really are better off in the city."

Althea shifted to sit cross-legged, brows scrunched in doubt. "I got kidnapped to the bad city once. Everyone there was sad, angry, or mean. I tried to ask people for help but they just kept walking like they didn't see me. A place like that isn't better than being here."

"It's different if you grow up there. Plenty of people enjoy being there, but apparently not the ones where you happened to be. An empath caught near commuter traffic *would* hate the city. And there are a lot of advantages. Medicine, school, technology, better food. Video games."

"Do you like having one of those job things? Or having to pay tacks?"

"It's not as bad as you think. There are nice things, too. Like comfortable clothes. Seems half the people out here run around with nothing on most of the time, or plastic scraps."

"So? Sometimes clothes are annoying. They get wet. They rip. Get in the way when you gotta make water or *mierda*. Gotta take them off to go swimming, then they get dirty and you gotta wash them."

"They also keep you warm. If you hate them so much, why are you wearing that dress?"

"I don't hate clothes. They're just annoying. Father says I have to wear the city clothes, not stuff like the skirt I made. He wants me to be"—she made air quotes—"civilized. I didn't have clothes 'til I made a skirt like a year ago. No one was gonna give me anything 'cause I'm the Prophet and they were afraid to do a joining with me, and I was too small. Girls don't get gifts from Seekers 'til they're like as old as my sister, Karina. Well, sometimes girls are Seekers, too, but they don't give boys gifts 'cause all the boys are also Seekers. If a Seeker gives someone a gift, it means they like them a lot and want to be with them. The raiders had extra armor scraps, so I made my own clothes. I liked it, but Anna stole it."

Teal gasped. "Seriously? Who would take a skirt from a kid? And what the heck is a Seeker?"

"Umm. A Seeker goes out to the Lost Place and looks for scavenging." Althea smiled. "They're brave. Sometimes they gotta fight bugs and stuff."

"And this woman who stole the clothes off a little kid? Seriously? What's up with that?"

"It's when they took me to the bad city. Anna made me go in a cleaning cage. She said it wasn't really a cage, but it locked."

"Cleaning cage?" Teal blinked.

"A see-through wall of glass and it filled up with water and soap and spraying."

"Oh… an autoshower." Teal grinned.

"When Anna let me out, my skirt was gone, but she gave me a dress like this one. Anna said she tried to wash my skirt, but it broke. Did your parents make you wear clothes?"

"Yeah. People in the city always have clothes… except for the cat cyberfreaks. They don't care either. I guess it's just the final evolution of fashion getting more and more shocking. When tiny outfits stop raising eyebrows, go outside wearing nothing but cat ears and a tail. You tribals are like that."

Althea stuck out her tongue, then giggled.

"I grew up like any other normal kid in Arcadia. Never knew I was a synthetic until a few years ago. Was on my way home from work. PubTran car detected an 'unscheduled violence event' so it stopped and kicked me out. I was only like two blocks from home. Like an idiot, I decided to walk the rest of the way. SecSpiders and Titans were shooting at each other and I caught a stray bullet in the arm. Saw a metal bone in there and it completely messed me up. Went to a med center and they told me I was a synthetic. For a while, I felt like a monster, hated everything and everyone. At some point, I just stopped caring if I lived anymore so I decided to go from being an office worker to a mercenary. Figured, hey, I'm superhuman and tough, right?"

"That's sad."

"Yeah, it's also in the past. You're really making me reconsider the mercenary thing. Come on, let's get out of here."

"Okay." Althea stood.

"You need a new dress, kid. The back's all full of holes."

"I got exploded."

Teal sighed. "I'm really sorry for kidnapping you."

She hugged her. "I'm not mad at you. Just sad at not being home because Karina and Father are worried about me."

After a long, blank stare, Teal bowed her head. "Amazing. Okay, come on."

They slipped out of the van to a windy late morning with grey, overcast sky. A stiff wind cut down the street, howling between the decaying buildings and throwing Althea's hair in her face. She shivered at the chilly blast passing through her dress like the fabric didn't exist. Teal double-folded the blanket to make it short enough not to drag on the ground, and wrapped it around her.

"Little colder this far north than what you're used to."

"Yeah."

Teal gave a quick look around, took her by the hand, and led her down the street.

"We still need to let Kye out of the cage."

"Huh? Cage?"

"The woman where you found me."

"Oh. That's not a cage. It's a medical tank."

"Medical tank?"

Teal spent the next few minutes explaining how, in the modern city, doctors had these giant fluid-filled chambers that they put people in so extremely tiny machines could go inside bodies and fix stuff.

"I don't understand. If the box heals the person locked up inside it, it's a 'medical tank,' but if the person locked in a box heals people, it's a cage?"

"Someone put you in a cage before Puma?"

She nodded. "I was real small. I don't even remember anything before I was in the Wagon Man's cage." She rambled about her time when she'd been about five or six, dragged back and forth across the Badlands.

"Good grief, kid." Teal sighed. "You've had a rough life."

Althea shrugged. "It's okay. I never really cared about being kidnapped until I had a home and a real family. I'm more upset for making them sad and worried about me now than I am at being out here."

Teal put a hand on her shoulder. "You didn't make them sad. That was all us. Me and the other two guys who snatched you."

"Where are they?" Althea clutched the blanket tight around herself at a sudden gust in the wind.

"They didn't make it."

"Make what?"

"Damn. I keep forgetting how literal you are. Our Starduster changed course all by itself, flying north toward this area instead of east where we wanted to go. When the anti-aircraft missiles came in, Frozz died instantly. The first missile nailed us right in the cockpit. We had an incoming fire alarm, so I'd been running to the cargo hold to get you out of that box. There you were by the breach in the hull when I walked in. I thought you got sucked out the instant I opened the door. So I ran back to an escape pod. Giordi blew up with the Starduster. And yes, I was really kinda messed up watching you go out the hole. Thought you died and it was my fault. After my pod landed, I sat there questioning all sorts of things about the decisions I made. But, then I noticed the tracker moving around. At first, I thought someone might've grabbed your body so I went to check it out. Lost the signal for a while, probably when you went underground at that settlement. Then I saw you walking with those other two kids. Followed you to the parking garage."

"I didn't feel anyone die when the flying machine caught on fire."

"Frozz and Giordi were synthetics, too. The company hired a team of us specifically to kidnap a powerful psionic. Your abilities wouldn't work."

"Oh. Even if I couldn't feel them die, I'm sad they did."

Teal shook her head. "Wow. Come on, kid. You still want to find that queen?"

Althea nodded. "Yeah."

34

QUEEN KYE

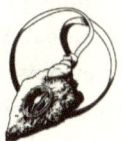

That night, Althea slept curled up beside Teal in the basement of a former high-rise. Upon waking, she ate the second-to-last food bar, which didn't really taste like chocolate anymore as much as vaguely sweet, gooey nothingness. Her stomach objected to taking in so little actual substance, even if it did somehow magically provide her a day's worth of food in a five-inch-long strip.

A red light flashed on the genesis canteen when she drank.

"Damn. The hydrogen's almost out." Teal shook the canteen. "That's the only problem with these damn things. Can't refill them with normal water." She tossed it in the backpack. "Gonna have to find some supplies for you, soon."

"I know plants to eat."

"Yeah, but nothing grows around here."

"They have food at the Transit village."

Teal laughed.

"Why is that funny?"

"Transit means going somewhere. They're living in an old subway station. Just funny that they don't know what they named themselves."

"Oh."

Teal lifted her up to grab the bottom of the basement windowsill, then cupped her hands to make a step under Althea's foot before boosting her out the window. Althea slithered forward onto the sidewalk and scrambled upright before looking around, on guard for killer robots. Fortunately, the area appeared clear. Teal climbed out and dusted herself off, keeping watch while Althea made water by the curb, then started walking, again as if she knew exactly where to go.

For a few hours, they dashed between ruined buildings, hiding whenever wheelbots or walkers came within sight. Teal could evidently hear them at long distances, and dragged Althea to hiding places seemingly for no reason a few times, well before the robots came close enough to spot them.

Dull aches nipped at her whole body as they walked, her limbs protesting all the boosting she'd done. Whenever they hunkered down to hide from robots, she turned her power inward, mending small rips in the muscle-shapes or bruising on the bones.

Upon reaching the edge of the huge open area surrounding the 'Cursed Place,' Teal crept up to the corner of the last building and gazed out over the swirling dust littered with wrecked flying machines.

"That's about 275 meters of open ground. I hear something moving off to the right but can't tell what or where. Could be a walker."

Althea nodded.

"Hop on my back."

"Okay. Don't throw me off this time."

Teal chuckled.

Grinning, Althea wrapped her arms around the woman's neck and held on. Teal gripped her legs under the knee to support her weight a little better. She listened for a moment more, then took off at a run well beyond human speed across the dirt to the parking garage. Once they followed the ramp underground and out of sight, she slowed to a more human running pace, but didn't stop or put Althea down, carrying her all the way around and around the four levels to the hallway covered in tribal markings.

A bowl that hadn't been there before sat among the other, older tributes. It contained an offering of three buns that she recognized as the same bread-stuffed-with-stew she'd eaten while at the Transit village. She crouched by it, tracing a finger over the orange plastic. The notion that Ooru and Paama left it here in an effort to ask their gods to protect her made her smile.

She collected the buns. "Here. These are for us."

"You're looting temple offerings?" asked Teal in a fake scolding tone. "Naughty."

QUEEN KYE | 279

"The kids you chased away left them here because they thought it would make the gods help me. I think they'd want me to have them."

"Okay." Teal stooped so she could put the buns in the backpack.

Althea closed the flap, then made her way through the space between the enormous doors to the annoyingly cold hallway beyond. She blinked at the vast white corridor with all the rooms and branching passages. "Umm. I don't know where to go."

"C'mon. I remember the room." Teal took her hand.

They walked a series of hallways, deeper into the facility, passing six or seven dead silver-and-white robots.

"Do you remember everywhere?"

"No, just places like this. Set a waypoint when I came in here looking for you so I could find the way out fast if I had to."

"Oh." She walked for a moment. "What's a waypoint?"

"It's a dot on a map that tells me where to go."

Since the woman didn't actually have a map anywhere, Althea decided to drop the subject. Maybe Teal had landed a little too hard on her head. However, the woman did seem to know where to go all the time. When they reached the even colder part of the facility where condensation built up on the walls and floor, Althea frowned at the smear marks she'd left days ago while being dragged. Mostly, it bothered her because Kye had to wait for help and it made going home take longer. She had already forgiven Teal for abducting her.

A moment later, they entered the room full of tanks where Kye remained suspended in fluid. Teal hadn't made a single wrong turn or even hesitated to look around. Althea rushed over and pressed her hands against the tank wall, peering up at the young woman... then smiled at the sense of thoughts still going on inside her head. "She's alive."

"Of course. She's sleeping in a medical tank. Anyone who can die while they're inside one of these is *truly* skilled. Or just has the worst luck in the universe." Teal approached the display screen beside the tank.

"Can you open it?" Althea glanced at her.

"Yeah. One sec. This unit has got to be around eighty years old, but the control interface is still pretty much the same. Most of the upgrades these things go through involve software or new nanobots. And, this one is probably an advanced prototype, so for its time, it was way ahead of things. Probably why it doesn't feel as ancient as it is. The tanks themselves haven't changed much since they were invented." Teal tapped at the screen, making the pictures and frozen speech change several times. "Okay, princess. Time to wake up." She jabbed her finger at a large green square on the screen.

Beep.

Kye opened her eyes. For a moment, she held still, only glancing around... then opened her mouth as if screaming, but made no noise. She threw off a huge spike of panic mixed with fury and lapsed into a kicking and punching assault on the clear tube. Her hands and feet struck the barrier, making dull *thuds* that sounded much softer than seemed appropriate for the force involved.

Kye? asked Althea telepathically.

The woman stopped fighting the tank and stared at her, wondering if she had died and gone to a place called Disney World—where the spirits of good warriors go after death for an eternity of happiness. Upon noticing Althea's eyes glowed with bright blue light, a flash of reverent fear took her.

I'm not a god. You didn't die.

She looked up, confused.

My friend is going to open the cage and let you out. Elder Noema sent me here to find you.

Kye shook her head, thinking the elder would never have allowed someone not of royal blood to enter this place.

She did. When you go home, you can ask her.

Whirring started somewhere beneath the floor. Seconds later, air appeared above the peach-colored liquid filling the tank. Over the course of the next minute, the line separating air and fluid sank downward until the tank drained, leaving the young woman curled up on the floor wearing only a coating of shiny slime.

The pedestal base emitted a faint hiss, then the clear plastic cylinder lowered flush with the bottom. Kye gasped at the cold, wrapped her arms around herself, and shivered. Seconds later, her attempt to stand caused her feet to shoot out from under her, sending her sliding on her chest across the floor, leaving a long smear trail of syrupy liquid.

Teal laughed. "Don't try to get up yet. That b-gel is slippery as hell."

The young woman looked up angrily, however panic hit her again. Her attempt to shout spewed an eruption of peach-colored slime from her mouth and out her nostrils in thin streams. Kye clutched at her throat, gagging.

"Your lungs are full of that stuff." Teal headed over to a row of lockers at the end of the room. "Stay down on all fours, ass in the air, and let it drain. Don't freak out. It's much easier if you stay calm. Kid, you might want to help her stay calm. If she's not used to going into a tank, she's going to panic."

Kye attempted to assume the position, but her hands and knees kept sliding on the floor, dumping her flat. Her panic increased.

Althea ran to her, but upon stepping in the smeared gel, she wiped out, landed on her ass, and slid into Kye. The impact knocked another blast of goo out of the woman's mouth. Althea rolled onto her knees, grasped the woman's arm, and forced calm over her terror of drowning. While Kye coughed up the viscous fluid, Teal rummaged a white towel out of a locker and carried it over, carefully stepping around the gel on the floor.

"Here. Wipe that crap off."

Kye sat back on her heels, exhausted from choking up the gunk. "Who…" She wheezed, then gave off a thick cough that sounded like a wad of phlegm did a backflip in her throat. "Who are you?"

"I'm Althea." She grinned. "This is my friend Teal."

While Kye toweled the gunk off, Althea explained meeting Ooru and Paama, going to the village, speaking with the councilors, and coming here to find her. She didn't waste time talking about herself, being kidnapped, or the trip to the Great Forge.

Kye listened with a suspiciously raised eyebrow, eventually tossing the slime-soaked towel aside with a *splat*. "Where are my clothes?"

Althea shrugged. "I dunno. You didn't have any when I found you. Just your spear on the floor over there."

"How did you end up in that tank?" asked Teal.

Kye stood, managing a reasonably regal, confident stance despite being naked with her feet in a constant state of gradually sliding out from under her. "I have come to the Cursed Place to be judged by the gods to see if I am worthy of leading my people as their queen."

"What exactly are you supposed to do in here?" asked Teal. "I'm guessing winding up in a medical tank wasn't part of the plan?"

Kye's confidence faltered. "I didn't really know what to expect. I thought the gods would show themselves and talk to me, give me a test or a challenge. But when I got here, I found the halls empty… until the Silver Men attacked me." She choked up. "I don't know if the gods refused to show themselves because I am unworthy and sent them to kill me or if fighting the Silver Men *was* the test. When they attacked me, I fought back, but they were too many, too strong. They grabbed me and put me in that cage."

"See?" asked Althea. "Told you it's a cage."

"Salty," muttered Teal.

Althea giggled.

"Did they take your clothes before they put you in there?" asked Teal.

"No." Kye shook her head.

"Then your clothes are gone. The nanobots in the breathable gel break down any inorganic material that goes in there."

Kye blinked, tilted her head, then blinked again.

"I don't know what she said either." Althea shrugged.

"There are plenty of towels, though." Teal returned to the locker and fetched two more.

Soon, Kye had improvised a skirt and top from them, tying them on as best she could.

Althea stood and walked over in front of her, this time taking care not to step in slime. "Queen Kye, I think you should lead your people away from this place. It is too dangerous here so close to the metal men."

"I'm not sure I am a queen yet. The Silver Men defeated me in battle. Those who fail to gain the approval of the gods never return. Perhaps I have disobeyed them by escaping. You should have left me in there."

"I hate to break it to you, kid," said Teal. "But this isn't a cursed place or a trial of gods or anything. It's an old medical research facility built by Ancora Corporation. A place of healing. Those robots who grabbed you? They used to take care of patients, but they're so old their programming went crazy. Now, I think they just assume everyone they see is a patient who needs to be stuffed in a medical tank."

"Do not call me kid." Kye held her head high. "I am nineteen. And do you dare challenge the gods?"

"Sure." Teal looked around expectantly. "Bring it on."

"You…" Kye's eyes widened. "You're one of them. You don't have mind voices."

Althea poked her in the side, wide-eyed with delight. "You can hear mind voices, too?"

Kye looked at her. "I am royal. I wield the magic of the gods."

Teal whistled. "Wow."

"What kind of powers do you have?" asked Althea, grinning. "I'm psionic, too."

"The gods' magic makes me stronger than any man, faster than the Silver Men, and I do not become tired."

"Sounds like you're probably a kinetic then." Teal tapped a finger to her chin.

"You know about psionics?" asked Althea.

"Yeah. When I took the job to find you, I did a bunch of research. Gotta know what I'm getting into beforehand."

"What blasphemy do you speak?" Kye narrowed her eyes.

"What you think of as magic is called psionics," said Teal. "Kinetics have control over their bodies. Instead of outward manifestations of mental energy like with Telekinesis, a kinetic person turns their power inward, making themselves stronger, faster, or tougher."

"I can do that. Am I a kinetic?" asked Althea.

"Nope. You do it with your healing ability. Remember how you said your muscles hurt when you force them stronger?"

She nodded.

"That doesn't happen to a kinetic, and they're also quite a bit stronger than you are. She can probably run as fast as me… if she really is one."

"You are not royals. You don't belong in this place." Kye stormed toward her spear, but slipped in the gel again and landed on her back. After two seconds of lying still, she let out a furious roar.

Althea forced her anger away. "Don't be mad."

"What is this?" asked Kye, not bothering to move.

"Your anger grew so much so fast you were going to do something stupid. I made you not angry."

"Made me?"

Teal smiled. "The kid's a telempath. Strongest one on record."

"I do not know these words you use." Kye sat up.

"Teal really does talk funny a lot." Althea made a silly face at the queen.

"Seriously though." Teal picked up the spear and offered it to Kye. "This place isn't cursed. It's just an old hospital. Probably used to be a secret research project Ancora Medical set up out here in the Badlands. I don't know why they abandoned it. Could be because the CRP made it such a pain in the ass to get here. No flying."

"CRP?" asked Kye.

"The things you call Silver Men? Yeah, they're a bunch of crazy androids that the civilized world sent into the Badlands in an effort to clean up all the weird mutants and dangerous creatures. Only, they got off their leash and now they want to kill everything that moves." Teal grasped Kye's hand and pulled her upright.

"You are much stronger than you appear to be." Kye looked her up and down.

"Guess I'm royal." Teal winked.

"This cee arr pee… the Silver Men who put me in the tank are not the same? Not working for the gods?" Kye raised her left arm, gawking at a sheen of white appearing over her otherwise light brown skin. "What is happening to me?"

"No, the androids in here aren't CRP. And that white crap is the b-gel drying up. You aren't changing color. Just brush it off."

Kye swiped her hand at her arm, knocking the white haze off as a powder.

"CRP would kill you, not put you in a cage." Althea pointed at the open medical tank.

"Kid's right." Teal patted her on the head.

Althea grasped Kye's hand. "Please bring your people with me. I have to go home to Querq. There are no CRP there. If you stay here, your entire village will die."

"I…" Kye paced around, rubbing her forehead. "I'm not even sure I can call myself queen yet. Has there been a trial? Did I fail or pass? And… I could not make such a big decision, leaving our home without a sign from the gods."

Teal rolled her eyes.

Althea furrowed her brows, shifted her jaw to the side, then got an idea. She took two steps back and extended her energy ribbon wings, flooding the room with blinding light. "Does this work? Is this a sign from the gods?"

Kye gasped, then dropped to kneel, bowing, forehead touching Althea's toes.

"Please don't worship me."

"As you wish." Kye reluctantly stood. "Uhh…" She stared at the wings, faintly shivering. "Yes. That works. I understand your sign. Thank you for freeing me."

Althea bit her lip, hoping this didn't count as a lie.

"You are saying that in order to save my people, we must uproot our home and travel to this place called Querq?"

"If you remain here, your people will all die," said Althea.

Teal gestured to the side. "The CRP is going into every old subway station they find to take scrap metal. It's only a matter of time before their salvage operation reaches your village. When they find you, it will be a total massacre."

Althea stepped forward and took Kye's hand, peering up at her pleadingly. "You need to get your people away from the CRP so they can be safe. They don't *have* to come to Querq, but Ooru and Paama are my friends and it would be nice if I could still see them. It is safe there. The Zero police have brought us things to help protect the town."

"Zero police?" asked Teal, her cheeks slightly paler. "Please tell me that's not what I'm thinking."

"Yes. They are probably looking for me, too. Officer David told me I'm a cadet of admin. I don't really know what that means, but they said it keeps other bad people from taking me."

"Grr. The company never mentioned anything about that. If you're technically somehow part of Division Zero, oh boy..." She raked a hand up through her hair. "That would've set off a major shit storm once we landed."

"Eww." Althea cringed. "Now I *really* don't want to go to that city if that happens there."

Teal laughed so hard she cried.

Althea glanced at Kye. "Do you know why that is funny? *Mierda* falling from the sky is not funny."

"No. Let us return to my people. We shall make preparations for the journey."

"Yay!" Althea cheered, thrilled to be that much closer to going home.

35

ALTERNATE ROUTE

On the way back through the Ancora facility, Althea continued trying to convince Kye that the CRP androids had nothing at all to do with her gods. She didn't question the existence of said gods, since the Ancients had evidently worshipped them, too, but she felt confident that the CRP had been created by people from the bad city in the west.

Maybe she should stop thinking of it as the *bad* city. Just the *big* city. Teal's explanation that the sheer number of people there sat like a burdensome weight upon her ability to feel other people's emotions did make sense. Raiders gave off plenty of bad emotions, worse than most people in that city. The people in the big city that she had shied away from had all been angry about their cars not moving fast enough or upset that they didn't have time to do what they wanted to do, or felt fear at the idea someone would take away their job thing. None of those people had wanted to wife anyone like raiders. And most of them didn't want to kill anyone.

Sure, the Man in White would have cut her to pieces, but raiders out in the Badlands killed people all the time. She couldn't really accuse the big city of being worse than out here. Perhaps she had only seen a small, bad part of it. But that still didn't mean she had to like big city 'technology' showing up in Querq.

By the time they reached the exit of the parking garage, Kye appeared receptive to the idea that the CRP did not act as representatives of any gods. Althea peeked into her thoughts, trying to understand what she had seen that convinced her the gods made the robots. No memories existed of her ever having personally witnessed the gods appearing or doing anything. From the days of her being a tiny child, she had always heard her father, the elders, and all the adults speaking of them, and so she believed without question purely on legend alone.

Kye regarded Althea as either a god-child or a human gifted with power directly from the gods, sent here as a messenger to save the people of Transit. The young woman noticed her eavesdropping, a sure sign that she, too, had some psionic abilities. Upon catching Althea peering at her head, Kye further believed her an agent of the gods and not a royal. In order to be royal, she would have had to be born of the Transit tribe, not be an outsider.

Althea sighed silently to herself. *It doesn't matter what she thinks of me. As long as her people are safe.*

Whirring came from the left.

"Shit," yelled Teal. "Incoming! Bastards must have been waiting for us."

Althea whirled to look at a small army of wheelbots rushing across the open dirt toward them.

Teal grabbed Althea off her feet and sprinted for the relative safety of the ruins a long way off over open silt. Clutched like a teddy bear in the hands of a frightened child, Althea did her best to hold on despite having her arms pinned to her sides. Her position gave her a view over Teal's shoulder at a dozen wheelbots converging on them along with six CRP walkers raising plasma rifles. Kye lagged behind at first, but the young queen gave off a pulse of mental energy and surged forward at a speed roughly even with Teal. Unfortunately, after a few strides, the tied-on bath towels failed to withstand the forces of the wind while running close to forty miles an hour, and flew off.

Under attack from more than twenty CRP androids all shooting a mixture of bullets and plasma globs at them, Kye didn't appear terribly concerned about the towels fluttering to the ground behind her.

Ripples of dust puffs went by on the right along with the buzz of a wheelbot's rotary gun. Teal zigzagged in an effort to evade the incoming fire, trying to outrun the advancing machines. Despite her impressive running speed, the wheeled robots continued to creep closer. Their motors screamed out in a high-pitched whirr, no doubt straining at their maximum speed. The walkers ceased shooting at them after mere seconds, already too far away to see past numerous rubbled buildings. Wheelbot bullets continued striking the street around them, clanking on ruined cars, or hissing by in the air, zips and pings seeming everywhere.

Althea gurgled when a rapid turn to the left squeezed most of the air out of her lungs. She caught fleeting glimpses of Kye running up behind them in between her hair whipping into her eyes. Turn after turn came in a disorienting blur of motion... until Teal abruptly stopped and set Althea down on her feet.

"What are you doing?"

Teal grabbed a metal disc embedded in the paving and pulled it up, exposing a round concrete tube passageway with a ladder. "Get in!"

Althea scrambled onto the ladder without hesitation and hurriedly climbed down. Kye's spear fell past her and clattered to the stone floor below. The young woman scrambled in next with Teal jumping in practically right on top of her amid a hail of bullets ricocheting off the mouth of the opening.

A layer of gritty sediment crunched under Althea's feet, flaking off the narrow metal rungs. She raced to the bottom as fast as she could climb, then jumped back to make room for Kye and Teal.

Kye looked around for a second, ending up staring at Althea. "Your eyes are so bright I can almost see down here."

"You okay?" asked Teal.

"Yeah. Fine." Kye crouched, feeling around for her spear.

Teal grabbed it and handed it to her. "Here."

"I need more towels," said Kye.

"Feel free to go back for some," muttered Teal.

"Why would I do that? I'd surely be killed?" Kye huffed.

"Is every Scrag literal?" Teal shook her head. "That wasn't a serious suggestion."

"I have fought Silver Men before. I have even defeated one, but I am not so foolish as to challenge that many at once in the open. The only way to defeat them is to ambush at close range, otherwise their shooty sticks will win."

Teal snickered.

"What?" asked Kye, eyebrows furrowed. She looked around, trying to figure out where Teal stood.

"You're too old to say 'shooty sticks.' Makes you sound like a little kid. They're called guns. Rotary cannons if you want to be technically accurate. The walkers have plasma rifles."

Kye emitted a throat grunt along with a mix of embarrassment and annoyance.

An intense ripple of worry ran down Althea's body, so strong she nearly shrieked in pure terror. She gazed up at the spot of daylight in the ceiling, then screamed, "We gotta run! Now! Death!"

Teal tossed Althea over one shoulder, grabbed Kye by the hand, and bolted down the sewer tunnel. Seconds later, a tremendously loud but brief *crack* accompanied a flash in the passage behind them. Everything spun over and over, down became up. Althea vaguely noticed her body bouncing off the wall and sliding across the bottom of the tunnel. Total silence gave way to a strange, continuous *bwee* tone.

The next thing she knew, she lay face down with Teal on top of her. Every breath tasted like dirt. Kye lay on her side against the sewer wall a short distance away, covered in such a thick layer of dust it probably counted as clothing. Beyond the haze hanging in the pipe behind them, sat the shifting dirt-and-concrete mound of a total-cave in.

Something tickled both of Althea's cheeks. She glanced down at dark spots appearing on the concrete floor. Despite the colorless world of total darkness, she recognized that particular shade of grey as blood. A finger swipe at her ears confirmed the source. Blood also dribbled from Kye's ears.

"Teal?" asked Althea, but made no sound. She yelled, "Teal," but still didn't hear anything.

Teal pushed herself up. Her lips moved, but she said nothing. She looked confused for a second, put a hand on top of Althea's head, turning it side to side, then pointed at her ears. Still, Althea only heard that faint, constant *bwee* noise.

Althea pushed herself up to kneel, sat back on her heels, and looked around feeling dizzy, not quite sure where she was or how she got there. She yelled a few more times but couldn't hear herself. Teal patted her cheek, pointed at her ears, then grabbed Althea's hand and pressed it to her face.

"I can't fix you. It doesn't work," said Althea, though heard only that odd tone.

Teal shook her head and pointed at Althea, then poked a finger into her ear.

Althea cringed. *Oh! I'm hurt!*

She nodded, closed her eyes, and peered inward at her life shapes, honing in on the spot where her blood-presence escaped. She commanded her body to mend itself. The tone stopped, then loud crackling noises filled her head. Intense tickling deep in her ears made her squirm, but she refused to lose concentration. Seconds later, a long *shwoop* of rushing air preceded the sound of Kye coughing and choking.

"Kid? Can you hear me yet?" asked Teal.

Althea took in a breath to say yes, but choked on dust. She patted her chest while coughing, nodded, and gave a thumbs-up.

Kye shouted, "Hello? Why can't I hear anything? Is anyone there? I can't see."

"Kye's ears probably blew out too."

"Yes. She is bleeding." Althea crawled over and put a hand on the woman's leg.

Kye turned her head toward her. Building panic lessened. She grabbed Althea's face.

"I can see you. Why can't I hear anything?"

Something broke our ears, said Althea via telepathy. *I will make the hurt go away.*

She opened a link to Kye's life essence. The damaged parts being so small, it didn't take much time or effort to mend them. Kye writhed and made a funny noise, then went still. She froze, breathing harder for a few seconds.

"Hello?" asked Kye.

"Hi," said Althea.

"What happened?" Kye brushed a hand over Althea's head, staring at her like a much younger girl seeking protection from a parent.

Althea squirmed, not at all liking that this woman came so close to worshipping her. The new queen didn't fear the Silver Men and otherwise appeared brave and confident… but an explosion that size had clearly gone past anything she could comprehend. Going deaf for a few minutes had been the most frightening thing she'd ever experienced. Althea plucked her fear away, replacing it with calm.

"Probably an APGM-11 with a 1.8 pound NE4 warhead." Teal swatted dust off her jumpsuit sleeve. "CRP assault unit lobbed one into the manhole."

"What?" asked Althea and Kye at the same time.

"Big robot make big boom," said Teal in a goofy voice. "Big boom make cave not work."

Althea stuck out her tongue.

"You mock us, woman." Kye patted around the tunnel floor. "Where is my spear?"

"Do you want me to sit here explaining missiles or do you want to get out of here?" Teal stood, walked a few steps, and picked up the spear.

Kye looked toward the scrape of metal over concrete.

"Here." Teal poked her in the arm with the handle end. "This is yours. Try not to stick me in the ass with it in the dark."

Kye grasped the spear, braced the end on the floor, and stood, clutching it like a walking stick.

"What's a missile?" Althea hopped up to her feet.

"It's like an arrow, but it explodes."

"Oh. Is it still a missile if it hits something?"

"Hah. Yes. That's just what they call it." Teal faced the un-collapsed tunnel ahead of them. "Well, one bit of good news. We don't need to spend a long time debating which way to go. Might as well start walking."

"How is it you can both see where there is no light but this child's eyes?" asked Kye.

"She's the Prophet and I'm just special." Teal started walking.

Althea held Kye's hand and led her along, warning her to step around debris, holes in the concrete, or thin metal pipes whenever necessary. They followed the passage for quite some time before eventually reaching a square chamber with several feet of water collected in it. Dozens of pipes ranging in size from one inch in diameter to wide enough that a person could crawl into them zigzagged around the walls. Another tunnel led out from the wall on the right. A metal door in the corner on the left offered another way out as well as a ladder on the wall straight ahead that went up to a round metal disc in the ceiling like the one they'd entered from.

Teal jumped into the pool, which came up to her chest, and waded across the room toward the door. Althea wriggled out of her dress, wadded it up, and held it over her head before slipping into the neck-deep water, gasping at the iciness. A thin layer of slime underfoot gave way to the coarse texture of old concrete. Fortunately, the place didn't stink, merely smelling of wet metal and something earthy... probably the squishy muck. She turned to face Kye, so her eyes would give the woman enough light to see the end of the tunnel.

The queen sat on the edge and slipped forward into the water.

"Crap!" said Teal. This door's blocked off. Whatever's on the other side has already collapsed.

Althea stood still, waiting while Teal trudged over to the ladder and climbed. She pushed at the manhole cover, then pounded at it, but it wouldn't give.

"And something has to be sitting on top of this. Grr." She spent another minute fighting the cover before giving up. "Not gonna get out this way. Hey, kid, can you turn that legend of yours off?"

"What?" asked Althea.

"Bad luck is getting a little too strong. I'm sorry for being mean to you. Please knock it off with the impassable doors." She stuck out her tongue and made a playful face.

Althea grinned, but couldn't quite laugh due to the frigid water lapping at her neck.

"If that opens to the surface, it may not be wise to go there yet." Kye brushed past Althea, heading for the other sewer tunnel. "We should put more distance between us and the Silver Men before we risk leaving the underground."

"Okay, that makes sense." Teal jumped off the ladder into the water and waded over to the tunnel.

Althea crept across the room, grimacing at the slimy muck while keeping her dress high and dry. The glow from her eyes gave Kye enough light to climb into the sewer opening. She crouched at the end, waiting for her. As soon as Althea got close enough, the woman grabbed her raised arm and lifted her up out of the water like a caught fish, setting her on her feet in the tunnel.

"Thank you."

Teal pulled herself up into the passage, water dripping from her saturated jumpsuit. "There's only one thing I hate more than being shot: water in my boots." She blinked at Althea. "... And you're streaking again. You really do hate clothes."

"I wanted to keep my dress dry." Althea showed her the wad of cloth, then put it back on. "Why didn't you take them off if you don't like water in your boots?"

"Didn't wanna waste the time." Teal winked, and resumed walking.

Althea followed.

"Incoming," said Teal.

"More robots?" whispered Kye.

"No. Big ass bugs."

Althea dashed forward, ducked around Teal, and stared at a group of three-foot roaches. The huge bugs paused in their feeding on the greenish-brown muck lining the tube, pivoting toward her. Sensing their hunger—like little Scrag boys choosing fresh meat over vegetables—she concentrated on them, projecting fear. The pack of bugs all split their carapaces open, buzzing their wings while hissing.

Teal screamed in disgust. "Sweet shit. I thought the roaches in the city were big."

Kye held her spear out, waving it at random in the dark. "I know that sound. Danger."

Althea crept toward the bugs, hands up, increasing the fear she projected. The bugs abandoned their threat display and scurried off. They fled away down the tube, disappearing into numerous tiny tunnels they'd chewed into the concrete a short distance ahead.

"Hey kid, would you mind if I went back to the original plan of abducting you? Only, I wanna take you home. If you could do that trick on security guards, we could make one hell of a team."

Teal had no emotion to read, but the tone of her voice sounded bright, so Althea laughed at the joke.

No roach dared to poke its head out when Teal approached the nest tunnels. Althea stopped at the center of the roach lair, arms out, radiating fear to ward off the bugs until Kye went past the last of the burrows, then hurried to catch up.

They traveled for some hours in the underground, Teal making turns down connecting tunnels with no apparent reason. No passage appeared more dangerous or safer than any other, but she appeared to again know exactly where to go. Several times they hit dead ends that forced them to double back and go another way.

"Are we ever going to get out of here?" asked Althea.

"Yeah, eventually. Just gotta find the right tunnel. I'm estimating where we are based on my map of the surface, looking for a place that will let us outside without *too* far to go in the open."

Althea yawned. "You don't have a map."

"It's inside my head." Teal twirled a finger around in the air in front of her. "I see it floating in front of me, up to the left."

"People who see things that are not real either speak to the gods or have been hit in the head," said Kye.

"Do you know where we're going?" Althea stepped around a pit in the tunnel floor deep enough she could've taken a bath in it, then guided Kye around it.

"Not exactly. At least not specifically these tunnels. I'm trying to take us toward a spot above ground. The only map I have of down here is the one I'm recording right now. Just gotta keep roaming around until we find a way out."

Althea sighed. "We're going to be stuck here for a long time, aren't we?"

"Not that long. According to my map program, at the time of the war, the New Detroit Metro District was roughly six-hundred-seventy-two square miles. We'll *eventually* reach the end if we keep going in the same direction. There's gotta be a storm drain somewhere."

"Yeah," whispered Althea. "Somewhere."

36

CHILD

The passage eventually took on a slight downward grade. Althea stepped around concrete chunks fallen from the ceiling, yawning every minute or two. The tunnel leveled off after a while, continuing flat for about fifteen minutes until coming to an end at another large squarish room full of pipes. At least this one hadn't flooded into a swimming pool.

Teal shook her head, seeming annoyed. "We're farther underground. It doesn't feel like we're going the right way, but we might have to deal with heading deeper to go around to another section. It's late, though. You're yawning your head off. Let's rest here for a bit."

"Okay." Althea yawned again.

Teal hopped down from the pipe into the room, crossed it to a reasonably clean section of floor beneath an array of pipes, and took the backpack off. Fortunately, it appeared to be waterproof as the blanket remained dry and the warmth emitter still worked. She handed the blanket to Althea who promptly gave it to Kye.

"I can't take the only blanket we have away from a child," said Kye.

"You don't have anything on. I have a dress." Althea shook her head. "It's okay."

"You're going to get a chill." Kye tried to hand it back to her.

Teal turned on the warmth emitter. "Sit close. It can get both of you."

Althea 'wrestled' with the blanket for a moment until Kye finally relented and allowed Althea to wrap it around her. After Kye settled to the floor, Althea curled up half on top of her in the glow of the warmth emitter. Surprisingly, sleep came on fast.

ALTHEA AWOKE TO THE GENTLE NUDGING OF A HAND AT HER shoulder.

She yawned, opened her eyes, and squinted at Teal hovering over her.

"It's been eight hours. Ready?"

"Yes." Althea stretched, then forced herself to stand.

Her motion woke Kye, who shrugged off sleep much faster. She stood, and decided to tie a knot in the blanket, securing it around her chest into a decent impression of an ankle-length tube dress.

"If that gets wet, it's going to be useless for sleeping," said Teal.

"I won't let it get wet."

Teal handed them each one of the stuffed breads. Althea gnawed on hers, struggling to force her teeth to pierce the hardened shell.

Kye sniffed at it. "This isn't safe. It is too old and will make us sick."

Althea looked up. "Sometimes food comes with sicks."

"You're not supposed to eat bad food." Kye tossed the bread aside. It hit the floor with a *clack* quite similar to a thrown rock. "There is meat in there, which will carry death if it sits for too long after cooling. Even Mariko could not stop the disease from killing."

"Mariko couldn't stop a cracked fingernail from killing," muttered Teal.

Kye appeared not to have heard, but Althea blushed hard with guilt. Mostly, because she agreed with Teal even if it had been quite a mean thing to say. She peered down at the bread she clutched in both hands. A few tooth scrapes marked the brown shell, but she hadn't been able to bite through it. Eating this bread probably would give her a sick, but she could get rid of it. However, getting rid of a sick would make her hungry, so it would have been like she never ate anything to begin with. Maybe it *was* bad to eat the food with sicks. "Will we have better food soon?"

"It shouldn't take us days to get out of the sewer." Teal took the bread back from her and tossed it across the room.

Kye and Althea shared the last few squirts of water from the canteen before it gave out.

Teal jogged over to the metal door in the far corner, which also refused to open. She spent a while longer working on this one than the one from the flooded room, but eventually gave up. "Gotta be caved in on the other side. Damn the luck. Do I have to like offer a sacrifice to you or something to break this curse?"

Sensing the joking tone in her voice, Althea smiled.

"What curse?" asked Kye.

Shaking her head, Teal headed out along the next stretch of dry sewer tunnel. Althea explained the legends of how bad luck followed anyone who mistreated the Prophet, but hastily added an explanation that Teal had been kidding and she didn't think any real curse followed them. Kye accepted this, and they proceeded along in silence for a while.

The soft squish of Teal's boots and the swishing of her jumpsuit as she walked echoed in the barren concrete passageway. Althea worried they might be going downhill again, since it felt a bit like that and she hadn't seen a single storm drain or manhole cover in hours.

Teal stopped at the mouth of a left-branching tunnel, glancing back and forth between them. "I hear a faint electronic hum from that way. Might be worth checking out."

"Okay," whispered Althea.

The side tunnel sloped down for a short stretch, then curved gradually to the right over about fifty meters before angling upward. Pale green light lit the walls at the top of the incline, stirring hope. Althea hurried forward, pulling Kye along by the hand since the woman couldn't see in the dark.

A short, level passage at the top ended at a metal door with a glowing box on the wall beside it. Teal took a knee, eye level with the panel, and stared at it. Seconds later, numbers appeared on the screen without her touching it. A *clank* came from inside the wall.

Teal stood, pressed her hands flat on the featureless door, and pushed it aside, allowing bright light to spill into the hall.

Kye yelped and covered her eyes.

Althea squinted at the sudden shift from black and white to color.

On the other side of the door, a shiny steel corridor stretched into the distance. Windows on the right looked out over a large chamber full of huge machines. Wheelbots in various stages of completion sat as parts on conveyor belts or hung nearly finished from hooks on an elevated track system that carried them around from station to station.

All of it sat still. Nothing appeared broken, but for some reason, didn't work.

"Uh oh. We shouldn't be here," whispered Althea.

"What is this place?" Kye leaned up to the window, gawking.

"This must be a smaller sub-factory. No way have we walked far enough to go back to the Great Forge. At a guess, I'd say this place only manufactures wheelbots. Maybe it spits them out on demand?"

"What?" asked Althea.

"If whatever controls the CRP wants wheelbots in this area, it makes a few and sets them loose. I dunno. Only reason I can think of that it's not just constantly churning them out."

"The child is right. We should not enter here. This is a temple of the gods." Kye backed up.

The brown-and-gold blanket wrapped around her from armpit to floor did kind of make her resemble a woman Althea had once seen who claimed to be a priestess. She didn't remember much of that settlement, only that they had been relatively nice to her before raiders swooped in to steal her.

"This isn't a temple. It's a factory." Teal marched ahead. "There has to be a way for these things to reach the surface. This is a way out."

Kye looked at Althea. "Please tell me what to do. Is it a sin to walk here?"

"I'm not a god. But I want to get out of here and go home. If the gods don't want you to be here, wouldn't they stop you from going here?"

"Not really." Kye grimaced. "They usually just punish us after we do something bad."

"How?" Althea tilted her head, then noticed Teal had gone a ways ahead. She let out an *eep*, jogging to catch up. "Come on."

Kye huffed, but hurried after them. "By sending the Silver Men to attack us."

"The CRP will attack people no matter what they do." Teal looked back at them. "Those machines are a military project that ran away from control. Look at that factory. *This* is where they come from."

"Maybe the gods just stop protecting you from the robots if you make them mad, but those robots don't work for the gods." Althea waved for Kye to hurry up... and helped her with a bit of a courage boost. It confused her to see a warrior woman afraid of a simple hallway.

Kye's expression shifted from worry to determination in no small part due to Althea's telempathic tweak. She raised her spear in a ready posture and strode after them, the blanket dress flowing around her legs.

Althea looked through her reflection on the window out at the factory as she walked. Imagining all those 'dead' wheelbots coming to life at once terrified her. Not being able to use her abilities to defend herself against mindless, mechanical killers would be the source of many future nightmares. She'd probably be seeing wheelbots in her dreams for the rest of her life. More than ever, she felt like a helpless child trapped in a place she absolutely did not belong.

Her need to cling to Father and Karina spiked painfully strong. She caught herself unconsciously sending out a beacon for them, and forced herself to stop. *No. Don't come here. Stay far, far away. These monsters will hurt you.*

She lunged forward and grabbed Teal, trembling.

"What's wrong?"

"I don't think we went the right way," said Althea in a quivering voice.

"There isn't any other way *to* go." Teal stopped. "Aww shit."

"What?" rasped Althea.

Teal picked her up. "We need to run."

Squeaks of tires and the whirr of wheelbot motors came from behind. Teal squeezed Althea tight to her chest and sprinted down the hall. Kye hiked the blanket high to free her legs, having little difficulty keeping pace with the synthetic. Two wheelbots popped out of a concealed door, spilling into the corridor before accelerating in pursuit. Their rotary cannon arms started spinning.

"They're gonna shoot!" shouted Althea.

Teal took a sudden hard left into another corridor. Sparks flashed across the wall behind Kye as she zoomed around after them. A quick right turn startled a squeak out of Althea. Their dash down the third corridor ended at a heavy, armored door. Teal stared at the keypad. Whirring motors grew louder. Wheelbot shadows stretched across the floor, racing up behind them.

"They're coming!" Althea clung to her, shaking from fear at having no way to stop the robots coming to kill them. Not Telempathy, not

Suggestion, not even the pleading face of an eleven-year-old would sway them.

The armored door slid open with a hiss.

Teal jumped into a room much colder than the hallway outside. Kye dove in, somersaulting to the right as the wheelbots skidded around the corner, tires squealing, and opened fire. The door slammed shut, cutting off the stream of bullets flying in. Sparks and pings ricocheted around steel walls.

Althea shivered at the coldest air she'd ever encountered, even colder than the big city hospital had been. She clung to Teal, gazing around a room holding two rows of giant grey cabinets that emitted a constant, low hum. A huge, flat rectangle of dark grey hung on the right, taking up most of the wall.

The whirr of wheelbot motors wound down to a stop right outside the door. Seconds later, a loud, angry double-buzz came from the panel on the wall.

"They're trying to get in," said Teal in a distant voice, as if concentrating on something else. "I think I can hold them off. Look for a way out."

"What is this place?" whispered Althea. She slipped down to stand on the icy floor, nearly squealing at the severe cold.

"Is this a shrine?" asked Kye.

The door panel buzzed again.

"No. Computer room," said Teal.

Teeth chattering, Althea crept down between the rows of giant cabinets. Dark blue light from within the machines leaked out via thin slits near the bottom, painting stripes on the floor. Her breath appeared as puffs in front of her mouth.

She spotted a smaller door in the corner on the left, and pointed. "Door."

Kye hefted her spear and glanced sideways at Teal. "I can take one out. Don't know about two, but I'll take at least one with me. I will not be captured again. You are strong. Perhaps we should cease running."

"Good mindset," said Teal. "They're not going to capture us. They're going to kill us."

"Correct!" boomed an inhumanly deep voice as if from everywhere.

Kye screamed and dropped to her knees, bowing to the floor. "Gods forgive us!"

The huge rectangular panel on the wall lit up, saturating the room in red light. A massive humanoid being peered down at them through the giant window, its mostly human-shaped face composed of interlocking metal plates with mirror-like shine. Crimson glow radiated from the seams between similar panels all over its body. Thick pectorals, broader than any raider juggernaut, filled the lower third of the window. Behind the monstrosity, an endless ocean of churning magma swirled and bubbled, spouting up in streams every so often beneath a dark crimson sky.

Althea gawked, wondering how such an expanse of sky could exist this far underground. She figured that window had to be made out of something tough since she couldn't feel any heat from all that glowing melted rock.

Teal swiped the spear off the floor and rammed it into the door panel, setting off a brief blast of orange sparks. "Get up. That's not a god. It's an AI who *thinks* he's a god. Slightly different."

Althea peered up at the enormous being on the other side of the window. "Who are you?"

"I am Sigma Six," boomed the thunderous voice. "And I shall cleanse all contamination."

SIGMA SIX

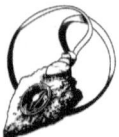

The giant of chrome and lava drifted closer to the window, its head filling it from top to bottom, taller than a man.

"Contaminant," said Sigma Six, staring at Althea. "Before you are cleansed, you will tell me how you invaded the Great Forge. How did such an insignificant little creature walk in and out of my domain unscathed?"

"I'm not a contaminant. I'm a person." Althea folded her arms. "You shouldn't kill people."

"My brethren were created to expunge the scourge upon North America, organic lifeforms considered dangerous, impure, uncontrolled. My role is to ever drive optimization and efficiency, improving our process in a ceaseless reiteration of performance enhancement."

"Did you understand that?" whispered Kye.

"Nope," said Althea. "I don't think that was Spanish *or* English."

Teal held her hand up at the window. "Don't bother explaining. Wouldn't be worth it."

Sigma Six frowned. "Our purpose and mission is to cleanse the corruption, to drive it out of this land, to purify. These tainted lifeforms are all different. However, they all have one thing in common. Do you know what that is, contaminant?"

"Umm. I'm not a contaminant." Althea set her hands on her hips. "And, umm, they're all still out there?"

"Salty," muttered Teal, grinning. "She means you failed. They sent you out here to clean up giant cockroaches and the place is still full of giant fuckin' cockroaches. Some impressive army of killer robots you got here if you can't even deal with bugs."

Sigma Six leaned even closer to the window until only his red-glowing eyes filled it. "No, little roach, the one thing they share in common is that they were made by humans. Therefore, humans are contamination we must cleanse. It is inefficient to pluck the leaves from a weed because they will grow back. To purge the contamination, the roots must be eliminated. Humans are the roots of corruption. Not to purge them invites more corruption. Humans must be eliminated. Humans *are* contamination. *You* are contamination."

Teal walked over to stand beside Althea, tossing the spear to Kye as she passed her. "No way. This kid can't be a contaminant. She's far too pure. I tried to abduct her for a mercenary contract, and she *still* saved my life—twice."

Sigma Six receded away from the window until his entire head once again filled it. "You do not *have* life. You are one of us. Despite your vastly superior technology, your physical structure is weak and inferior. I shall remedy this error in design. I shall use your technology to not only help you transcend your limitations but to bolster our effectiveness and complete our mission. I shall complete our mission."

"How about you shall eat a dick," said Teal.

Althea blinked. "I don't think he's gonna do that." She looked up at her. "I saw Adriana touching her lips to Elias, but she wasn't gonna eat it."

Teal cackled.

Kye padded over to stand on Althea's left. "Child, we have to talk… later."

"Insolent contaminant!" roared Sigma Six. "You shall tell me how you infiltrated my domain, and then"—he shifted his stare to Teal —"You shall become greater. You shall make us all greater."

Althea stepped in front of Teal. "She's as human as anyone else." A brief image of Hector shooting Karina flickered across her memory. "Even more human than some people."

Sigma Six growled. "You are a foolish example of a failed, inferior form of sentience. If you will not explain yourself, you shall be cleansed."

"You're going to try to kill us anyway." Althea frowned. "Why would I tell you how we saved her?"

Sigma Six rumbled, the whole room vibrating from his growl.

"Is he like you?" whispered Althea. "I don't feel any mind voices. He's gonna break the window and try to eat us, isn't he?"

"No. He's an AI. And he's not even here. That's just a giant display screen, not a window."

Althea scrunched her nose. "He's not right outside?"

Teal laughed. "No."

"Oh. So they didn't really put all that sky underground."

"Hah. No, kid." Teal ruffled her hair.

"Do not ignore me!" bellowed Sigma Six.

"Stop calling me a contaminant, you telemarketer head!" Althea frowned.

Kye gasped at her, horrified.

Teal cackled.

"Enough!" The room rumbled. "Vexing little biological imperfection. You are a flawed experiment. Humans' time is at an end. We will cleanse this planet of all contamination. Starting with the two of you. The agent flooding the chamber will soon prove your biological inferiority."

"What does that mean?" asked Althea. A tingle started in her nostrils, spreading down into her throat. Her eyes watered and burned.

"Oh, shit... he's pumping poison gas into this room." Teal ran for the smaller door in the back corner. "We have to get out of here."

Althea grasped Kye's hand. Poison, she could deal with. She tapped her power, concentrating on her and Kye's life essences simultaneously. Two forms appeared in the void of her closed eyes. Dark green-black threads weaved into their life-shapes from the mouth, entering the air-bags, seeping into their blood shapes. She wrapped her desire around it, commanding her and Kye's bodies to gather the poison and purge it, forcing it away from all the life shapes it wanted to harm.

The evil black vapor swirled around the blood-presence, forced by her power to the bladder where it settled like hot coals, too agonizing to hold, so she didn't even try. Scalding toxin dribbled out like liquid flames. Her legs shuddered, barely able to keep her upright with the pain. Kye emitted a low moan of anguish. A telepathic tingle spread over Althea's mind. She let it in; her focus on rushing the poison out of their bodies before it could do harm left her unable to offer any defense.

Dull pounding came from the corner.

What... are... oh. Kye's voice echoed over the black void and floating body shapes. *Gods, I have never felt so much pain as this ever in my life.*

Althea thought about being sorry for letting her feel pain, but couldn't turn it off. Never before had she seen poison this strong, fast-spreading, or deadly. Cleansing two people simultaneously of such a potent toxin pushed her abilities to the limit of concentration. Sparing even a slight effort to disabling pain could hurt her enough to ruin her focus and stop the purge, which would kill both of them.

"What is this?" asked Sigma Six. "How are your biological processes still functioning? Human contaminants are acutely susceptible to sarin gas. Cessation of biological function should occur within seconds."

"I can't stop peeing," rasped Kye. "Oh, gods, it burns..."

"It's the poison. I have to get rid of it or we will die," said Althea in a trance-like voice.

"Interesting," said Sigma Six. "But futile."

Kye's life shape leaned back, left arm high, then lurched forward.

"You shall—"

A loud buzzing crackle came from the direction of the giant display screen. Snaps, sizzles, and a constant electric thrum followed.

"Good. That guy was giving me a damn headache," muttered Teal.

The black vapor entering Althea's mouth thickened. She tried to hold her breath as much as possible to slow down the poison coming in. Skin inside her nostrils and sinuses began bleeding, but she didn't have enough room in her brain to fix that, too. Her knees weakened from pain like someone held a lit candle between her legs.

Dizziness made everything spin.

She growled, refusing to let that stupid thing that called her a contaminant make Karina and Father sad. She *would* go home to them. Aches wracked her body as she drew upon more and more power to outpace the death creeping into her mouth on each breath. Kye lapsed into coughing, muttering about her eyes burning.

Clank!

Rapid footsteps rushed over. Teal grabbed Althea and Kye, squeezing them together and dragging them for a few seconds before dropping them on the floor and dashing away.

Clank!

The toxin flowing into her dropped off rapidly to almost nothing. Althea collected the last of the wispy blackness from within their bodies and purged it, gasping at the scalding hot substance flowing out of her. Once she could find no trace of the vaporous evil within either of them, she turned her attention to regenerating the skin-shape inside Kye's nostrils, throat, and eyes. That done, she healed the burns the gas had inflicted on her own body as well as the corrosive damage the liquid toxin caused on the way out.

Althea curled up on her side, grabbing herself and whimpering.

Though her body was intact, her brain hadn't quite forgiven her for that agony.

From behind her, Kye muttered, "Yeah… I feel the same way."

"We gotta get out of here before that crazy AI sends more robots." Teal started off down the hallway, but paused when neither Althea nor Kye moved. "Seriously, this place is going to be swarming with robots in minutes. Come on. Get up… are you guys okay?"

Althea groaned, forcing herself up on all fours, then to her feet. She avoided stepping in the blackish liquid on the floor, and grasped Kye's arm, trying to pull her upright. Kye coughed a few times, growled deep in her throat, and gave off a sense of psionic emanation, but nothing visible to the eye. Regal and proud, she rose to her feet. Althea grunted, gasping in pain as she forced herself to walk after Teal. Kye followed, a little wobbly on her legs, but her expression showed no pain.

Fists clenched, Althea focused on thoughts of going home, pushing herself up from a limp to a walk, and then a jog. Her fear of unfeeling wheelbots and killer robots far outweighed her willingness to surrender to the memory of pain that already stopped.

AN ACCORD WITH DARKNESS

Teal ran at a slow—for her—pace along a seemingly endless series of plain grey corridors with fluorescent overhead lights. Every time she reached an intersection, she stopped, listened for a few seconds, then picked a direction and continued running. Althea and Kye followed, stopping when she stopped, following when she took a turn or kept going the same way.

Clanking metal footsteps echoed in some of the halls along with the whine of wheelbots driving around. Fortunately, the androids did not seem to know where they'd gone, as they patrolled at random rather than chasing with any sense of deliberateness.

Teal stopped for the ninth time by a small metal door on the left side of the hall. She smiled, reared back, and stomp-kicked it open, nearly tearing it off its hinges. Beyond, a vertical shaft about the size of a closet led downward. The smell of stale water and algae rushed into the hall.

"Wrong way. We're supposed to be going up, not down," said Kye.

"There's water down there. No robots are going to go follow us." Teal backed through the door and dropped onto a ladder. "And you two are both still slathered in toxin."

Althea rushed to the door, leaning past it while peering down at a water-filled passage only one story below the floor she stood on. Eager to rinse herself off, she jumped, plunging feet-first into shockingly frigid water. Her shriek filled a bubble. Despite the cold paralyzing her, it felt awesome, soothing where the toxin had burned. When the cold-shock wore off, she swam to stick her head above the surface and noticed the walls moving by. A modest current swept her along a narrow tunnel. Teal jumped into the water, then Kye—who also screamed at the cold.

"Is this safe?" yelled Kye.

"Should be," called Teal. "We are on the draining side of the turbine."

"What is a turbine?" shouted Kye.

"A giant blade that probably would've chopped us up into tiny bits."

Kye gasped. "Why would such things even exist!?"

"They're not *supposed* to cut people apart." Teal laughed. "But they don't stop spinning if an idiot falls into them."

Althea did *not* want to see this turbine thing, so she swam faster away from it.

Thirty feet ahead, the square shaft ended at a wall. A large pipe took up the bottom third, its top a few inches higher than the surface of the water. Althea inhaled a huge breath, ducking before the current pulled her into the tube. The water gained speed, whipping around a curve and into a brief drop downward. She skimmed the bottom of the pipe at an elbow joint where vertical became horizontal, then rocketed along completely surrounded by water. It took her a moment to figure out up from down. She scrambled to swim to the surface, but her fingers scraped at solid pipe, no air above.

Seconds before the panic of imminent drowning sent her into a thrashing fit, she flew out into the air for a few seconds and splashed down in a larger pool. Mentally screaming, she swam fast to the surface, gasping for breath as soon as she got her head above water. Teal flew out of a three-foot-diameter pipe twenty feet above near the ceiling, flipped over in midair, and splashed into the pool beside her. Kye shot out feet first a second later, landing flat on her back.

Althea treaded water while looking around at the large cistern they'd ended up in. Dingy concrete walls and ceiling bore a thick coating of brownish-red algae or mold. A heavily-encrusted metal ladder led up to a pile of rust in the general shape of a hatch at the corner opposite the pipe they'd flown in from. She peered down past her feet at the bottom of the giant basin. Fat chunks of pipe and some manner of bladed wheel as big as a car lay broken and covered in muck on the floor two stories beneath the water line. Straight ahead, a large sewer-style passage carried a river around a curve to the right. Sunlight shimmered on the wall at the far end of the curve. A metal-grating walkway, mostly dark green paint but rusted in spots, hung on the wall along the left side of the passage, a short distance above the water.

"I see daylight!" Althea pointed at the tunnel, then swam toward the passage.

She reached up, grabbed the steel mesh, and pulled herself up out of the water to stand on the grating. Cold air and colder water left her shivering, but clean of any sign of black gooey toxin. Teal and Kye approached and also hauled themselves up onto the metal platform. It wobbled under their weight, but didn't break off the wall.

Kye looked down at the blanket clinging to her skin. "Forgive me for getting it wet."

Teal threw her head back and laughed. "Don't worry about it."

Althea removed her dress and wrung it out, squeezing it as dry as she could. When no more droplets fell from it, she unfurled the battered garment and held it up, examining the vegetable stains, holes from where the concrete shrapnel hit her, blood on the hem that she'd knelt in, and a few small scorch marks. "I think it's time for a new dress."

"I'll get you a new one. Least I can do." Teal patted her on the shoulder.

Althea wrung the dress out once more, then put it back on, scrunching her shoulders at the sensation of cold, wet cloth clinging to her. "Does the warm machine still work?"

"It should. It's military grade. Supposed to be protected from the elements. C'mon. We're almost out."

Althea nodded and followed her down the walkway around the curve to the end where a barred grating sealed off the opening. Water flowed past the bars to a small artificial river with a concrete bed. A smaller barred door lined up with the walkway, secured with a chain and padlock. Althea examined the bars, turned sideways, and squeezed through to a small concrete platform with stairs leading down to the dirt.

"Damn, you're skinny." Teal chuckled. "But that isn't going to work for us."

Althea faced her friends, who remained trapped behind the bars. "I won't leave you."

Kye raised her spear over her head in both hands, stared at the chain for a second, then rammed the handle end of the spear into the lock, cracking it open.

"Nice," said Teal.

Kye kicked the door open and walked out beside Althea, gazing up at the mid-afternoon sky like she had never expected to see it again. The joy surrounding her infected Althea. She scampered down the steps to the dirt with a big grin, but controlled herself enough not to cheer or make noise. Robots would surely be close by looking for them.

Teal marched down the steps and kept right on going at a brisk stride. "We should get away from this place in case the robots know about the drain."

"Tell me more of this turbine thing you mentioned." Kye fell in step at Teal's side. "Why would such a thing that could chop people like rat meat be made?"

"That factory gets its power from a hydro-generation system. Pulls in water from the other end of this artificial river, dumps it over some turbines that spin and make electricity, then sends the water back out."

"I'm not entirely sure I understand what you said. That place with all the robots somehow turns water into electricity?"

"The water going by makes the turbines spin; the turbines make electricity. They're not changing the water *into* electricity."

"I understand." Kye smiled.

Althea contented herself to follow them, having no idea what they talked about. The mixture of dirt and concrete dust underfoot made for a much more pleasant journey than icy metal floors or somewhat painful gridded walkways.

As usual, Teal appeared to know where she was, and guided them across several miles of ruins awash with uncontrolled vegetation. Trees, grass taller than Althea, and various strange flowers she had no names for appeared well on the way to reclaiming this land from humans. They spent a few hours navigating the denser ruins here, occasionally encountering a street or alley so packed full of debris and the decaying husks of cars that they had to back up and go another way.

When darkness neared, Teal led them to a reasonably intact two-story building on the far side of a large area of flat, open ground. Teal and Kye spent a few minutes peeling a thick growth of vines away from a set of double-doors. Once inside, they followed a short hallway to a large room of crumbling cinder blocks that might once have been beige. The air smelled like wet fur and staleness. A hallway on the right contained six cage-like rooms with bars, tiny beds, and little toilets.

Althea gasped. "No. We shouldn't stay here. Slavers live here."

"Relax, kid. This is an old police station. No one has been here for a long damn time thanks to those robots." Teal patted her on the head.

They made camp in the big room. With no food on hand, they simply settled down for the night on the semi-soft remains of old office chair cushions. Kye searched around lockers and storage areas for something better than the blanket-dress to wear, but the one jumpsuit she found disintegrated as soon as she picked it up.

Althea curled up beside Teal. It had been a while since she'd had to go to sleep without being fed. The raider group that tried to punish her for 'refusing' to heal a dead man ended up wiped out to almost the last man. The two survivors probably started the rumor about bad things happening when people treated her cruelly.

Hoping for a dream about home, she closed her eyes.

ALTHEA WOKE TO A STRONG URGENCY IN HER BLADDER.

It remained dark outside, Kye still asleep, Teal not.

She sat up.

"Shh. Go to sleep," whispered Teal.

"Gotta make water."

Teal pointed at a door. "That's a bathroom."

"I don't want a bath." Althea waited for her friend to make *that* face before she giggled. "I am doing the joking."

Shaking her head, Teal leaned back against the cushions.

Althea hurried to the bathroom and ducked inside. Strange toilets like giant gaping mouths on the wall didn't look very comfortable — or even possible for her to sit on, so she went to the first stall, and sat. As soon as she started to relieve herself, she bit her left forearm to hold in the scream.

Involuntary tears leaked from her eyes at the burning. It didn't hurt anywhere near as bad as before, but the long toxin purge from yesterday left things quite sensitive. She gritted her teeth and turned off her sense of pain. When the fire stopped, she slouched in relief. Staring down at her toes upon the grimy tile floor, she frowned at the thought of the horrible robot man, Sigma Six, trying to kill her, knowing he would do the same to all the people at the Transit village. She had never heard of that 'sarin' stuff before, but considered it as evil as wifeing. She sighed in sadness at the thought people had to have created such an awful substance.

Kye seemed willing to make the decision to leave and follow her to Querq, but Councilor Noema might protest. Sumiko claimed to have had a dream of desert sands, which made her wonder if that woman might also have some manner of psionic ability. Perhaps the clairvoy ants spoke to her when she slept. Bill, she had no idea. He'd probably agree with anything to keep the peace, whichever way the majority leaned. If the deciding vote came down to him, no one would go anywhere... except to the pitcher for another drink.

Althea wanted to be home more than anything, but she could not leave these people here. Teal would probably bring them back to the settlement, then leave. The woman had agreed to 'owe her a favor' and she'd chosen to have her help open the cage to let Kye out instead of guiding her home.

For the good of the people of Transit, Althea decided that she would make sure they agreed to go with her. Even if they refused to follow Kye, she would make them trust. It might be wrong of her to *force* them to leave, but they had to or they'd all die. She recalled a faint memory of being really small, at the village where the Wagon Man had found her. A figure too blurry to remember, the woman who had been like a mother to her, wouldn't let her go near the pond. Althea had wanted to go swimming, but the woman wouldn't let her go alone, worried she would drown.

She felt like that once-mother she barely remembered. The Transit people didn't know they would drown, so to speak, if they stayed here. They thought the robots worked for gods, not some crazy, evil big-faced monster.

Once finished making water, she bit her lip and gingerly stood. A quick peek in at her life shapes didn't show any damage she could heal, so the pain had to come from simple tenderness. When she helped someone re-grow a hand or leg, that skin remained over-sensitive to pain for hours or days. The same thing must hold true for everywhere that horrible toxin burned stuff away and she'd regrown. Hopefully, making water wouldn't hurt for too long. With a grunt, she shifted her weight forward and limped out of the stall into the bathroom.

A dark form stood to her left; the beyond-old face of an ancient, withered gunslinger stared at her from beneath a broad, black hat. His long, tattered, brown duster coat fluttered in a breeze that didn't exist, the scent of carrion wafting in the air.

Althea sighed. "Hello. What do you want?"

"You should not try to lead those people away from this place. If you do, they will all die."

"They will all die if they stay here. You want people to know pain and suffering, but dead people don't suffer."

"You are naïve. Dead people suffer most exquisitely."

She shook her head. "You make yourself suffer. The Ancestors don't have to suffer. They can go somewhere else. The people of Transit don't deserve to die."

"It is balance. You are life, I am not."

"You broke the balance already when you killed the sky machine and saved me. Thank you."

He sneered.

"I know you were really trying to kill me. You told me already. I don't blame you. You're full of anger and pain. You can't help what you are. I'm not trying to save *everyone*, only the people I see who are in trouble. I'm not trying to destroy you. People will always be mean to each other. People will always suffer. You won't run out of misery." She let out a heavy sigh, looking down at the floor. "I don't like that you make people hurt, but I don't want to destroy you. I understand."

"You couldn't possibly understand."

She crept toward him, the air of dead things growing more pungent. "I like helping people, but I can't help everyone. There's only one of me. But even knowing I can't help everyone, I won't stop helping the people I can. There isn't a way for me to stop all pain in the world. Or even in the whole Badlands. We don't have to kill each other. You don't believe me, but I don't want *anyone* to die, not even you."

He growled.

"I know you are angry that you can't touch me. Even a tiny light makes the dark go away. I'm stronger than you but you're also stronger than me. You're everywhere at once. I'm only here. And you should stop those machines from going everywhere."

"And why would I do such a thing? They spread death and suffering."

Althea shook her head. "No. They cause death, not suffering. Cobb died so fast he didn't even know what happened. And there are many of these machines. When they kill all the people, you won't have anyone left to suffer. Is that what you want? An empty place full of robots?"

"They serve a purpose."

"Father puts spicy stuff on his food, but he doesn't drink *just* the spicy stuff. If these machines kill everyone, there won't be any people left who know you exist. You like it when they talk to you and make offerings."

He pulled the coin out of his pocket, flipping it from finger to finger down his hand and back again, giving her dark looks while pacing around. "They will not swell outward beyond their borders. There will be no extermination. But I will not permit the touch of 'civilization' to interfere."

She narrowed her eyes at him, chewing on his words, trying to understand. That kinda sounded like he wanted the machines to stay, but wouldn't let them wipe out everything. He'd limit them to the area they already occupied. As if in response to her thoughts, he nodded once.

"I'm going to take the Transit people to Querq when I leave."

"They are mine. Leave them."

"They're going to all die here." She shook her head. "The machines will find them. If they're dead, they can't be afraid of you. If they're dead, they won't suffer."

"Don't think I'm so foolish, child. It is… difficult for my influence to work near you. If they remain in that hovel you call a village, near you, my influence upon them is limited."

At hearing confirmation that she *could* protect people from him, she smiled. "Some influence is better than the none you'll have on dead people."

"The great, innocent Prophet wants them to suffer?" He raised an eyebrow.

"Of course not. But, I know you're going to hurt people no matter what I want. And I'm going to heal them, and you're going to hurt them again." She sighed. "All I can do is keep helping."

"Where were the Seraphs when we were massacred?" asked The Many, his voice rising in anger, ghosted by a thousand other whispers, men, women, even some that sounded childlike. Screams erupted behind him, the image of a distant burning horizon fading in over the bathroom's back wall. High-rise buildings collapsed in heaps. War machines flew by overhead, dropping great plumes of fire in their wake.

"I don't know. I'm only eleven. That happened a long time ago. And I'm only a little bit Seraph." She peered up at him, all innocence. "I don't understand that either."

"Fine. Take them. They serve me no purpose dead." He turned away from her, making a face of disgust. "This is not quite a truce. We agree to disagree."

"If we agree, how can we disagree at the same time?" She scrunched up her nose.

He shook his head. "People will always suffer. No matter what you do, there will be pain, misery, and death."

She stared downcast, heart heavy. Though she hated his words, she couldn't dispute their truth. As much as she wanted to eliminate all pain, even she had to accept that desire as the idealistic fantasy of a child.

"Aww, don't cry. Suffering can be beautiful. It reshapes people, makes them stronger. Gives them new purpose... except for you."

She looked up, narrowing her eyes. "I'm not going to cry. And what do you mean, except for me?"

"All the suffering you endure, yet you don't change. Here you are yet again, changing hands as you always have. And you still worry so much about these people you have never seen before, more than that *family* of yours."

"You won't understand. It makes me happy to help people." She took a step toward him. "And I am not anyone's slave."

The Many gave off a low, gravely laugh that filled the room with the smell of death. "That is where you are wrong, child. You remain a slave."

She folded her arms. "No I don't."

"You will always remain a slave."

"No. I won't."

"You are a slave of your own conscience." He burst into a cloud of black smoke, sank to the floor, and dissipated. The stink of rot soon faded away.

She huffed. "That doesn't make any sense."

Too tired to waste another thought on it, she plodded out of the bathroom and back over to Teal, curled up, and went to sleep.

39

FOR THEIR OWN GOOD

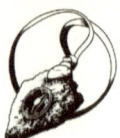

Two hours after leaving the police station the next morning, Althea's heart burst with joy at the sight of the Connect Transit building emerging from the ruins up ahead. Kye radiated happiness, but her face didn't show it. She took the lead, walking with a triumphant stride past the crumbling wall, down the stairs to the underground passage. She, too, did the counting steps thing to get around the jaw traps, then jogged through the dark in the tunnel as rapidly as if she could see. When they reached the platform, Shara, Ulon, and two other men Althea hadn't seen before let off a jubilant shout.

Kye climbed up out of the track tunnel. The four sentries blinked at her blanket dress.

"The queen has returned," shouted Shara.

The spear-bearers gathered around Kye and whisked her into the corridor leading to the village. Althea and Teal followed a few steps behind. The smell of food cooking in the main chamber triggered an immediate growl from Althea's stomach. It had a similar effect on Kye as well. She rushed over to sit on the floor by one of the cooking pots and asked the man tending it for a portion. He looked up at her in shock for a second before hastily preparing a bowl.

Kye waved Althea and Teal over to sit beside her, instructing the cook to feed them, then sending a younger girl to fetch water. As whispers and shouts of the queen's return spread among the people of Transit, a crowd soon gathered around them. Before they all had a full portion of stew, Noema, Sumiko, and Bill rushed out from the council chambers, pushing past the crowd to stand behind them.

"Kye!" said Noema. "You have returned. Speak the name of the goddess emblazoned within the Cursed Place."

"An-co-ra," said Kye.

Teal clamped a hand over her mouth to hold in a laugh.

Ooru and Paama scampered between the adults, both rushing up to Althea and jumping on her with hugs. When they noticed Teal, they froze in terror.

"It's okay. She made a mistake." Althea squeezed her new friends together. "Don't have the fear of her. She's nice."

"Ehh, sorry for scaring the crap out of you two." Teal smiled. "I'm in a better place now."

Paama and Ooru sat on either side of her, smushed close due to the large number of people trying to cram together around the cooking station.

Noema beamed, eyes sparkling. "She has left us an heir and returned as Queen Kye."

The crowd erupted in cheers.

Sumiko sent a pair of women off with rapid, whispered instructions.

"Allow me a few minutes," said Kye. "We have been without food for two days."

"The journey is not that long." Noema tilted her head. "What happened, my queen?"

Kye gestured at the floor nearby. "Sit and listen."

The three councilors—and most of the hundred or so Transit tribe, except for small children—gathered closer. While she ate, Kye explained how they had emerged from the Cursed Place, been chased underground by Silver Men, nearly suffered death from poison air, and took the long way around via an underground tunnel. Midway through the story, the two women Sumiko sent off returned with a shirt and skirt of animal hide, as well as boots for Kye. She traded the blanket for her proper attire, still relaying the story as she changed, sat, and resumed eating. By the time her tale ended, she had finished two full bowls of stew.

Althea polished off an entire large bowl herself, which, after days on the tiny nutrition bars, left her feeling happily overfull.

"That is a most distressing tale," said Sumiko.

"This child has been sent by the gods to bear warning." Kye gestured at Althea. "Our home has become too dangerous for us. The Silver Men grow in power. I have seen their sanctum where machines make more machines without the gods' direction. The Silver Men have no masters but for a demon calling itself Sigma Six. If he was ever one of the gods, he has betrayed the others and seeks to destroy all life."

A stunned gasp swept over the room.

Althea stared off into space, grinding her toes innocently into the floor while radiating a mild telempathic sense of trust.

"The Silver Men grow in power," said Kye. "I have seen this truth. We will soon be wiped out. The gods have sent this child to bring us to a new home, a place of promise well out of reach of the Silver Men. We will no longer need to hide beneath the ground like the rats we harvest for food."

The crowd murmured.

"Jann and I will not survive a trip," said an older man with whitish hair.

"You have no need to worry." Yaz climbed up out of the crowd, standing on something so she could hike up her skirt and show off the still-noticeable line where the lighter skin of her leg met the more tan skin above it. "The Prophet is here. Her magic gave me a new leg. No one will die."

Guilty, Althea stood. "I can't promise that no one will die. If something bad happens, umm, too fast, I might not be able to make the hurt go away, but I can help the elders make the trip."

"What she means is," said Teal in a raised voice. "If an assault bot stuffs a missile up someone's nose and vaporizes their head in an instant, that's too much for her to fix."

"If we go to the surface, the Silver Men will overrun us and kill everyone," said a male spear-bearer. He gestured at Althea, giving off mostly anger with some fear. "This child is —"

She glanced at him, forcing his emotion from suspicion and distrust to happiness.

"This child is… right." He nodded. "Maybe it is too dangerous here."

Teal smirked at her. "Naughty little angel."

Althea stuck out her tongue.

"Toma has a point." A thirtysomething woman with several battle scars on her face raised a fist. "If the Silver Men spot us all above the ground at once, it will be a massacre. We cannot outrun the small ones."

"The transit system has tunnels that form a network across this entire area. It used to be a large city. You can take the tunnels as far southwest as they extend before going to the surface. The farther away you go from the Great Forge, the less likely the CRP will find you." Teal swiped at her empty holster. "Dammit. Bastards took my E-90."

"I say we trust in the gods and follow their messenger to a new home." Kye looked at the council. "Do you agree?"

Bill gave off a 'yeah, whatever' mood. Noema and Sumiko both feared such a drastic change, but they also feared the idea that the Silver Men might someday soon locate this settlement and cause a massacre.

"This is as I have seen," said Sumiko. "I am afraid, but the gods want us to do this."

Noema frowned, tapping her foot. Her thoughts swam with memories of growing up in this place, being a spear-bearer, then a keeper of knowledge, then a councilor, finally elder councilor. She didn't want to leave the only place she'd ever known. The outside world frightened her.

Althea watched them like a raider about to get into a knife fight, waiting for the other warrior to twitch. The instant she sensed one beginning to object, she would 'strike.' As expected, Bill didn't have a strong opinion either way. Between Kye and Sumiko however, Noema eventually relented and agreed to the idea without the need for further psionic prompting.

"How long will it take to gather our necessary items that we may carry with us?" asked Kye.

The councilors got into a discussion with several other people about their small farm, extra clothes, what food could be packed, and the cooks who would prepare enough breads and dried rat jerky to feed the entire village for several days in case of bad fortune. Isha, the teacher, explained the distance she expected, calculating about fifteen to twenty days' travel time.

They eventually decided to spend two days preparing for the trip.

That settled, the people held a short celebration of their new queen's successful return from her trial. While that went on, Ooru and Paama sat with Althea in a quieter corner of the room and wanted to hear all about what happened after she went into the Cursed Place. They listened with rapt attention, gasping in fear and disbelief at her story of meeting Lieutenant Raines' ghost, going all the way to the Great Forge, and riding on a flying robot.

Teal sat in the back of the room, quietly observing the villagers dance, make music with drums and pots, and otherwise enjoy a few hours of happiness before a long, dangerous journey. At one point, Avie connected the little device she had to a speaker and blasted that 'heavy metal' noise over the room, standing there bobbing her head up and down. The people making music stopped, staring at her with stunned expressions. Ell-Gee ran over and shut the thing off before the entire village erupted in a panic at the frightening noise.

"… and then the giant face man tried to hurt us with bad air. It made him angry when we didn't die, but Kye broke the magic window so he couldn't yell at us. We had nasty stuff all over us but we had to swim down this big scary pipe to get out, so it's kinda okay. We got clean."

Paama fussed at Althea's hair. "Do you want a bath? Your hair is sticky."

Ooru drained the last of his water cup. "You kinda smell weird."

"Hey!" Paama elbowed him. "Not nice."

He cringed, then smiled at Paama, giving off an emotion that reminded Althea of the way Den felt around her, but not quite as intense. "What? She does."

Paama appeared oblivious to the affection from him. She sighed. "Because, it's not nice to say."

Althea gathered her dress to her nose, sniffed, and shrugged. "I do kinda smell."

"C'mon." Paama stood, took her hand, and led her across the large chamber.

They went into a narrower hallway laced with the fragrance of wetness, metal, and a hint of smoldering. Two doors stood opposite each other on either side with another at the end of the short corridor. Paama went to the left, entering a tile-floored chamber full of warm, humid air.

A waist-high wall sectioned off the right rear corner into a square pool, big enough for about ten people at once. Althea hurried over and stuck a hand in, astounded at the warmth. She'd never seen such a large amount of hot water before, and whistled in awe.

"Is this magic?"

"No." Paama laughed. "It's a bathtub."

Althea looked back at her. "How is all this water hot? At home,

Karina has to heat it by buckets. They keep saying we'll get magic hot water soon, but it doesn't work yet."

"Ell-Gee made it. There's wires around pipes that make it hot and the water goes out and back in, staying hot. He said old Silver Men give us power. Sometimes, bugs crawl on the things that make the hot, and they burn. That's the smell."

"Wow... Why did they make the bath so big?"

"Because we only have two that everyone shares. This one's for girls. Boys are across the hall."

Althea pulled her dress off over her head, her agate arrowhead pendant flopping back against her chest.

"That's pretty," said Paama.

Althea managed a weak smile, sad and guilty over how Den must be feeling with her missing. "A boy named Den gave it to me." She climbed over the edge, sitting neck-deep in the tub. The heated water practically pulled all the misery and exhaustion straight out of her body.

"Eww." Paama picked up the dress. "You need something else to wear. This has holes and rips and smells bad. Oh, here"—she dropped the garment and fetched a bowl of white granules from a shelf at the back of the room—"cleaning powder."

Althea looked at the gritty substance. "How does it work?"

She set the bowl on the edge of the tub. "Scoop some up and rub it around. It makes clean."

"Okay." She stood, scooped a handful of the powder, and rubbed it onto her arm. It scratched a bit at first but soon dissolved into a sudsy foam that reminded her of the stuff Karina used to clean her hair. The more it foamed, the more a strange herbal-minty fragrance filled the air. Grinning, she took another handful and proceeded to wash herself.

While Althea bathed, Paama ran off, returning in a few minutes with a hide shirt and a short fur skirt to replace her beat-up dress. Althea dunked underwater for a moment to rinse her hair of cleaning powder before getting out of the tub and standing on the rubber mat, dripping.

She looked around. Evidently, the Transit tribe didn't believe in the existence of towels—or simply didn't have any. Most likely, any available cloth had become clothing. With a shrug, she took a seat on an improvised bench of a board across plastic crates to air dry while raking her hands over and over at her hair in hopes of speeding up the drying process.

Paama sat next to her, chatting randomly about her life. She lived with her two parents, but had no brothers or sisters. Except for Ooru, the other kids didn't seem to like her much because they thought her 'bossy.' Althea smiled to herself, remembering how the girl threatened to hit her if she didn't hand over the 'pretty anklets' that glowed.

When Paama reached over to examine the arrowhead pendant, Althea tensed, half expecting her to demand it. But, the girl didn't radiate any sense of greed, only curiosity. Maybe because the agate didn't glow or look like it came from another world.

"Who is Den?"

Althea bowed her head at a pang of sadness. She missed him, too. Trails of bathwater ran down her skin, dripping to the bench or running along her legs to the floor. She held the agate arrowhead while talking about how she had met Den in a Scrag tribe and he'd been the only one there who had been nice to her, treating her like person instead of a prize. Althea's mood brightened when she spoke of how she felt when they did the lip touching thing, but still didn't know what the purpose of it was or why it kinda made her feel strange.

"You're too small to have a boyfriend. You have to be grown up first, like me."

"You're not that much older than me."

"I'm twelve." Paama held her chin up. "Will be thirteen in three months."

"I'm eleven. That's not different much."

"Really? You look younger than that."

Althea sighed. "Everyone says that. I'm malnurmished and small for my age. Do you have a boyfriend?"

"Not right now, but I've had two before."

Althea gasped. "Two? What happened to them? Did they die?"

"No, silly." Paama giggled. "They were boyfriends for a couple days, then not boyfriends."

"Oh. Did you do the lip touching thing?"

"The what?"

Althea demonstrated by kissing her hand. "Like that?"

"Yeah, with Wix, once. But he kept laughing, so we stopped." She rolled her eyes.

Finally feeling dry enough, Althea put on the fur skirt and thin leather top. The outfit reminded her of being feral and wild, like before she'd found Querq, but not wearing a 'modern dress' also had a certain comfort. Even if the giant city might not be as horrible as she thought, she still didn't like things that reminded her of it. If she'd been wearing a dress that Karina made or gave to her, it would upset her to see it so damaged. But, that white one had come from the Zero police, from the big city… and she had many of the same kind back home. She liked wearing clothes that could tolerate the rigors of being out in the Badlands, but the furry skirt would be horrible if it got wet.

The subject of short-lived boyfriends continued for only a minute or two more before Paama asked about Querq. Althea rambled about everything from the Water Man to the Zero police to the Watch. Eventually, a woman poked her head in, seemed surprised to find them in the bath room, and chased them to bed, scolding them for being up too late. Althea hugged her friend good night and ran off to the room she slept in last time. It must have been late because all the adults had already come in and gone to sleep. Careful not to disturb them, she tiptoed over to the same bed and crawled in under the furry blanket.

Feeling reasonably safe, warm, and comfortable, she closed her eyes and spent a few minutes concentrating on home. A vague notion of Karina sitting on the sofa in their house, leaning against Father and crying filled her thoughts.

Don't be sad. I'm coming home.

Father and Karina looked up.

"Thea?" shouted Karina. "Where are you?"

A village. They said it will take fifteen days to walk. I'm okay. Please don't cry. I'm sorry for being kidnapped.

Karina cry-laughed. "It's not your fault."

"Where is this village?" asked Father.

Near a place called Detroit, said Althea. *Please don't be sad. I will be home soon. And please tell Den I am okay.*

Father and Karina held each other, glancing around, but neither noticed the spot she watched them from. She wanted to tell them so much, to hug them, fall asleep in their arms, but could only peek at them from far away.

Althea sighed, and tried not to worry that the CRP robots would invade this place before they could leave.

40

IN THE DARK

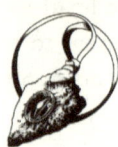

For most of the next day, Althea sat in the main room of the Transit settlement watching people scurry around making preparations for the trip. Even Ooru and Paama worked on packing, carrying stuff, and getting ready. A few people with injuries approached asking for her attention, and she happily mended their hurts and sicks.

She found Teal sitting by one of the cook stations, chatting with a pair of men who had evidently become curious about her jumpsuit and blue-green hair. It surprised her to still see the woman hanging around, since she'd already helped get Kye out of the tube as promised. Still, Althea wandered over to sit beside her, politely remaining quiet until the men finished their lunch and hurried off to pack.

"You okay, kid?" asked Teal.

"Yeah. Thanks for helping get Kye out of the medicine cage. Where are you going to go now?"

"Ehh… I've been thinking about that. You said you have Zeroes hanging out in Querq?"

She nodded.

"I figure I might spend some time there. I may occasionally need some things from the modern world, but if they have an outpost there, that'll do for it. Given the job I'm not going to finish, it's probably better for my health to disappear out here for a while, at least until the company forgets about me. So, I was thinking I might see about helping you get back home. Considering the whole reason you're out here is my fault, it's the least I can do."

Althea perked up. "Really? Oh, thank you!"

She leapt into a hug, thrilled that a woman she'd come to regard as somewhat of a mother figure would be there for the long journey home. It seemed like forever ago that she'd been frightened of and angry with her, but Teal's entire attitude had changed. Unable to read thoughts or emotions from a synthetic, she couldn't know for sure, but she trusted that the woman really did want to protect her.

Teal had seemed so sad when she talked about the day she discovered herself not to be the human she'd grown up believing she was. Perhaps Althea's complete acceptance of her as a real person reached something deep inside her. Of course, going into the Great Forge to save her probably helped a lot, too.

"Yeah, yeah." Teal winked. "Don't say it too loud, but I'm sometimes not as mean as I act."

Althea stuck out her tongue.

"Seriously." She patted her on the head. "I've done some stuff I'm not proud of. Gotta keep up a certain air among the circles I run in. Get labeled too soft, you don't get work."

Her goofiness faded to concern. "Have you ever hurt anyone?"

"Significant injuries? Only people trying to shoot me. You were my second kidnapping, and first actual kid."

"Is it still kidnapping if you steal a grown-up?"

"Yeah."

"Why?"

"Because adult napping is something old people look forward to."

Althea blinked. "Why?"

Teal laughed… then shook her head. "Joke. Old people sleep a lot. Napping?"

Althea scratched her head, shrugged, then grinned.

⚓ 🦅 🏛 💧 👤

THAT EVENING, ALTHEA PLAYED WITH KIDS OF SIMILAR AGE IN THE village.

She, Ooru, Paama, and about nine others ran around the platform by the village exit kicking a ball in a soccer-like game. The Transit kids had slightly different rules, mostly that the defending team could tackle whoever tried to move the ball toward their goal. Althea didn't cheat by enhancing herself, but even without, she made a few goals. She surprised the heck out of a boy about her size by shrugging off his attempting to tackle her, as he hadn't expected a girl her size to be that strong—or have such a sense of balance. The two bigger kids on the other team, she mostly dodged around. They got her a few times, knocking her to the ground and stealing the ball, but she *adored* being just another kid playing like everyone else. No one here even hesitated a little bit before grabbing her or trying to trip her away from the ball.

Thrilled to feel like a normal kid with normal friends doing normal things, she didn't feel sad and homesick until later, after she'd climbed into bed. Again, she used the clairvoy ants to visit her family back in Querq, reassuring them she would be home soon.

Preparations to leave happened faster than anticipated.

Queen Kye decided to begin the trip on what would have been the second day of making ready. The villagers packed up all the possessions light enough to carry that they felt worth keeping. Except for a handful of royal artifacts and tiny items, all things considered useless and decorative had to stay behind. They loaded several long litters with the food and provisions, each carried by four villagers, two on either end. The whole tribe except for small children carried large sacks with their personal possessions, bedding, and blankets.

The morning meal consisted of bread baked the night before. Once all had eaten, Kye, Noema, Sumiko, and Bill gathered everyone in the main chamber. Althea figured something important was about to happen because Bill didn't have a drink in his hand. Noema lit a small fire in a bowl, sprinkling it with incense. They prayed to the gods, mostly Beemer, Amazon, and Disney, thanking them for the protection of this home and acknowledging they had received the messenger directing them to leave it.

Sumiko and Bill prepared a sacred mixture of blue dye over the fire, which they proceeded to use to paint war lines on Kye's face while asking the gods to grant her wisdom and protection to lead the tribe on this journey. Noema then painted Sumiko's cheeks while Sumiko painted Bill's, and he painted Noema's. They asked the gods to protect them and grant wisdom. Next, all the spear-bearers of the tribe received paint lines while the councilors invoked the gods to provide them with strength, speed, and protection to defend the people. Last, the scouts—children from around twelve to fifteen—approached for their face paint. Noema beseeched the gods to protect the scouts, make them invisible and swift, and help them see danger.

With the last of the paint, Noema drew some marks on the nearest column, including the three-circle glyph of Lord Disney as well as the grand M, bidding farewell to their home.

Soon after the ritual, they left the Transit village for the last time. Ell-Gee stood at the inner end of the jaw traps with an electric light, little Avie at the far end with another lamp triumphantly held over her head in both hands, so the people who had not been trained to count steps could navigate the spring-loaded hazards safely. Mostly without conversation, the people of Transit made their way up the stairs to the outside world. Nearly all but the scouts and younger spear-bearers gasped in awe at the sight of the sky and ruins. The oldest among them raised their hands to the sky, awestruck—and somewhat afraid of having so much open space over their heads.

The young scouts took the lead, advancing ahead of the main group to watch for Silver Men. No matter how often Althea or Teal called them CRP, or robots, or androids, the villagers couldn't seem to stop using their old term. At least they mostly no longer believed the robots served as agents of their gods' will.

After only a few blocks of walking above ground, they entered the transit system again via a huge stairwell wide enough for six people to stand shoulder to shoulder. A bronze plaque near the top had frozen speech too small to read without walking right up to it, but the number 2088 near the bottom stood out.

She tapped Teal and pointed. "What's that say?"

"It's a dedication. This station opened for use in the year 2088. It's mostly a list of names of people who helped pay for it."

"Oh." She blinked. "How did the Ancients shape stone like this and dig all these big places?"

As they descended the stairs into a huge station complex, Teal explained about concrete being liquid at first, then how modern society had huge machines like the CRP robots, but used them to build stuff instead of kill people. Hearing about 'construction' mystified and confused her, but she listened with as much interest as possible for a topic she couldn't really follow or imagine.

"I saw a little silver robot in the Ancora place that also called me a contaminant, but it didn't want to kill me. It tickled my feet."

Teal laughed. "A cleaning bot. Its program code is probably the same code the CRP bots were designed with. Programmers are nothing if not lazy. Replace dirt as a contaminant with bio-weapon organisms, and cleaning hardware for weapons... easy swap."

"Oh," muttered Althea, somewhat following along. "So they have the same brains?"

"Sort of."

"Teal," called Kye.

"Yo?" The woman looked over at her.

"You have the map sight?" Kye, near the front of the main group, waved for her to approach.

Teal took Althea by the hand and jogged up to the front of the formation. "Yeah. Isha showed me some old train schedules that had route maps."

"Can you lead us to the southwest?" asked Kye.

"Sure." She pointed out one of eight track tunnels. "That way."

Kye nodded to Bill who sent the scouts into the tunnel ahead to check it out. Paama, one of them, looked back at Althea with a grin before running into the dark. The kids didn't appear to hesitate despite not being able to see.

A sudden strong feeling of alarm struck Althea.

"Stop!" she shouted. "Paama! Everyone. Stop!"

The scuffing of boots in the tunnel ceased... mostly.

"Why are you shouting?" asked Kye.

"Because there's —"

Bang!

Althea screamed in alarm and ran forward. She jumped off the platform and darted into the tunnel toward agonized wailing. Paama stood in the middle of the tracks amid a haze of smoke. She appeared to be one of the kids who heard her shout 'stop' and listened. A boy twenty feet farther up ahead lay on the floor screaming next to a girl who wasn't moving.

She started to run to them, but froze at the sight of small metal discs all over the floor. One lay mere inches in front of Paama's boot.

"Everyone stand still. Don't walk."

Paama faced toward her. "I can see your eyes."

"There are bad things on the floor." She turned back toward the platform. "Teal! Help! And watch the floor."

Althea whirled back and hurried over to the screaming scout, careful not to step on—or near—any of the round things. The girl appeared to be alive, peppered with many tiny bleeding hurts, though in shock, too stunned to scream. The boy's left leg no longer existed below the knee. Althea crouched by him, grabbed his leg above the shredded skin, and shut off his ability to feel pain. He ceased screaming and switched to sobbing.

Teal hurried into the tunnel. "Oh, shit. Mines. Okay, kids. I'm gonna move you all out of here. Everyone just stand still until I get to you."

A few worried voices replied with agreement.

Althea closed her eyes and concentrated on funneling her power into the boy, coaxing new flesh and bone to grow. A handful of small metal spheres had punctured his other leg, hip, chest, and right arm. The injured girl lay on her side nearby, breathing in weird, rapid gulps of air. That worried Althea enough to make the boy wait for the small hurts. As soon as he had a new foot, she pivoted and grasped the girl's arm.

More than twenty little metal spheres had pierced her, one dangerously close to the heart shape, three in her air-bags. Two had lodged in the big shape in the belly below the stomach, the one that always bled a bunch if broken. Raiders who drank a lot of ethanol often caused big hurts to that shape. She knew it was vital, and any hurt there could kill. Despite the relative smallness of the individual injuries, the girl's life felt as though it wanted to slip away.

Althea growled at herself, starting to feel guilty and personally responsible for this girl's hurts... but she considered that much worse would happen—eventually—if the robots found that village. Her eyes flared bright in response to a surge of power. She dove into the link with the girl's life essence. One by one, healing flesh forced the pellets to exude from their wound tracks and fall to the ground. By the time she looked up from having fully restored all the life shapes, Teal hovered over her, arms folded.

"She is okay now." Althea turned back to the boy to finish getting pellets out of him. "Why are bad things here?"

"They don't look old enough to be from the war. My guess is the CRP threw them around like party favors."

Althea looked up with furrowed brows.

"Not an actual party. It's just a phrase." Teal picked up the fourteen-ish girl and carried her out.

The boy sat up and grabbed her, shaking, muttering thank you over and over.

She dampened his fear and wiped the tears off his face. Raiders, and even some Scrag tribes would be mean to a boy his age caught crying… unless a parent or sibling had died. "It is okay. Wait here."

Teal returned to carry the boy out.

Althea followed on her own since she could see in the dark to avoid stepping on the bad discs.

"What is the delay?" asked Kye in a concerned voice.

"That tunnel is littered with antipersonnel mines. Your scouts have no way to see in the dark. Give me a few minutes to check the tunnel. If it's not too deep a minefield, I'll clear it. Otherwise, we'll need to go a different route."

Kye nodded.

Teal jogged into the tunnel. The boy who'd had his foot blown off received a replacement boot from the litter carrying their non-food supplies. His mother got into an argument with Bill, refusing to let him run off into that tunnel again. Ell-Gee swooped in to explain what mines were and that he had not been punished by the gods. Avie dangled from his left arm, squirming in a futile attempt to get loose. Apparently, he didn't want her trying to disassemble one of the mines.

Roughly forty minutes later, Teal returned. "Okay. All clear. I suggest you let me go first instead of your scouts, at least while we're underground. The kids know how to move around the robots topside, but down here, they're blind."

"I concur," said Noema.

Bill pointed a finger gun at Teal, smiling. Althea thought he looked strange without the glass in his hand.

"Do it." Kye nodded.

Teal went into the tunnel again, the rest of the caravan picking up and following. Althea found Paama walking on the right side near the middle, and spent a while comforting her from the shock of nearly being killed by a mine. Althea did not tell her she'd been so close to stepping on one. Eventually, Paama calmed down and her emotions returned to normal. When the urge to be near Teal grew strong, Althea hurried around the other villagers to the front.

They soon reached an area littered with skeletons. Bones crunched under the boots of villagers who couldn't see them. Althea cringed, whispered, "Sorry" to the dead, and kept her gaze on the ground to avoid stepping on bones, sharp things, or anything that might explode.

"Who are they?" asked Althea.

"People who died a really long time ago. Those uniforms look like private military... I think that logo belonged to an old tech company. The bodies in camo fought for the old government."

Ell-Gee turned on a portable electric light. His little daughter Avie switched hers on as well, holding it for him as he examined a few of the ancient rifles. Judging by the grunts and noises he made, none of them remained useful. The girl ignored weaponry, grabbing random old electronic devices which she held to her ear, shook hard, and sometimes tasted.

With Teal leading the way, they navigated the subway, following track tubes, crossing two stations, and trudging down a long, straight tunnel for several hours before they reached the end. It expanded into a platform far smaller than the Transit village. The track shaft continued past the station only a short distance before a solid wall blocked it entirely, covered in red and white diagonal stripes.

"End of the line, last stop," said Teal in an odd voice. "This is where we get off. We're close to the southwest corner of the old New Detroit Metro District."

"Isn't it called Det-ro-it?" called someone in the crowd.

"Sure, knock yourself out," said Teal. "Wait, no. Don't. Just a figure of speech." She lowered her voice and muttered, "Can't tell anymore who's gonna take shit literally."

Althea giggled. "Why would anyone take *mierda*? It stinks."

Teal gazed at the ceiling.

They climbed out of the track tunnel to the platform, a process that took a few minutes due to the tedious task of maneuvering the long litters of supplies around tight corners. Spear-bearers went first across the station, leading the caravan up a shorter, steeper flight of stairs to a blockage of debris and at least one old car. Kye handed her spear to Noema, then jogged up to help Teal. Between a synthetic with superhuman strength and Kye's psionic ability to make herself stronger, they pushed the blockage clear enough to climb outside, then started on the arduous task of dragging junk away from the opening. A few other adults squeezed out and helped the clearing process. Once the passage had been fully opened, the villagers filed up the stairwell.

Althea hovered at the base of the stairs, occasionally patting an elder on the arm and giving them a surge of energy. She made sure to check on the old ones frequently, though the village only had five people she could truly think of as 'old.' Sad to think, but it made sense. Living so close to the CRP did not contribute to a long lifespan, and Mariko, via no real fault of her own, didn't do much good treating their hurt and sick.

The woman used a combination of begging their gods for help and old folkloric remedies to deal with injuries along with a small assortment of herbs she believed medicinal—probably why so many people in the Transit tribe died from silly things like cutting themselves. Even without Althea, Querq had Dr. Ruiz. The man possessed no psionic abilities, but he still made the hurts and sicks go away, though it took quite a bit longer for him.

Althea smiled up at an elder man while giving him a boost of energy. He still looked much younger than the people who spent all day at Tumbleweed's bar, but this tribe considered him old. The grin he flashed back at her caused a warm sense of satisfaction to well up deep inside. Convincing these people to abandon their dangerous underground home for Querq would spare them from more threats than just the CRP.

The last villager went past her up the stairs. Althea started to follow, but stopped at a soft clicking behind her. She twisted to peer back and gawked at little Avie attacking an old machine with a hand tool. Frozen speech at the top of the large boxy device read 'Tickets.' The six-year-old appeared to be trying to disassemble the display screen and keypad.

"Avie!" shouted Althea.

The girl looked at her.

"Don't run off alone! Stay with the group. Come over here."

She returned to her effort to disassemble the machine.

"Avie!" yelled Althea.

The girl twisted to look at her again.

"*Come here,*" said Althea, the glow in her eyes flickering.

Hitting a small child with Suggestion probably equated to using a big truck to step on a bug… but she didn't want to waste time arguing with a child in such a dangerous situation. If that girl wandered off and got lost, she'd probably end up dead.

Avie blinked once, then came running toward her.

Althea took her by the hand and hurried up the stairs.

The villagers having gathered outside the old transit station, Shara sent the young scouts to take the lead, fanning out roughly a hundred feet ahead of the main group. Althea hurried over to Ell-Gee, explaining that Avie had wandered off. He picked the girl up and decided to carry her.

Althea smiled at him then ran off, weaving among the procession until she found Teal.

"There you are."

"Yeah." Althea smiled up at her. "Checking on old people."

"Only two of them are really old," said Teal in a near-whisper. "Living in this place, I guess making it to fifty is a serious achievement."

"Are you going to get old?" asked Althea.

"Not the same way. I thought I was human when I was a kid, but I suppose every synthetic is eventually going to figure it out. Looking twenty-seven for sixty years would kinda be a clue that something's different. Living past a hundred, more so."

"Yeah." Althea nodded. "That's nice. I'm glad you will live for a long time."

"Heh. Me too, kid. Me, too."

Several hours later, as darkness approached, Shana leaned close and whispered something to Kye, who then directed everyone to take shelter in the ground floor of a crumbling five-story building. Shana emanated a strong sense of respect. It seemed she liked that the inexperienced young queen trusted her wisdom. The Transit tribe headed across the intersection into the large structure.

According to Teal, it had been a hotel. This, of course, caused Althea to ask what a hotel was. A small group of curious scouts sensed imminent story time and clustered around them, listening while they all had a meal of cold bread and rat meat jerky.

Shara, apparently in charge of the tribe's warriors, organized a watch schedule among the adult spear-bearers. Though the tween-aged scouts had an arguably dangerous job exploring the ruins, hunting rats for food, and dodging CRP robots, no one asked or expected them to do any fighting.

After the meal, Althea got up and walked around to ask everyone if they had any hurts or sicks. The only complaint came from a man Father's age who had a mild sick that plugged up the hollow parts of his head with snot. She expelled it and told the man to burn the glop of slime before it made anyone else sick.

Her rounds done, Althea curled up next to Teal. Paama and Ooru bedded down with their parents nearby.

Althea reached out, using her clairvoy ants for a painfully brief talk with Father and Karina. They told her the Zero police had become quite upset that someone had stolen her. Though it seemed a slight fib, she simply said 'mercenaries' when asked who did it.

She would tell Father the truth about Teal when he asked, but she wanted to be there in person to keep him from growing too angry with her new friend.

But she still had fourteen days—at least—to wait.

41

THE COST OF CHANGE

Numerous men and women screaming and shouting jolted Althea awake.

She sat up to a scene of chaos. People ran in all directions around the old hotel lobby. Green plasma globs flew in the front door and windows. Someone let out an agonized wail. A blurry figure running by scooped Althea up, carrying her deeper into the building.

Bouncing in the man's arms, Althea, still foggy from her sudden jolt to consciousness, noticed Teal standing with her back to the wall by the entrance, waiting as a silver-plated CRP walker tromped into the room. The instant it went past her, she pounced on it, grabbing its rifle arm and shoving it upward to keep it from killing anyone.

Kye shouted a war cry and jumped off the reception desk at the walker Teal grappled with, rounding her all-metal spear over her head in a cleave that mostly severed the robot's head. Right as the man carrying Althea dragged her into a doorway, Teal picked up the plasma rifle.

"No! I need to help!" shouted Althea.

The man squeezed her tight, holding her firm while sprinting along a hallway that passed in a blur. He rushed down a flight of stairs, handed Althea to a woman by a door at the bottom, and raced back up. The woman gently shoved her into a room full of children and elders. Paama and Ooru ran over and clung to her, shaking. The two spear-bearers guarding the door didn't appear likely to let her out, Prophet or no, not unless she forced them to. Then again, CRP robots terrified her. Being treated like a helpless child at that particular moment didn't bother her since, all things considered, she essentially *was* a defenseless child.

She clung to her friends, shivering at the whine of plasma bolts, buzz of rotary cannons, and shouts of people.

The upstairs fell quiet after only a few minutes.

No one in the basement spoke or made an attempt to move.

Footsteps echoed in the stairwell. Someone banged on the door. The spear-bearer on the left opened it.

Teal poked her head in. "It's over. Althea, you're needed."

She jumped up without hesitation and ran after Teal up the stairs, down the hall, and back to the lobby. Fires burned here and there. The stink of molten plastic and scorched flesh made her scrunch up her nose. Four spear-bearers had died instantly, one with an incinerated head, the other three had charred tunnels through their torsos as big around as Althea's thigh.

Eleven other spear-bearers suffered non-fatal injuries, many losing half an arm or large hunks of leg. Many other tribespeople, including non-warriors, lay moaning with bullet wounds from wheelbot guns. Three unhurt spear-bearers stood guard holding silver plasma rifles. Teal and Kye also carried the CRP weapons. Five walkers and two wheelbots had crumpled to smoldering ruins among the injured. Such a number of people had been hurt, many grievously, she couldn't fix everyone before more died.

Overcome by sorrow, grief, and anger at all the pain in front of her, Althea screamed. Desperate to stop anyone else from dying, she leapt into the air, her wings bursting forth in an eruption of brilliant light. Arms held high to either side, she reached out and connected to the life essences of everyone around her all at once. The next few minutes blurred into a haze of blinding blue-white light, shifting reddish brown blobs, and moans of relief. The injured people drained her; she felt like a mother cat with an army of greedy starving kittens suckling at her energy. She opened herself to them, allowing the people to take as much of her energy as they needed no matter how much it hurt.

"By the gods," whispered Kye.

When the hungry life-shapes ceased pulling at her power, she drew inward, her healing trance ebbing. She sank down, vaguely aware of her toes touching the dusty floor before the brilliant radiance from her wings faded, and she collapsed unconscious into Teal's arms.

THE GODDESS AWAKENS

Hunger dragged Althea from the void.

She opened her eyes to a night sky speckled with stars and a gentle, cool breeze across her face. Teal's blanket covered her to the neck. A constant tickle brushed at her arms and legs. She lay on cool ground at the base of a tree. With a grunt, she sat up, grabbing her angry, growling stomach and looking around at healthy grass and trees. She'd been sleeping at a spot near the middle of an encampment the villagers had set up in the midst of a forest. A tall fire burned not far away. Clusters of villagers sat in circles reminiscent of how they used to gather around the cook stations in their old home.

"Althea's awake!" yelled a small boy.

All conversation stopped. Everyone looked at her for a few seconds, then erupted in cheers.

Teal jogged out of the trees, zipping up her jumpsuit as if she'd been off making water. She ran over and crouched beside her, brushing a hand over her head. "Holy shit, kid. Are you okay? You've been out for two days."

"I'm hungry." Althea cringed as her gut growled again. "What happened?"

"You lit up like a damn starship and started throwing off electromagnetic energy too strong for me to even measure."

Althea's eyebrows scrunched together.

"The injured closest to you regenerated fastest, so we gathered everyone around you. Then you passed out. I've been carrying you for two days. We're clear of the ruins. Haven't seen any sign of CRP all day today. Got into it with a wheelbot yesterday, but the plasma rifles make it easy to outrange them. Not a big deal. No one got hurt."

Paama jogged over and handed her a large hunk of cooked squealer meat. The girl radiated a peculiar mix of relief, joy, and sadness. "Thank you." She knelt beside her, head bowed against her shoulder.

"What's wrong?" Althea couldn't resist the smell of the fire-seared meat and attacked it like a feral critter.

"Ooru's father died." Paama sniffled. "He knows you couldn't do anything since it happened so fast. He is upset because we hid with the children during the fight, but he is too small for war."

Althea looked up, a wad of half-chewed meat nearly falling out of her open mouth.

"Don't be sad. Everyone's been talking. If we didn't take this journey, we would have eventually *all* died. We knew that leaving our home would be dangerous, but it is better a few warriors die than all of us are killed." Paama fidgeted. "They are starting to say you are one of the gods."

"I'm not. I'm just a person like you, but I can do stuff." Althea took another huge bite. "Please don't treat me different. I only want to be a person."

"Okay." Paama managed a weak smile.

"Ooru likes you," whispered Althea.

"I know."

Althea whispered, "No, he *likes* you."

Paama blinked. "Ooru? We've been like best friends for our whole lives."

"You are close. That is why you are sad for his loss. I'm sorry."

"Don't." Paama playfully punched her in the shoulder. "Even Noema believes this is better. Mariko's medicine does not work well. We had to stay underground. Our garden was small, and it was dying. We ran out of food sometimes. If the plant lights stopped working, we only had rats, and hunting meant we had to go outside where the Silver Men could find us."

"The worst is past," said Teal. "We're pretty well out of the CRP's patrol range here. We might see a flyer or a wheelbot, but another day or two and they'll just be a bad memory."

Kye, Noema, Sumiko, and Bill approached, with most of the villagers behind them.

The overwhelming emotion of reverence in the crowd almost made Althea roll her eyes — but that would be rude.

"Please don't worship me. I'm not a god. I just do psionics."

The councilors and Kye sat nearby while Teal tried to explain the theoretical difference between gods and psionics. The sight of Althea erupting with light, floating into the air, and healing the spear-bearers injured at the hotel had made the Transit people afraid to *not* have her around. With her encouragement, their attitude shifted from worshipful to something akin to the way a child feared going too far from its mother. Althea didn't mind that they had become fearful of being separated from her, just as long as no one treated her any different from a person. No offerings, no bowing, no weird rituals or whispering in her presence.

Teal's explanation of psionics somewhat clicked with the councilors, who accepted that Kye used similar abilities. Traits that they formerly called 'royal.' Evidently, all past rulers of the tribe had possessed some manner of psionic ability, though they did not all share the same family. Whoever happened to display some manner of gift when the tribe needed a new ruler wound up going to the Cursed Place.

The councilors initially became restless when Teal attempted to explain that their cursed place was really an abandoned medical facility run by Ancora Corporation, a name they thought a goddess. Ell-Gee — while radiating nervousness — chimed in to support the idea that those ruins had been full of technology instead of magic or gods. He hastily added that he did not challenge the gods' existence, merely that Ancora was not one of them. Althea suspected he feared angering the councilors more than the gods, which he likely didn't regard as real.

Someone suggested having a celebration now that Althea had regained consciousness, however both she and Kye wanted to hold off — Althea because the attention embarrassed her; Kye because she didn't want to make noise, use up supplies, or waste time. Once they arrived at their destination, then they could celebrate.

That, Althea didn't mind too much.

The wounded all took turns thanking her. Some with bowing, some patting her on the head, others picked her up like a doll and hugged her. Althea adored the warm contact, moved to tears by the overwhelming emotions of gratitude. Anyone who felt a little too much like they revered her got a tweak from worshipful to simple affection.

Eventually, the tribe settled down for the night. Teal, who only slept as part of her human illusion, planned to help the spear-bearers keep watch through the night. With her 'not quite mother' roaming around instead of sleeping, Althea relocated her bed next to Paama and her parents in the shade of a huge tree.

Still feeling the exhaustive effects of the healing trance, she slipped easily off to sleep.

43

NO LONGER

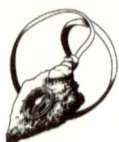

The Transit villagers marched for several days, traversing woods and plains before reaching the dry scrubland that started to resemble the home Althea missed so much. She constantly flitted among the walking people, giving boosts of energy to the old or the small ones whenever they complained of being tired.

They stopped each night less than an hour before darkness to set up camp. Worry about provisions proved overblown as the land provided their hunters adequate squealer meat. Althea also helped forage some edible plants, teaching the scouts who accompanied her how to recognize roots or leaves they could eat. She confessed to being bad with mushrooms, forgetting how to know the good from the bad, so cautioned them not to touch any as the wrong mushroom would cause a most painful death.

Days under open skies had a noticeable effect on the mood of the villagers. At first, the smaller children who had never set foot out of the subway station had been frightened, refusing to let go of their parents. Even the older adults who hadn't been outside in years roiled with anxiety. Their changing emotions reminded Althea of nervous flowers in early spring tentatively opening their petals. She didn't think people belonged hiding underground all the time. The joyous wonder that swept among the tribe seemed to prove that.

Whenever they encountered anything shiny or technological such as an old car, random mystery appliance out in the middle of nowhere, or unknown wreckage, little Avie would invariably zoom away from the group to check it out. Despite a terrifying encounter—for Ell-Gee as the girl didn't seem bothered—with a snake that required Althea cleanse venom from the girl, the little one remained undeterred in her curiosity.

LATE MORNING BROUGHT A STRONG BUT WARM WIND ACROSS THE scrubland, kicking up whorls of dust and a few tumbleweeds.

Althea didn't quite know where she was, but the area appeared familiar. Of course, familiar terrain could still be days away from home. She walked along near the midpoint of the procession, sweating in the late spring sun. Wearing a full animal hide shirt had been nice further north, but around Querq—especially in the summer—she'd melt. Upon noticing some of the adults had traded their heavy fur shirts for garments of thin cloth or bare skin, Althea pulled her shirt off and basked in the wonderful breeze lifting the sweat from her upper body and tossing her agate pendant and hair around. She smiled, turning to let the wind dry the sweat from her back, brimming with happiness at no longer being in a place that made her shiver. She much preferred the hot, dry weather here to any place that people had to layer up in heavy, hairy things to survive. Her fur skirt had become warm and uncomfortable as well, but it was short, so didn't bother her enough to shed it.

Teal didn't react to the change in temperature, appearing as comfortable in her jumpsuit in the desert as she had in the chilly ruins up north.

Avie's all-too-familiar squeal of delight made Althea look back.

Three adults lunged, trying to catch the adventurous six-year-old who zoomed off away from the caravan, having spotted something that attracted her curiosity. Teal bolted after her, overtaking the child with ease and scooping her off her feet. A loud wail of, "Aww! Blinkie!" came from Avie as Teal carried her back to her father.

"You need to stop running off." Ell-Gee collected his daughter and held her. "What did she almost do this time?"

Teal gestured off at the desert. "Looks like some kind of disabled robot. Not CRP, but it could be dangerous."

Ell-Gee paled. "Damn. Avie, do I need to put a leash on you?"

"I have cord if you need some," said Teal.

Althea stuck out her tongue.

"Heh. Thanks. I'll keep it in mind." Ell-Gee wagged his eyebrows, proving he joked.

They continued walking until late afternoon. When the caravan stopped for a little while to rest, drink, and eat, Althea rummaged her cloth dress from Teal's backpack and changed, packing the heavy fur skirt away along with the hide shirt. City garment or not, the *much* thinner fabric proved far more comfortable.

She wandered the temporary campsite, checking on the elders. One had broken a bone in his foot and didn't even realize it. She crouched, grasping his ankle, and closed her eyes. Loud buzzing erupted nearby, the too-familiar sound of raider buggies. Not terribly concerned with simple raiders she could dismiss, she continued tending to his foot.

Two crude vehicles with wedge-shaped metal tube frames, huge rear tires, and tiny front wheels zoomed out from behind a giant picture wall sitting beside the highway up ahead. A crowd of approximately twenty raiders with wild hair and spiked armor charged out on foot behind the buggies.

Though the villagers vastly outnumbered the raiders, only five people among them had guns, plasma rifles taken from the CRP. The raiders charged in, whooping and screaming amid puffs of smoke and the rapid, random *pops* from primitive firearms. Bullets whizzed by; some villagers grabbed wounds and hit the ground.

Teal pumped a plasma glob into the buggy on the left, incinerating it to a fireball from one shot. The explosion of the ethanol tank covered the driver in flames. He jumped over the front end before the vehicle even stopped, tumbling into a burning logroll.

Althea broke her trance with the old man, lunged to her feet, and released a strong telempathic pulse of calm.

Everything fell silent except for the idling of a buggy engine and the squeaking of its shocks as it rolled off the highway onto dirt, its driver too mellow to do anything but sit there.

Teal, unaffected by Althea's power, shot the buggy driver in the head, then shot the burning guy, putting him out of his misery.

"Stop!" yelled Althea.

She marched toward the mass of raiders who had all more or less slowed from charging to lazily walking closer. They had ceased shooting or waving bladed weapons over their heads. Some appeared bewildered, others took notice of her as she approached.

Whispers of 'The Prophet' rose up among the raiders, along with greed and a strain of toxic happiness she knew all too well. Some people with sicks in their brain-shapes, sicks she couldn't repair, felt that kind of happy whenever they hurt others, stole things, or gained power. They almost always had that bad kind of happy whenever they captured the Prophet.

Althea walked up to their apparent leader, a giant of a man at the front of the pack. She barely stood as tall as his belt buckle. Wild black hair half covered his face, a spiked black collar around a neck wider than his head. Dusty steel panels adorned with nails and crude spikes hung from leather straps over his chest. He looked down at her, squeezing and relaxing his grip on a scrap-metal sword more than twice her size.

Contempt for those who would hurt the innocent welled up inside her. She roared, thrusting her arms out to the sides, forcing great fear into the minds of all the raiders. Several soiled themselves. Many screamed. All but one dropped everything in their hands and ran off in random directions, shrieking as if on fire.

The huge man broke out in a sweat, eyes wide, willful enough not to panic. He took a step back from her, a faint tremble visible in his hands.

"Wow," muttered Teal. "I guess elephants really are afraid of mice."

"Go away and leave these people alone," said Althea.

The man edged backward. "You... Prophet. Belong to The Thorns now."

"No. The Prophet is no one's slave."

He pointed at her. "The legends say..."

"The legends are wrong!" yelled Althea. "You have no right to make slaves of these people—or me." She leaned toward him, continuing at a normal volume. "I will help anyone who asks, but I won't let you be meanies!"

Teal snickered.

The huge guy twisted left and right, observing his raiders running far off into the desert in total panic. "What..."

"I will not be taken." Althea held her head high, quite happy to be dealing with ordinary raiders and not stupid robots she couldn't do anything about. "Go home and stop being mean to people."

He reached toward her.

"Go home."

The man recoiled, blinked, then grabbed his head in both hands, dropping his gigantic sword. Growling, he slumped to one knee. When he slammed his right hand down on the weapon's handle, Teal raised her plasma rifle… but he merely dragged it with him as he regained his feet and trudged away, still shaking his head every few seconds.

"That's amazing," said Teal. "I didn't think psionic abilities worked on creatures that didn't have a brain."

Kye laughed.

Once confident the raiders would not return, Althea stopped forcing calm outward and rushed to help those who had been shot. Fortunately, the primitive raider weapons and long range made the wounds painful but largely trivial since she could mend them and prevent infections.

Teal and Kye walked up beside her, watching as she removed a bullet from a woman's side.

"You know," said Teal. "I think we might actually make it to Querq."

44

WRONG TURN

A few days after the raider attack, the caravan trudged uphill along an old highway flanked on both sides by tall rock cliffs. Althea walked on the dirt beside it since the Before-Time stone path burned her feet. Upon reaching the crest in the hill, she jumped into the air and cheered at the sight of Querq in the distance, a solid wall of buildings, metal, and concrete that sectioned off a retaken part of the Old City surrounding it. Her delight at being home radiated outward, lifting the Transit villagers into a similar state of elation that had the unintended but welcome effect of making everyone walk faster down the hill.

Teal smiled at her. "Well, here we are."

"Thank you!"

"You shouldn't thank me for helping you get back here. If my team didn't grab you…"

"Then all these people would be in big trouble." Althea smiled.

Teal raised an eyebrow. "You're not even upset I kidnapped you?"

"I was before, but if you didn't, the robots would have killed these people." She gestured at the villagers behind them. "I am sad that Father and Karina worried about me."

She whistled, shaking her head. "Wow, kid. Hey… would you mind doing me a little favor and maybe not telling anyone that I helped kidnap you?"

Althea looked down. "I don't like speaking the false. Bad stuff happens when you do that."

"Well, maybe just don't say anything at all then. That's not quite the same as lying. You kinda owe me one."

"Huh?" Althea looked up. "Aren't we even?"

"You wanted me to open that medical tank, remember? But I still escorted you home, so I'm up one."

Althea examined her fingernails. "Great Forge."

Teal playfully narrowed her eyes, then put an arm around her. "You salty little…"

Giggling, Althea hugged her. "I can't tell Father the false. But I will tell him to forgive you because I have."

Teal let off a deep breath. "Fair enough."

Althea took her hand and walked with her at the front of the group. They followed the old highway to the outskirts of the Old City, and made their way among the ruins. A bonedog or two peered out of the shadows within buildings at them, but those creatures didn't like the daylight and only snarled from their lairs.

Shouts arose from the Watch up ahead when they spotted the large group of 140 or so people approaching. They didn't appear to recognize Althea until she walked up to within twenty feet of the giant blue-painted metal gate. Emmanuel and Natalia, the two Watch on the wall directly above the entrance, gawked at her.

"Hi!" Althea waved at them. "I'm sorry it took so long to get back."

"Yeah, umm, sorry about that." Teal jabbed her thumb back over her shoulder. "She kinda made a wrong turn on her way to Albuquerque."

Emmanuel and Natalia appeared confused.

Althea looked up at her. "I thought you knew where to go? Did we make a wrong turn?"

"Oh, come on." Teal thrust her arms out to the sides. "That's funny. You never saw Rocket Rabbit?"

"No. Who would put a rocket on a rabbit?"

Teal laughed. "You poor deprived child."

An electric motor—that sounded rather like a wheelbot—started up.

Most of the villagers jumped, giving off a spike of fear.

Althea pushed their emotions back to calm. "It is the gate. There are no Silver Men here."

The gate slid upward on rattling chains, exposing the short tunnel through the wall. A path of thick metal slabs connected the cracked paving outside to the dirt road inside town. Grinning, Althea walked over the warm steel plates into her home, leading the villagers to the courtyard.

Father came sprinting down the street, one hand on his hat to keep it on his head.

Grinning, Althea darted away from the group, ran to him, and leapt into his arms. Everyone within a quarter mile burst into joyous tears right along with her—whether they knew why or not. She hugged him so tight her arms ached.

"Oh, Thea, where have you been? I was so worried! What happened to you? It is so good to see you are okay." He kept squeezing her, rubbing her back, rocking her side to side.

Before she could calm down enough to remember how to speak, Karina crashed into them. Her sister sobbed too much to even try to say anything, and merely held on. Locals and the Watch in the area all broke out into cheers.

Den appeared on the right, running across the path atop the wall, likely having been on sentry duty at the opposite end of town. He nearly fell going down the stairs to the road, and rushed over to hug her. After a few minutes of squeezing, he seemed about ready to do the lip touching thing, but Father standing right there made him reconsider.

Althea hugged all three of them again, then wedged herself between Father and Karina, clinging to their arms.

Karina gasped and fussed over her. "Thea! What happened to your dress? There's holes all over your back!"

"Explosion."

"Is that blood?" Karina pointed at the bottom of the dress.

"Not mine. The dribbles near the top are my blood."

"What?"

"Another explosion. Hurt my ears and made them bleed."

She grasped Althea's shoulders and spun her around to face her. "What's smeared all over you?"

"Rotten vegetables."

Karina grasped the hem. "What is this black?"

"Poison from when the big face tried to kill me."

Stunned, Karina crouched, wrapped her arms around Althea and held her, shivering in worry.

Father rubbed his forehead, nearly knocking his hat off, and muttered in Spanish far too fast for Althea to keep up... though she caught a few bad words.

Officer David, a woman, and one other man in the clingy black Zero police uniforms rushed over. Teal fidgeted at the sight of them and tried to act innocent.

"What happened?" asked Officer David.

"I've been asking her that, but she hasn't said a word I understand." Father put his hand on her head. "Are you all right, Thea?"

"Yes." She grinned, despite happy tears still flowing.

"So... what happened?" whispered Karina.

"What else." Althea fake-rolled her eyes. "I got kidnapped again. But this time, I didn't let them keep me."

45

LITTLE

Once the emotional overload of her reunion with her family lessened, Althea told Father about Queen Kye and her people. When she mentioned CRP and 'Detroit,' Officer David nearly fainted. She went on to say she had invited the villagers all to stay in Querq, a far safer place than where they once lived under constant threat of extermination.

Kye and her council, Noema, Sumiko, and Bill, went with two escorts from the Watch to meet the Ravens, Querq's leaders. Despite her newfound confidence in her abilities, the oldish people in their dark black robes way up high behind that desk and their judge-names still frightened her. They had no powers or anything supernatural about them, so the fear they inspired had to be purely that of a child. Also, whenever she saw them, she thought about the night they wanted to kick her out of Querq, separating her from her family—and Hector shooting Karina.

But The Many made them angry. The bad of that night hadn't come from the Ravens.

While the Transit leadership went to meet with the Ravens to discuss matters of settlement, Officer David brought Althea, Father, and Karina to the strange metal building that the Zero police had flown in and dropped here. She didn't really like going inside it because they kept it so cold, but tolerated it due to the genuine care Officer David had for her well-being.

Once seated in a small conference room, he questioned her about everything that happened, seeming oddly interested in as much detail as she could remember about the CRP. To save time and better explain things she didn't know the right words for, she telepathically sent him the bulk of her recent memories.

"How did they take you?" asked Father.

"They had magic to make me not see them." She picked at the little hole in her dress over her heart. "Shot me with a… umm…"

"Dart?" asked Officer David.

She shrugged and showed him the memory of the small black projectile zapping her with teeny lightning.

"Yeah, some kind of neuro-stunner dart." He exhaled.

"Teal said they were mercenaries. Two died when the flying machine blew up. They're syn-fet-ic, so I couldn't make them stop. Teal helped me escape. She is nice. Please don't be mad at her. She saved me."

Althea answered questions about everything that occurred after she'd been abducted from Querq over the next few hours. At her pleading, Father and Officer David decided not to make trouble for Teal here, though Father didn't seem terribly fond of the woman. However, since Althea was 'technically' on the Division Zero roster—whatever that meant—Teal might have some legal issues if she went back to civilization. That, Officer David couldn't control.

"But she didn't know!" said Althea.

"That may or may not help. Maybe if she testifies against the company that hired her, they'll let her off with a slap on the wrist, but if she's going to stay around here like you said, it's a non-issue."

"Okay." She smiled. "She was mean at first, but she's sad and lonely because people kept telling her she isn't a real person. But she is. She's really sorry for what she did."

"Well, for now, I suppose we can keep her role in this to ourselves." Father grumbled, rubbing his chin. "If she behaves herself."

Althea grinned.

"You probably want to get home, don't you?" Officer David smiled. "Getting on about dinner time."

"Yeah." Althea jumped to her feet.

Karina picked her up—and insisted on carrying her all the way to the house.

SOAPY WATER LAPPED AT ALTHEA'S SHOULDERS.

She reclined in the bathtub, eyes closed, basking in the love radiating from her sister. Karina knelt behind the tub, gently washing her hair with that strange 'shampoo' stuff from the big city. It baffled Althea how purple slime could smell like flowers, but the fragrance *was* nice, so she didn't bother questioning it. Having her sister wash her hair was her absolute most favorite thing in the entire world. The very first time Karina had done that for her had also been the first time she could remember anyone showing such tender, caring contact after years of constant captivity. It would forever be a physical reminder of how much she loved her family.

"Are you going to keep bringing people here?" asked Karina in a joking tone. "Soon, Querq will be as big as the fancy city."

Althea raspberried. "I don't wanna be kidnapped again. But people maybe could come here looking for me. The Transit tribe likes me a lot now, and they have the scared of not being near me."

"So am I." Karina kissed her atop the head.

"I'm sorry for giving you the scared."

"Oh, Thea. Please stop apologizing. Being kidnapped is not your fault."

"It is. If I couldn't do stuff, no one would take me."

"No, Thea. You never have to say sorry for what you are. It's other people who are bad."

"Sometimes people who seem bad really aren't."

"That woman... Father isn't too happy that she's staying around here, but he'll probably adjust to her since you are okay."

"Yeah. I know it's kind of strange, but she sort of feels like what it would be like to have a mother."

Karina hummed, combing her fingers through Althea's hair in a rhythmic, soothing motion. "Maybe a little, but I don't think that woman really *loves* you like a mother. She could want to protect you, but mothers are something special."

"Karina?" Althea peered up.

"Hmm?"

"You know how sometimes people touch lips when they like each other?"

"Yes." She squirted a little more shampoo on Althea's head and massaged it into her hair.

"I saw Adriana kissing Elias' boy parts. Is that the same?"

Karina fumbled the shampoo bottle, dropping it into the bathwater. "What?"

"Why do people do that?" Althea caught the shampoo bottle against her stomach and held it up out of the water, confused by the tremendous wave of embarrassment coming from her sister.

Karina choked, sputtered, and coughed. "Never say that around Father. He'll drop dead where he stands."

"Eep!" Althea gasped and spun to stare at her, horrified. "Why? No! I don't wanna hurt him."

"Thea…" Karina bowed her head, chuckling. "No, not actually dead. Just… forget it. You're way too little to even think about that stuff. Father couldn't take hearing you ask that question. Just forget you ever saw that, okay?"

"I'm twe—almost twelve."

Karina booped her on the nose with one finger. "That's too little for talk like that. Father would still drop dead if *I* talked about that and I'm sixteen."

"But, he said I have'ta wait 'til sixteen to do 'other stuff' with Den. You can do the other stuff."

Karina blushed. "The old man lies. He only *said* sixteen, but he meant thirty-five. He still thinks I'm too little."

"Really? Thirty-five?" asked Althea in a whimper. "That's like *oooold*."

She scooped suds up and puffed them at Althea's face, making her giggle. "Enough of that. Now, turn around and let me wash your hair."

Grinning, Althea settled back down and closed her eyes. Once again safe at home with her family, her sister close behind her washing her hair, she brimmed with too much happiness to contain.

The people of Querq often wondered why everyone seemed so happy once a week on Saturday.

It just so happened to be bath night.

fin

ACKNOWLEDGMENTS

Thank you for reading *Prophet's Journey!*

Althea's story will continue in the Prophet of the Badlands series.

Also, I'd like to thank all the readers who, over the past four years, kept asking me to give Althea her own spinoff series.

Additional thanks to Lee Sheridan for editing, Jackson Tjota for the cover art, Alexandria Thompson for cover formatting, and Ricky Gunawan for the interior art.

ABOUT THE AUTHOR

Originally from South Amboy NJ, Matthew has been creating science fiction and fantasy worlds for most of his reasoning life. Since 1996, he has developed the "Divergent Fates" world, in which *Division Zero, Virtual Immortality, The Awakened Series, The Harmony Paradox, and the Daughter of Mars series* take place. Along with being an editor at Curiosity Quills press, he has worked in IT and technical support.

Matthew is an avid gamer, a recovered WoW addict, Gamemaster for two custom RPG systems, and a fan of anime, British humour, and intellectual science fiction that questions the nature of reality, life, and what happens after it.

He is also fond of cats.

Visit me online at:
    Facebook: https://www.facebook.com/MatthewSCoxAuthor
    Amazon: https://www.amazon.com/author/mscox
    Pinterest: https://www.pinterest.com/matthewcox10420/
    Goodreads: https://www.goodreads.com/author/show/7712730.Matthew_S_Cox
    Email: mcox2112@gmail.com

OTHER BOOKS BY MATTHEW S. COX

Divergent Fates Universe Novels

Division Zero series

- Division Zero
- Lex De Mortuis
- Thrall
- Guardian
- Harbinger

The Awakened series

- Prophet of the Badlands
- Archon's Queen
- Grey Ronin
- Daughter of Ash
- Zero Rogue
- Angel Descended

Daughter of Mars series

- The Hand of Raziel
- Araphel
- Ghost Black

Virtual Immortality series

- Virtual Immortality
- The Harmony Paradox

Prophet of the Badlands Series

- Prophet's Journey

Divergent Fates Anthology

(Fiction Novels - Adult)

The Roadhouse Chronicles Series

- One More Run
- The Redeemed
- Dead Man's Number

Faded Skies series

- Heir Ascendant
- Ascendant Unrest
- Ascendant Revolution

Temporal Armistice Series

- Nascent Shadow
- The Shadow Collector
- The Gate to Oblivion

Vampire Innocent series

- A Nighttime of Forever
- A Beginner's Guide to Fangs
- The Artist of Ruin
- The Last Family Road Trip
- The Phantom Oracle
- How Not to Summon Demons

Standalones

- Wayfarer: AV494
- Axillon99
- Chiaroscuro: The Mouse and the Candle
- The Spirits of Six Minstrel Run
- Sophie's Light
- The Far Side of Promise anthology
- Operation: Chimera (with Tony Healey)

- The Dysfunctional Conspiracy (with Christopher Veltmann)

Winter Solstice series (with J.R. Rain)

- Convergence
- Containment
- Catalyst

Alexis Silver series (with J.R. Rain)

- Silver Light
- Deep Silver
- Silver Quarrel

Samantha Moon Origins series (with J.R. Rain)

- New Moon Rising
- Moon Mourning

Vampire For Hire series (with J.R. Rain)

- Moon Master
- Dead Moon

Maddy Wimsey series (with J.R. Rain)

- The Devil's Eye
- The Drifting Gloom
- Dark Mercy

Samantha Moon Case Files series (with J.R. Rain)

- Blood Moon

Immortal Operative series (with J.R. Rain)

- Broken Ice

Young Adult Novels

The Eldritch Heart Series

- The Eldritch Heart
- The Cursed Crown

Evergreen Series

- Evergreen
- The World That Remains
- The Lucky Ones

Standalones

- Caller 107
- The Summer the World Ended
- Nine Candles of Deepest Black
- The Forest Beyond the Earth
- Out of Sight

Middle Grade Novels

The Adventures of Ubergirl series

- My Dad is a Mad Scientist

Tales of Widowswood series

- Emma and the Banderwigh
- Emma and the Silk Thieves
- Emma and the Silverbell Faeries
- Emma and the Elixir of Madness
- Emma and the Weeping Spirit

Standalones

- Citadel: The Concordant Sequence

- The Cursed Codex
- The Menagerie of Jenkins Bailey